ALIEN FUGITIVE REQUIRES MECHANIC

Starborn Circus – Book I of II

Published by Entrada Publishing.

DEDICATION

To my Noeline and to the Joy of my life

A stray thought wondered if there was a market for that, chocolate Salome Malones, but smaller because one this size would kill him.

"Gratitude." She glanced around, no doubt looking for the garage, so Jamie held out the house boots.

"Put these on, please, and follow me. Don't cut across the grass or ass... er, the gardener will complain about you messing up the neat lines. From mowing?" Jamie headed for the back door into the garage, fumbling for his pass-card, which posed a question. How the hell had a naked woman gotten past the wire and alarms around the perimeter?

"When we get near the door, keep to the path or the alarms will go off." Then Damian would think Jamie had smuggled someone past the security and would be less than pleased she was wearing his wife's clothes.

"We perceived the precautions. We could propel ourselves faster without this protection. Serpents or barbed vegetation will not affect us."

Jamie ignored the strange phrasing again. So English wasn't her first language, big deal—half the refugees coming over the Mexican border needed a translator. The odd phrasing might mean she'd learned from a dictionary rather than the usual ways, street corners and kid's ed programmes. "My garage is in the, er, near Turnbull, a couple of miles south, but I've got a car." Telling her it was in a part of Albuquerque that was once a war zone, and might still be if it was worth fighting over, might put her off.

Once inside Damian's garage, Jamie hesitated. He was used to his heap of junk, but it looked worse than ever in the middle of a line of classy cars. Just for a moment he was tempted to take his sister's convertible. She'd added his biometrics to the security settings, so he could drive her home if she was drunk.

Instead, he pointed at his obviously not-new and not-expensive transport. "The red one with rust. It's temporary, because I wrecked my usual ride." Not quite—he'd wrecked his street racer, which had been sprayed recently. This one was more rust than red, and lacked a few things like windows, door handles, or back seats.

Jamie was tempted by the convertible, again, but last time he'd 'borrowed' it, Shania had reported it stolen. He'd been picked up, and she'd left him to rot in a cell all day. The cops would have been pissed off if most people had 'forgotten' they'd lent the car to a friend, but she dropped a wad of cash in the widows and orphans jar on the desk, and everyone smiled. It might have been the cash, but her married name was probably enough to smooth out any little difficulties.

~~

Swinging in through the driver's window, Hazzard-style, Jamie reached across to open the passenger door. He snatched his hand back when boots flew through the window, along with the skirt, shirt, and half-bikini, and landed in the back. Seconds later, the woman followed.

From the way she slid her feet through the window and the rest of her followed, twisting to land in the seat, she knew someone else with a car like this. Her ass hit the upholstery, her feet hit the floor, and Jamie winced. Her bare feet were now firmly placed on the remains of a carpet that had, at one time or another, been soaked in beer, cheap wine, curry, tacos, and on one memorable occasion, cat puke. He'd bleached it since, but wasn't sure he got it all.

Too late now. He reached under the dash and reconnected two wires, his anti-theft device and ignition combined. The thumbprint reader under the steering removed the engine and steering locks, then a button transmitted the code to open the garage doors and let him out. The gentle rumble of the engine was totally at odds with the bodywork. His car might look like junk, but Jamie was a good mechanic so the essentials worked perfectly.

trade. Most of the locals only get their cars fixed when they really have to, and haven't got much cash so they give what they can."

At least that got a reaction. "Barter?"

"Yeah, I guess so. I get cash from the racers, but most of that goes on my own racing." Though most of the local street racers were broke as well, so they sometimes paid him in spares, methanol, nitrous, or parts from the wrecks when they wiped out.

"Competition. Speed." She looked around the inside of the car, probably wondering how something like this could race.

"Not this car. I've got another, or had another. You'll see the heap of parts, everything I could strip from the wreckage." Jamie sighed, speaking to himself as much as her. "Now I've got to find a scrap chassis and body, something tough enough to take the punishment."

"Punishment. For racing?"

That made Jamie smile. "Not unless I'm caught actually racing. I meant the stress because it's street racing, not on a racetrack and not always on a road. There are potholes, curbs, walls, parked cars, hydrants, and posts, but no sandbags or crash barriers. Though if any of us does well, and the right person notices, then we might move up to organised street races. Then the roads are clear, and there are medics and a fire truck."

Jamie laughed quietly, because he rarely admitted the dream. "What we really hope for is a scout from a real team, IndyCar or something like that. That won't happen without a car." He sighed, because he was out of that for the foreseeable future.

This time, there was more interest in her voice. "Our transport is also defective, malfunctioning."

~~

He opened his mouth to ask if her transport would be safe, then Jamie remembered she'd been using we instead of I, and had just said our transport, not mine. Someone was looking after it, in which case why was she on her own—and naked? He glanced at her, and she was looking straight at him. Jamie looked back at the road, knowing he had to answer, but he didn't really need another job with no cash. If she had a bank account, she'd have a chip in her wrist, and could have paid for clothes, or a cab, instead of lurking in bushes.

He desperately wanted to know why she was in Damian's garden, but so far she hadn't even given up a name. "I'll take a look, but can't promise anything." With luck he'd find out who she was, and where the hell she came from. Then either the rest of her party had money, or he could phone someone to come and pick them up.

It crossed his mind she might have gotten stoned or drunk and wandered off. The others could have gotten the car fixed and be looking for her instead of waiting wherever she left them. If so, Jamie really hoped the mystery "we" had left a clue, or he could drive right past them.

Miss Mystery broke into Jamie's mental whirlpool. "Gratitude. Thanks. Are these your clan or family? These are their domiciles? Residences?" Her voice didn't seem worried, despite the hunched, scruffy figures lurking in the shadows, the trash and stripped cars, vacant overgrown lots, and the rough repairs or boarded windows on many homes.

"No family, not now. Papa died and left me the garage, or I might have left entirely. Nearly there. Don't get out until we're inside and the door is closed." A woman looking like her, out on the street at night, would be like waving catnip at tigers.

Jamie turned the last corner slowly, watching for odd shadows as his lights swept across the vacant lot on one side, and the dirt track on the other side of home sweet home. No crackheads, no muggers, nobody parked on the vacant lot, so he thumbed the switch. The lefthand garage door went up, quick and smooth, and he accelerated.

~~

He watched his mirrors as the door slammed down just as quickly, but nobody tried to dive inside. The look of the place wouldn't put off Jamie's customers or neighbours. They knew what sort of gear he had, and the racers would be happy just to score the parts from his old car. "Okay, all clear. The door handle..." He was talking to her belly, then legs, then the grubby soles of her feet.

Reaching up, Jamie pulled himself out of the window to find the mystery woman already walking towards his workbench. He waited for some reaction, but grease, oil, cracked concrete, and occasional nuts or scraps of metal didn't bother her bare feet. Maybe serpents and barbed vegetation really weren't a problem.

Since she was occupied, Jamie headed through the door at the back and began picking up scattered clothing and oily rags, tossing the lot through into the bathroom. He collected a few tools, and two projects that were in bits on the table, and shoved them into what used to be his bedroom. His breakfast dish and mug were still there, but when he went to put them in the sink, it was nearly full. There wasn't time to do anything about the dirty dishes, so he laid a towel over the lot.

When he looked back into his workshop, the woman was inspecting the heap of parts he'd salvaged from his racer. She didn't belong in a place like this, except maybe on a calendar, but she looked as if she was really interested. Then again, she'd looked interested in everything. "There's a drink and a seat back here. My name's Jamie."

"Greetings, Jamie. You are a mechanical engineer. Do you have experience with a wide variety of propulsion?" Turning away from the spares, she headed towards Jamie.

His mouth was answering automatically, luckily because

Jamie's brain and eyes were fully occupied with the approaching vision. "I guess so. Everything from scooters up to gas injection, nitrous. I even worked on a couple of rocket-powered bikes, for racers who thought the extra speed was worth the risk. I don't see any new cars, or only parts of them, but the principles are the same. There's one guy who uses methane from trash and his hogs, and others use bottles of propane. I don't get any hovercraft, aircars, just kiddie toys and sometimes drones." He realised he was babbling, so Jamie shut up.

He stood aside as she came past, and saw the oil on her hands. Enough brain cells diverted their attention from her shorts to realise she'd been more than looking. "You can wash your hands in there." That was pure manners, compliments of Papa, but then Jamie managed to get between her and the bathroom door. "In a moment." In a few frantic minutes he hid the dirty laundry, wiped most surfaces, and tossed the flannel, sprayed aftershave to kill the smell, and dumped cleaner in the pan. He came out and left the door open. "All yours."

While she was in there, Jamie had another go at tidying up the rest, but it was never going to look like anything but a dump. A rummage in the bedroom dug out clean sheets, and he hid the grubby ones behind the couch until he could get at the bathroom. More spray cleaned up the air a bit, and the rest of his clean bedding covered the oil stains on the seats. Jamie was just considering setting into the dirty dishes when the creak of the door warned him.

He threw the towel back over the lot and turned. The young woman spoke before he could make any excuses. "Are the facilities here traditional?"

~~

That stopped any babbling. At first Jamie thought she was yanking his chain, but she didn't smile, sneer, or sound sarcastic. He hadn't figured out where she was from, so maybe she meant it? "I suppose so, in this area. Coffee, Coke, or beer? Are you hungry? There's stuff in the fridge, or the freezer."

Gesturing towards the fridge, Jamie hoped that her food preferences would give him a hint. "No name brands, and most of it is homemade. Some customers pay that way, or their wives do." Jamie eased off when he registered the slightly puzzled look, and gave up on subtlety. "Are you from abroad? Not this country?"

"Correct. Not this country, political division. Do you use coin, valuable metals, as well as barter? Barter is unusual in a mechanised society, unless it is in catastrophic decline, dystopian." By then she'd opened the fridge, and bent to look inside.

Jamie tore his eyes away from her ass. He really shouldn't have given her those shorts, but Shania's skirt was probably a mini so it might have been worse. He concentrated on answering her question. For someone having difficulty with the language, she sure used a lot of big words, but once again that seemed like a serious question. "The usual way of paying is with coins, dollar bills, credit cards, or a wrist chip."

Mexico and Brazil, everywhere he'd seen on TV, had cash and bank cards—he didn't know of anywhere that didn't. Jamie tried to match the weird choice of words, unusual for someone still learning a language, with her complete ignorance of how Americans lived. He seemed to remember North Korea didn't have proper TV, or maybe it was just because he'd mentioned getting paid in goods.

He had another go at clearing up the confusion. "It's not really barter. They know I can't cook, and can't afford to buy ready meals. Well I can, but only cheap cr— stuff. The home cooking is a lot better." It was a sort of barter, maybe, because those who sent food knew he hadn't charged them the proper rates, because *he* knew they couldn't afford them.

"We would appreciate nourishment. Our system can utilise

most types except for some potent toxins. We believe you would find those inimical, so any of your food should be suitable, and interesting." The woman pulled out several dishes, plates and plastic tubs, and a carton of milk. "Are there rituals before partaking?" She frowned, obviously thinking. "Imbibing? Eating?"

"Heating and a fork usually, and real plates for special occasions." That was a test, and when she nodded without smiling, Jamie just plain asked. "You're not from Mexico, or even South America, and you don't know anything about America, the United States, do you? How did you learn the language?"

Miss Mystery hesitated, but then answered. "We are utilising a translator, which is still learning your language. Without background knowledge, choosing the correct term is difficult." She paused, but when Jamie just waited, she pushed on. "Names are of little use without a visual, or context. When you point, or your speech has an obvious subject, the programme updates both the database and phrasing."

"So where are you from? It must have a name, even if it's not what I'd call it." Looking at the amount of food, Jamie wondered when she'd eaten last. A quick glance confirmed she definitely wasn't starving, but he didn't look for too long or he'd lose track. Jamie thought about the avoidance of her name and origins. Add in hungry, naked, and not knowing anything about the place, and Jamie remembered some recent stories about illegals arriving from overseas. "Are you on the run? Escaping from someone or someplace?"

The answer wasn't reassuring. "In a way. The name of the place will have no meaning to you, but would translate as Starborn Circus, or possibly Zoo. Yes, we have absconded, escaped, but our transport was not optimal, and exceeded its performance parameters."

He'd been thinking more of her escaping from a smuggling

A couple of swings later, Plug froze with his eyes wide open, so Jamie took the opening and clouted him. When the Hellbat spun and fell, there was a knife stuck in his back. Jamie raised his eyes to see that Skid was on his face, with a pool of blood under his neck.

Beyond Skid there was guy on his back, with a knife handle sticking up from his chest. Fiend was knelt with a knife in his right shoulder, and had reached for his fallen pistol with his left hand. The woman's bare foot pinned hand and gun, while one hand grabbed Fiend's hair and pulled his head up. The other hand pulled the knife out of his shoulder, and it slashed across under his chin. She spun aside as blood spouted, almost balletic, and neatly avoided getting a single splash on her shorts.

~~

Jamie started forward but her smile died, her face hardened, and she threw the knife past him. He turned in time to see that Imp had made it up onto one knee. The knife was firmly planted between his ribs and, as well as Jamie could judge, through his heart.

"No!" The one holding his wrist, Cha, had made it to his feet. He stared down at Imp for a moment, then turned towards Jamie, scrabbling for a knife with his left hand.

Jamie crouched and brought up his wrench, but as Cha got his knife free, another knife came over Jamie's shoulder. It took Cha in the throat, and he spun against the fence before falling and kicking a couple of time. Jamie turned as she came past him, and saw the knife was gone from Plug's back. Damn, she moved fast.

He turned back in time to see her pluck the knife from Imp's chest, and turn towards the last Hellbat alive. Pills was still bleeding through his hands, his visible eye wide in shock, so Jamie tried to stop her. "No!"

She stopped and frowned, then turned with a small bow.

"That is just. He did not offer death."

"What did you do that for? They'll kill you, burn the place down." Sheer shock must have overcome pain, because Pills had taken his hands from his face. A deep cut had opened up his forehead, carved through his nose, and left a bloody line across his left cheek. The wounds were still bleeding, so a red mist sprayed as he kept talking. "The others will come after you. You killed *Fiend*!"

"Blood feud?" Her hand hit him in the throat and his eyes bulged. Jamie watched Pills drop to his knees, all thought of his wounds gone as he fought to breathe. She picked up Cha's knife, ignoring the man kicking and choking on the floor, then collected Imp's machete. One in each hand, she turned towards Jamie. "We must arm ourselves and finish them before they can organise. How large is his clan? Do you know their home burrow or nest, stronghold?"

~~

Jamie was in some sort of shock, watching Pills as he stopped twitching and his body relaxed. He turned towards her, still trying to make sense of her killing seven men. "Finish them, the Hellbats? What planet are you from?"

"We told you; the name would have no meaning. Ah, when did you realise?"

It took two tries, but then Jamie managed to answer. "Just now." Because that hadn't been a literal question, just a figure of speech when someone acted really weird. After all, everyone came from the same planet—or not, apparently. That presumably explained the problems with speech, and food, and possibly the bodies.

The last one kicked Jamie's brain back into gear. Before he dealt with the alien elephant that had just strolled into town, Jamie had to deal with the bats in the alley, the dead Hellbats. "We can't just go and kill a bunch of people."

"There are too many? Do you have allies?" Pulling the belt off

Imp, she cleaned it on his jeans, then started collecting the rest of the knives and attaching their sheaths. Since they all carried at least two, the belt was going to be crowded.

Jamie watched her, and thought hard, and for once he wasn't thinking about how goddamn sexy she looked. Maybe the circus or zoo part was a bad translation, or a lie, and she'd been locked up for a reason. Maybe mass murder, because that hadn't been a fight—the Hellbats never had a chance. If she had a gun as well, she really might kill the other eleven or twelve.

Most people would consider that a public service, cleaning up the neighbourhood and gene pool, but whichever gang took over the drug dealing wouldn't be happy. They definitely wouldn't want that sort of threat in their neighbourhood, and the simple solution would be to burn his workshop down, with him inside. Jamie thought about what she'd said, and done, and looked around to check what evidence there was. Very little—she'd avoided the blood, and the only marks on the baked, beaten earth were old tyre tracks.

~~

"We are ready." She'd tucked Fiend's gun in her belt as well, so Hellbats had just hit the endangered list.

Taking a breath, Jamie tried logic. "Do you have any reason to kill the other Hellbats?"

"These offered death, but died. That is balance." She turned and gestured towards Pills. "This one declared blood feud, clan war to the death."

That sounded like some mystical martial arts crap, or maybe aliens usually killed each other in job lots. The alien bit threw him for a moment but Jamie pushed on—one problem at a time. "He wasn't a leader, so he couldn't declare anything for the rest. If we go indoors and pretend we don't know what happened, they won't know so there won't be a feud."

He glanced at the seven bikes parked near the front of his home. With luck someone would steal at least some of them by the time the cops arrived, which would give them suspects. They probably wouldn't make more than a token effort at looking for the thieves, not in the Pits—they'd want to get the bodies bagged and tagged and get out.

Jamie thought about not reporting the bodies, but they'd stink eventually. Someone else would call the cops to get them shifted, then they'd give Jamie a hard time and think he was involved. He was tempted by the bikes, just for a moment, and then sanity prevailed. Even if he managed to hide a couple, he'd never get to sell them. There'd be eyes already watching, and then the locals would get a lot more serious about breaking in.

His resident alien diverted Jamie from temptation. "How do you disclaim all knowledge of this?" Her gesture took in the seven bodies and all the blood.

"Indoors first, now?" Jamie heaved a sigh of relief as she went towards the door. "If I wash this wrench and those knives in acid, and the belt goes in the furnace with my other trash, that takes care of the evidence." He thought back, and she hadn't touched anything else. For a moment he wondered if she had fingerprints, then concentrated on the problem.

Though Jamie had to smile, because her look back at the alley spoke volumes. "I meant any evidence we were involved. The cops, the local law enforcement, will take a quick look for anything obvious, report a gang fight, and call the meat wagon. If they knock on the door, we heard nothing." Jamie paused to put on shoes, then headed straight through into the workshop. He'd have been embarrassed, but from the way she dressed, he didn't think she'd realise he was in underwear.

"Your guardians of the law will not detect omissions and untruth?" The alien looked up and around as Jamie put the knives and wrench in the big sink, and poured battery acid over them. He headed for the trash can with the belt and sheaths, but she wasn't letting it drop. "You have an interference field? They will notice when their veracity checker is unresponsive, or reports function errors."

Veracity was truth, and Jamie figured aliens with spaceships and that translator would have more fancy tech. "Your cops have a lie detector, yeah?" She nodded. "Ours don't, so we're safe as long as you don't look guilty. They'll think they already know what happened: war with another gang. The questions will be to make sure the paperwork is all neat, stop the boss giving them a hard time."

She still looked unsure, so he tried again, hoping she didn't have some alien hang-up about lying. "Just say you didn't hear anything, and didn't go outside so you didn't see the alley. That's a good point; they'll want a name." So did Jamie, and this time he might get one—hopefully not obviously alien. He put the belt and sheaths into the trash bin, tipped in the contents of the recycling bin, and tied the bag firmly shut. Dropping the pistol in the bin, he put the bag back in to hide it—he'd sort it all out later.

~~

When Jamie turned around, she was watching him, maybe deciding whether to tell him. "We listened to local transmissions last night, so the translator has a wider database now." She stood straighter, almost at attention. "One possible form of our name is Ghost Claw of the Purple Hills Slashtails."

A name like that needed some sort of explanation, but not right now. "Slash or Claw might work, considering the state of the alley, but that's also why it's a bad idea." Jamie remembered his first impression, before she had clothes and the sexy part overwhelmed everything else—she'd moved like a ghost. "How about Ghost Hill, then it's familiar so you'll answer? You've got no ID, but I'll give you an address that's far enough away they won't bother going to check. If they're pushy, just promise to drop by the station sometime with your license."

Jamie headed for the coffee pot, hoping he still had two

clean mugs without having to investigate the sink. Just for a moment he wondered what transmissions, but the radio had been on while they ate. He also debated telling her where the Hellbats lived, then leaving town before she got back.

That was bloody tempting, but would leave a murderous alien loose in the neighbourhood. It wasn't much, but the residents didn't deserve that. She seemed to be willing to follow his suggestions, so Jamie figured he should get her out of town if possible. He definitely wasn't reporting her to anyone.

If the FBI or National Guard turned up, she'd fight, and would probably get a couple before they took her seriously. If she could use Fiend's pistol, or get hold of a rifle, the assholes wouldn't care about the locals—they'd level the Pits to get her. Jamie remembered she had friends somewhere, so maybe the whole of Albuquerque would end up flattened. He checked the alley, and three of the bodies had lost their boots and jackets, Plug had no jeans, and two bikes had been stolen.

That kicked his brain into action and Jamie took off his tee, wrapped his hand so there'd be no fingerprints, and checked the bodies. The three nearest the road had already been searched and robbed. The rest had a hundred and thirty-five dollars in cash, but Jamie left the wallets, ID, and credit cards with the bodies.

As soon as he was back indoors, Jamie took out his phone, then paused. He should talk to the alien before calling the police. There was at least one big problem if she was going to meet the cops, her obvious resemblance to an infamous adult movie star. There should be a solution—Jamie didn't believe there was an alien race someplace that all looked like Salome. "Ghost, can you change your appearance a little, still human but so you don't look like anyone famous?" Especially a sex goddess, Jamie thought, though the cops might not look at her face.

shouldn't take more than an hour. The last time he'd seen the cops in the Pits, they'd brought five patrol cars and an armoured SWAT truck, so the delay was reasonable.

Once he was dressed and had a mug of coffee to help him wake up, Jamie tried to persuade Ghost that her rules didn't matter on Earth. Eventually Ghost confessed that no other Slashtail would ever visit Earth—it wasn't on the permitted list. She could defer telling the Hellbats, but must do so before leaving, then they could follow if they wished to declare feud.

Leaving Earth seemed to involve Jamie, to start with, at least. "We must find out if our transport can be repaired, and if we can negotiate an acceptable price with you. We hoped to barter, as the accepted currencies are not used here, but we must be careful not to exceed local tech levels."

"I can't fix a spaceship!" Though even as he said it, Jamie knew he'd like to look at it, especially the engines and the electronics. He realised it might not have electronics, or anything he recognised as an engine, which just made him keener. "Though I could take a look?"

Just too late he remembered the ship would have more murderous aliens, but now he daren't change his mind. It would help if Ghost didn't look like that, but then Jamie realised that anonymous aliens would be worse. She'd accidentally bump some guy in a store, he'd object, and half the customers would be bleeding out before Jamie could explain. People tended to be more tolerant of hot women—unless they started cutting throats.

Ghost had been answering while Jamie's head ran around in circles, and he registered what she'd said. "When? The ship is clear of the crater, and any search will concentrate there."

"Search? Crater?" She'd done it again, Jamie was lost. On the plus side, a crater had to be out of town, which had been Jamie's first step—get her away from people. *He* wanted to get away from her, but wasn't sure she'd let him, not until he'd repaired her ride.

Ghost must have been listening to the radio properly, not just as background music. "Transmissions spoke of investigations but not of discoveries, so the ship is still hidden. There was talk of excavations to find the remains of a shooting star, meteorite." She looked quite smug. "We left some remnants in the crater to suggest that."

A crater sounded like a really bad landing, so Jamie asked about the state of the spaceship. The exterior wasn't damaged, but the engines were. Ghost didn't have a lot of technical information. They were the sort that went into most similar types of spacecraft—which was a bit like saying a car had an engine like all other cars.

He tried to narrow it down, getting her to describe what she could, but his best bet would be to take a wide variety of tools and parts. Thrusters sounded promising. That meant it was some sort of jet, just bigger than the bikes or toy rockets he'd worked on.

According to Ghost there were electronics, and electricity must work the same everywhere. There were also computers of some sort as the ship made calculations, and had pre-programmed functions, which Jamie hoped he didn't have to touch. He felt better when Ghost assured him all programming followed the same basic principles. The simpler the better, then Ghost and her alien friends could head for the stars—preferably without meeting any more people.

When she explained that the computers controlled internal functions, including atmosphere, food, and seating to suit different races, he started worrying again. Jamie almost asked what Ghost was really like, but if it was too horrific, he'd never be able to pretend to relax and be friendly. Then she might decide she didn't need him, or force him to help.

He wouldn't mind her leaving, but that could include leaving no witnesses, and a bloodbath when she kidnapped the staff from a repair shop. As long as her friends didn't have nineteen legs and horns, or he could stick to dealing with Ghost, he could manage. Jamie tried to pretend she was human, but it wasn't easy. It was like those drag queens. They still looked like sexy women, but once you knew it was a guy, it didn't have the same effect.

Jamie hoped he could fake it long enough to get her the hell away from his planet, so the quicker the better. He took his second coffee into the workshop but Ghost followed, still trying to answer his questions. That wasn't helping the pretence, but he needed to know.

Jamie had no idea what he'd need, but any programming would need his cracking gear. Papa's cracking gear, really, upgraded to get around the programming that stopped people fitting salvaged electrical spares to cars. It could be used to steal spares, or electric cars, but Papa taught Jamie to use it for repairing, much cheaper than the approved workshops.

Manufacturers kept upgrading the protection, which was why Papa set the test kit up to adapt, to crack the codes. Since Papa died, Jamie had kept it up to date as best he could, but it wasn't easy. Some pirated upgrades cost hard cash, and the locals couldn't pay much for repairs so he had to save up. To earn anything, Jamie had to accept any sort of work, fixing stuff like toasters, air conditioning and dishwashers. That meant the kit learned to talk to pretty much anything, so with luck it could include a spaceship.

All the repairs and salvaging left Jamie with a toolbox full of used connectors, adaptors, and reprogrammable chips. Even an alien computer should need something similar, Jamie hoped, and the same reasoning led to him throwing in a wide variety of tools. Hammers, cutters, and big spanners joined the smaller tools once Ghost revealed that the propulsion involved grease and moving metal. Jamie had thought a spaceship would be gleaming, delicate instruments, but the more Ghost told him, the more he thought he might fix it.

It might look like a car outside, but inside, Jamie's vehicle was more like a truck in some ways, a racing truck. A big steel box replaced the rear seats and small trunk, built into the car, which provided a lot of secure storage. Even so, he couldn't pack his whole workshop in there. For once, Jamie loaded enough so he could see the suspension settling, and hoped he wouldn't be going cross-country or end up in a high-speed chase.

Despite trying to work without looking at Ghost, or thinking about what she looked like, Jamie couldn't help it. She still looked like a sexy woman, but now he was trying to see a hint of alien.

~~

As he worked, Jamie was trying really hard to forget he'd spent a night in bed with a naked shape-shifting alien, one who looked like a movie star but killed seven men in seconds. It had the opposite effect, so by now Jamie's nerves were shot. Three times he ended up outside, walking away, but he kept coming back.

Jamie wasn't a hero, but he'd brought her here, so the least he could do was take her away. One thing was certain—any dreams he had about last night weren't going to be the sort he'd been hoping for. He'd feel better if the copy wasn't perfect, but she moved totally naturally, and that finally firmed him up. He'd stick it out because even if Albuquerque had written off everyone in the Pits, he didn't want an invisible murderous alien anywhere near Shania.

The two interruptions didn't take long, but the first one seemed to last a lifetime. The cops turned up with four squad cars, a bus with mesh over the windows, and two ambulances —but no SWAT. The cops in the bus sealed off the track and the road out front with barriers and shotguns, then pairs of them went house to house. Jamie had called it in so he was first.

All that saved him was that the cops just went through the

motions. He was a bag of nerves, and Jamie was sure he looked guilty, but he managed to stick to his simple story. He'd heard some noise, looked outside, and there were bodies. Luckily there was no interrogation—the cops didn't even check the workshop. After they left, Jamie realised they hadn't expected any information that would help.

The cops barely spoke to Ghost once she'd given her name and explained she had no ID, no phone, and no vehicle. With her staying overnight, the cops probably assumed she was a prostitute but didn't care. As agreed, Ghost didn't even admit to looking outside, and said as little as possible. The police were more interested in leaving before someone started throwing bricks. Since the worst troublemakers would be nursing hangovers or still asleep, they got out with nothing more than shouted insults.

The Hellbat banged on the door about half an hour after the cops and medics had taken the half-naked bodies and two remaining bikes. Jamie told him what he'd told the cops, without mentioning his visitor. The biker never got inside the door, or saw Ghost—Jamie didn't trust her not to claim the kills, or the Hellbats to keep their hands to themselves.

~~

He waited until the gang finished rousting the neighbours, and the sounds of cursing and bikes had died away, then Jamie told Ghost they could go. He suggested she changed her clothes, wore the shirt in public, which gave him time to write a quick note for Shania. He explained he was trying to get an alien back into space with minimum collateral, but skipped over where he found Ghost, and stealing clothes. Now, if he didn't come back, and Ghost didn't leave, someone would be looking for her. Looking properly, because the FBI would listen to someone like Damian.

At the last moment, he chickened out of calling his big sister —she'd tell him to run, get out, and sod the neighbours. She'd be right in a way, because his neighbours were a long way from helpless—they'd kill any stranger as soon as he pulled out a gun or knife.

The problem was that Ghost was female, and looked harmless. They'd warn her, or hesitate before shooting. Ghost wouldn't, and she had a pistol and plenty of knives to throw. If she was hurt, she might turn into an armour-plated killing machine, or slither down a drain, or spray them all with poison or gas.

Jamie settled on texting, just to let Shania know he'd be gone a couple of days and had left her a note. He turned his phone off so she couldn't ask questions, and tried not to look guilty as Ghost spoke from just behind him. "Will this be acceptable for travel?" Jamie looked, and debated trying to get her into some of his clothes.

He'd asked her to change to get some privacy, but had also thought it might make her blend in better. It wouldn't help as much as he'd expected. The shirt covered up more than the bikini, even if it was tighter than it would have been on Shania. Unfortunately, she'd put on the skirt as well—and it would attract more attention than the shorts.

The skirt was a mini, because that was a part of Shania's trophy wife thing, especially at a pool party. The trouble was that Shania was fashionably thin, and Ghost wasn't. Presumably it wasn't a micro-mini when Jamie's sister wore it, because it sure as hell wouldn't curve out like that. Everyone who saw it, especially the guys, would remember her.

A relieved Jamie remembered she'd be in the car, so nobody would see it. While most guys behaved around hot women, a really short skirt just encouraged some. They'd figure she was easy, or selling her ass, and end up with a busted arm—if they were lucky. Once they reached the ship, she could put on her own clothes. "Those will do until you can wear your own stuff."

He tried to suppress the flinch when he mentioned her own stuff—that meant her own shape. He'd wondered about Shania's or Damian's reaction if they knew he'd nicked the clothes, but now it didn't seem as important. "Most people don't go barefoot, so you should wear the boots if they'll fit. If not, I can stop somewhere and buy something." The seat might be covered, but the floor was a lost cause.

"We cleaned these, as you suggested." She proffered the clothing, so Jamie took the small bundle.

"I'll get cleaned up as well." Jamie showered and put on a clean shirt, and last night's jeans because they were his decent pair. He took a moment to settle his nerves, and remind himself why he was doing this. Ghost hadn't threatened him, yet, but she'd shown no remorse over killing so he had to keep her away from others. She wasn't threatening in human form, so once out of the Pits, there'd be less chance of casual violence.

~~

Jamie hadn't asked how far the spaceship was, but if Ghost insisted on him inspecting it, or actually trying to repair it, he probably wouldn't get home tonight. He might disappear without a trace, but for now he daren't think about that. He packed an overnight bag and his work jeans, then took the emergency cash taped under his sock drawer. Less than three hundred dollars, but he'd got the cash from the Hellbats.

Taking one last look around, Jamie spotted something on the bed, and when he looked closer there were three long, pale mauve hairs. Leaning down to pick them up, he caught a faint aroma, maybe scent, and realised it seemed familiar. A sniff confirmed it was from the hairs, which explained—he'd slept next to that smell last night.

A quick check proved the shorts had the same faint smell, and he wondered how she'd cleaned them. It was quite pleasant, a good thing because that had to be Ghost, and he was going to be in the same car for an indefinite period. Realising

Ghost only had the clothes she was wearing, and ought to wear the shorts if she left the car, Jamie put the clothes in his bag.

As he made sure everything but the fridge, freezer, and alarms were off, Jamie kept thinking about that hair. Instead of being put off, he thought long, pale mauve hair might not be too bad. It would be a lot better than spines or slime, even if it was all over.

Maybe the hair meant there wouldn't be either, maybe alien women were like those on *Star Trek*. Most of them were hot, which fitted, but had something a bit different, maybe like mauve hair? She'd altered her chest and face a little, but Ghost's basic human shape hadn't wavered at all.

When he came back into the workshop, Jamie forgot all about hair, or scent. He'd put the Hellbats' knives in a bucket under some scrap, in case the cops wanted to look around. Now they were laid on his workbench, fifteen of them, and a machete, a hatchet, and what looked like a short sword. So was his wrench, and Ghost had been in the trash can because she was inspecting Fiend's revolver, and had retrieved the belt and sheaths. "Be careful with that. Does your world have guns, pistols?"

"Not like these, but there are various types of projectile weapons on other worlds. We cannot see any way to programme this, and these appear to be inert, just metal, unless the explosive is part of the projectile?" Ghost held out a dozen rounds, so she'd searched Fiend's pockets.

"The explosive is propellant—the lead is what does the damage." Jamie hesitated, then went for it. "I was going to leave the gun and knives behind, in case we were stopped. There might be some blood on them."

"We should be armed, and none of these have any trace of bodily fluids." Nor acid, Jamie noticed, so she'd dried them all. Her hand tapped the wrench. "We included your weapon of choice, though you should carry something smaller for close

the USA as well as other countries, which was embarrassing. Papa had always said the news was all about rich people, lying politicians, and wars, so Jamie didn't usually watch it. School hadn't helped, but maybe that was his fault. He was more interested in getting home to help Papa than dead people, or places he'd never go.

An hour later Jamie was jerked out of trying to remember stuff when a bike roared past, well over the limit. He was relieved when the picture on the biker's back was a truck with ram's horns. Now he wasn't driving on automatic, concentrating on answering questions, Jamie realised there wasn't a single vehicle in sight, front or back, not even a truck in the slow lane. Watching the other highway confirmed there wasn't much traffic the other way, which was reassuring, but now Jamie was uneasy.

He'd had as little as possible to do with the Hellbats, though he'd been warned it was a bad idea to refuse to repair or service their bikes if they asked. He'd also been warned they wouldn't pay full price, but insisting might mean a mystery fire, but he'd thought leaving town would be enough to avoid them. His neighbours always said that if someone crossed the Hellbats, they'd hunt them down, and that bike had gotten Jamie wondering how hard they'd try.

Another five miles passed without incident, but then a glance down the ramp as Jamie passed the next junction showed jammed-up cars and trucks. There weren't any buildings, and from the people getting out and waving their arms, they didn't want to take Country Road Four. "I think we might be in trouble, Ghost. Hellbats or your Hunter, though I'm not sure how either could clear the traffic."

"Hunter should not act openly. It is illegal on a primitive world like yours, one that does not know about other races." Ghost checked her knives. "We will be ready."

That wasn't reassuring—Jamie didn't think a knife would

stop an alien hunter with a disintegrating ray or a laser sword. The alternative was another heap of human bodies, so Jamie slowed to take the next off-ramp. A bike accelerated away just before he got there, and Jamie saw a diversion sign laid where it could have been thrown off the road.

A quick check showed there still wasn't any traffic behind, so he slowed right down, then accelerated without turning. There weren't many vehicles at the bottom of the turnoff, and this time there was a truck stop, but there was a line of cars wanting to get back on the freeway. Barriers with flashing lights were stopping them so far, but there weren't any uniforms in sight.

He quickly explained, but Ghost was confident it wasn't Hunter, as he wasn't allowed to act openly on a primitive world. Jamie was more worried about humans. He eased off a little and looked ahead for the ambush, but kept glancing at his mirrors, so he saw the dot coming up behind. He debated for a moment, weighing up giving Ghost another weapon against his current odds of surviving.

Jamie opted for not dying just yet. "Ghost, there's a bike coming up, and the rider might have a gun so be ready to duck. Can you reach back between the seats? The two centre bolt heads on the big chest behind the seats are loose. Turn one clockwise as far as it will go, the other anticlockwise."

A glance showed her concentrating, probably on the translation, so he tried again. "They only turn one way, and the bike is getting close, so be quick." He heard the click as the panel unlocked. "Pull the front down, and take out the weapon clipped to it. Please keep it down, out of sight. If anyone sees it, we'll be locked up for life." Maybe not, but Papa's little souvenir definitely wasn't registered, and might have been stolen. The ammo could be worth jail time on its own.

Papa had always seemed kinda boring, but when Jamie first saw the weapon, he wondered just what his usually mild-mannered father had done during the rebellion. Shania was seven when the National Guard came through, and remembered living in a house. There was noise and panic and flames, and then the workshop, and she thought that might have been when Mama left. Jamie couldn't really remember Mama, just a vague impression, maybe—his first memories were of the workshop.

There had never been any explanation, or any mention of the rifle, but it seemed like the sort of thing that would have been useful back then. Either the rifle or what he used it for might be why the locals treated Papa with respect, and never tried to break into the garage. That changed when he died, and Jamie learned to immobilise any repaired vehicles until the bill was paid. After the third time he was woken up by some asshole robbing the workshop, Jamie electrified the doors and the only window.

The key to his wall safe had been with Papa's car keys, and there'd been two boxes with the rifle. One with three rounds was labelled 'practice' in Papa's handwriting, and Jamie used them up doing just that. The one with nine rounds said 'armour-piercing,' and the internet reckoned armour-piercing ammo would break an engine—so Jamie had modified his toolbox. A pistol might have been handier to stop a carjacker, but you use what you've got, and anyway, he wasn't sure he could shoot a person. Right now, that ammo would sure as hell stop a bike.

"This is another projectile weapon? A firearm?" Ghost was keeping it down as requested, but also giving the rifle a really good inspection.

"Can you use a projectile weapon?" Damn, she had him doing it. "A rifle? Hold on tight; we won't need a weapon for this." The bike behind had suddenly accelerated—very suddenly, so probably a race bike, methanol, or maybe even nitrous if it was a Hellbat bike. A moment's thought and Jamie pulled into the outside lane so the bike had to come past Ghost.

He figured she had a better chance of dealing with whatever.

~~

Sure enough, the bike moved over to come past on the inside—without slowing down. "Watch out, he might have a machete or a pistol." Hoping it wasn't just some guy showing off, Jamie waited until the last moment, then tapped his brakes and swerved into its path. He only needed a glancing blow, or for the idiot to try swerving at that speed, so Jamie straightened up immediately. A direct hit could leave the bike engine in his lap, and his legs in the road.

Most of Jamie's attention was on getting his car under control as it fishtailed down the road, but the bump meant he'd done the job. From the corner of his eye, he'd seen Ghost lunge, and beyond her there might have been a bike, briefly. Then she was back down, and his car was back under control.

Jamie's mirrors showed a wreck bouncing across the highway and off into the dirt, and two smaller soon-to-be-wrecks that were completely airborne. Once again, he hoped they'd been Hellbats, but stopped worrying when he glanced at Ghost. He was damned glad he'd switched lanes, because she was examining a big semi-automatic pistol. He'd never have caught it, which would have given him a hell of a headache.

"Another firearm, bigger than the first, shorter than the rifle. Why do you need all the different sizes?" As Ghost turned the weapon, examining it, Jamie reached out to push the barrel out of line with his favourite head.

He looked at the road ahead as he explained, but there still wasn't any sign of a road block. "There are quite a few types of firearms, not all legal, and they aren't all for specific uses. First rule, don't point it at someone unless you might want to shoot them. Second rule, finger off that bit underneath, the trigger."

Jamie took a slightly longer look, because the road ahead was still clear, and the empty road behind meant the Hellbats were backing up traffic. He hadn't thought there were more than a dozen of them left, unless these weren't Hellbats? "When you caught that, did you see if either of them was wearing a Hellbat jacket?"

"The one with the firearm had a skull with Hellbat wings on his hand. Look." Ghost leant down towards the floor, then held out a hand with a skull and bat wings tattoo. She hadn't caught the gun—she'd cut his bloody hand off! While Jamie was replaying the lunge in his head, or the part he'd seen while trying not to crash, Ghost continued. "He was pointing this at us, so we disarmed him. Was he a Hellbat?"

"Oh yes. That hand belongs to Fiend's second, Lucie, short for Lucifer. Guess someone talked after all, and you've got your blood feud." Jamie glanced at the hand again and shook his head. If the Hellbats had any idea what they'd tangled with, they'd run far, far away.

~~

Jamie had thought about running away, and still did, but Ghost seemed to consider him an ally, or maybe just useful. She'd never even hinted at threatening him, so he stuck with his first decision—to try to keep her away from other people until she hopefully left. That would help if other people, Hellbats in particular, stayed away from him, but he figured they'd get the message eventually.

He reconsidered running, but the last few minutes reminded Jamie it could be fatal—even if Ghost let him go, the Hellbats wouldn't. He knew that part of him was willing to take risks to see an alien spaceship, but that didn't mean it was the wrong decision. Jamie did another round of the mirrors, and two dots had appeared on the highway behind him. "I'll have to stop so I can use the rifle, so keep your head down."

"If the tube on top is target acquisition, and what you called the trigger is the release lever, we believe we can operate this weapon. The principle is common among ranged weapons, and the target is close, so the lack of programming should not be too detrimental."

Ghost sounded confident, so Jamie nodded. Stopping wasn't the favoured option, and she didn't have to be really accurate. The mesh across the back, there instead of a window, would have absolutely no effect on the bullet, and if she clipped a speeding bike, goodnight asshole.

Jamie reached over and jacked a round into the chamber. "That lever will load another round, projectile." Jamie glanced down and tapped the safety. "Flick this off before operating the lever underneath, the trigger. Make sure this end, the butt, is tight into your shoulder because it will kick, hit, very hard. I'm going to accelerate, pull away from those two, which will give you a little more time to get ready. Aim right for the middle of your target. That bullet will stop the wheel, or if you're off-centre, it'll make them crash."

It might rip an arm or a handlebar off, or just make the rider flinch, but by then they'd be going well over a hundred so it would probably be enough. Jamie looked in the mirror again and this pair were cruising up, so they'd open fire from behind. "There will be a jerk when I accelerate, and they'll drop back at first, but I can't keep it up for long. Turn around and brace your back on the dash, and rest the barrel on the back of the seat. When they start to close again, nail them. If the first one hurts your shoulder too much or you miss, say so." He'd stop and try to get his shot off fast enough.

~~

He'd never aimed a gun at a person before, and had only fired the rifle three times, so half of Jamie hoped Ghost was a crack shot. The other half hoped the bikes behind would let him go when he accelerated. Jamie stuck his foot down, but as expected the pair were still closing, so he took a firm grip on the wheel with one hand and reached down with the other. He'd never used this car for racing, or let others look at the engine, so this was going to come as a hell of a shock to the pair behind. It might also mean a serious overhaul, but if he lived that was cheap.

Praying there were no potholes, Jamie flipped the switch. Moments later, the nitrous kicked in, and his car did its best to rip the wheel out of his hand and go airborne. Jamie grinned at the high warbling cry from the passenger seat. It wasn't anywhere close to human but the sentiments were clear, and it wasn't fright—Ghost was a speed freak.

When he spared a glance at the mirrors, they were vibrating too hard for a clear view, but the blobs behind had disappeared so he shut the bottle off. The two very small dots started to grow, so they'd accelerated and were coming like, well, hell bats. Jamie opened his mouth to warn her, but Ghost was already turning. Just for a moment she looked alien, too supple, but then she had her back to the dash, and the rifle up and resting on the back of the seat.

"Don't worry about range; it won't matter this close." Jamie flinched as he remembered what the damn thing sounded like when he'd fired it outside. "Shit! Here, ear plugs."

"Our ears will not be affected now we have warning." Jamie didn't answer, busy jamming his ear buds in before she fired. Not quite earmuffs, but they must have been good enough because his ears survived. He heard a loud clicking sound, followed by the sound of the bolt and the ping of brass hitting something.

The clicking had to be Ghost, and alien, and was unmistakeably annoyed. "High." A glance in the mirror showed the blobs much nearer, but one was shorter than the other. As it drifted off to one side, Jamie realised she'd shot the rider clean off. He was about to say that was near enough when she fired again.

The second bike stood on its nose and began to cartwheel, then bounced high above the tarmac, shedding components. The two Hellbat components flailed their arms, trying to fly, but failed so they bounced along the tarmac after the wreckage. A satisfied "Hah" was followed by the sound of another round going in.

"Forget the riders. They're dead, or very lucky and will be in intensive care for months. Nice shooting." It was, especially for an alien who'd never seen the weapon before. Jamie remembered wondering if she was special forces, an alien SEAL, or maybe shark. Squid?

Ghost still sounded a little annoyed. "We allowed for the influence of gravity the first time, but the trajectory was as straight as a laser." Jamie had eased off the pedal, and a glance showed her inspecting the rifle again before giving it a pat. "Primitive can be very effective. We had not realised such a small amount of lead would have that effect on a machine."

Jamie answered automatically, still trying to get his head around killing five people. Maybe not all dead, but in intensive care, and even if he hadn't shot anyone, the cops weren't going to believe an alien did it. "Jacketed rounds, so the first one would have gone right through the body. Hollow nose or plain lead are better against people, but those bullets are meant to stop a car. That's why I keep it in here, though this is the first time I've needed it." Jamie eased off even more, as he'd reached what was probably the rest of the Hellbats. "I think this might be as far as we go."

The freeway rose gently, then dipped out of sight, and beyond the rise he could see the tops of four trucks, blocking both lanes. A semi at each side, sideways, stopped him driving around them, while two more blocked the other highway, even if he'd managed to cross over the rough ground in between. Maybe the two bikes were only meant to chase him into the real ambush.

~~

A look back showed twinkling red and blue lights, so the cops had finally turned up. They were in the distance, and seemed to be stopped by the wreckage, but Jamie didn't think the Hellbats would let him wait. There were other reasons for not waiting, five of them, probably dead with only one convenient suspect. "I don't fancy trying to get away on foot. If the Hellbats don't cut us off, the boys in blue will lock us up. Self-defence might fly, eventually, but I'm not hopeful." Jamie had considered going forward on foot and shooting at any Hellbats with the rifle, but not with the law already in sight behind.

Jamie knew he shouldn't be this calm, but presumed he was operating on pure adrenaline, and sheer panic was keeping him on his feet. Sooner or later he'd collapse, it would all crash in, and he'd have a gibbering fit. The alley had been bad enough, then there was the alien thing, but gunfights on the open road were just too far outside his comfort zone. *Any* gunfight was outside his comfort zone!

His sister needn't worry about him turning up at the wrong time and outing her. After this he'd be staring at padded walls or a barred window for years, maybe life. Ghost broke into Jamie's thoughts about his lack of a future. "If we leave now, and you keep them distracted by driving slowly closer, we can outflank them. These firearms are not familiar weaponry, so we will revert to Ghost Claw traditional skills."

~~

As Jamie tried to work out if the "we" meant he was supposed to leave as well, Ghost put the rifle back in its clips, placed the ex-Hellbat pistol on Jamie's lap, checked her knives were in her boots, then without any warning, dived out of the window. Instead of breaking a couple of bones, Ghost rolled onto her feet and ran to the verge, and within seconds Jamie lost sight of her.

That settled who was leaving—Jamie wasn't trying that! He caught a flash of mauve, which had to be her natural look. A human shouldn't be moving that fast, or keeping out of sight without more cover. Jamie was getting more and more curious, and worried, because that meant she wasn't anything like human. He consoled himself with the thought she must be small to hide in the grass—then realised that a long, slimy, spiky snake or giant centipede would have no problem.

When Jamie crested the rise and got a proper look at the roadblock, he stopped worrying about Ghost. There was just enough room between the trucks for a man to walk, and his car couldn't fly, so unless he moved a truck he was stuck. A glance back showed that the flashing lights weren't moving, so they were still checking the Hellbats. The top of the rise meant the cops couldn't see the blockade, so he had a bit of time, but only until the Hellbats were declared dead or unfit to answer questions.

Jamie glanced at the big pistol on the passenger seat. He'd need two hands or it would break his wrist, but Jamie still had Fiend's pistol as well. Maybe he could give Ghost some covering fire? He'd been trying to stop her killing people, but the bikers weren't making it easy and now it was decision time. Hellbats or alien possibly-monster? Jamie made his mind up—he stopped the car and reached for the pistol.

This wouldn't be the sort of covering fire seen in movies—if he aimed anywhere near Ghost, there was an even chance he'd hit her. As Jamie opened the door and got out, seven figures stepped out into the gaps between the trucks, and two stood up on top. He squinted and some had pistols, but he thought the long barrel was a shotgun. He hoped it was, and not a rifle.

Jamie would have considered shooting them all, despite the police, but the Hellbats would dive for cover if he hit one. He might miss entirely as he wasn't an expert with the rifle, and anyway Jamie didn't have enough ammo for nine. Even if he got a couple, the rest would hide, which wouldn't help Ghost. A diversion, attracting and keeping their attention, was easy enough.

A flicker of mauve in the verge, very close to the end truck, told him Ghost was closing in, so Jamie stopped dithering. He'd stopped about sixty yards short, hopefully too far for a pistol, because it didn't matter to him. He'd be lucky to hit a truck at ten yards, but if one of these was a real shooter, he'd find out the hard way. Cupping his hands, he shouted. "What's the problem?"

~~

For a moment Jamie thought he was too far away for the shout to be understood, but then two men climbed out of a lorry and walked forward. One stopped but the other took another two steps, then shouted. "One of your neighbours gave you up, Jamie. We only wanted the whore, but Lucie and three bikes should be right behind you. I'm guessing you stopped them, unless you're gonna say it was the whore?"

Jamie told them the truth—it would work better than anything he could make up. "You're right; Ghost stopped them. I keep telling you assholes she's not a whore, but Hellbats keep insulting her, or trying to hurt her. Then you act surprised when she tops them." Jamie shrugged, exaggerated enough so he hoped the Hellbats could see it. A flicker of movement caught his eye, and there was a body laid between the first two trucks. Damn, he'd better make sure none of them looked that way. "Hang on a minute."

Jamie remembered a character in a movie, and very obviously patted his pockets and looked around. "Nope, sorry. I was looking to see if I'd got a shit I could give, you know, for Fiend and Lucie, but I'm all out. Why don't you step out here and have a look for yourself?" There was a body between the next two trucks now. Jamie assumed it was a body, because Ghost didn't seem to go for knocking people out—then a man on top of a truck flew backwards out of sight.

"Cruise, show him why we don't have to go out there." The Hellbat just behind the spokesman pulled out a long-barrelled pistol, but as he brought it up to aim, he collapsed onto his face. Jamie could see something jutting up from his back, a knife hilt presumably. "What's the matter? Just shoot the arse." The spokesman turned. "Look out, the bitch is behind us!"

~~

Talking wasn't going to divert anyone, not now, so Jamie raised the big pistol. Holding it with both hands like he'd seen on the TV, he braced himself and fired at the truck between the highways. At least the sound brought a couple of heads around, but the bullet was probably trying to make orbit. Jamie shook his wrists, reflecting that movie heroes had hellish wrist muscles or cheated, then had another go. That one might have frightened a bird if one had been perched on the semi's cab, but he daren't try again.

Though Ghost didn't need any help. There were flickers of mauve under vehicles and in shadows, and some were too far apart for one Ghost. Those had to be decoys, though he'd no idea how Ghost managed something like that. The whatever were working, because Hellbats were shouting and pointing, or shooting, in all directions. If Jamie managed to keep the barrel down and hit a truck, Murphy's law would make it the one hiding Ghost, so he just watched in case she got into trouble.

He didn't think it was Ghost who needed help. Men were being dragged out of sight, sprouting knife hilts or spraying blood, and then mauve flowed up behind the last but one, on top of a truck. Blood fountained from his throat, he dropped the shotgun and toppled over, and Ghost was stood looking down on the spokesman.

"We are Ghost Claw clan of the Purple Mountain Slashtails. Will you give your name and lineage, for our kin to sing of?" She glanced each way. "A small song, but a name would make it a little better."

The Hellbat froze for a moment, possibly because she was

stark naked apart from one knife, but then he screamed something probably obscene. He brought his gun up, and started shooting as fast as he could, but the target was already moving. Mauve flickered as Ghost seemed to pour down the side of the truck, more like water than a person, and came at him in a weaving, flowing movement that was more dance than running.

She ran on all fours like an animal, a big cat—and she was fast, much too quick to see details. Then Ghost was right in front of the man, and she stopped and snatched the weapon from his hand.

She tossed it behind her and stood up straight, pulled the knife from between her teeth, and lashed out. The Hellbat spun away in a splash of blood, which she once again avoided with one of those balletic twirls, and Jamie saw the flash of teeth as Ghost smiled at him. She looked down at herself, then raised her voice enough for Jamie to understand. "We are inappropriate again, one moment." Then she was off, running behind the trucks, while Jamie was still blinking, torn between admiration, relief, and sheer horror.

~~

The wailing and whooping of sirens behind banished the sight, but only temporarily—Jamie doubted he'd ever forget and he might have nightmares. The way she'd come down the side of the truck, then run at the Hellbat, hadn't been anywhere close to human. *Star Trek* got it wrong. Aliens weren't human-shaped, which left Jamie's imagination to run riot.

The avoiding-killing part wasn't working, so he seriously debated jumping into the car, turning around, and driving away. A distinctive sound closed off that option. A glance back and Jamie dived into his car and drove forward, because the cops were coming. He came out of the door running, heading for the nearest truck, but when he stood on the step and peered in, no key. The next had keys, and what was presumably the driver—tied, gagged, and bug-eyed.

Jamie put a finger to his lips. "All over in a minute, cops on the way, but I'd like you to forget me." He slid into the seat, turned the key, and gave a little "yeah" when the engine started. No finesse, Jamie crashed it into first gear or possibly second, and revved the hell out of the engine to move it clear. As he jumped out and began to run for his car, Ghost came out from between two trucks.

She'd dressed, including her belt, and it was already crammed with extra knives and several pistols. She'd also picked up a shotgun. "Take these while we collect the other trophies."

"No chance, leave the rest. The cops are coming." Jamie beckoned as he went past, but she passed him the shotgun and darted off to the side. He was already in his seat when she ran towards him, with the long-barrelled pistol in her hand. Ghost must have taken a fancy to it, or wanted her knife back. She slid in through the window, and Jamie dropped his car into gear and shot through the gap. The cops were coming slow and steady, so just maybe?

His mind registered what he'd seen at the side of the road, and Jamie swerved and screeched to a halt, flipping the switch for the tail lift. He'd turned down the last opportunity, but if Ghost liked trophies, he should have one as well. Jamie pulled Fiend's pistol out of his belt, put his hand out of the window and aimed at the sky, then pulled the trigger. That would slow the cops up.

"We will stand and fight here?" Ghost looked around, then back at the trucks. "The vehicles would give cover."

Maybe it was adrenaline, or he'd finally cracked, or it was just that Jamie had always wanted a street racing bike. He'd chickened out of his first chance, and immediately regretted it, but now an alien Lady Luck had given him another. "I'd like a trophy as well. Give me a hand to push one of those bikes around the back, please?"

She may have had a puzzled look, but Ghost followed as Jamie ran to the row of parked bikes, and chose the best one. That was easy, because he'd repaired or serviced all of them at least once. Once she had the idea, Ghost helped him muscle it into place across the forks he flipped out at the back of his car, and held it there while the tail lift picked it up.

Jamie quickly fastened the straps to hold the bike in place, stopping several times to fire into the air. He could see glimpses between the vehicles, and as he'd hoped, the police had parked sideways. Several were out of their cars, but using them for cover. "Time to leave, quickly." Hopefully before a chopper appeared.

As he pulled away, Ghost transferred the extra guns and knives from her belt to the glove box. "If we need to fight, we have replacement projectiles." A quick glance at her pulling ammo from inside her shirt, and Jamie moved his eyes quickly back to the road. She'd been in a hurry, obviously, as she hadn't bothered with the bikini top.

That barely registered—he'd just realised the rifle didn't matter anymore. The alien killer had picked up a whole armoury, with reloads! He couldn't even be reassured by them being alien weapons to her, not after the way she used his rifle.

Jamie concentrated on his mirrors, watching for the police, and only half-listening to what she was saying. "Many weapons have not been operated, fired, so they will not need replenishment. So many different sizes. Your people must have many different types of warfare. This rifle is very different."

A glance told Jamie what she was talking about. "Shotgun. I was about to say I'll explain later, but it isn't optional. Shove that lot out of sight, in with the rifle if it will all fit, and shut the compartment. I doubt it will make much difference, especially with Lucie's hand and a pool of blood on the floor, but there's no point making it easy for them."

Jamie pointed ahead, to where two cars with flashing lights had crested the next rise and were pulling across the road. An officer came out of one car and stood in the middle, raising his hand.

~~

The three policemen looking over the cars, and pointing weapons, weren't asking Jamie to stop—they were insisting. Ghost had stopped hiding weapons, and had a knife in one hand, but despite that a sudden thought made Jamie laugh. "It's a pity you aren't really Salome Malone. You could wiggle over there, tell them it's a shoot for a movie, then let them take a few selfies. If they're fans, they might even let us go rather than upset you."

"Like this?" A quick glance showed the light golden tan and pale blonde locks of the one and only Salome Malone, though actually not the only one now. Her new double smiled, and tried a couple of pouts. "If we are asking for help from males, should we remove our coverings, clothes?"

That was tempting. The cops would be really screwed, because they couldn't handcuff her without risking a molestation claim. "Very few clothes work just fine. Can you do it, manage the sexy walk and speech?"

The more Jamie thought about it, the more it was worth a try. From the occasional glimpse between the trucks, the cops from the cars behind still hadn't reached the trucks. He didn't blame them. By now they'd be close enough to see bodies, and probably blood, and they knew someone was alive and had a gun. Now he just had to get clear before they found out the blood was real, and told these cops. "You need them to be thinking of sex instead of procedure."

"We remember the transmissions. Oh Jamie, do you like me?" Ghost was smiling as Jamie looked over, in some sort of shock because the last part had been the right voice, with *exactly* the right breathy, sexy emphasis.

"Er, maybe tie the shirt together under, er. Tease rather than a clear view?" She'd adjusted her sizing and opened the shirt, and he was really pleased he'd stopped the car. Otherwise, he might have run the cop over, but not because of her breasts. He was horrified because she'd transformed in seconds. If Ghost ever decided to hide, the cops would never find her—*he'd* never find her!

Ghost was a perfect copy of Salome, and the slow lick of her lips and flutter of eyelashes were spot on. Jamie concentrated on escape—a lot more hopeful now. "Just remember, movie shoot, and you want to get back to the trailer for a shower. Ask if they want a selfie, and if they'd like to come and wash your back. They won't accept, but they'll sure as hell be thinking about it. Ah, I like your scent, but it isn't human."

"Anything you say, Jamie." Ghost smiled, a slow, seductive Salome smile, and as she slid out of the window, a whiff of perfume hit Jamie. He'd no idea what it was, but seriously considered chasing after Ghost and dragging her back into the car. The scent cleared, so did his head, and his hormones settled down.

Not completely, because that scent, or gas, was more frightening than the shape-shifting. Jamie forgot the gas as he watched her, and wondered how much of a Salome movie she'd watched. Enough to get the walk right—Ghost was rolling her hips as if she was dancing to something slow and sexy. The officers' eyes weren't sure where to look, but her face wasn't on the list. Jamie had to look away before he laughed, because the ones with guns were standing up, eyes riveted, but then he remembered that scent.

Oh shit, they really might come along to scrub her back. On the other hand, that would mean a police escort clear of the area, so it might not be all bad. All four were clustered around her now, taking a good look down her shirt. He was damn sure cops wouldn't act like that normally, so the scent must be some sort of alien gas. Just for a moment, Jamie wondered if the scent he liked meant he was being dosed as well, but she'd been in different rooms and had left him during the attack.

Ghost/Salome turned to point back to where the cops had stopped again. The first officers were waiting for the rest of the cars to catch up, still well short of the trucks. Those on foot had their weapons out, covering the trucks and no doubt looking for survivors, but so far they were ignoring the car stopped by their colleagues. The four colleagues were totally distracted, all of them taking the chance to eye up Ghost's ass when she turned.

Jamie knew exactly when selfies were mentioned—all four fumbled for phones. Each one had a kiss on the cheek, and her arm around them, then she turned and beckoned for Jamie. He wiped the smile away, not easy because three took the opportunity to get a picture of her ass and legs. The other one stepped back to get the full view—those pictures were going to puzzle the hell out of the real Salome.

A wave, a blown kiss, and then Ghost rolled her hips to meet the car and slid in through the window. As Jamie drove sedately through the narrow gap, she leant out of the window to wave, giving them a wonderful view down her shirt. All four took a picture. The poor schmucks were going to get crucified, and it wouldn't be long because the other cops had reached the bodies.

They'd be puzzled by some wounds, the ones that looked as if they'd been inflicted using a chainsaw. They'd definitely baffled Jamie, but then he lost track of that and pretty much everything else. He was fighting off the hint of that perfume that came in with Salome, damn, Ghost, but was losing—then a strong waft of her natural scent blew it away. Jamie sighed in relief.

~~

The road sign promised an off-ramp into Santa Rosa, but Jamie wasn't sure that was a good idea. In the rear-view mirror the cops were still watching instead of jumping into cars and chasing—surely their radios were screaming at them by now? Though Jamie needed another question answered before that. "How the hell did you learn to move and talk like that? And what was that smell, scent?" Jamie smiled as he remembered when he first saw her. "How come you didn't do that when we first met?"

She didn't answer straight away, and a glance showed Ghost looking guilty, a neat trick in a borrowed body-shape. "The scent was to arouse a human male." The smile was all Ghost, which seemed odd since those were Salome's lips but it was true. "We could not do this until we had the human pattern. Our external body shape was human, but our bones and internal organs could only be approximated. Then when you allowed us to share your night-nest, we relaxed the shape and exchanged a sample."

"What do you mean, exchanged?" All those possible nightmares reappeared in Jamie's mind—a bed full of sample-sucking monsters.

Now she looked worried, possibly at whatever expression was on Jamie's face. "A small amount to tell us how humans are constructed, and a similar amount of us for you. That allows us to recognise you should we be in a fight in the dark, so we do not attack you by mistake. It did not hurt you."

Jamie took a deep breath to calm down, and looked in the rear-view mirror. He was over the rise and out of sight now, so he slowly pressed on the accelerator, still thinking hard. Understanding human construction meant a DNA sample, which didn't take much, and he didn't fancy being mistaken for an opponent. Bottom line, it was too late now, and getting upset could be fatal. "Okay, fair enough, but ask in future, yeah? Will it give me mauve hair?"

He'd meant it as a joke, but Ghost was dead serious. "Not unless you accept much larger samples, and even then the result varies. How do you know?" Jamie explained the hair in the bed, and flashes of mauve. "The colour is natural. A full melding into another form isn't hard to maintain, once it is locked in place. Smaller variations are harder as they tend to drift back to Slashtail, and the pelt on my head is close to normal. When I am distracted, fighting, or altering shape, I may not catch it in time."

Trying to ignore the full melding bit, Jamie concentrated on a mauve pelt. Pelt meant all over, which wouldn't be too bad, and might rule out slime or spines. "I don't mind mauve hair if that's easier, and then it won't alter and maybe attract attention. It'll make you even less like Salome, so people don't connect you with your fans back there."

He realised that what she actually looked like didn't really matter anymore, not if a drop of DNA was enough to copy an alien species. If Ghost disappeared, knowing her true form wouldn't help—the FBI would have to include cattle and goats on the Most Wanted. Ahead of him, off to the right, Jamie saw a lot of trucks around several buildings.

~~

He'd rejected going into town in case the cops caught up, but now Jamie realised what was going to happen. Behind him the cops at the blockade would be talking to the ones Ghost had met, then radio messages would alert other squad cars. There would be road blocks on I-40 and every turn-off, and then choppers would search the whole area.

Out on the highway with absolutely no-place to hide, he'd be a sitting duck, but that didn't mean they'd catch Ghost. By the time he explained she'd changed into a horse or maybe a pack of coyotes, and they'd tested for drugs, she'd be long gone.

Then if she caught a couple of officers on their own and took a sample, Ghost could put on a uniform and drive off in a squad car. If she blasted them with that gas, there'd be no blood—they'd take their clothes off before she stabbed them. Nobody would even know until the bodies were found, and by then she could have switched out and look like anyone, or maybe a tree.

Jamie recovered enough to stop inventing even more what-ifs, but the time-out had made up his mind. Hiding had to be better than forcing Ghost to go on the run on her own. Turning off I-40, Jamie could see that further along the road was what looked like a breaker's yard, while a sign told him this was Santa Rosa.

Glancing down the side road just before the yard, there weren't any buildings behind it, so Jamie turned. As soon as he could, he swung off into the stunted trees and brush, hidden from the highway by piles of scrap vehicles. A quick look around was reassuring. He should be out of sight of passing traffic, unless they turned down what rapidly deteriorated into a dirt track.

Jamie pointed through the bushes. "I should be able to buy paint in the place with all the junk cars, then we can respray my car. It won't stick too well over the rust, but should be enough if nobody gets too close. Every bit will help, because we're going to be on Most Wanted once those four cops get their hormones under control."

He was sure the other cops would slap some sense into them once they'd seen the bodies. Jamie frowned, wondering again why the cops behind hadn't used their radios to tell those four to stop anyone getting away.

"Does my natural pelt look human enough?"

Jamie's first reaction was to stroke her head, really odd, then he had a sudden image of being snuggled into a big wriggly rug made of the stuff. It wasn't Salome hair—it looked thicker, softer, silkier, and yes, he still wanted to stroke it. The mauve looked exotic, but sexy woman has a fancy hair job exotic, not alien, and it was longer and straight, a completely different style.

"Oh yes, better than the other hair." He'd get lynched if Salome's fans ever heard that. "It changes your whole look." So did changing her skin colour—she didn't need more DNA to hide.

~~

Jamie took a deep breath, quashed another impulse to reach out and stroke her head, and got back to repainting his car. The big lung-full of Ghost's scent was a reminder—he might be drugged. "I'll be back in a few minutes. If you stay with the car, you can divert anyone who wants to know why we are parked here. Tell them I'm buying spares."

The smile and agreement were a big relief—she wasn't worried about him leaving. He wondered briefly if that meant he was already infected or otherwise controlled, but if so, it was too late to matter. He'd just watch out for doing things totally against his nature, like running off with a total stranger, or engaging in gun battles with a biker gang. Smiling quietly to himself at the thought of Shania's face when his sister found out, Jamie headed for the junkyard.

As expected, the place sold a wide variety of accessories for drivers. Jamie bought two pairs of shades, drinks, snacks, and a cheap Stetson-type hat—in case the cops had actually noticed him. Remembering how much Ghost ate, he bought plenty of sandwiches from a machine. He'd eat some, and they were in sealed packets so any that were left would stay fresh for a while. Thinking of Shania, he also bought a cheap phone, so he could text her without using his own.

A quick look through the paint colours, and the only one that would do the job in one coat was orange. He didn't have time do it properly, remove the rust and use two or three coats of an entirely different colour to cover the red completely, but it wouldn't matter if the orange looked reddish. He only bought six spray cans, because buying food had reminded him he didn't have much money.

It was a good thing Jamie had picked up a Hellbat bonus from the alley, and a pity he hadn't had a chance to search the bodies at the roadblock. Jamie would have usually considered four hundred and twenty dollars a small fortune, but it wouldn't last long if he ended up on the run. They'd still reach the ship today, but with a long detour so it would be late, and they'd need two rooms. With the toolbox behind the front seats, they wouldn't recline properly, so Jamie had no intention of sleeping in his car.

Worrying about finances, Jamie forgot about pursuit until a cop car roared past, then another, heading into Santa Rosa. The hat and shades had been enough for him, and they hadn't turned down the side road, but they'd be asking around. Mauve hair or not, anyone who saw Ghost in that mini and shirt would remember her, though the instant extreme tan might throw them off.

Jamie relaxed when he came in sight of the car, because Ghost was leant against it with mauve hair and wearing the bikini top and shorts. The cops would be asking for someone white, blonde, top-heavy, and wearing a miniskirt. They even had pictures. As he came nearer, Jamie could see she'd reverted her shape and face to the not-Salome-but-actually-sexier version. There was a good chance that any guy coming past wouldn't have noticed the colour of the car, or even that it had a bike hung on the back.

He should change clothes as well, at least his shirt, though the two cars hadn't slowed up so maybe not. The four cops that stopped him might not have noticed what he was wearing. "I've brought you shades, but that hair works better than a hat. Now we just need a few minutes without witnesses, then we'll find somewhere to park while it dries. Did anyone come past?"

"No." Ghost lifted her head and sniffed. "You have food? Changing shape uses resources, though we can manage for a while." When he opened the bag, she smiled. "We remember Coke. This food is different."

"Sandwiches, bread with different fillings. Try them all, and the chips, the packets." Jamie was hungry as well, but he could eat any she didn't like. He hesitated for a moment, wondering if that was safe, but he'd been in a car with her all day so he'd already breathed in any alien bugs. On second thoughts, that wasn't reassuring, but right now Jamie had bigger problems.

~~

Ten minutes later they were looking at an orangish car, reddish-orange in places, but not too bad as orangey rust took the edge off it. "It's still wet, and a rough job from close up, but that won't be too obvious if we're driving." Jamie looked regretfully at the bike, which he'd taken off while they were spraying. "I didn't think that through. It'll be obvious, stuck on the back. The cops will stop us regardless of the colour of the car, so we'll have to leave it."

The license plate wasn't a problem as he always carried several sets, and rarely used the legitimate ones. He always put them on to visit Shania, but switching them out was almost automatic. Jamie didn't want his car identified on someone's clip of the street races, the ones that were splashed all over the internet.

All the plates came from vehicles with the same bodyshell as his car, which would be enough for any casual check. The donor vehicles were wrecks, either abandoned at the side of the road or racing accidents. Collecting spare plates was almost a reflex, and he'd considered walking around the yard before buying the paint.

While he switched the plates, Ghost had been looking at the car and bike. "We have been watching you drive and we believe we could do so. The authorities will not be looking for two vehicles, each with one human." She gestured towards the bike. "We would like to learn to use your trophy, if you will

chest, plastering herself up his back. Her breath tickled his ear. "Now we will lean whenever you do." Jamie tried to ignore the waft of her scent and accelerated slowly away. Even so, he felt her arms tighten.

Not for long. Within a couple of miles Ghost was sat upright, barely holding on and shouting, asking how much faster he could go. Jamie remembered that noise when he'd hit the nitrous and opened the throttle. Ghost wasn't as loud this time, but the occasional high warble as he took a bend, or left the ground over a hump, confirmed it. Regardless of species or form, she was either a speed freak or an adrenaline junky.

Though Ghost wasn't human, so it wasn't adrenaline, and Jamie still had no idea just how crazy Ghost Claw were.

FLOAT LIKE A POD

Just over an hour later, it wasn't adrenaline that prompted Jamie to pull over near a clump of trees and bushes, it was his bladder. The bike was still moving when Ghost leapt off the back. Jamie looked around, startled, but Ghost whirled away, leaping and writhing, with her arms out wide or above her head and giving little yips, chittering noises, and warbles. Almost human, but sometimes her body curved where it should bend, as if she had extra joints in her spine—and possibly springs in her heels.

A last twirl brought her back to the bike, eyes wide and a huge smile on her face. "We must learn to control this, and take one when we leave." Her face dropped a little, but recovered. "If we leave, but if we must stay, then we will ride this every day!"

He didn't want to rain on any parades, but Jamie was sure she'd said life pod, which didn't sound very big. Science fiction tended to show them as large coffins with life support. "Will there be room to take a bike?"

"Oh yes. The life pod had six night-nests. We sacrificed two rooms and extended the front to install bigger thrusters, the missiles, and an interstellar jump, but there is still room for one of these." She produced a perfect Salome pout. "Not your trophy of course, but if we do this and remove coverings, perhaps someone will give me one?"

"Probably. Now stay here because I have to hide behind a tree." Jamie laughed as she looked around, puzzled. "Not a problem, it's just that bodily functions are kept private."

"We should watch, as this body is now human so we must learn how."

“Wrong sex, your plumbing is different.” Jamie thought frantically. He hadn’t processed Ghost now having a near-human body, but not knowing how to operate the machinery, as it were. Considering how much she ate, it would be a problem sooner rather than later. “I’ll show you a toilet, the right place for this, the next time I see one. I’m sure it’ll come naturally.” He hoped so. Babies had no trouble, but they also had diapers. “Just don’t let anything out of any orifices, and let me know if you feel too full.”

As he went behind the tree, Jamie hoped it came naturally—Ghost certainly had no trouble operating the rest of her new body. He sniggered as he remembered that pout. With that and no sense of modesty, she’d get away with bloody murder. The next thought sobered him. The way she used a knife, and collected guns, she might *need* to get away with a murder—or a massacre.

As Ghost snuggled in against his back and they took off again, Jamie thought about what else she’d said, that she might have to stay. He wasn’t sure how she’d make a living, but her first problem would be a place to live. It might be safer for the rest of humanity, but Jamie wasn’t keen on sharing accommodation. He had a nasty suspicion she’d want to share the night-nest.

Now he knew that was a real human body, the ‘knowing means it isn’t sexy’ thing wasn’t working as well. Since she could also turn into a monster in a heartbeat, the combination of physical attraction and horror would send him crazy within days. It occurred to Jamie that if he accepted the Maldives pad from Damian, he might persuade her to sleep in separate rooms—with locks and bolts.

He wondered how long Ghost would live, and if he could keep her there, out of trouble, if she couldn’t go back to the stars. If he couldn’t, the war zone would be a long way away from anyone he cared about. Nearly wrapping the bike around a rock jerked Jamie back to the present.

~~

Avoiding rocks, and hitting the throttle now and then to get Ghost to warble, kept Jamie from worrying about the spaceship and Hunter thing. So did taking her behind some rocks, because there weren't any rest stops on the side roads. He explained removing coverings, squatting, and cleaning, then handed her a fistful of tissues and got out of there as her shorts came down.

While she dealt with that, he texted Shania with the new phone. *"Hi Frankie. All okay so far."* He hoped her phone didn't treat the strange number as spam and junk it, and the FBI might treat it as a wrong number if they got that far. Frankie was a reference he didn't think anyone would pick up on, but Shania would know who'd called. He turned the phone off—he still wasn't ready for Shania's opinion on what he was doing.

There was some light relief when a police chopper swooped down to investigate the dust plume behind them. As instructed, Ghost waved with both hands and blew kisses, and it veered away again. Even so, Jamie was glad they hadn't taken the direct route. The dirt roads kept their speed down, and meant detours, but now he didn't begrudge the extra time.

If there was a chopper this far off I-40, there must be cop cars all over the road itself, and any towns along it. They'd stop everyone, if only to ask if they'd seen the car, and would want IDs. As it was, although Jamie had to drive under the highway, the only person they met was a guy in a pickup truck. Not so much a meeting as a raised hand as they passed each other, and he might not have noticed Ghost on the back. Avoiding the outskirts of Tucumcari, and the larger clusters of buildings here and there, meant that by the time Jamie pulled onto the 54 to Nara Visa, the sun was setting.

Floodlights and a couple of big diggers in the distance, off the road to the north, started Jamie worrying again. There wasn't any sign of movement, but he'd just remembered what

Ghost said about a search at the crater. If she'd parked the spaceship too near, and there were still people on-site, they might notice his lights. They might see the pod when it moved—then there'd be jets and all hell would break loose.

Ghost tapped him on the back, then shouted in his ear and pointed south, off to the right. "The lights are where we left a crater. Our pod is that way, but still a long way."

Jamie looked at the broken ground, stopped, and took out his phone. Google showed dirt tracks here and there, enough to move in roughly the right direction, and then Ghost could have a look around again. The shadows were spreading and joining, and the sun had started to dip below the horizon, but he still didn't use his lights. It was too late to fix the pod tonight, so he hoped there was somewhere to sleep in Nara Visa, a cheap motel somewhere.

It seemed to take hours as Ghost occasionally pointed, and Jamie looked on his phone to find tracks in the right direction. The sun finally disappeared, but it was a clear night, and the quarter-moon and starlight were enough until he ran out of road. Not exactly road, more like ruts where someone had driven often enough to make them, but they'd been enough for a bike. Now Ghost was pointing, but neither Google nor Jamie's eyes could find any sort of track.

~~

When the slope dipped and the arroyo sides rose, Jamie pulled up rather than try to ride down a cliff. The shadows hadn't been hiding the track—the ground stopped. Ghost said they were near enough, so Jamie laid the bike down and looked all around. Ahead, there was a steep slope down into what he could now see was an arroyo, maybe four hundred yards wide. "Is your spaceship in there? If we backtrack and head north or south, there are ways to get down, then there's a track along the bottom."

The whole area looked completely deserted, bare scrubland

except for several unconcerned steers. Nara Visa was about four miles away to the north, but there wasn't a direct route, even in a four-by-four. Jamie had passed several buildings along the dirt tracks, but now all he could see were a couple of house lights in the distance. The crater floodlights had disappeared behind a rise some time ago.

Ghost pointed straight ahead and down. "We are very close, as we left it well away from tracks. Once we were near enough, I activated the beacon to head straight for it. It is very low-power so Hunter will not detect it, but we should hurry." She looked either way. "If you can take us down this slope, we can send the code for it to hover lower, and unlock the airlock. We still can't get too close to the pod, or we could set off an alarm or maybe a trap."

"Send the code with what?" It had taken him long enough, but Jamie had finally realised that despite all the talk of listening to communications, Ghost had arrived starkers. "Where's the transmitter, or receiver? I thought you were totally human now?" Even as he said it, Jamie realised the translator must be under her skin, so there could be a radio as well.

"Ninety percent, less now our pelt has reverted, because part of us must remain Slashtail to trigger the reversion. It is not a quick or easy conversion, not with such a small sample of what you call DNA to guide us." Ghost gestured towards the invisible spaceship. "That small amount of Slashtail permeates our body, every cell, and is enough to be detected by advanced sensors. Your body cannot do that, so your portion of Slashtail is smaller, a package hidden deep inside where nothing but another Slashtail can sense it."

Tapping just below her shoulder, opposite her heart, Ghost shrugged. "The communication unit is neither human nor Slashtail. It is organic to avoid scans, but adapts and remains operational regardless of the body surrounding it. The unit automatically listens on all available channels, and we asked it to watch for mentions of space or aliens. We used it to prevent transmissions to and from the police at the roadblock."

It took a real effort, but Jamie ignored what was apparently a living comms centre—for now at least. "So because my added bit is hidden, I can just walk out there and Hunter won't shoot me?" At least Ghost wasn't controlling him or Jamie would be marching out there—but that wasn't much consolation just now.

"You are an indigene, a native of this planet. His instruments will ignore you as they ignore the other animals, or every cow, bird, and moth would trigger the alarm." Ghost pointed down again. "Could you ride your bike down there first? If you leave us here, you will have to fly the pod up the slope, and if you catch the ground, you may disturb the disguise."

Looking along the slope, there were a couple of places Jamie thought he could get down, even on a road bike like this one. "We stole the wrong bike for this, but yeah, I can do it. Just sit still, even if you think we're going over." It was close in a couple of places, but Jamie got down without dropping the bike, though he wouldn't get any further. "I hope this is good enough, or you've got a way of flying a bike over there."

"It would be best if we, and your bike, stayed here."

Jamie hesitated until Ghost stuck a pistol in the back of his belt, then pointed and pushed him, just a little. "There, now you can shoot suspicious shadows. Perhaps we should emit human pheromones and remove coverings, then ask again?"

Jamie hoped the smile meant that was a joke. "That might encourage me to stay. I'm on the way." If she really was a human, he wouldn't have minded a hug or kiss for luck, but the alien equivalent could be a lick. As he hesitated, his hand came up and stroked her head, right down her back to the end of her hair. "Er, for luck? Sorry." It was just an impulse, one he kept having, and this time his hand got away from him.

At least the quiet smile wasn't annoyed. "That was unexpected, but pleasant. Please, stroke our pelt whenever you wish, or for luck." Her smile widened a little, and the next part might have been teasing. "You will be popular on my world if you stroke all the Slashtails." That was bloody tempting, because her pelt was really soft, and just for a moment he'd had that image of being buried in a wriggly soft blanket. Dragging his mind back to the job in hand, Jamie stood up and set off in the direction she'd pointed.

~~

Jamie wanted to look around, to try and spot any traps or the pod, but he had to watch his feet or he'd trip. Ghost insisted he should walk slowly until he felt resistance, so he did, except for when he had to scramble across two hollows. He hoped the pod wasn't just above either one, or he'd missed it. Looking around, Jamie tried to see any sign, but he had to stop before he veered off-course.

He was beginning to think he'd missed, that he'd gone off-course or it had been above those hollows, but then he felt his hair pushed down against his head. Jamie reached up to scratch his head and could feel definite pressure, so he took a slow, casual look around. He was alone, because he'd laid the bike down and Ghost must have crouched down out of sight. No Hunter, unless he looked like a steer—Jamie had a nasty moment where he realised Ghost could probably look like a steer, but she must know these were real.

Reaching up, slowly, Jamie's hand met what felt like a metal plate. A glance up showed that the night sky was distorted, as if he was looking at a reflection in a slightly curved mirror. He felt the surface slide slowly sideways, so he moved his hand up and sideways to follow it, but he had to take a step to find an edge, which meant a large opening.

Feeling around over the edge, Jamie stopped for a moment as his hand disappeared. He pulled it back and it was fine, so he pushed it upwards very slowly. It looked really weird as his fingertips, then fingers, and then hand apparently sank into the night sky! He concentrated, but there wasn't any tingling, though his skin might be a little warmer.

Reassured, Jamie felt around and found a bar he could grip, then put up his other hand and took a quick look around. Still nobody in sight, so Jamie pulled with both arms and jumped, and got up far enough to throw one elbow past the edge. Even close like this, there was only a little distortion where his arms ended. The top of his head must have disappeared as well, and he wondered if anyone inside could see his brain, then Jamie concentrated on the job at hand.

Using his elbow and forearm to hold on, he felt further into nothingness with the other hand, and found another convenient bar. This time the heave brought his eyes above the level of his elbow, and suddenly Jamie could see the inside of what Ghost said was the airlock. So could anyone nearby, as the lights came on and lit up the ground below.

On the plus side, Jamie could now see he'd grabbed the bottom two of a series of bars that made a ladder, and he used them to scramble inside. The opening closed, then a soft beep announced a door above him opening. Resisting the urge to investigate the boxes and some sort of machinery, Jamie started climbing.

The ladder made it easy, and then there was a handhold on the nearby wall to pull himself up and out of the hole. Ghost had explained, but it was still a relief to find himself standing in a dimly red-lit corridor. Remembering the warning, he touched a yellow panel. It turned orange, and a cover slid across the hole in the floor.

An orange touch-plate at the nearest end of the corridor opened a door, which, as Ghost had promised, revealed a room. The control room she'd called it, which seemed odd in a life pod, but she'd been right, of course. Directly opposite the door was a long console right across the end of the room. Above it, set into the wall, were what looked like a dozen TV screens of different sizes, with banks of lights under small glowing panels.

One of the panels cleared to show what must be alien figures or writing, while a larger screen showed the view outside. The console was tilted to show more lights, panels, switches, and two joysticks. In front of each joystick was a circular seat with a low rim, covered with scratched leather or plastic, and as he moved forward, Jamie saw pedals.

Red, yellow, and orange lights glowed or flashed, and some changed colour. No green ones, he realised, which wasn't reassuring, but there weren't any blaring alarms. More of the TV screens lit up, with the largest showing his bike, and Ghost, so she'd stood up. Jamie worried about the floodlights for a moment, then realised they would have created shadows—the pod was using some sort of night vision.

Ghost was beckoning so he sat on the right-hand seat as instructed—and shot to his feet again! It felt alive! A long look didn't reveal any movement, so he tried again. This time he stayed put, relaxing as he realised the seat was altering to suit his shape. Jamie moved back instead of perching on the edge —just in time, as the bit behind him surged up to provide a backrest.

The whole seat narrowed, and raised up so his feet naturally reached the ground instead of being too high, and Jamie wondered if that meant Ghost was short. He could have been diverted, trying to work out a shape from the seat and where the controls were, but he didn't have time. Ghost was still beckoning, but now she was using both hands.

Looking at the big screen directly ahead, the pod wasn't aimed directly towards her. Jamie took hold of the stick and pushed gently sideways, and the view moved across until she was in the centre of the screen. It kept going when he didn't quite centre it, so Jamie moved it back. This time he let go, and the stick centred, stopping the movement.

He pushed it gently forward, and Ghost began to grow as the pod eased forward. Pushing more made it go faster, then Jamie let go. He can't have pushed dead straight as it had started to veer off. Ghost had been right, the control was simple, but operating it was harder than expected.

He'd have probably done better if he'd relaxed and treated it like a gaming joystick, but he couldn't—he was flying a bloody spaceship! Jamie let go, and the pod stopped as the stick snapped back to its default position. He lined up again, and this time concentrated on keeping straight.

Jamie was just congratulating himself, and relaxing, when Ghost pulled the long-barrelled pistol out of her belt, and aimed it at him. He had a few very bad moments before he realised—she was shooting lower, at something below him. Jamie pushed the stick forward, resisting the urge to spin around and look, and the ground scrolled past faster. He wavered a bit but corrected without stopping—he had no idea what was chasing him.

Ghost dropped the pistol, but pulled out another and kept shooting, which wasn't reassuring. Jamie suddenly realised he'd kept pushing too long and pulled back on the stick, but he'd already overshot. He flinched because he might have hit Ghost, or the slope, then realised she was in a hollow.

~~

Finally stopped, Jamie spun the view around, then back because he went too far, and there were three little robots and three holes in the ground. The holes were in a triangle, with the nearest half-blocked by a heap of scrap that had apparently been digging itself out. Tracks showed that the next heap of scrap, stopped but still smoking a little, came out of the left-hand hole, while the mechanical mole on the right was still operational. It was leaking smoke from a hole in the front, but although it was dragging two broken legs, the other six were still making progress.

At the moment, it was climbing out of the second of the hollows Jamie had navigated. As it reached the lip it rocked back on its suspension, and two smaller holes appeared, while the arm with a pointed lump on the end spun away. Jamie was pleased—that had looked like a weapon aimed right at him, or maybe a missile. The robot rocked back again, and this time a bright flash scattered half the dome on top across the landscape. Smoke trickled out, and Ghost's voice rang out above Jamie's head.

"Let go of the controls, Jamie, and move away from the seat. Now you have activated it, the pod will accept remote instructions." As Jamie moved away from the seat the view turned, and showed a quick view of the bike before it disappeared underneath. *"Come to the airlock, please, and lower a cable."*

A few minutes later, Jamie had passed pod loading 101, using a powered winch to lower a cable and hook and then hauling up the bike. Ghost followed with one athletic bound, lunging sideways for a grip once she was inside. "There was a trap, three buried devices, arranged so the pod had to pass close to one if it tried to leave. We destroyed the one that came up beneath you, but that one must have activated the others."

Jamie was hurrying after her as she headed for the controls. "I saw a gun on one, I think."

Ghost glanced back and smiled. "Launcher. The drones were meant to transmit an alarm and fire a tracker. They also carried short-ranged weapons meant to immobilise us. Their simple programming prioritised the threat, the firearms, rather than the pod, so they tried to reach me. Then the rough ground slowed them just long enough."

She inspected the seat adapted for Jamie, then sat and waited as it reformed just enough to fit her. "The head wouldn't have penetrated a pod hull, so it would have broken and spread a very tough, fast-setting adhesive. Dissolving the glue without the correct products would be almost impossible, so the fastest way to remove the tracker would be by cutting a piece out of the hull. That would have compromised our shield, the disguise, then Hunter's ship would have spotted us."

As she spoke, Ghost was flicking switches and moving sliders, and more lights turned orange or red. "Hunter will be heading this way so we must leave, but first we will deal with Hunter's spies."

Jamie was more worried about someone from Nara Visa, especially the people investigating the mystery crater. At the moment the lip of the arroyo cut off any view of the surrounding countryside, but the gunfire would have sounded like a full-scale battle. He wasn't in charge so he headed for the other seat, but kept an eye on Ghost.

A joystick with a yellow button popped out, with a screen above it showing the scene and a targeting circle and cross. It was like a game—Ghost put the crosshairs on each robot in turn and thumbed the button. A flickering beam hit the robot, just for a few seconds, but the result was impressive. Each time metal glowed and then slumped, melted, while sparks flew and things inside burst into flame.

Ghost quickly targeted the larger bits that had blown free, melting them. "Now they won't tell him which way we left, and humans will not be able to salvage any technology. There are severe penalties for technological pollution of primitive worlds." She took hold of the joystick and the pod flew along the arroyo for a while, before lifting up over the lip to head cross-country.

When he'd first entered the pod, Jamie had considered ramming the arroyo wall, disturbing the disguise. He figured that this was as remote as he was going to find—a good place for an alien battle—but then he realised he needed Ghost on board. The shooting would have gotten people looking this way, so once they were high enough, opening the airlock so the light shone out would have been enough. Now he totally abandoned any idea of attracting the military, or Hunter.

The escape pod name had fooled him into thinking it would be small and harmless, but now he knew that whatever it was called, he was in an alien war machine. It was invisible, bounced off rocks without a dent, flew around without a sound —*and had a bloody ray gun that melted metal!* That beam would burn a hole right through some poor sucker in a plane or tank, and they'd never see it coming. Now Jamie was just hoping anyone who heard the gunfire had ignored it.

Coming out of the valley confirmed Jamie's worst fears. "What about those?" He pointed at the lights coming their way, four vehicles at least, though they had to be a couple of miles away. A lot further for them, as the rough ground meant that none could head straight towards the pod. "Shouldn't we stay in the arroyo so they can't see us?"

He was more interested in making sure Ghost didn't decide to hit them with that beam, but she laughed. "They cannot see us unless we wait until they are very close, and then we will just be a vague distortion of the sky beyond us, and perhaps a couple of odd reflections. The wreckage will keep any interest centred here, well away from Albuquerque."

Jamie nodded, remembering he couldn't see the damn thing from a few inches away. When the searchers arrived, they'd assume a few guys had been having fun shooting at home-made robot targets, or maybe remote-controlled cars. The melting metal part might puzzle them, but most people didn't think of aliens as the first explanation for a mystery.

~~

Ghost flew west, away from the wreckage, cross-country rather than following Jamie's tyre tracks, while Jamie sat in the other form-fitting seat. Once she reached Highway 54, she accelerated until the road was hurtling past about fifty feet below them. "I can't see why you were so keen on the bike. This is a lot faster."

"But no bumps, no wind, no chance of an accident because if we let go, we just stop." She did so and the stick centred, then although the pod slowed quickly, there was no sensation inside. Ghost accelerated again. "All transport is like this, or not quite, as we disabled some features in here. Otherwise, the pod would have warned you when you turned quickly, and told you not to fly so low, or over us and your trophy. If you had been going to hit us, standard programming would have stopped you automatically."

Turning towards him, Ghost smiled, ignoring the finger Jamie pointed at the screen she should be watching. "We will not be allowed to ride our bike on the more advanced worlds, or not where anybody can see. Except at home, where Ghost Claw clan are allowed to be different—most laws do not apply to us."

"If I visit, I'm applying for membership." Jamie relaxed as she turned back to the screen, and looked around. The instruments and screens, most of them still dark and silent, reminded him this was a sort of spaceship. He thought of Earth's attempts to conquer space, and the safety stuff made more sense. Not just space, everything these days had safeguards on the safeguards, and the safety laws were gradually tightening.

He'd seen people on the internet, complaining that some countries were already strangled by regulations, but others wanted the US to do the same. There was talk that some places only had electric cars, driverless on main roads, while trucks, trains, or buses only had drivers in case the automatics broke down. A couple of people he knew reckoned some states, and foreign countries, wouldn't allow anything but electric cars on main highways and freeways. Some states insisted they were driverless, and Jamie had heard the whole of Europe was like that, but so far New Mexico was holding out.

He figured there might be a point to the electric cars, if it really would help with the spring floods and the water shortages in the summer. The global warming thing didn't really affect Jamie, and some guys on the internet reckoned it was bullshit, but Shania reckoned it was real, and serious. Even so, there wasn't any real need for driverless cars and all the other regulations, but they were creeping in.

All of Damian's cars were electric, and three were self-drive. Just like the pod, they stayed a minimum distance from other vehicles, so they couldn't crash. They also kept below the speed limits, and followed sensors so they couldn't swerve off the road, or even switch lanes without a reason. Even gas-powered vehicles were computerised, regulating this and controlling that to stop emissions, while the government and manufacturers seemed determined to stamp out independent repairers. On top of that, the price of spares and gas kept rising, so eventually older cars and non-electric engines would disappear.

Jamie realised Ghost was looking at him with a little smile, instead of watching the countryside ahead—which sort of proved the point. "You might want to see us at home first, before joining our clan. We are a little wilder there." She laughed and leant towards him. "Some of the other clans might kidnap you just to stroke their pelts."

He could take a hint, so Jamie stroked her head right down to the small of her back, the end of her hair, pelt. It really was incredibly soft and silky. Ghost sighed and leant back into her seat, then her smile disappeared. "We used the wrong weapon against Hunter's devices. The shotgun would have destroyed them quicker."

He hesitated for a moment, but Jamie had to reassess making Ghost more dangerous. That Hunter type might squash Jamie if he got in the way, but he was beginning to think Ghost wouldn't. She might even save his life—if she knew enough about guns to deal with Hunter. "The buckshot would have spread, so I doubt you'd have hit the first one at that range, and maybe not the second. The long-barrelled pistol was the right weapon, or the best option without my rifle. Pistols and shotguns aren't long-range." Jamie glanced back, though there wasn't a rear window. "Though you got all three, so maybe it's just that most shooters aren't that good."

"Here, these smaller screens show other directions, including up and down, though alarms will tell us if there is any chance of a collision." Ghost flipped switches and a row of the smaller screens lit up, showing views including the night sky above. "The usual sensors would also avoid the collision, but sometimes Ghost Claw want to hit something."

She frowned, definitely not happy about something. "We had hoped to do better after the rifle, but the smaller weapons have very primitive aiming facilities, and are badly affected by gravity. Without ranging equipment, we wasted some projectiles." She shook her head, sharply, and made that annoyed clicking noise. "We know the correct terms now, so accepting the translator's first suggestion is lazy. If we persevere, it will learn the preferred usage."

~~

Ghost took a breath and tried again, speaking a little slower. "With only the small metal sights we wasted bullets, then when we switched to another weapon, it had different characteristics so we wasted more. We didn't use the shotgun because it has no sights, but then we had used up the rest and we have not practiced reloading."

Ignoring the screen, she pulled a pistol from her belt and pulled the trigger, proving it was empty. "If the shotgun hadn't worked, I would have been left with throwing this, knives, and rocks. We must practice with all the weapons, aiming as well as reloading so we will need more ammunition."

Jamie thought Ghost already had enough ammunition, once she knew how to reload, but there was a simple answer. "The hardened rounds for the rifle, and maybe ammo for Lucie's gun, the magnum, are illegal because they'll go through armour. There are places that might sell the rest, but I don't have the cash. I'll use up most of what I've got left just renting rooms for us tonight." He'd end up broke, but that wasn't new, and this time it was for a good cause—world peace.

"Perhaps not." Ghost had a little half-smile now. "You allowed guest-share of your sleeping nest, so we should do the same. Providing you will follow Slashtail tradition?"

Jamie was wary, because if that half-smile meant what it did on humans, she was teasing him. "What tradition?"

Ghost's smile widened. "You must stroke our pelt before sleeping, to help us relax. It is very close to a Slashtail greeting-to-kin, which might be why we like it."

"Greeting-to-kin? But we aren't related." Jamie was completely confused when Ghost burst out laughing.

"But we are, once you took in a little of us and we absorbed a little of you." Her laughter died and Ghost looked very serious for a moment. "No Slashtail would extend sleeping-nest-share to anyone not of their clan."

Her voice stopped any jokes—she was more serious about that than killing. "Er, in that case I am honoured. What will the rest of your clan think?"

"We are content. Ours is a small clan now, and believe your mechanical aptitude will be an asset." Ghost looked up at the screen as a tone sounded, and a series of alien characters scrolled down one side. "We are close enough to activate the tracker we placed in your vehicle. Now I have the bearing, I will turn it off so Hunter doesn't use it to trace us. We must find somewhere for you to leave the pod without being seen, and where we can meet later."

That might be a problem, and would get more urgent with time. "I'll need someplace out of sight so I can bring tools inside. When they can't find my car, the cops will issue a dozen pictures of it in different colours, and send patrols to check any parking. Eventually they'll find it, and then we'll lose anything left inside. Is there any way to hide it, like this pod?"

Even then, Jamie wasn't sure where to put it. There were a limited number of places where he wouldn't leave mysterious tracks, and someone or something wouldn't bump into an invisible car.

~~

That wouldn't be a problem—Ghost couldn't disappear a car. "Not while it is contact with the ground. The field must go all the way around, but if we lift something that large, the power signature will be too obvious. Hunter will detect us, and some of your military facilities may show anomalies." Ghost pointed ahead to the first buildings. "But first you must leave the pod unseen."

"First we find a place to hide a car." Jamie used his phone to bring up Santa Rosa on Google.

"How effective is human detection of transmissions?" Ghost pointed to a small yellow flashing light, and some gibberish on the screen above it. "The pod had already detected your device, and now it is warning me you have started transmitting. If Hunter realises it is yours, he will be able to trace our location. Unless it is using a directed beam?"

"No." Jamie had bought a phone to text Shania, in case the FBI read the messages, but hadn't thought about them tracing his own phone. It was Papa's phone because it had all the business contacts, and was still in Papa's name, but now he wondered if the FBI would make the connection. He immediately turned his phone off, then remembered some things that had been said about cell phones.

Jamie wasn't sure which was true, so he took out the battery,

SIM, and additional memory. The flashing yellow light went out when the phone was turned off, but the orange light persisted until he took out the battery. "I wanted to find out which houses were for sale, then use an overhead map to find one with hidden parking." A view of the ground below came up on a screen, then a portion of the view zoomed in on a street sign.

The pod cruised above Santa Rosa while Jamie and Ghost looked for 'For Sale' signs, then she checked each hit for hot spots, people. The overhead view also allowed Jamie to look for a place where both his car and the pod would be out of sight of passers-by, or neighbouring properties, but there wasn't anywhere. He began to think they'd have to risk driving out into the countryside, but Ghost found one she thought was worth risking. The car would be hidden and then the pod could hover above it, low enough to hide anything going up or down.

~~

Leaving the pod was easy, once Jamie realised how near to the ground or a wall the pod could hover. With Ghost giving him a bird's-eye view, Jamie could see that the cops had checkpoints on the accesses to I-40, but weren't actively searching Santa Rosa. Most of the lights were around the ambush point, though one lane was open for traffic. His car was still in among the rest, with no watchers, or none that Ghost's instruments could detect.

Well before midnight, Ghost descended into the narrow, shallow valley containing the creek, still invisible despite the lights from the town. A quick check to make sure nobody had a clear view, and Jamie jumped down, landing crouched. He gave Ghost time to move away, so he didn't bang his head, then stood up. There were no shouts of alarm, so he walked towards the buildings and the Blue Hole sinkhole. There were always a few pedestrians around there, so he didn't stand out as he headed into town.

Even if a camera had seen him appear from mid-air, investigation would only show footprints leading to the sidewalk. Relieved, he diverted into the all-night store to buy a cheap plastic sheet and another very cheap phone, then headed for his car. Now that he'd shut his own phone down, Jamie wanted a second option.

There was no hurry, so Jamie took his time, drinking a can of Coke while watching the cars and nearby houses. Knowing that Ghost was also watching, and could snatch him in seconds, was very reassuring. There were a few people about, and the occasional car parked or left, but nobody looked suspicious.

Eventually Jamie plucked up his courage and headed for his car. The hooked end on his telescopic rod detached the driver's-side mesh, and he slid in through the window. At least the paint was dry. Even if Jamie caught the edges, he wouldn't have more orange streaks on his jeans. A short pause while he waited for searchlights and shouting, then he drove away.

It wasn't far, but seemed to take ages as Jamie was still waiting for the wail of sirens, but so far the quick disguise was working. He would love to check on the news, but he'd have to wait, though Ghost promised she could access whatever he wanted once they were parked up.

~~

Jamie headed for the best option, a bungalow with bushes hiding the end of the driveway and garage door from the road. There'd been nobody inside when the pod drifted above the roof, and when he drove past, Jamie still couldn't see any signs of life. A loop around the nearby streets, and this time Jamie killed the lights as he turned up the drive.

When he turned in behind the bushes, the ladder extending from a black hole in mid-air, just outside the garage, meant Ghost was already here. Jamie threw the cheap plastic sheet over his car, in case a helicopter came over, and put a foot on the ladder. It shot up into the darkened hold, which solved the problem of someone seeing him climbing.

Since they finally had some time when they weren't travelling, or trying to avoid sudden death, Ghost gave Jamie a tour of the pod. He'd always pictured escape pods as a sort of coffin with protection and life support, but this was much bigger. According to Ghost, this one had been modified for Slashtails, so all the sleeping rooms held proper night-nests. That was a large, round, padded dish that could probably hold five or six friendly humans, so it didn't give any hint of her real size or shape.

This one was a little higher off the floor than usual, as there was a second night-nest below it. If the night-nests were too crowded, the top one was raised halfway to the ceiling, like a giant bunk-bed. There was one cleanser per sleeping room, an advanced shower with blow-dry the way she described it, which was behind a curved door cutting off one corner of the room. Some races wore coverings, which could be cleaned in the same unit.

The engine room had a few big pipes running along the wall, but the actual workings were tucked away behind panelling. Several warped panels, shattered gauges, and some scorch marks warned Jamie this wouldn't be a quick fix. He might have asked more, but finding a safe hiding place, and the tour, had relaxed him. That led to a problem, and there wasn't a tree or convenient rock.

The toilet seemed odd to Jamie, though the operation was easy. Drop pants, then reverse into or sit on a daffodil-shaped pipe. The end would respond to the contact and allegedly spread to form a seal, then clean him afterwards. Jamie tried it and wasn't keen, but it did the job.

~~

Mention of food diverted Jamie from the facilities—it had been a long time since those sandwiches. "This time we will feed you, though it will not be very exciting. A spoon rather than a fork, unless you have a long snout or tongue." Ghost pointed to the pad next to a spout above a bowl. "That will take a very small DNA sample, then the machine will extrude a paste which will contain everything necessary for life. Some forms of life require extra liquid." This time she indicated a different spout and bowl. "Since humans seem to be mostly water, that is what you will be given."

The food spout three-quarter-filled a bowl, but Jamie struggled to find anything complimentary to say about it. "At least it has colour." The bright pink paste was thick enough to spoon up without risk of dripping, and cool enough to eat. "Pink pea soup?" Sort-of pea soup, the very faint hint of taste had a pea-ish sort of flavour. "Is this what the er, people on other planets eat, thick soup?"

That prompted a curled lip, so gloop wasn't Ghost's usual food. "No, this is to keep survivors alive, perhaps for a long time. The colour and what is considered taste will vary, but there is no way to choose. The uncertainty is meant to alleviate boredom." Ghost gestured to the machine. "Providing there are the basic constituents, this would keep everyone in a filled life pod alive for about one of your years. If they were stranded longer, there is a facility to slow life processes."

Ghost put her own bowl under the spout and touched the pad. "Since this body requires local food, we collected suitable nourishment on the way here, animals and vegetation." She spooned up gloop, light blue in her case, and grimaced. "We hope we can eat local food most of the time and save this for emergencies, or never."

Jamie was still coming to terms with the pod hoovering up parts of the New Mexico countryside. He was trying to remember if they passed over crops and herds, and hoping she didn't mean grass, a few bushes, and a stray coyote. Then he realised they couldn't afford anything else. "Me too, but you might remember me saying I didn't have much cash." Once he explained properly, finance could be less of a problem—depending on Jamie's stance on counterfeiting.

He was flexible, but worried about being caught, though Ghost swore the paper, ink, and any security features in Jamie's remaining cash would be duplicated. He wouldn't be going mad, buying luxuries, because that included identical serial numbers, so Jamie couldn't spend more than the original amount. On the other hand, he could spend nearly four hundred dollars as many times as he wanted to—as long as it was in different places.

He was wrong. "I did not have time to search all the bodies, but you looted paper currency from the first bodies." Ghost offered a small bundle of notes. "If we duplicate this as well, it will give us more flexibility." A quick count and an extra three hundred and forty-five dollars was more flexibility than Jamie usually had. Over seven hundred dollars of flexibility, a fortune before he met Ghost, but now he'd need it copied more than once.

Before going down that route, Jamie wanted to know just how much trouble he was in.

~~

When Ghost used the pod's comms equipment to log onto the web and TV, Jamie couldn't help but smile at some of it. Not the official pictures, but someone had leaked the photos taken by at least one cop. Those on TV showed a lot of Salome, some of them including her smiling face, but not the ones down her shirt. The internet, however, had them all, including close-ups down her shirt and the view as she left.

Apart from accidental glimpses in the background, the pictures didn't include the car or her driver, and neither were news. Jamie would have trouble identifying himself from the half-shot of the back of his head, though enough sections of his car were in backgrounds to give make, model, and colour. He'd be spraying the bike orange, because part of that was in two of the shots as he drove away.

The rest wasn't funny at all. There were some long-range shots of broken bikes and the sprawled figures of the riders, and two had survived. The line of trucks didn't look too bad, until the cameras zoomed in enough to see the bodies—and splashes of blood. No survivors and no close-ups, though Jamie knew some would leak onto the web eventually.

The police wanted to talk to any witnesses, especially anyone who knew Hellbats, and issued a picture of a jacket to help people's memories. The pictures of Lucie and other Hellbats had to be from driving licenses, and the ones identified as Salome Malone had enough clothes on to be official releases.

Her lawyer must have insisted on the disclaimer straight after those were shown, and might be the man who came on straight after the news clip. "Salome Malone denies any involvement, and can prove she was nowhere near the gang war or the four police officers. The alleged pictures are clearly a fake, and we will be insisting that all sites remove them." Not a chance. Those pictures were spread far enough across the web to be immortal now.

Salome gave an interview where she confirmed it wasn't her, but implied she wouldn't mind being accosted by four guardians of law and order and offered them real pictures. The news was more interested in her than the actual shootings, but Jamie finally got the gist. "Even if I resprayed the car, properly, I reckon the law will want to talk to me. They'll go back to interview everyone near my workshop, properly this time. Nobody cared about Hellbat bodies in the Pits, but a shoot-up on a public highway is the sort of crime that gets people excited."

The dirt track and Jamie's place were on the TV, background in the official shots taken by the cops, though nobody but a local would recognise the place. That would include Shania, so even if she hadn't picked up the note, she might now. He hoped nobody connected them, or Damian wouldn't be happy.

Jamie was trying to see a way to go back to his old life, but couldn't. If a neighbour had told the Hellbats he was involved, the cops would find out. Then even if he strolled in and tried to bluff it out, they'd want to talk to the mystery woman.

~~

The mystery woman was busy working through the firearms: cocking, firing, and swapping magazines. There wasn't any danger because Jamie had unloaded everything and emptied the magazines. "Will these Road Rams also declare feud?"

"Probably not." Jamie fervently hoped not, or Hunter and the cops wouldn't need his car—they'd just follow the trail of bodies. "If they stick to claiming that stopping the traffic was because they'd heard the Hellbats were going to hit us, that might be enough to keep them out of jail. Since the Road Rams also diverted traffic from in front of us, and on the other highway, they must have had really good info. I reckon they either knew the Hellbats and it was a favour, or they were paid. Claiming it was a public service to prevent innocent deaths is smart."

Jamie was relieved—they were a local gang, but none of the jackets near the trucks had been Road Rams. If Ghost hadn't killed any, the gang would want to keep well away from any fallout.

He gestured at the man in a suit. "From that lawyer's statement, some of the Road Rams got caught. The truck drivers only saw masks and coveralls, so unless the cops can tie them to the hijackings, it's just interfering with traffic. Though if the two Hellbats in intensive care survive, they'll serve time. The Road Rams will dump the lot on them." He sat back and heaved a sigh of relief. "The cops really, really want to talk to us, but haven't got a clean ID, not yet."

“Hunter will be searching, but he will start where we destroyed his mechs. Would you like to start on the engines?” There was just a bit of anxiety in her voice, and Jamie realised —Earth police weren’t Ghost’s real problem. She was fretting about getting the hell away from all things Earth.

“I don’t think I’ll be able to help. Perhaps if you take me to see them, not just the panels, and tried to explain?” When the pod started zooming about, silently, Jamie had realised there was nothing on Earth like these engines. He still wanted to look, partly because Ghost expected him to, but also because he was a mechanic—and they were *alien spaceship engines*!

The inspection had mixed results, but left Jamie feeling more hopeful. The hovering thing had nothing to do with the main engines—it was an entirely different process. He’d dealt with thrusters, controlled rockets, but the electronics, controls, and readouts in the pod were nothing like anything he’d ever seen before. That wasn’t a total deal breaker—he’d never seen the controls on a plane, a submarine, or even a loco.

The physical part, the pipes that moved fuel and fed thrust to the nozzles, were different but only in scale. The jets that Jamie had dealt with were on bikes and a couple of toy rockets, but the basic process was the same. More complicated because there were a lot and some had to steer, but he tried to persuade himself the process was just larger repeats of a straight rocket bike.

Despite the obvious damage, Jamie could see that the setup had been modified, rather like street racers in a way. There were marks where something had been cut away, and homemade brackets, visible welding, and rerouted wiring and piping. His first impression was that extra or larger components had been crammed in, presumably to boost the performance.

~~

Leaning against him, Ghost looked over Jamie’s shoulder.

"Can you fix it? We paid to have this installed, but escape pods aren't meant to be modified so there are no proper schematics. The parts were from different scrap vessels, not necessarily the same type." She was jigging up and down a bit, obviously impatient and on edge. "We just need to break clear, get far enough from Earth's gravity to use the Stellar Jump safely."

Ghost pointed off further along the ship. "There is no Standard Jump or Stellar Jump system fitted in pods, but we gave up rooms to add a Stellar Jump and the missiles. Thrusters and repeated skipping, up to one hundred thousand of your metres at a time, will take us away from strong gravitic influences. Once we are clear, the Stellar Jump will take us to our home system. There we will commandeer another ship, and then we can deal with Hunter and the Starborn Circus."

"I thought you were running away from Hunter?" And the Circus, Jamie remembered.

Jamie flinched as he heard what sounded very much like a growl, right beside his ear. "Only until we are properly armed. Both have caused grievous harm to Ghost Claw, and our reputation insists we take appropriate action." A glance back showed that Ghost was deadly serious—her lips were peeled back and she looked as if she wanted to rip out a throat.

Jamie had the distinct impression that, as well as the mauve pelt, she usually had sharper teeth. At least she stopped growling to speak. "This pod has weapons to deal with small space debris, but nothing that will harm his ship. It is our ship, impounded and then given to Hunter to help him recapture us, which is an insult in itself."

Ghost sighed, deliberately stepping back and relaxing, but Jamie could see it wasn't easy. "If we could get aboard, we could take it away from him. His employers may have hacked the control interfaces, but a drop of our blood will open many back doors into the software. With access we will reinstate our own control."

~~

He'd thought her comrades, the rest of the we, were with the ship, but there'd been no sign. Now Ghost had been talking about capturing a spaceship, but not on her own. He was frightened of the answer, but now Jamie had to know. "Where are they, Ghost? You kept saying we, so I thought there'd be more of you. Now I don't see anyone else, but I remember you saying Ghost Claw agreed with me being clan." He paused and concentrated so his voice wouldn't falter. "Where are the rest of your clan?"

There was a long pause as Ghost looked at him, and Jamie wondered if she was deciding whether to lie. Even when she sighed and her shoulders slumped, she was an alien so it might not have meant anything. "The rest of Ghost Claw, almost all of them, are aboard. It is something humans can't do, but means they aren't able to greet you, not yet. If you can fix the pod, I swear that you will meet them before we leave Earth." The quick smile after that looked mischievous. "Then you will understand why pelt stroking is close to greeting-to-kin."

That wasn't really an explanation, but Ghost obviously didn't want to give details. Jamie wondered if it was some sort of cold storage, but Ghost could just as easily mean their brains were downloaded into a computer, and a new body was grown when they were needed. The others might have told him more about the engines, but if they couldn't, the reason didn't matter.

Thinking of storing brains on computers reminded Jamie of a big problem. "We might have a problem with software. I've got a test kit, but it's for Earth. Can you get me into these systems, or supply some way to highlight problems?" Jamie pointed at the screens, gauges, and lights on the panels. "Or persuade my test kit to talk to the software, and translate whatever language that is? I don't even know what the different coloured lights mean."

"The colours are easy. Yellow is bad, while orange means activated, either in use or ready for use." Quick gestures at orange lights below active screens, and the orange panel for opening the door, demonstrated. "Red means inactive or safe. Some builders use green instead of red, but both mean the same as several races can't tell the difference. Other races can't differentiate blue and yellow, but yellow is favourite as danger signs should be bright."

Ghost patted the dials. "The language is Slashtail, but we can transfer the human equivalents from my translator and reset the display. Pod systems are kept simple and designed to be adaptable, as they may have to communicate with a wide variety of rescuers. The pod and your kit both use electricity so they will connect, and then we'll just have to hope."

Looking around, Jamie couldn't see an obvious way to get outside. "While you deal with the translation, I'd better get my tools in here in case someone spots my car. Do I have to bring everything in through the airlock? Hauling it up a bit at a time will take ages."

"Sorry, but we will help once I am finished here." She must have seen the disappointment on Jamie's face, because Ghost explained. "The loading hatch for provisions and engineering supplies would be too obvious, as the building stops me getting lower. With the lights turned off, the bottom opening for the airlock can't be seen except from directly beneath it. If you load a container, we will bring it up with the cable and winch and send down an empty. While you fill that, we will unload the first one, then switch them."

Gesturing towards the airlock hatch, Ghost turned to stand with her back against a panel. "If you go and get started, we will reset the displays. We will have to stand here to make sure the transmissions from our translator are clear."

~~

By the time Jamie had filled the low-sided box on the end of the cable, Ghost was ready. He rode up with a selection of tools, spares, and his testing and cracking kits, to check how they'd be stored, and found the screens were in familiar numerals and English. Jamie had intended bringing up what he thought he'd need, but now he'd realised that wouldn't work.

Ghost couldn't leave the pod here in daylight, in case a bird or smoke hit it. Even a comment on Twitter might be picked up by Hunter, and once he had her pinpointed, he might open fire. The pod might survive the first volley, but Jamie was sure that anything powerful enough to harm it would wreck the nearby houses. His car would end up like those robots, and with that as an option it was easier to consider abandoning it.

Maybe he'd get it back after Ghost left for the stars, but for now it was a liability. Jamie put the genuine plates back on, then took all the tools, spares, weapons, and enough parts and wiring to immobilise it. When he came up with the last load, Jamie watched through the hatch as it closed, wondering if he'd ever see his ride again. Unless someone who knew cars checked, and realised it was in first-class condition under the shell, it would be crushed.

There was one outside chance, and he should contact Shania anyway. Jamie unboxed the new phone, and there wasn't much credit but he only wanted to send texts. The actual wording took some thought, as eventually someone official might see it. *"Hi there Frankie, just to let you know that your favourite charity project is doing okay. The new partner isn't what we expected, but since it's only temporary we should manage. Once this stage is over, we should relocate, possibly abroad. Our transport has been stolen, so someone should let the cops know. Will be in touch."*

Jamie read it through five times, and then deleted the part about transport. He wasn't sure if Shania could report the car anonymously, and the car would lead the cops to his workshop and the dead Hellbats. Remembering the blood on the carpet, from Lucie's hand, made up Jamie's mind. When the cops got the car, it was a straight link between him and both the Hellbat massacres.

Jamie really hoped the Maldives offer was still open. If he couldn't fix the thrusters, Ghost could fly them there, which would definitely break any trail. Even if he did fix them, he might persuade Ghost to drop him off there before leaving.

After sending the text, Jamie pulled the phone battery, in case Shania's phone was already being hacked. He wasn't sure how easy it was, but he knew that cops, criminals, and even reporters hacked phones, and Papa's phone had Shania's number. Jamie distracted himself by storing everything in a small room with shelves, one of the holds. That led to him wondering how many holds a life pod needed, or if this was another Ghost Clan addition.

Ghost's voice, right behind him, made him jump. "We are parked a long way from any road or track, high enough that nothing will run into us, and too low for aircraft. When can you start? Tomorrow morning?" Ghost managed a smile, but it was definitely forced. "We need to relax, and having our pelt stroked will help."

Jamie didn't mind that part, but remembered the rest. "Ah, right. If this is nest-share, does it mean you'll be sucking out more DNA?" That would mean her changing form, and this time he might see it. He was still wary about her combat skills, but a mauve pelt might mean Ghost's real form would stop him imagining spiky, slimy monsters.

"We swore we would ask, so would you mind, just a little?" She looked down as if she was shy or embarrassed—Ghost must have been studying human mannerisms. "It would help us if we need to adapt our form radically. Adapting quickly during the ambush was very painful, which is why we need to sleep now, to recover properly."

Put like that, Jamie felt he probably owed her a bit more DNA, but now he worried about the actual method. "Exactly how do you get the sample? Like the machine, or a needle or something similar?" Not long hollow fangs, he hoped.

Though if he'd known the full range of options, hollow fangs might not have seemed too bad.

FREAKS AND WILDCARDS

Ghost's relieved smile was a relief to Jamie—she wouldn't have been worried if he'd been under control. "No, we need more than that. Though since we are more human now, and you are willing, we can use our mouth. Similar to the Salome transmissions?" Ghost looked a lot happier now. "If you find that idea distasteful we could remove some coverings, or all of them, and emit pheromones? That seemed to make the males agreeable."

Jamie wrestled with the idea that she wanted to kiss him, then realised no, she was just teasing him again. She'd stick a tube in his mouth and hoover what she needed. "No striptease and no scent, thanks. I told you; I like *your* scent." If Ghost took everything off, then gave him a blast of what she'd used on the police, his alien cherry would be cherry soda. Jamie definitely didn't want to go there, regardless of percentages and packaging. "Where do you take the sample?"

"In the night-nest, bed, after you stroke our pelt, so that we can sleep afterwards and absorb it." She turned and headed for the night-nest and Jamie followed, still not sure about the teasing—or sleeping in her night-nest. He debated saying no, but daren't, though he wasn't as frightened of her as he had been.

Maybe that was because she never threatened him, or it could be her personality—if it wasn't an act. Could an alien adopt a realistic human personality? He stopped worrying when Ghost slid under a thin cover, still dressed.

Just as he relaxed, she started moving under there, then threw out her shorts and top and laughed, probably at his face. Rolling over onto her front, Ghost wriggled in a little and sighed. At least that meant she was covered, and he could sit next to her and stroke her hair without getting personal. Jamie debated, but then took off his shoes, socks, shirt, and jeans, because that was how he slept at home and this bed was wider.

He sat down and reached over, then, rather self-consciously, stroked her hair or pelt. "All of it, please. Push the cover down, or off." Jamie pulled the cover down just past the end of her pelt, halfway down her back, then stroked it all from top to bottom. Ghost gave a happy sigh. "You really will be popular at home."

Jamie kept stroking, eventually lying down because it was very soothing for him as well. He wondered if it was like the dog thing. Stroking dogs was supposed to release some sort of feel-good chemical, which might explain why he drifted.

He was still awake, not quite in a trance, so it took a while to realise the gentle background music was Ghost. She sounded like some sort of musical instrument, a wind thing but not harsh like brass, softer and haunting. The most important part was that the sound seemed happy.

Drifting, half-lost in the music, Jamie had no idea how long he kept stroking her pelt. Presumably long enough as Ghost stopped singing, lifted herself up and over, wrapped her arms around his neck and head, and kissed him. Jamie ended up on his back with Ghost half-laid on him, frantically trying to tell himself DNA sample, it's just a DNA sample. The trouble was that when Ghost lifted up, she'd given him a wonderful view of a very human-looking, half-naked woman. The not-sexy-because-I-know-she's-not-human failed completely.

Now the naked part had made contact, and her tongue was swabbing DNA from the inside of his mouth in a gentle but very persistent and appealing way. When she finally released him, Jamie was quite proud of himself. He'd slipped now and then, kissed her, and his arms had definitely tightened around her, but his hands hadn't strayed at all.

Ghost raised herself on her elbows, looking definitely guilty. "That really was a good way to get my sample, but also an experiment. I'd wondered, after seeing the transmissions?" Her soft, gentle smile reassured Jamie. "This body finds kissing surprisingly pleasant, but you need more Ghost Claw to grow a proper pelt."

She patted his chest, then her eyes dropped. "Oh, we are inappropriate." Ghost turned away and shuffled back under the cover. "My thanks, Jamie, for the stroking *and* DNA."

"You're welcome." Jamie needed a bucket of cold water, but he couldn't complain. Despite what his human body thought, Ghost hadn't been trying to be sexy. He looked down at his none-too-generous chest hair with a little smile—she was right about his pelt. Jamie rolled to the edge of the bed, as far as possible from temptation, pulled the cover up over him, and found it surprisingly easy to sleep.

The stroking must have relaxed him as well, but Ghost had left a definite impression. Jamie dreamt of that soft, snuggly, furry mauve blanket, but now he felt sure Ghost was in there somewhere.

~~

This morning Jamie felt Ghost leave the bed, and opened his eyes before his brain engaged. As a result, he had a lovely view of Ghost stepping into the cleansing cabinet, holding her shorts and top. That definitely woke him up, in a much better mood than usual. Slashtails seemed to think sleeping and walking about naked was normal, and once again he wondered what Ghost really looked like.

Jamie was almost certain she was covered in that soft, very strokable mauve fur, but could be any shape from a long, thin snake to a tree stump. He was also sure she had teeth—and with that snarl they were sharp. Ghost was definitely a killer, with no hesitation, and he'd assumed no conscience—but that didn't match her personality.

When she wasn't fighting, Ghost was generally cheerful, more cheerful than Jamie would be in her position. She'd also started teasing him, which might be an act but it seemed natural. It definitely wasn't seduction. He was an alien so she wouldn't fancy him, but it could be deliberate, to encourage him to keep being helpful.

The cleaner unit opened so once again Jamie abandoned the subject—he'd know eventually. Ghost came out wearing her clothes, and he noticed the smear of orange paint on her shorts had disappeared. That explained why she'd taken them in with her, and now Jamie wondered if the 'cleaning' at home had just been leaving them in the shower cubicle.

Though the missing paint solved one problem—Jamie didn't need a change of clothing. He picked up his clothes, said good morning, and went into the cubicle. He was still looking around for controls when the space filled with mist, a warm draught wafted over him, and he felt as if something invisible was scratching him all over, gently. Remembering the cleaning, Jamie dropped his boxers and shook out his clothes. He wondered if he should rub them, or his skin, but the scratching was getting down to his scalp so he didn't bother.

The mist disappeared, the draught briefly became stronger and warmer, then it stopped. Jamie checked his hair and it was dry, as were his clothes, but a quick sniff at the shirt armpit proved it was clean. When he put his jeans on, an oil stain was gone, so the alien shower worked better than his washer.

He came out to find Ghost leant over the nest, definitely a nest, Jamie decided, and she stood to show him a few long mauve hairs. "Stroking was very relaxing, so we slept well." She turned sideways and tipped her head forward just a little, so Jamie stroked her pelt. Like nest instead of bed, pelt felt right instead of hair.

"Me too, but now I'd better start on the engines." Once Ghost showed him how to open more access panels, Jamie made a tentative start. He tested some wiring and found what seemed to be normal electricity at a slightly different voltage, so he attached an adaptor and plugged in his kit.

For a while it seemed to be searching without finding anything, then the screen cleared and the pod offered an upgrade. Not usually a good idea from a strange source, but his software was backed up, hard copy, and he wasn't going to get any further without it. Jamie reluctantly accepted.

While that downloaded and installed, Jamie brought more spares from the hold, because opening panels had revealed a lot of burned wiring. The kit reported the update was completed, but as soon as he asked it to start analysing, it ran out of computing space. A check showed that the hard drive and RAM were full, which was a shock.

Programmes had become more complicated, but the actual programming was getting tighter, so multi-gigabyte drives usually had plenty of space for calculating or data. Either the alien software was trying to carry out an insane number of simultaneous checks, or alien programming was sloppy, wasteful. Jamie plugged in his prize, a salvaged solid-state ten-petabyte high-speed drive, and an adaptor with eight five-gigabyte USB sticks, and tried again.

This time the kit beeped and a lot of lights lit up. They must have been a good sign as the screen began to report errors, though Jamie had no idea what most of them meant. He started with the obvious, swapping charred wiring for new, and hoped that would change the reports and readings. That would at least tell him which part of this mess some reports referred to, and the new readings should eventually tell him what was normal. Then all he had to do was figure out what the hell that part did.

~~

Still hoping that he'd recognise the normal readings when

he saw them, Jamie pushed on. Electricity obeyed certain rules, and testing had determined which coloured wire matched Earth's, so he knew he wasn't making it worse. There was plenty to work on, just replacing charred wiring all around the blackened and melted components. When Ghost reminded him to eat, Jamie had started removing a few components, and was trying to find out what they did.

"You will be able to fix it?" Ghost looked and sounded nervous.

He thought about what he'd done so far, and Jamie could fix the physical damage, but a lot depended on the damage to the software. Most important human systems had a backup, so if it wasn't too bad the pod might rewrite any damaged sections. "Possibly. It's making more sense than I expected. Once I get the damaged part doing something, then I can refine it. It won't be exactly repaired, more like adapted so it does the same job, maybe. Probably not quite the same way, so I hope you won't be trying any fancy moves."

He didn't have the components to fit new replacements, but that was how Jamie did most repairs. He rarely had the right spares, but he usually got the whatever to function. Sometimes they worked better, like the lawn mower that one of his neighbours now used to go shopping. It was fast enough to stay with the traffic, easier to park, and the grass-box held a lot of groceries. Or the microwave oven that picked up radio, and could be turned on and off using a phone, though remotely accessing the pre-set programmes was a bit hit or miss.

Ghost nodded, still frowning. "We thought so, after looking at the components from your vehicle. They also showed signs of alteration, non-standard deviations that still operated. If my impression is correct, the result probably worked as well or better than the original. That won't be necessary this time. If the main thrusters work, and the pod has basic steering, that will be enough. That may be possible as you are a freak, similar to the entity that adapted these engines in the first place."

"Papa was the mechanic." Meeting Ghost was forcing Jamie to face up to some unpleasant truths. "I'm just an amateur, good enough for a cheap repair, and the only freak about it is the number of things that actually work afterwards."

She'd relaxed a little now, not completely but she managed a smile. "That might be why Ghost Claw like you. We do not believe in conventional solutions, but we get the job done." Her brow furrowed again as she concentrated. "Wild card? Prodigy? The translator has several alternatives that are not quite what we meant."

"I'll take the wild card. You'd better hope it isn't an ace or joker." The puzzled look was exactly what Jamie hoped for. "Look up card games, especially brag and poker. That will stop you worrying. Just don't get into an on-line game and lose your ship."

He stood up and put his bowl in the cleaner, still nearly full. The brown sludge was spicy enough to destroy any taste and threaten blistering. "I'll get back to work for now, but we'll have to go shopping eventually." Ghost was already deep in thought, either searching or looking at translations, so he left her to it.

Jamie broke off several times for water and twice for gunk, and both meals were edible, even if one was borderline. Eventually he was too tired to concentrate, but wiring was all that Jamie had replaced. He'd collected a heap of charred boards and chips, and made sketches and notes, but was still working on what to put in their place. He could bypass the damaged part, but then there'd be no thruster controls.

There was also physical damage, torn and twisted metal, but he should be able to rebuild that. He might need some new piping or sheet metal, and welding, but that didn't involve anything alien, even if the result was. From the pattern of damage, either the burnout had created a build-up of pressure, or the pressure had blown pipes and burned out the controls.

When Ghost asked about progress, Jamie confessed he could only get so far with what he'd brought. For starters, he needed a lot more wiring of different sizes. Then he needed more clips, so he could disconnect in a hurry if he connected the wrong things, and fuses for if he was too slow. "We'll go shopping tomorrow. It will help if you've got something that can cut and bend metal without flame, especially if it's small with variable heat settings." Jamie hoped that aliens had better tools than his. He didn't fancy getting in among that lot with a cutting torch, especially when he wasn't sure what might be carrying fuel.

"Very variable." Ghost brought him a small, hand-held device like a utility knife without a blade. When activated, it emitted a variable-length glowing beam that ranged from gentle heat to cutting or blending steel, welding. "There is a larger version that will cut the hull, but once again it is variable."

Ghost was looking more relaxed since she'd seen the heap of scrap—she seemed to think it was a good sign. "The main problem is to persuade the safety cut-outs to allow you to operate in some places. The slightest hint of flammables in the air and they will cut out."

She must have read the question on Jamie's face. "No, these are not the correct tools, but those can only be operated by suitably trained personnel, those with implants to do so."

"Since you are smiling, I'm guessing Ghost Clan are allowed to use the wrong tools or turn off the usual safeties?" He was getting very curious about that, but Jamie wasn't sure he'd like the answer. Maybe Ghost Clan were intergalactic criminals, and Hunter was the sheriff or alien FBI?

Ghost's smile disappeared. "We are Ghost *Claw* Clan, and usually make sure other entities remember our full name, your name now you are related. It is more a case of if we aren't told specifically that we can't do something, we don't ask." That teasing hint was back in her voice, and the smile returned, though the bit about her name had been dead serious. "Sometimes we do things even after being told not to, occasionally *because* we were told not to. The first Slashtail reactions to a motorbike will be amusing, then it will be banned, and then we'll ride it anyway."

"I'd like to see that one day." Jamie chickened out of asking why Ghost Claw Clan were different, again, though he really would like to visit one day. They were beginning to sound like Slashtail Hells Angels, especially with the Claw part, so they might be disappointed in their new member. "I suppose you'll want the greeting-to-kin before you sleep?" Each time he'd seen her she'd presented her pelt, by turning sideways and bending her head slightly forward.

"But no DNA tonight." As she turned away, Ghost murmured, "Or kissing." Despite the comment, she lay still and sang quietly as Jamie stroked, then sighed and wriggled back under the cover. That didn't stop Jamie's furry mauve dreams. He could feel Ghost in there somewhere, but without a hint of teasing or sexy, more like comfortable because she belonged.

~~

This time Jamie remembered to keep his eyes shut until Ghost was in the cleanser, so his wake-up was gentler. He was definitely a fan of the cubicle—shower, laundry, and drying all in one, and quick. Today's pale orange gloop tasted of apples, but over-ripe, which made him grateful the taste was very faint.

A check on the news wasn't much more palatable. The police had a description and his first name, probably from a neighbour, but they hadn't connected him with his sister. Ghost was causing them trouble, though some postings suggested Jamie was travelling with two underdressed women with different hair and skin. So far, mauve hadn't been mentioned. At least there weren't any other pictures of her, just the Salome ones with a big "This Is Not Salome Malone" across them.

His car was there, and the different guesses included orange, while the picture of a bike was the right type but without the racing enhancements. "That's awkward. We'll need several trips on the bike, so the chances are someone will spot us and call it in." Jamie shelved his own problems—getting Ghost clear was more important.

If *she* was discovered there'd be an alien scare, then the government would try to capture her. Not kill her with a sniper or guided missile, relatively cleanly, the spy bosses would want the shapeshifting at least. There'd be a huge fight, and anything from a couple of houses to most of New Mexico would end up wrecked. If she lost, then alive or dead, Ghost would disappear into a government dungeon for vivisection.

Jamie found himself rejecting any idea of betraying her, leading her into a trap, and wondered why. His original decision still made sense—he didn't know how much damage Ghost could inflict if she was trapped or went on the run. Now, though, he realised she was growing on him, becoming less horrific. It wasn't how she looked, because he knew that wasn't real, so it had to be her personality.

Once again Ghost broke into his musings. One thing was certain—she couldn't read minds. "We can move the pod nearer the suppliers, so you can make shorter trips?" She looked at the police sketches of Jamie, and the partial-pictures of him in the car. "We are not on any pictures, so we could try to purchase what you need? We would also prefer food like the first meal."

~~

So would Jamie, but right now he had to concentrate on alien electricity. When he had tried copying what was on a damaged component, and wired the chip into place, the pod had offered to upgrade it. That had been a relief as whatever he'd copied across had gaps, sections where his laptop couldn't read everything. Damage or alien software his laptop didn't recognise, he couldn't tell which, but now it didn't matter.

A check on how the pod was getting on spoiled Jamie's mood. It had filled his chip, then aborted the upgrade for lack of space. He would have tried splitting out any surplus files, but Jamie couldn't tell what the programme did, or which bits were individual files, or if it was actually in files. He'd thought the problem would be access, but that had been relatively easy. He should have realised aliens might not use anything that resembled Earth's computing principles.

He'd checked the upgraded programme on the hacking kit, thinking that might translate, and aliens had a different definition of upgrade. The whole lot had been overwritten, even the formatting, so he couldn't read a thing. That settled one thing—his laptop and any programming skills were useless.

A quick check showed that even if he relied on the pod backups, and they reformatted his chips or hard drives, Jamie's collection wouldn't hold enough data. Petabyte RAM chips would be expensive, if he could find any, though Jamie might be able to use high-speed hard drives. Unfortunately, multi-petabyte drives, fast ones, weren't cheap, especially for someone with a limited budget.

If he could work out how to split the programming, a lot of plug-in second-hand drives might do it, though the quantity he'd need would mean copying his cash a *lot* of times. At least one worry had been settled. Ghost confirmed that the life support and internal power and gravity were still working, so he wasn't going to cut them by mistake.

Jamie knew people who would supply any quantity of tech, off the books as long as he paid in cash, and some of them would sell ammunition as well. The problem was raising more than seven hundred dollars in one bundle. There was a way, providing he went home, but then he'd need transport he could use openly. If his car was found in Santa Rosa, attention would move away from the Pits, so he could sneak in and talk to the right people.

He could also get a message to Shania, without using a phone. He could warn her, if her phone had junked his texts and she hadn't got the note. He'd texted her about it before leaving, but Shania hadn't been near the place since Papa's funeral, and then she'd only parked outside to give him a lift. If she saw the pictures, or was asked, she had to swear the guy in the car couldn't be him—because her brother was in the Maldives.

He didn't want to get Shania involved, and not only because she was his big sister. If he brought the cops down on Shania, Damian would be upset, and might decide to solve the problem before his family was involved. Jamie had a feeling the sort of hit men Damian could afford would find him long before the police, or Hunter.

~~

When he mentioned leaving his car to Ghost, the reaction surprised him. "But we will keep your trophy?" She obviously had different priorities. "We can check there is nobody inside the building, but later, as Hunter might be watching for a return to Albuquerque. Will you be able to keep working today?"

The answer was simple and might break the trail, get the cops and Hunter searching elsewhere. "I've changed my mind about shopping. I should spend the next couple of days, maybe three, removing burned wires, cutting away the burned controls and wrecked piping, and using up the rest of my cable. That should give me a better idea of what I need, and we can go to Oklahoma City for the cheap stuff. If we're spotted, it will pull the search further east, away from home, my home. Where are we?"

It had just occurred to Jamie that they could be parked just outside Santa Rosa, unable to move yet because there were a hundred Hunter drones looking for them. The answer was a surprise, but the good sort. "We are about seventy miles from Albuquerque, in the mountains. We expected more people here, visiting at least, but they seem to prefer air with pollutants."

He was one of them in a way—Jamie hadn't been to the mountains since he was little. His strongest memory of the yearly trips was a crowd of kids, and teachers shouting at them to stay together. They were lectured on not touching stuff, and not annoying animals, though he couldn't remember ever seeing an animal. The noise probably scared them all away.

Now he was thinking about it, they were shown some leaves and told not to touch or eat them, but it never made any difference. Someone always ended up crying because they'd touched the wrong leaf, or thorns, or fallen down, or got splinters, or been bitten or stung by insects, and one year someone broke their arm. As he got older, Jamie skipped the trips. He preferred helping Papa in the garage, and the teachers were probably happy to have one less to supervise.

Though Ghost had gotten one thing wrong. "It's the same air. Albuquerque isn't a big city like New York, and the wind blows off the mountains sometimes." Jamie had been outside Albuquerque, and never noticed any change. Only when the races were on the outskirts, and not for long, and now he thought about it there were a lot of bikes and trucks as well as the racers. "Shania reckons we've polluted the whole planet, and she knows about that stuff. That's why we've got electric cars, to fix the air."

Ghost spun around and stared at him, then stopped and sniffed. "We have a human nose, and we can tell the difference. Come on, you can spare a few minutes." With that she was gone, off down the corridor and presumably outside.

From her reaction, maybe the air really was different. Remembering the school trips, Jamie called after her. "Watch out for leaves and animals, and insects. And snakes." Maybe not, some of the guys went hunting and never mentioned stuff like that. That might be because, from what some of them said, hunting didn't involve trees and animals. Their version meant driving out of town to drink beer, then shooting at the empty cans and anything that moved.

~~

When he reached the ramp, Jamie stopped. His memories of the actual hikes were of being surrounded by huge trees, and the trees were still here. Not surrounding him, so they weren't as overwhelming, because Ghost had landed in a grassy clearing. The ground sloped away, and there were enough gaps to see water, a lake, but what caught his eye were the mountains.

They stuck up the other side of the trees and lake, probably miles away, and from the slope there was another one behind him. There wasn't a sign of a house, road, or even a trail, and for a moment Jamie panicked. He didn't even know why—it was all just too much. It was gone after a couple of very deep breaths, but the place was still a shock.

Maybe it wasn't the place—it could have just been the realisation this was on his doorstep, and he'd never seen it. No wonder Shania told him he had to get away from the garage now and then. She'd probably been to lots of places like this, with Damian. Jamie had never been interested in her holiday snaps because he knew they'd be fancy rich places, and she'd use them to try to get him to leave the Pits.

Remembering why he was here, he sniffed, but the air was flat with no smell at all. It was like a couple of places he'd been in that had decent air conditioning. Jamie almost laughed at himself when he realised why—he was still inside the pod. He'd stopped dead when he saw the mountains, but now Jamie took the first step onto the ramp—and then it wasn't the air or the mountains that caught him out.

The lack of noise came as a big surprise. There wasn't any traffic, no voices or radios, no screaming kids or slamming doors, none of the usual background noises. It was quiet, but he realised it wasn't silent, there was a different background. Even in Shania's garden he could hear traffic in the distance, but not now. Jamie had no idea what all the birds were, but looked around in alarm at the buzzing.

After watching a few, Jamie realised the bugs weren't interested in him. They were all busy doing their own thing, which didn't include dog crap or whatever trash someone had dumped on the vacant lot next door. He relaxed and walked down the ramp, which was when the smell hit him. Maybe that was what Ghost meant by clean air?

The second breath wasn't as bad, so maybe it had just been the contrast with the pod air. Jamie had always figured clean air, not polluted, meant no smell, but he was wrong, again. He sniffed again and it had to be all the green stuff, even if he couldn't see many flowers. Shania's place smelled of flowers, or maybe it was just their air conditioning, but even that big garden didn't smell like this.

Sitting down on the ramp. Jamie tried to remember the last time he'd been out of town, properly, not just to race, and he couldn't. Apart from picking up spares and groceries, and visiting Shania, Jamie realised he rarely left the garage. The Pits was dangerous, but not that bad—it was just that there was always something that needed doing, fixing stuff, either his racer or trying to make a few bucks.

~~

He was still sitting there, trying to figure out how he'd ended up like that, when Ghost's voice disturbed him. "Does it smell that bad?"

"Huh? Oh, no, just, er, different. Okay, you got me, but this air is polluted as well, with plant smells." He was smiling because Jamie knew that wasn't what pollution meant, then something else struck him. He waved a hand to indicate the trees and mountains. "It's a pity I've never been hunting, or we wouldn't need to buy food."

Ghost looked around, puzzled. "The local clans do not object? At home, valuable hunting grounds like this would be reserved for clan members. We had wondered why the pod couldn't detect any humans, and when we landed there was no human scent."

Now she'd mentioned it, a clan might claim this land, only they were called tribes. There were a bunch of reservations near Albuquerque, but Jamie didn't know if the tribes stopped others hunting. He was realising just how much he didn't know, though he'd already gotten a hint on the way to Nara Vista.

Ghost hadn't said exactly where they were. "These might belong to someone, local First Nation tribes, so you might be right. If I could use my phone, I could tell you if we're on their land, but?" He shrugged, and looked around. "It doesn't really make any difference. We can't risk attracting attention with a shot, and I don't have a fishing rod."

A big smile split Ghost's face. "Fish? Your internet says they are delicious, and I won't need a rod or spear." She started down the slope. "You had better stay here, unless you want to hold my coverings, clothes, while I swim?"

Jamie laughed, he had to. If she'd been human, he would have been tempted to find out if she meant that. Jamie remembered wondering if Ghost was trying to make sure he stayed helpful, so she might mean it. He wasn't sure, because the teasing fitted with the way she usually acted, and she'd never tried to take it further. Rather than get lost in trying to figure out if Ghost was acting naturally, again, Jamie went back to how he'd somehow ended up a hermit.

Not quite, but he didn't really have a social life. He'd thought he had friends, but now he realised they were all people who sold him spares, wanted stuff fixed, or raced cars. Now he was thinking about it, it had started long before he left school. All the kids knew they shouldn't hang about on the streets, but as they got older, they'd roam around in groups that weren't quite gangs. Jamie liked helping Papa from when he was old enough to fetch him a spanner, so he never joined them, and then Papa was gone and he had to make a living.

~~

He was never sure how long he sat there thinking through his life, or lack of it, before Ghost disturbed him. "Fish!"

When he looked up, Jamie almost asked how she'd caught them, but although her bikini and shorts were dry, her skin was wet. Ghost was holding up four fish, fresh enough for one of them to twitch. "That was quick. How did you catch them?" Jamie had read books where people caught fish with their hands, but they always made it sound like it took ages. They definitely didn't jump in the water and chase them.

Lifting one of her feet, Ghost waggled it. "Maybe we swim faster than other humans, and your fish aren't used to being chased." As she came nearer, she shook her head. "Humans need a pelt, so they can shake off water." She turned to present her pelt, and when Jamie stroked it, it was barely damp.

"We have towels." No they didn't, he realised, because this was a Slashtail vessel.

Ghost headed up the ramp. "We will use the cleanser to get dry, but perhaps we should buy some of these towels. Then you can show me how they work." She held up the fish with a finger stuck in their gills—at least Jamie knew that much about them. "We assume you will want these cooked? Humans seem to spend a lot of time making sure food doesn't look or taste like it did when it was harvested."

Jamie almost pointed out fruit was eaten without being

altered, but Shania told him most of it was poisoned with chemicals so it lasted longer in the stores. He'd tried to find the stuff that wasn't, but it cost a fortune. With a smile he realised that most of the fruit he ate was in pies, or canned peaches as a treat, which kinda proved Ghost's point.

By that time it was too late to answer—Ghost was gone, which looked weird. He knew the ramp led to the entrance, but it looked as if she walked into the landscape and disappeared. The interruption had stopped Jamie worrying about his life, so he wandered around the clearing.

He didn't touch anything, so those childhood lessons had worked, though he couldn't remember the actual plants. Even the grass wasn't like Damian's lawn, or the one across the road and the patches of grass some of his neighbours kept alive—it had other plants mixed in with it. They were probably weeds, but they looked a lot better than the stuff growing on the vacant lot next to his workshop.

"If you want them cooked, you could have collected firewood." When Jamie turned, Ghost was back.

That had to be a joke. "Isn't there anything in the pod that can cook?" There was, Jamie realised, but he didn't fancy fish gloop. "Forget I asked. I'll have a look for firewood, but I'll have to be careful. The teachers told us which plants and bugs to avoid, but I've forgotten."

~~

As he set off for the trees, Ghost joined him. "Another reason humans need a pelt. Then they could walk in the woods without worrying about leaves, barbed vegetation, serpents or flying pests." She paused, and then sounded puzzled. "How did humans survive long enough to learn to make clothing, if the plant life is so dangerous?"

It was embarrassing, but at least Jamie's recent trip down memory lane gave him an answer. "Humans managed for a long time without clothes. It isn't that dangerous; it's just that

I've never really left Albuquerque for years. You picked the wrong human for a guide."

"We don't think so, and exploring is fun so we can find out together." She trailed her hand through a bush. "We heal quicker than humans, so we will test the leaves. Just make sure you pick up sticks, not sleeping snakes." When Jamie turned towards her, alarmed, she laughed. "Though you make so much noise you are waking up all the snakes for miles."

More teasing, though he probably was making a lot of noise, so Jamie smiled. "As long as there aren't any bears. They might come to see what was happening."

"We will hear the splash. She will have to swim across the lake, and we don't think she will leave her baby." Jamie looked at her, trying to work out if Ghost was being serious, and then she smiled. "They will be too busy eating fish. Mama Bear wasn't having much luck so we threw some up onto the grass. Baby bear was frightened and climbed a tree, but came down to eat when we swam away."

He was just about to say that wasn't how people usually treated bears, then he remembered Ghost wasn't people. Though maybe she was, just not human people? Rather than head off into a mental whirlpool again, Jamie picked up some branches. "I don't suppose they'll be cooking theirs. Aren't you worried about smoke from the fire being seen?"

Ghost picked up some branches as well. "No. There were no humans in this valley when we landed, and if Hunter had followed us, we would know by now. If Hunter is scanning for signs, he will be looking for the pod, not a cooking fire."

Patting a tree trunk, she looked up. "These will help conceal us. There are trees back home, but not like these and not in the Purple Hills, so this is new for us." Ghost touched her shoulder, where the comms system was hidden. "This does not provide visuals from your internet, but the translator will record images that we can compare later. We can find enough wood for a fire without risk, if we are careful."

~~

By the time the fish were on the ends of sticks, close to a neat fire surrounded by a ring of rocks, Jamie was feeling embarrassed. There were some things like poison ivy, oak, and sumac that he should keep clear of, but the list was small—unless he was stupid enough to start eating random leaves. He actually knew some of it, but hadn't connected garden plants like oleander with wild ones.

Jamie couldn't even use the excuse that he lived in the middle of a city. Albuquerque wasn't that big, the Pits wasn't in the middle, he had a car, and the buildings stopped four miles west. The countryside there was semi-desert, but if he wanted trees, the Rio Grande was only half a mile from his home. There was woodland on both banks, and the gangs of local youths and older schoolchildren went swimming, but Jamie never had.

Maybe it was a good thing Ghost was so interested in everything, as she kept Jamie from plunging into another mental whirlpool. She was in a terrific mood, teasing him about the mess he made of pulling the cooked fish off the bones, and offering to take him hunting, or fishing, Slashtail-style.

That meant without weapons, though even when she conceded he could take a knife, Jamie wasn't keen. Ghost started adding weapons, to encourage him, and by the time she'd worked up to allowing him armour and a rocket launcher, he was laughing at himself.

From some of her comments, Jamie knew part of the reason she was so happy. They'd shaken off the police and Hunter, but that wasn't all. Ghost was impressed by the heap of frazzled wiring and twisted, scorched metal, and confident that Jamie had the repairs in hand. He didn't have the heart to tell her the problems, or not until he couldn't find a way around them.

At least part of her mood had to be the wild country around them. When Jamie went back to work, and over the next two days, Ghost spent a lot of time exploring. She brought back a wide selection of feathers, flowers, bits of tree—and a turkey. The first Jamie knew of the latter was when he was called outside to find it above another fire, ready to carve and eat. He agreed with Ghost—it was a lot better than gloop of any colour.

The following day he saw her come back with what looked like the entire back legs of a deer. A mule deer, according to Ghost, and the black bear and her baby were eating the rest. Ghost had taken a real shine to them, and left them the rest of the turkey the previous day, and more fish. After eating part of one leg, roasted above another fire, Ghost insisted on Jamie coming for a walk. She could show him what was safe, allegedly in case he had to hide in the woods sometime.

Even with the teasing, or maybe because of it, Jamie enjoyed himself. At first, Ghost insisted every single bush or tree they passed was deadly, but even Jamie knew things like grass wouldn't hurt him. She burst out laughing when he challenged her, and he had to join in.

Ghost still claimed that almost every plant they passed was dangerous, but described increasingly ridiculous symptoms. Various leaves would, allegedly, turn his skin green, make his hair, nails, and teeth fall out, or make his feet swell into balls so he kept falling over. The trip wasn't much good as a lesson, but Jamie felt much better afterwards. Shania always said he was too serious, and perhaps she was right.

The third day Ghost took him to see Mama Bear, but was dead serious, insisting he walked quietly without stepping on twigs. She took a roundabout route because of the wind, so by the time she stopped, Jamie was ready to sit down for a break. He'd thought he was reasonably fit because he lifted lumps of metal, and had to free off things like rusty bolts, but Ghost wasn't even out of breath.

Trying not to puff and pant, he crawled forward and peered through the bushes, safe ones, to find Mama trying to sleep. The cub, however, wasn't tired, and wanted to play, or maybe eat food. The result kept Jamie amused as the cub persisted, and Mama kept fending it off and trying to rest. Eventually the cub won, and they headed off somewhere.

On the way back, Ghost stopped by the lake, and she had her bikini under her shorts so they could swim. Jamie put his hand in and it was icy, so he watched her swim for a while. She didn't look fast enough to catch fish, and he wondered if she'd changed shape, but for once it didn't worry him.

During the last three days, Jamie had come to realise that some things were just Ghost acting naturally. The pelt stroking, for instance, really was a way to relax before sleeping, and the name gave him the other hint. When Ghost kept tipping her head a little each time they met, he remembered she called it greeting-to-kin. Her people really must do something similar, so it wasn't a joke or tease.

The other thing that he was now accepting was a surprise. Her occasional mistakes, and generally brief clothing, really weren't at all sexual or teasing, human-style. Ghost really didn't care about clothing, but the shock was Jamie realising he was getting used to it. Shania would have hysterics when he told her he'd gotten used to an attractive woman occasionally forgetting to dress.

Ghost and her strange habits were alien, but by the time they got back to the pod, Jamie had realised he didn't have to go to the stars to find new things. There were plenty right here on his doorstep, almost, if he'd ever bothered to look. She might have been an unwelcome interruption, but Ghost had literally changed his life forever, in a good way.

~~

It came as a shock in a way when, on the evening of the third day in the wild, Jamie realised he'd done all he could. Most of it had been destructive, removing ruined components, so there was a big heap that was junk and a lot of gaps that needed filling. Before he could do much of that, Jamie would have to go shopping. That evening, after their roast deer, he stopped Ghost before she went for another walk.

In between ripping out stuff and walking in the woods, Jamie had been planning. "We need to go shopping in Oklahoma, as I suggested. Even if I only spend seven hundred dollars at a time, I can get a lot of the straightforward stuff: cable, fittings, and piping. As long as you can be sure we can get away and hide, it won't matter if some computer programme picks up an unusual shopping pattern, because we won't be going back there. If the pod can identify the rest of the components, we might get some of those as well."

"Then you will be able to fix the engines? How long?" Ghost was suddenly tense, concentrating, and totally focused on getting away. Jamie wondered if all the walks, and hunting, had been her way to avoid thinking about it.

He hesitated, but not because he was frightened of Ghost —he just didn't want to disappoint her. Maybe it was gas or drugs, or maybe just getting to know her, but Jamie couldn't help hoping that she got home safe. She might be trying to encourage him to feel like that, but Jamie was almost sure most of it was just Ghost's natural personality.

Hesitating was just making her more worried, so Jamie got on with it. "It could take a week or more, though first we have to collect all the materials. I'll need a lot of simple electrical stuff, which I can buy from several different places. We also need pipes, tubing, several different sizes, with connections and bends, or a pipe bender. If Hunter is tracking things like that, that's the sort of thing that might show up."

Ghost was looking more worried, so Jamie gave her the solution. "If you can get us out of Oklahoma City afterwards, we could use the shopping to deliberately throw Hunter off the scent. A definite sighting would also divert the police, and if he's hooked into their computers, that would convince Hunter we've gone that way. Can you definitely get clear afterwards?"

She thought about it for much too long for Jamie's peace of mind, but then Ghost nodded. "Will you get everything you need in Oklahoma? If so, we can fly to the coast, submerge, and come out somewhere remote. We can stay there while you finish the repairs."

That sounded wonderful, but unfortunately it wasn't possible. "Not everything. There are some components without an Earth equivalent, so I can't buy replacements until I know what to get. I will definitely need more high-capacity computing parts. They will be expensive, and since I can't order from the internet, there aren't many people that stock them." Jamie knew of one way, maybe. "Can you get me back to my place without being seen? There are locals who can get it all, and there might be a way to pay."

He'd thought sneaking back there might be a problem, but Ghost didn't hesitate. "If we leave Oklahoma in daylight, we can get back to Albuquerque unseen, then move to your home while it is dark." She licked her lips, slowly, and smiled. "Though if we have to change shape to elude pursuit, more DNA would help, once you have stroked our pelt to relax us."

Since he'd already said okay once, for the same reason, Jamie could hardly say no. Though as he followed her to the night-nest, he realised that some things were going to be harder to get used to.

~~

The following morning, just before they left, Jamie put his two cheap phones back together. There were three messages from Shania, all from a different phone number, and none mentioned their names. The first one was straightforward. *"Frankie said to thank you for her card, and the message. I hope your new friend doesn't attract the wrong sort of attention."* That had to mean Shania got the note from the garage, and wanted to know more about the alien.

As he opened the second one, Jamie wondered if Shania had the same thoughts as him about Ghost's natural shape. *"Frankie says the weather where you are is stormy. Keep well clear of strangers, there are some awful stories about hitchhikers."* Shania must have heard that the Hellbats were chasing him, or just found out about the bodies and guessed. The second part was telling him to get rid of the alien, but now it was Ghost giving *him* a lift.

The third text made him laugh. *"Surprised when I recognised your friend, but then I realised my mistake. When you get back, I'm going to want to know ALL about it."* His big sister was going to want every detail, or else. Shania would recognise the car and the partial shots of his head, but she didn't seem as worried about his companion. Maybe that was because he'd been alone in the car, but waited for Salome/Ghost to get back in.

Jamie had thought hard about what to say, and the truth wouldn't hurt. *"Hi Frankie, I was out of touch in the mountains. I've been camping, and walking in the woods with my new friend. We've had trout, turkey, and deer, cooked over a camp fire, and I met a momma bear and cub. If school trips had been like this, I might have gone on more of them. The air smells very different. Will be on the move, but will get in touch when she goes home, maybe before. Don't believe wild rumours, the truth is a much better story."*

Jamie shut down both phones, quickly before Shania phoned and demanded explanations, and dismantled them. If the Feds or Hunter were tracing the phone, it would bring them to the mountains, and a cold campfire. When he reached the control room, Ghost was already there, waiting, and took off immediately.

The holiday was over, and the memory would stay with Jamie forever—even after he'd been hunting Ghost Claw–style.

NOT-VERY-SECRET SHOPPING

Instead of travelling cross-country, Ghost headed for I-40, and Jamie learned more about alien technology. Ghost flew above a truck heading for Oklahoma, so that any faint emissions would be masked by the vehicle below. Hunter would stay up high in daylight, so it wasn't strictly necessary, but it was good practice. Unfortunately, travelling like that was comparatively slow and boring.

Too boring for Ghost, especially with five hundred miles to go, so she began to fly faster. She chose the fastest vehicle, then when it caught up with a group of cars or trucks, accelerated briefly to the front. Jamie had never realised vehicles tended to form loose groups with gaps between, though not many gaps as Ghost also used the oncoming traffic and any buildings as cover. She also flew a little faster than the traffic in the gaps, so the trip only took five hours.

Once they reached Oklahoma City outskirts, just before midday, Ghost slowed and began looking for a parking lot. With all the emissions and metal in a busy city, she could use Google, so they were soon hovering above one within easy reach of several big stores. The concrete and metal, and the vehicles coming and going, were an extra layer of camouflage for the pod.

Jamie had a list of what he'd need, but there was still one non-electrical mystery item. It was part of the steering thruster pipework, but he didn't recognise the wreckage, and what it did wasn't obvious. He'd found markings, letters, and numbers according to Ghost, but Ghost's translator didn't recognise the computer identification.

Since then, the pod computer had been working through a huge amount of information from the web, but still didn't have an answer. Ghost wasn't surprised. "The pod computer is identifying as much as possible, searching for any similar components by shape, size, or apparent purpose. You can't say what this item does, the shape isn't distinctive even before it was ripped open, and the identification code doesn't give any hint of its purpose."

That didn't sound promising but Ghost was busy again, and symbols scrolled down a screen. "We have altered the search criteria. The pod computer is looking at how the damaged component is constructed, the actual materials, and is trying to translate them. Then it will look for anything that uses a similar combination. This sort of problem isn't unusual when dealing with a new language, but usually the locals will sell translation modules."

Jamie watched for a few moments, but he'd just have to be patient. "Once we know what to get, I can replace all the physical pipework. That just leaves the electrical components, but the pod seems to have some back-ups." Though when he looked at where they'd parked, there was a more immediate problem.

~~

The pod was about eight feet off the ground, so the bike would have to be lowered in case a van parked beneath it. Then so would Jamie, as he didn't fancy jumping that far onto concrete. If anyone even glanced at the surveillance screens, a motorbike being winched down out of mid-air would be noticed. "Can you blank the cameras up here and on the way out, temporarily?"

Jamie wondered if they could make one drop, not three, but a flying bike with two riders would be even more obvious. At least Ghost had a partial answer. "We can blank some but only have four drones left. The rest were left behind during our escape, or damaged during our landing." Reaching across to the wall, she pulled off a small grey disc. "This drone can stop all the electrical equipment within about eight of your feet, though most systems will recover when it leaves. We used one on the police car near the parking lot, so the officer couldn't report you or follow."

Gesturing to a screen, Ghost tapped keys, and displayed a wire-frame version of the parking structure. "The yellow lights are surveillance cameras, too many for these drones. We can hit those we can see with an electrical discharge to burn out wiring, or a laser to actually burn them?" Ghost checked through the firearms. "We could shoot them, but for accuracy we would need the rifle."

There was a pause before Jamie answered, while he recovered from finding out the police had watched him collect his car. At least the drone must have stopped them taking a picture, but that explained why orange had been the first suggested alternate colour. "We've only got ammo for seven, and the camera views overlap so I might be seen shooting them. Just seeing me carrying the rifle might be enough for the operator to check my vehicle. When they find they can't, that the cameras are down, that might cause more trouble than a picture of us dropping down on the bike. Will the electrical thing be seen, a lightning bolt or something similar?"

Ghost smiled, amused for some reason. "There may be a few sparks and some smoke from the cameras, just for a moment. The overload may burn out other equipment on the same circuit, then the drones can deal with any other cameras? The interference will be obvious, as the discharge will also affect electrical systems in nearby vehicles."

He thought it through again, but that only left one answer. "If you use the laser on the nearest, can the other four keep us off any screens while we ride down the ramps?"

~~

Shaking her head made something else obvious, and Jamie cut in before Ghost answered. "Ah, could you revert your pelt to black hair? We're trying to blend in this time and the mauve won't help, even if you're wearing a shirt and my smart jeans." Clean, undamaged second-hand jeans, the best he had, though Jamie had never made them look that good.

Jamie turned, keeping his eyes averted, because Ghost had turned away each time she changed. She obviously didn't like spectators. A few moments later her voice was just behind him. "There, now nobody will notice me."

Her black hair was now above shoulder-length, almost like a helmet with a short, neat fringe, which with the jeans gave her a leaner, more athletic look. For a moment Jamie tried to work out if Ghost had resized to be more athletic, which would make sense the way she fought. He realised he'd been looking too long, and quickly turned away.

Too late, Ghost had noticed. "You should check what this pelt feels like, for luck?" The cheeky smile as Ghost leant forward admitted luck had nothing to do with it—she liked her pelt stroked. Jamie was really hoping the stroking was that, and not some sort of joke, something that would make him look an idiot or an ignorant primitive to other Slashtails.

He stroked her head, and confessed that her pelt was softer. "Probably a good thing or you might be tempted while we are shopping, and it doesn't seem to be a human habit. If you pause on every ramp, the drones will reposition. I will use the laser on the nearest two cameras while you put the sling around the bike, and open the airlock."

As he accelerated gently away from between the cars, Jamie looked, and although one camera was smoking, the rest looked untouched. On the way down the ramps, he paused when told, startled the first time one of the little discs flew past. They were silent, and stayed up near the roof, so he didn't think the cameras would notice them closing in.

At the bottom, Jamie remembered another camera, and the barrier. "We don't have a ticket, so we'll wait for the barrier to lift for another car, then get out before it comes down. Duck down as we go through, then the car will stop the camera getting a clear shot."

"We will bring a drone from another camera."

"No, we need the electrical components working to lift the barrier." Jamie might have gotten his bike under the bar, but this one had a drop-down grid so maybe the locals had already tried that. Jamie had to pass up the first chance, but the next car left enough of a gap at the passenger side. They both crouched low, and he accelerated through the gap and away, weaving through the traffic until he was out of sight. A short warble in his ear reminded Jamie not to do that where people could hear Ghost.

~~

The first stop was to buy a couple of backpacks, but before they went into the store, Ghost had advice. "Save any notes that you are given; don't spend them in other places. We will take them back and duplicate them as well." That would increase the total amount he could spend in one place, a good idea, but now Jamie wondered how often Ghost copied the local money.

With extra cash in mind, he spread his shopping over several stores, and used twenties to buy small items like single frozen meals. He also insisted on buying her footwear, rip-off Nike copies and shoes with a small heel. Ghost preferred bare feet, but people didn't risk that in towns, and the house boots didn't look right with her other clothes.

When he started on the main purchases, like rolls of cable, Jamie didn't get much change. It was the same when he bought ammo. Jamie spent nearly a whole set of copies, seven hundred and forty-five dollars, and he'd only bought enough for a few minutes of gunfire.

He daren't risk buying more. It wasn't likely, but if someone noticed the identical numbers, even if Jamie got away, news would spread about counterfeits. If the shop had CCTV, almost a certainty in a place selling ammo, the cops would have clear pictures of them both. Fingerprints as well, if he touched the counter, so he diverted to buy them both a couple of pairs of gloves.

Jamie knew a couple of other places that sold ammo, and at least one person who would sell almost anything, maybe even magnum and jacketed. Not today, as the places were in Albuquerque. Then he'd have to be careful, as that source might also sell Jamie—turn him in if there was a reward.

Even with the saddlebags and both backpacks filled, they hadn't made much of a dent in Jamie's shopping list. Ghost carried two rolls of cable, but that meant people noticed them so she couldn't do it every time. He parked the bike clear of the parking lot so it wasn't a direct trail, but they were still conspicuously overloaded.

There was another reason for walking the shopping into the parking lot. If the cameras had caught his plates on the way out, the security system would have added them to the database. Then when it spotted him coming back in, someone would come to clamp or impound the bike, and check the damaged cameras. The pedestrian access had a camera, but it wasn't near the barrier so the drones covered their visit.

Ghost brought the pod lower and opened the airlock remotely, then threw her shopping up and disappeared inside with one athletic bound. The pathetic human waited for a cable with a loop to be lowered, then gave a little yelp when it snatched him upwards like a rocket. It kept going up until he stopped just below the hatch at the top of the ladder, his fingers just short of the pulley.

~~

"Your search has a hit! Several hits! You can repair the thrusters!" Ghost bounced up the ladder and past him as the hatch opened, then her hand came back and dragged Jamie through. Just as well, as his backpack was trying to pull him back down. He slipped his arms out of the straps, then Ghost wrapped her arms around his head and kissed him, thoroughly.

He'd put his arms around her automatically, and Jamie knew he'd kissed back—it was hard not to. When she let go, he didn't know what to say, so he went for ignoring it. "You're stronger than you look." Jamie glanced back through the closing hatch. "Good job there's a safety on that pulley."

Ghost stopped for a moment, and her smile was replaced by a puzzled look. "Safeties? On a Ghost Claw ship?" Her blazing smile reappeared. "Strong? Our world has more gravity than your Earth, so we can do this!"

She sprang up and twisted so her feet and hands were planted firmly on the ceiling, then flipped over and landed back on her feet. "If you wish to travel with us, you must train or you will be very slow and tired. Or I suppose you could keep stealing DNA?"

The smile as she turned away knew damned well it wasn't Jamie who'd been stealing DNA, or not at first. "I noticed that many Earth females wear shorts or skirts while shopping. They are more comfortable, so while you look at the search results, we will change. Not here of course, or we would be inappropriate. Unless you wish to help, which the internet suggests would lead to exchanging more DNA, or kissing as humans call it. More Slashtail would help your muscles adapt to higher gravity."

It was out before Jamie could stop it. "Maybe I'd grow a proper chest pelt, then I could find out why you like the stroking."

For a moment Jamie was worried, but Ghost was smiling

when she turned back. "Tempting, but too much too fast might be a bad idea." She stepped in close, and her hand came up and rested on his head, then stroked. "Still human, but I never asked. Do humans like their pelts stroked?"

"Not as much as Slashtails." As she turned away and headed for her pilot's seat, Jamie added the rest, very quietly. "It might depend on whose pelt, and who is stroking."

He wasn't quiet enough, because Ghost answered. "Truth, but luckily you seem to be an expert." Jamie watched in some sort of shock as she disappeared into the control room, but not about the DNA thing, or the hair stroking—that was Ghost having fun with him. What caught him out was that he'd responded as if she was a human woman.

She wasn't, and he didn't think of her as human, so why did he say that? Maybe it was just a natural response to what she said, and how she said it? He thought of the flashes of humour as human-like, but maybe they were alien, Ghost's own humour and personality. He'd wondered before, but now Jamie thought that as long as she wasn't too horrific-looking, he'd like Ghost in her natural shape.

As he set off after her, Jamie thought about her sheer happiness at finding the whatever. He hadn't come anywhere close to realising how much Ghost was worrying about being stranded on Earth. Determined now, Jamie went to check on the search programme—the sooner he fixed her transport the better. A happy warble and several little yips hurried him on his way.

It took him a couple of attempts to get the English version on the screen, but the translation of the first few components was enough. Jamie knew what he'd need even before he read the whole list. "Platinum, palladium, and rhodium, we can get those from catalytic converters. There are people who steal them just to try and reclaim the rare elements. Extracting the good stuff isn't easy, and there isn't much in each one, but they're all expensive."

Ghost was already back, in her shorts, and she picked up just one thing out of that. "But now you can buy them, so you can repair the thrusters."

Some quick investigation on the web and Jamie had even better news. "I might be able to use Earth catalytic converters instead of extracting the bits we need. The proportions aren't the same, but I'm not really confident I can alter that. Once we've finished shopping, I'll work out how many we'll need, then add extras to compensate."

~~

Despite trying to look ordinary, Ghost was noticed as they carried on shopping. It was nothing to do with how she dressed—as she'd said, there were others in shorts. Ghost was happy, almost bouncing as she walked, and laughing and chattering. At least she remembered to keep away from alien subjects, so she probably looked like she was on vacation, or possibly a little drunk.

Ghost was definitely more tactile, pulling Jamie towards whatever interested her, and hugging him for no apparent reason. He might have suggested she calmed down, but he didn't want to spoil her mood. Instead, he bought her the sparkly beads that caught her eye, a small long-haired teddy bear so she had a pelt to stroke, a bracelet that changed colour to match moods, and a purple slushy she said would suit her hair. It wouldn't because it was black right now, but she'd obviously forgotten.

Jamie remembered to change twenties where possible, and in between the fun stuff, managed to fill the rucksacks with more cabling and things like fuses. Ghost calmed down enough to redirect the drones, so they reached the pod unseen. Instead of calling it down, she jumped onto a car, then up through the open hatch. Once again, Jamie got a high-speed winch trip.

This time, once she pulled him through the hatch, Ghost grabbed him, picked him up, and twirled him around. Letting go, she put a finger on his lips. "No more DNA, not until we have absorbed what we have. Though pelt stroking won't make any difference?"

Jamie laughed and stroked her hair, and she stroked the toy because his pelt hadn't grown yet. This time they quickly emptied the packs and went back to shopping. There was a short delay while a couple walked to their car, and drove away, but then the drones got to work. Ghost thought some of the cameras would break down under the repeated assaults, but Jamie was sure they'd finish shopping long before anyone came to fix them.

~~

The fifth trip was different, and Jamie had to ride further than expected. Ghost had been sampling Earth movies and had seen milkshakes, then she'd used Google to find a retro milk bar to get the proper effect. She had both shakes covered in several different coloured syrups, and then chocolate and coloured sprinkles and chopped nuts, each one with a different combination. Jamie just kept nodding, letting her enjoy herself.

They had to sit facing each other, then after trying her strawberry shake, they had to try each other's. According to Ghost, or whatever movie she'd watched, that meant leaving the shakes where they were and leaning forward. That wasn't as easy as it sounded, though she admitted the movie couple drank from the same one. They tried that and Ghost voted it a success, as it meant the couple's pelts were in the right place for stroking.

By now several customers had noticed, and a couple were laughing, so Jamie was feeling embarrassed. Even so he kept smiling, and, when Ghost stroked his hair, he stroked hers. It didn't take long for the embarrassment to wear off, at least partly because Ghost in this mood was a lot of fun. She definitely liked milkshakes, as she drank all hers and most of Jamie's butterscotch shake, and stole his cream and toppings.

Her good mood persisted when they went back to proper shopping, so Jamie ended up with a mood bracelet. While they were in the store, Ghost spotted friend bracelets, so they ended up with six each, a mix of braids and embroidered bands. On the way back to the pod, Jamie had to pull over.

Ghost had spotted tee shirts, or one in particular. They both ended up with 'I Want to Believe' *The X-Files* shirts with flying saucers, and Ghost had one with an alien's head, and 'I Don't Believe in Humans.'

~~

This time Jamie was ready for the hug and head stroke, but as they emptied the rucksacks, he had to spoil Ghost's mood. "This is taking too long, and it will be worse when we shop for the piping. It will be unwieldy, and heavy, either on the bike or carrying it." He'd dismissed the idea at first, until he realised he was buying with counterfeit money. "We should steal it all in one go."

Ghost waited before answering, but when he didn't speak, she laughed. "I thought you were joking, because that is a Ghost Claw solution. Have you been stealing DNA while we sleep?"

"No!" That came out a bit sharp, as Jamie was remembering the purple furry blanket dreams. "Sorry. I just realised that I'd be paying in counterfeit money, which is stealing anyway. We can steal the converters from vehicles and the pipe from a wholesale shop, then leave town. By the time the cops and Hunter start looking, you'll be on the coast."

She nodded, but Ghost remembered something Jamie had forgotten. "What about the computer supplies from your friends?"

That stumped Jamie, until he thought about Ghost's evasion

lessons. "You told me that a town, all the electricity and metal, hides the pod. If Hunter can't come down low in daylight, we can lurk near my workshop while I buy everything. If we head out along a highway, any highway, before dark, he'll lose us again."

"As long as we stay above a truck. No speeding, skipping gaps, as Hunter will be looking very hard." Ghost looked at the heap they'd already bought. "Will we need more shopping here, in Oklahoma?"

"Yes and no." Jamie smiled at her frown. "We could buy more here, and steal what we need tonight, but that might be a mistake. We have been all over Oklahoma City, so someone might have recognised me from the sketches." That was more likely because of how Ghost had been acting, how happy she was, but Jamie would never say so. "If you are sure you can attract Hunter, then lose him, we can raid somewhere in Albuquerque tonight. He'll still be scouring Oklahoma, five hundred miles away."

Ghost thought too long for Jamie's peace of mind, but it wasn't about the escape. "If we adjust the pod disguise a little, it may not be enough to definitely attract Hunter. Too much and your military may investigate anomalies. If I use the Salome Malone body, I can make sure both are looking here?"

Jamie didn't hesitate. "Perfect. The police will have to check it isn't the real Salome, so by the time Hunter picks it off their computers, we can be clear. The sighting will confirm whatever hints the pod gives off, so he'll be certain we are here. As long as you are sure he won't come down low in daylight?"

The laugh was a surprise. "If Hunter brings Starlight Ghost low enough to find me, in daylight, the distortion will be visible. Your military or police will send helicopters, and if he is down low, they may detect the ship or even hit it. If he gives a primitive planet a clear look at an interstellar spaceship, Hunter will be running for his life. The central worlds will send a team of mercenaries after him, kill on sight."

Which would be very convenient, but then the search for Ghost and Jamie would go into overdrive. "I'd better bring the bike up, then we can leave as soon as you've made sure you are reported." Jamie headed for the exit, and it didn't take long to walk to the bike. The drones did their thing, and Jamie was soon attaching the sling, then riding up into the pod.

As he fastened the bike to the wall, Ghost called down from the hatch. "We will put on the skirt and shirt, to make sure everyone notices."

~~

By the time Jamie had climbed the ladder, Ghost was waiting —or Salome was, with blonde hair, tight shirt, short skirt, and the shoes. She also wore Jamie's hat and her shades. "Other famous people wear things like this as a disguise, but never enough to actually hide them. Very strange." With that she slid down the cable, and dropped to the ground.

Since there was nothing else for him to do but wait, Jamie tried to keep occupied, and he had one important job. He put his phones back together, but there was nothing on Papa's. As expected, one of the cheap ones had a message from Shania.

"Wow, did you get all your shots first, and put on a lot of sun cream? I suppose that proves you aren't a vampire. Did you mow the grass? I arranged to have your gardening done while you are away." That was an old joke of Shania's, that the reason he never left the workshop was that he'd burn up in the sun.

The mowing and gardening part was a surprise. The empty lot opposite the garage had a big flower bed in the middle, and the rest was grass. Papa had always kept it watered and clear of empty cans and trash, mown the grass, and weeded the flower bed, and when he'd died, Jamie kept it up. He wasn't sure how Shania knew, but he was pleased.

"How did you find canned raw trout, turkey, and deer? You should try to can some of that air, bring it back to remind you now

and then." That was another joke, that she fed him fresh food to remind him what it was because he never bought any. It had started when Shania found him eating peaches straight from the can.

"Ask Mama Bear if she can spare you a cub. Then you'll have someone to cuddle on cold nights. On second thought, bring me a cub. It will liven up the garden, and keep Frankie's gardener on his toes." Phillipe, her gardener, would clip off individual leaves to keep bushes looking nice and neat, so a bear would probably give him a heart attack.

"Just remember, Frankie has a spare room once you've finished with your adventures. You can bring a friend to visit if you like, so they can compare tastes in clothing. Keep in touch." Oops, Shania had recognised her clothes, the shirt presumably. Jamie wondered if the spare room was in the Maldives. The bit about a visit was a surprise—he hadn't expected Shania to want to meet the alien.

Jamie dismantled one phone, then wrote out his message a couple of times first. *"Hi, thanks for sorting out the garden. Wish I'd read this before shopping, then we could have collected an extra bear for you. Tell Frankie I will probably need the spare room, maybe for both of us. She likes milkshakes, old-style, and is a real tourist, wants to see everything. You might not-recognise her again, even if you look in the right places. We will come by if possible, just so you can see how much she's changed."*

If the FBI or Hunter were already hacking Shania's new phone, or this one, they might understand some of that, but they'd never work out the garden part. He didn't think there was anything to lead them to Shania if they weren't already watching her, or identify him. Once he'd dismantled the phone, Jamie thought about the last part. He'd love to take Ghost to see Shania, but was worried about getting her in trouble. Ghost would probably escape, possibly leaving a trail of bodies, and Jamie had accepted he might end up in jail, but he didn't want to mess up Shania's life.

~~

When he got back to the repairs, and looked at the shattered original, Jamie realised that calculating the number of converters he'd need wouldn't be easy. He tried to figure out how to extract the right stuff and build one big one, then how much of each element was in an Earth one and in the original, but gave up. He didn't know enough about them.

The alternative was to fasten a lot of the Earth type together, which would need a rat's nest of piping. Jamie finally worked out how to do it, and he was going to need another room. Even then it might not work, because now he looked at the details, the stuff in the original was more complicated than Earth versions. There was a simple solution, do without, but how long did Ghost need the steering thrusters working?

He was trying to work out the best way to give her more operating time when Ghost's voice disturbed him. "I think we had better leave, Jamie." When he reached the control room, she'd reshaped, re-grown her pelt, and was sitting in her seat. "There is a crowd downstairs, and they will get impatient eventually."

He wanted to ask, but Jamie could see that Ghost was concentrating, moving controls just a tiny bit, then checking screens. "I am disturbing the disguise just a little, as if there is a malfunction." The view below began to move slowly, and Ghost tweaked her instruments again. "It will get a little worse as we move across Oklahoma, then cut off as if I noticed. Hunter will hope that I stay on that course, to the southeast, and should check there first."

Silence fell for a few minutes as Ghost occasionally altered controls, until she nodded sharply. "That will be enough." Her fingers flew across the panel, and several orange or yellow lights turned red. Jamie started worrying until he remembered that red was the same as green. As Ghost relaxed and sat back, she changed course, sweeping around in a gentle arc to head west. "Now we want a fast car or truck going to Albuquerque."

The pod really did stick with the traffic this time, only switching vehicles when the driver turned off, so the trip took just over seven hours. They both slept for long periods, with the pod locking onto the target truck and staying with it. The alarm if it turned off I-40 was transmitted to Ghost, so it didn't rouse Jamie, but he woke up when she did.

Ghost made the most of it, insisting she needed pelt-stroking to sleep again. That might not have been strictly true, but she still seemed hyped from her shopping trip and Jamie didn't mind. He didn't quite trust the pod, but the stroking relaxed him as well, so neither was tired when they reached Albuquerque. Jamie directed Ghost to two stores, so she could decide on which one to rob, but now he had to decide how much to take.

~~

When Jamie had been looking at the damaged converter, he'd noticed that the insides of the pipe leading to it were crazed, as if it was coated with something. The rest of the thruster pipes looked like straight steel, but the inside of the sections still connected to the damaged converter were corroded. It had made holes in the thinner pipework nearer the steering jets, which explained what the converter was for.

Jamie's main problem was that he'd no idea how fast the exhaust would corrode thicker pipes. "How long do the steering jets have to last, Ghost?"

Her voice came back from somewhere near the control room, but was behind him by the time she'd finished speaking. "Fifteen of your minutes would be enough. Not continuous, just to set a course out of atmosphere and avoid satellites, then to pick a course that won't hit a moon. Once we are lined up, we will use the main thrusters and skipping to give us clearance for a Stellar Jump. If we can do that while Hunter is on the other side of the planet, we'll be gone before he can lock on and the missile can reach us. We hope he follows."

Ghost peered over Jamie's shoulder. "If we arrive before him, long enough to contact our orbital, our world's defences will deal with Hunter. A rescue vessel will retrieve us." Her smile should have more teeth, long, sharp ones. "Then we can deal with the Starborn Circus."

Jamie concentrated on repairs rather than possible dentistry. "You definitely won't need the steering thrusters again? Because I might be able to get them working for a while, but then they'll be shot, need replacement."

He'd turned to speak to her, and Ghost immediately presented her pelt. "For luck?" He stroked down to the end of the hair or fur, just past her waist, not totally sure her pelt came right down to her shorts before. He'd have to be careful or he'd be stroking her ass, which might mess up the getting-used-to part. A brilliant smile and then a quick kiss on the cheek distracted Jamie. "Just for luck, no DNA."

A kiss might not be enough. "I need as much luck as possible. You'll have to test it all very carefully first, and there won't be much gradual control, probably just on, half-power, and off."

The laugh was still happy about the progress. "That could be more exciting than the motorbike. If it is exciting enough, Ghost Claw might keep it that way."

Jamie wasn't sure when excitement turned to sheer terror, but had a feeling the latter was more likely. To keep that down a bit, he'd better make sure nothing burned through too fast. He wished he knew what material would last longest, but the simplest way was to go with overkill—use more than one layer with the thickest pipe on the outside.

Which wasn't a problem as long as Ghost could land the pod in the right place. "In that case we'd better take plenty of pipe, so it lasts longer. Have you decided on the best place to land?"

"To avoid the police and Hunter, or to make it exciting?" As he followed her to the control room, Jamie wasn't certain if she meant that. She might because the last day and night had settled one thing—Ghost wasn't putting on an act. Regardless of shape, this was her real personality.

Though if Jamie had known the truth, her personality wouldn't have been the part that worried him.

(ALIEN) COPS AND ROBBERS

As soon as the pod reached Albuquerque, Ghost checked Jamie's suggestions, and chose the best candidate. The long shed with big doors at one end, big enough for a truck, had to be where the stock was kept. Breaking in there and loading up would be less obvious than robbing the store, in full view of the street.

Enlarging the view, Ghost explained there was still a problem. "The gap between the shed and store is too narrow, and in front of those doors is clearly visible from the street. The pod would be in among too many lights and cameras in a confined space. Turning off enough of them to hide us would be obvious, and probably set off alarms."

That didn't make sense. He'd seen the pod, or actually not seen it even close up, but before Jamie could comment, Ghost explained. "We can't rely on the disguise. The deception programming deflects the view around us, but if the surroundings are too complicated, it may be overloaded. There will be distortions and partial reflections as it tries to deal with complicated, brightly-lit backgrounds in all directions, especially with us moving about, loading up."

Jamie realised that Ghost usually parked in a place without a lot of movement to deflect, with sky or something solid like a wall as a background, which now made sense. "There will be someplace nearby that is deserted at night, maybe an empty parking lot, and then we can go in on foot. If you can create a blind spot near the back door, between the shed and the store, we'll put everything there."

Reaching past her, Jamie put his finger on the spot. "We can stack the pipe, rope it together if you've got some, and bag up the fittings. Then we get the pod, hover overhead where it's nice and dark, and I'll ride the cable down to hook up. If there's a long-range shot of us from the rest of the CCTV, it will just show two people breaking in, or running off. We'll both wear shades, I'll wear the hat, and if you change your hair colour, that should be enough. Black will be better at night anyway."

Jamie thought about Ghost changing her face, but the cops were looking for a Malone clone and had his general description. A few long-range camera shots wouldn't matter as long as there wasn't a clear close-up of their faces.

After looking at the shadows and angles, Ghost sent drones to stop the electricity to two lights and one camera, then the pod hovered and waited.

Once both Ghost and Jamie were satisfied that hadn't triggered an alarm, Ghost went looking for a nearby parking spot. Finding one took time, as the nearby parking lots were busy, and gardens were either too small or too public, but eventually they spotted a vacant lot with a board fence. That would mean walking a long way, but riding the bike would be noisy, and he didn't have any fake plates. Checking the area again didn't come up with a better spot, so Ghost almost-landed and opened the hatch.

~~

Ghost pulled four planks loose to get out through the fence, gently so there wasn't much noise, and the pair of them slid through. She replaced the boards, using the handle of a knife to push, not hammer, a couple of nails back in, and Jamie remembered the strength comment. He remembered again when Ghost climbed up the chain-link fence and the post with the camera in seconds, leaving him struggling. Jamie wasn't exactly unfit, but he was going to need serious time with weights and gym equipment to keep up.

At least Ghost waited for him, using the time to connect a larger device to the camera. "Once the drone moves away, this will infiltrate the programming and take control. It will pause recording on any camera that might show us, so we never appear. It will take a few minutes, but the drones will cover us until then."

Standing in a deep shadow until the programme reported in, Ghost opened a trash bag and pulled out coils of rope. Once the cameras were looping recent footage, they walked down the middle of the gap between the store and shed, stopping opposite the side door. Ghost laid the three long, thin ropes side by side with three-foot gaps.

When they approached the door, Ghost pointed up to a box on the wall, and a drone flew in to land on it. "That will stop the alarm when I open the door. We'll stack the pipe across the ropes, and fasten it into one bundle so we can snatch it in seconds." Pulling out the machete she went to jimmy the door, and stopped. "The frame is steel, so this will not work. The door is timber so I can open it, but there will be some noise. Be ready to run."

Jamie moved back to the ropes so he could snatch them, and turned to nod to Ghost. He'd thought she was going to cut a hole but she had a sneaker in her hand. She took two quick steps and kicked the lock, and it twisted inwards, torn out of the door! Jamie remembered the comment about barbed vegetation not hurting her feet, then wondered if it was a foot, or maybe a hoof.

The angle meant he couldn't see, which he didn't think was accidental. Remembering she didn't like spectators while changing he looked away, and when he looked back Ghost was beckoning. A glance confirmed she was wearing both sneakers again. He listened for a few moments, but the sharp crack didn't seem to have attracted any attention.

When Ghost pushed the door to open it a little, the lock remained, hanging from the frame. Two drones flew through the gap and she waited, then turned and smiled. "One motion detector, now turned off." Pushing the door wide open, Ghost caught the lock as it slid free and placed it on the floor. She wasn't wearing gloves, but when he'd offered, she'd concentrated and smoothed her finger ends.

Jamie followed her in, and used a dimmed flashlight to read the signs as he walked down the aisles. No problem with quantity, he could have replumbed the whole pod with this lot. He found the first size on his list, and called Ghost.

He needed her because the lengths of piping were shrink-wrapped in bundles, so Jamie would have struggled with the larger diameters. Ghost could lift them, but found them difficult to control, and Jamie could manage that part. He was relieved in a way—she wasn't an alien Superwoman. He didn't want to repeat this, so Jamie took more than he'd need, making a big stack.

Once he thought he'd got enough, in three different diameters, Ghost pulled the ends of the long ropes up and around the heap. Instead of tying them, she placed a clamp where the ropes met, and pressed a button. The clamp tightened, though she tugged the rope to make sure. Glancing at Jamie, she smiled and waggled her fingers. "Easier than untying knots, cheaper than cutting the rope."

"Easier to learn than all the different types of knots." Jamie hadn't enjoyed those lessons, though he'd persevered and learned the ones Papa used in the garage. He wondered if he could persuade Ghost to leave a couple of the clamps, but then remembered she'd even melted alien metal.

Ghost was already moving back into the shed. "There were no fittings, but we saw a door at that end." Jamie followed, pausing when she tried the handle and it didn't move. She tried again, and a sharp crack loosened the handle but the door remained locked. Jamie was ready to turn away, even though he was tempted to peek, but this time the machete prised the door open.

Jackpot, one set of shelves was full of boxes with the right pictures. Once again Jamie checked his list, and they tipped the boxes into the rubble sacks. As he hefted one, Jamie was pleased he hadn't brought ordinary trash bags. Once they had as much as he thought the six sacks could carry, Jamie used ordinary Earth rope to tie them to Ghost's ropes.

Looking at the pipe, then the sacks, he could do with more. "Ghost, if we fill a couple of boxes we can carry them back, just to make sure there's enough." She followed him and he filled two cardboard boxes with a selection. Ghost offered to carry more, but that would have looked odd, where one box under an arm shouldn't attract attention.

~~

Despite Ghost's assurances, Jamie was relieved when they arrived back at the fence. Still no alarms, though three drones were blanking the cameras covering the stack and cutting off any alarm. The fourth drone came back to cover the fence and camera for when Ghost removed her gadget.

"Just one more problem." Jamie gestured up towards the top of the fence, and hefted his box. "I'll never climb up and over with this, and even if you do it, it'll make a hell of a racket." He hadn't really thought this through. The loose fittings in the boxes weren't too noisy just walking, but would make a racket climbing the fence.

Ghost eyed up the height, and the two boxes. "Could you catch them if we throw?"

Jamie wasn't sure, and even if he caught them, there'd still be a lot of noise. "No, but I've just had a better idea. We can use that gadget for cutting metal, the one you brought in case we cut any chains?" Jamie made a shape with his hand, across, down, and back to cut a door in the mesh.

"You said someone might spot a hole while we were inside, and raise the alarm." Though Ghost was smiling because she'd realised—even if the hole was seen, they'd be back with the pod before the police got here. The stack of pipe couldn't be seen from the fence, so even with someone standing here, they could hook it up and fly away. "That is a Slashtail solution. I'm beginning to wonder how much DNA you have absorbed?"

Jamie laughed and pointed at his head. "No pelt."

"Truth, and your little package won't give you one." As she spoke, Ghost took out the little gadget. It was the same one Jamie used for cutting, heating, and welding, but now a thin glow extended about fifteen inches. "Ready?" Jamie barely nodded before her arm drew the shape, the wire sagged open, and she scooped up her box and jumped through. By the time Jamie belatedly snatched up his, she was halfway up the pole to collect her gadget. That was a big step up from bolt croppers!

Since he used it for welding, the gadget could also hide the hole. "Hang on a minute." Ghost stopped as she was picking up her box, and turned, by which time Jamie was holding the mesh roughly in place. "If you spot-weld the mesh, the hole won't be obvious in the dark. I'd rather not risk the police getting here first. Flashing lights and policemen everywhere might upset the pod disguise."

"Boring. Maybe you should steal a little more Slashtail." Though even as she spoke, the gadget lit up and Ghost carefully welded the first links together. Three dabs at each side and one top and bottom was good enough, then they both walked casually away.

~~

Ghost's casual was a bit too fast, so Jamie called her back. When he caught up, she waggled her fingers. "If you give me enough DNA I could grow another arm, so you don't have to carry anything?"

Just for a moment she got him—Jamie wondered how the

hell that worked—then he grinned back. The weight wasn't the problem, and she knew it. Turning off the direct route, Ghost tried to pick a route where trees gave a lot of shadow. Just as well—it meant that when the red and blue lights started flashing just ahead, the pair of them weren't out in the open.

A glance back showed more flashing lights, close to the compound but moving slowly towards them. There were four cars pulled up ahead of Jamie, and the distinctive figure of an officer with a dog was inspecting the first one. "Put the boxes over the wall, in the garden. Then we stroll past, and pick them up later." Even if the boxes were found, Jamie figured they could buy or steal more connections.

Ghost put her box on the ground. "That animal is not a dog, and that police officer is an alien: Hunter. They will detect us, even looking like this. Hunter must have picked up some hint when we left Oklahoma, or left a drone. That might have detected our transmitter, as we have been monitoring police channels. We will divert him while you get these boxes aboard the pod, then we will join you."

Just for a moment, Jamie considered dumping the boxes once she'd left. One look at the determination on Ghost's face, and remembering her reaction to finding out he might fix her ride, and he let it go. "What if there's more than one Hunter?"

A sharp headshake dispelled that idea. "Hunters are greedy. They usually work alone rather than share the reward. He will have a crew to operate Starlight Ghost, and perhaps they are carrying the lights behind us, but he will want to make the capture himself. You are not the target, so you will be safe."

She kissed him quickly, on the cheek. "For luck, because you don't have a proper pelt." A supple wriggle and Ghost was gone into the shadows, leaving... Jamie leant down and picked up her clothes, half-unzipping his jacket to stuff all five items inside.

While he waited, Jamie watched the officer, looking for

something to show he wasn't human. With the flashing red and blue lights behind him it wasn't easy. The officer almost seemed to flicker and fuzz at the edges—which he couldn't be doing or the car's occupants would notice.

The search seemed to consist of asking the passengers to wind down their windows, then leading his dog right around the vehicle. Another car joined the queue, and Jamie began to worry. If one stopped near him, and the occupants saw the boxes, they might mention it to the officer—Hunter.

~~

Jamie was just about to break cover, head back up the road, when a roar got everyone's attention. A long cattish or short snakish predator, slim, pale blonde, and long-haired with a bald black lionish head and fangs, stalked out into the road on eight stumpy legs. It paused so everyone got a good look, then roared again, proving that most of its impressive fangs had been hidden. Lashing its tail, it glared at the officer.

He went for his gun, but what shocked Jamie as much as the lionish was the dog. It collapsed and curled up, then shivered and shimmered before standing up as something entirely different. It was now a slim, long-legged otterish or maybe meercattish creature, but larger and bald, with gleaming, dark purple skin and a fat bushy tail. It shrieked at the lionish and lunged, yanking at the lead so the Hunter's first shot missed. That was easy to see as, instead of the usual flash of flame, a thin beam of greenish light came out of the weapon.

It might have missed anyway, because the lionish creature was already moving—a lot faster than the short legs suggested. The beam hit the corner of a building as the lionish disappeared behind it, and a web of sparkling green light spread across the brickwork. When it stopped spreading, the whole web and attached wall crumbled away, revealing offices and, above them, a bedroom. The combination of weird noises, creatures, and lights caused absolute chaos as the waiting drivers panicked.

Two of the cars accelerated, one knocking the lights aside, while the people in two of them jumped out and ran. The couple left in the remaining car, which was trapped between abandoned vehicles, opted for ducking down out of sight. They could all have saved themselves the effort—none of the aliens were interested in them.

Hunter broke into a run as his prey leapt across the road and into the dark, and disappeared in hot pursuit along with his tracker otterish. As he did the image wavered, and for a moment he looked taller and almost egg-shaped, and there was some sort of big pack. Then he was gone, but the couple in the bed joined the screaming as more bricks fell.

Jamie gave it a few moments, then turned up his collar and picked up the boxes, one under each arm. He walked past the cars without looking towards them, and turned towards the pod—no point in a diversion now. It wasn't far, but he kept to the shadows as much as possible. He stopped worrying when two squad cars and an ambulance roared past, lights and sirens clearing the way. Right now, they were more interested in aliens.

For a moment, Jamie was relieved when he reached the fence without seeing Hunter, but then he realised he wouldn't see another pod. Another moment's thought and he couldn't do anything about it, so Jamie pulled off the boards, pleased the nails holding them were already loose. He pushed the boxes through the gap, propped the boards in place, and used the winch to load the loot.

Not much loot—Jamie didn't think Ghost would risk picking up the rest, not with Hunter looking for her. He wondered how long the drones would last before their batteries ran down, and how much trouble they'd cause her. Even if they kept working for hours, there would be cops all over the place, and someone would see the damaged fence. A blanked camera wouldn't hide anything when the yard was searched.

~~

A quick look confirmed Ghost wasn't in the control room, or her nest-room, so Jamie sat in the control seat and tried to spot her, or the Hunter. There were several screens giving views in different directions, but none of them showed green glows, and any flashing lights were in the distance. He couldn't redirect the cameras, so Jamie considered rotating the pod to cover any blind spots, but worried that might make it easier to see. A flash of movement in the air was followed by the sound of the airlock opening and closing.

There was a short delay, presumably while Ghost changed shape, before the door behind him opened. Three drones flew in, followed by Ghost. "We must get under cover, quickly, because Hunter's ship will search the area."

Jamie didn't answer, or move, because she'd leant across him to reach the controls, and Ghost was starkers again. He eased out from under her so she could sit, which earned him a quick glance and smile, but she was more interested in steering. The pod hopped over the fence into the street and accelerated, keeping just above the tarmac except when she hopped over the occasional vehicle.

Two of them stopped very quickly, and one swerved, so she must have gotten close enough for a quick glimpse of something. That didn't matter as much now, not after the alien death ray and the rest. Every alien hunter in the USA would be here tomorrow, along with the FBI and agents from secret departments with odd initials.

Jamie kept looking at the screens while pulling her clothes out of his jacket. Jeans, shirt, jacket, and sneakers—Ghost just didn't get the idea of underclothes. Actually, she didn't get the idea of clothes at all because she was still naked, and didn't seem to care. "Here, you might want these."

Ghost laughed, though when he glanced she was leant

forward in her seat, intent on steering. "Not really, but no clothes is inappropriate with you here. Unless you prefer my last look? It is a predator on my homeworld, endangered now as it is hunted for the pelt."

"I like your pelt better." He'd already tried to imagine her covered in pelt, and regardless of her shape, he thought Ghost would be beautiful. He nearly laughed when he realised he really was looking at her pelt, and not the naked and sexy part. Shania would never believe him. Maybe it was the alien part, or maybe it was because he liked her as a person. Had he just friend-zoned an attractive naked woman?

Glancing at the clothes, Ghost shook her head. "There is no point in dressing, as we must change again soon. We are sorry if this is offensive." The humour in her voice knew damn fine it wasn't.

"Not really, I'm getting used to it." Jamie concentrated on the screens—he hadn't meant to say that. At least there were plenty of practical worries to divert her. "I'm surprised we haven't seen any cop cars. Some of those people must have phoned in." Jamie wished he'd taken a picture himself, but it was all over too quickly.

Ghost was concentrating on escaping, so she took a moment to answer. "Hunter is still blocking phone and radio transmissions, so your police are having difficulty communicating. We had blocked police transmissions nearby, but stopped when we saw the red and blue lights. Hunter has better equipment, and must have detected our transmitter moving along that stretch of road."

She gestured to the three drones, now stuck to the wall. "We have lost a drone. I called them in and reprogrammed one to deal with the clamps. With their power packs drained they will fall off, and hopefully won't draw attention. The drone won't catch up now, so it will self-destruct, burn out the interior so it is an inert disc."

Jamie wasn't worrying about the clamps or drone. "Will Hunter be able to follow the pod?"

"Not until he reaches his transport. That will take time as it will be larger than this pod, so it will be hiding further away, and by then we will be hidden." Reaching up, Ghost tapped several yellow lights, and a screen zoomed in on a darkened building. "We have cut off all emissions so he cannot follow us to our new hiding place. We thought of hiding here before, but it is too busy in daylight."

"But if he followed us from Oklahoma, he'll be able to follow us now." Jamie wondered if they'd been moving too fast on I-40, but wasn't going to suggest it.

"He didn't follow us." Ghost seemed certain, but in that case, Jamie wondered if Hunter was psychic. The explanation was much simpler. "The more we think about it, the more we are sure he left drones everywhere we were seen, probably covering all of Santa Rosa, Oklahoma, and Albuquerque. Starlight Ghost would have dropped out of orbit at nightfall, so once a drone reported my transmissions, it wouldn't take long to move in."

She paused, looked at the two boxes of fittings, and sighed. "While we were collecting those, he had time to plan and land assets. At least he didn't get a clear fix, or he would have followed us to the pod." The second sigh was resigned, and disappointed. "Perhaps we should have left the police radios alone, and trusted our stealth."

She sounded forlorn, downhearted, and if she'd had clothes, Jamie would have offered a hug, or a pelt stroke. He settled for trying to look on the bright side. "If he's lost us, we can get more pipe. It didn't cost us anything, and if we move far enough away we'll be clear of his drones."

The attempt failed—Ghost didn't answer. As the structure came nearer, Jamie realised it was a major construction site, a partly-built multi-storey office or apartment block. Ghost took the pod high over the security fencing, then brought it right down almost to ground level, only a few yards from the wire.

When it stopped, she stood up. "The drones are stopping three cameras, just until we can fit what you called a gadget to a junction box. We will change into a nighttime hunter so no drivers will see us. We will stay with the gadget, monitoring progress as it infiltrates the programming and adjusts it, which may take some time."

As she moved towards the door, two joysticks popped up in front of Jamie, one with a yellow button on top. "The pod's computer will take over, delaying the views from the cameras just a little. It will adjust the signal to alter what is on any screens or recording devices, but only when it would reveal us. Just looping would be spotted if it carried on too long. Wait until I call, then head for those big doors."

~~

Jamie was wondering why he'd need the laser—he recognised the yellow button, when he realised. If Ghost was sneaking around out there, he might see what she changed into. One second's thought and he didn't want to. The lionish was strange without being gruesome, but he'd no idea what a night hunter might look like.

Jamie didn't want anything really gross in his head when he looked at Ghost, so he kept his eyes on the warehouse doors. An hour later, or that's what the four or five minutes felt like, Ghost's voice came from a speaker. *"All clear, Jamie. Stop the pod just before the doors, then use the laser to cut the lock. The small screen to your left is a scan of the area ahead, and will show any bars or bolts. Cut through enough to get inside, then open the rest without leaving visible damage."*

As he lined up on the doors, Jamie thought about that, and there might be a better way. The scan showed a central locking bar and bolts at the bottom, but as expected, there was a smaller door set into the large one. He hadn't had many lessons, but Jamie zoomed in on the smaller door and it had what looked like a house-type keyhole below the recessed handle. The scanner was the ultimate cheat—Jamie carefully aimed at the crack between the door and the frame, and a two-inch cut did the job.

He still might need a cut on the main doors, but he went to check first. On the way to the exit, he picked up his head torch, the one he'd been using to look at damaged piping in dark places. The metal either side of the crack was blackened, and a very small strip of paintwork was bubbled, so Ghost's camera programme should be able to deal with it.

No lights inside, and even if he'd seen a switch, Jamie wasn't daft enough to turn it on. He realised he was enjoying this, and grinned at the thought of Shania's reaction. Boring Jamie, the intergalactic burglar! More importantly, the small door opened almost silently, with hardly any resistance. The locking bar was manual, and neither of the bolts was stiff, then Jamie eased one door open.

Or didn't, because it didn't move. After turning his head lamp back on to inspect it for more bolts, Jamie figured it was the weight—he hadn't pulled hard enough. Turning off his light he tried again, and once it was moving it wasn't too bad, or as loud as he'd expected. Even so it was a long way from silent, so Jamie hoped any passers-by were in cars.

He stopped the door before it was all the way open and hit a stop or wall, and squinted to try to see if the pod would fit. He could see a little distortion, presumably because of the lights on the building and fence, but not enough to be sure. A moment's thought and from the rooms he'd seen, the pod probably wouldn't fit, so Jamie opened the other door.

~~

The voice nearly gave him a heart attack. "Move aside please." That had to be a loudspeaker of some sort, but turned right down, and then Jamie finally saw the pod as Ghost turned off the disguise. There was only reflected light from the nearest fence lights and some starlight, but the twenty-foot-square front of the spacecraft was close enough to almost run him down.

As he stood aside and it drifted forward, Jamie got a better look. The body was about twenty feet high, and the same wide as he'd just seen, and now he could see it was about sixty feet long. The first forty feet had no protrusions, and there were no signs of an opening, though he could see lines or scratches on the nearest parts. There were some discoloured patches on the matt black, but no serious damage as he could see.

The last twenty feet was the same height and width, but had antennae, bulges, and angled exhausts sticking out, so it just scraped through the doorway. Once it was inside, Jamie saw two big tubes with flared ends sticking out behind, the main thrusters. The whole thing looked like a blocky copy of a space shuttle without wings or tailfins. "Close the doors please, Jamie."

As he slid the second door closed, small areas of the hull glowed, illuminating the floor. Six thick legs telescoped out of what looked like smooth metal, and the pod lowered the last few inches so they supported it. That was when Jamie realised the scratches he'd seen on the way in weren't necessarily damage. The straight lines and smooth curves probably formed shapes if he could see them properly, so maybe it had wings when it flew properly.

~~

The external lights glowed enough to give an idea of the size of the warehouse, then an oblong section of the pod's hull slid aside. The brighter interior lights lit up a wider area, and the ramp that extruded. Ghost strolled down what had to be the cargo access she had mentioned, wearing the bikini top but still tugging her shorts into place.

She hadn't bothered with boots. "These clothes are more

comfortable than yours, and this top doesn't cover my pelt. We have turned off the shield and most of the rest of the pod. The electrical wiring, metal building and the equipment in here will interfere with scans, so even a close pass by Hunter's ship shouldn't detect us."

She paused to glance upwards. "We are safe for tonight, as Hunter will have had to break off, lose track. The ship will be forced to go higher now your armed forces are alerted, or one of your aircraft may hit Starlight Ghost. Then he must stay high in daylight, unless there is low cloud or mist."

That didn't make sense, considering what the pod could do. "I would have thought the spaceship's disguise would be better than an escape pod."

Glancing towards the pod, Ghost shook her head. "Pods have top quality concealment, to hide from primitives or enemies. Hunter's problem is size. Re-transmission on that scale can't cover every possible angle, and at close range, the small anomalies around something the size of an interstellar spaceship become obvious. Birds hitting solid air and falling in the street, or smoke bending around a starship, would be a big hint something was there."

"Won't he have something smaller?" Jamie frowned at Ghost's ship, because it was nothing like what he would call an escape pod. He upgraded his idea of how big the main ship must be. "If this is small?"

Ghost turned to look up at her ship. "Yes, very small compared to Starlight Ghost, our starship. The other pods do not have modifications so they are smaller and slower, with very little manoeuvrability. The ship has dedicated landing craft, but they will not operate without two key components. Finding out which two are dummies would take a workshop and real experts. The other options are not very stealthy."

~~

That came with a very human smirk, and then Ghost

pounced across the last two paces. She picked Jamie up in a bear hug and twirled him around. "We made it!" She plonked him back down and kissed him.

Startled, Jamie forgot, wrapped his arms around her, and kissed back. She spun away, arms out wide. "Oops, inappropriate, but tasty." When she stopped twirling Ghost had a big smile, and licked her lips, but then her smile died. "We are sorry. We did not ask first, as we did not mean to take DNA. This body reacted when we kissed."

Jamie almost pointed out so did his, but bit it off and just smiled. "My fault as well, I kissed back. You'd better be more careful in future, or you might find out about some other Earth habits." Damn, that slipped out. Turning away Jamie looked for another subject, quickly, and the light from the open hatch provided one.

Some of the spares in the workshop explained the size of the doorway and the open space in the centre—it was to let the big construction machinery come inside for repair. "Handy, lots of tools, and I can see sheet metal. I'll be able to shape the thicker steel for the heavy repairs, if I can work out what I actually need. There are some pipes as well, but I might have to adapt for different sizes."

Jamie didn't look back, but the humour in Ghost's voice meant the deflection didn't work. "But first we should sleep. You will be safe while you stroke our pelt, as we already have some DNA to absorb." The last bit was quiet, as she turned away, but Jamie was sure he was meant to hear her. "And we are not ready to learn more habits, or not yet."

At least the DNA part gave Jamie an excuse to bring up another subject, one he was beginning to wonder about. "How did you get the DNA for the lion thing? I doubt it was from stroking its pelt, or kissing."

~~

That didn't get the expected laugh. "Not quite DNA, that is

a result of Earth's local evolution. With any animal, collecting information is much simpler, we just need to eat enough. That is how the Hunter's tracker could look like an Earth dog." She sounded cautious now, which might be because she guessed Jamie's reaction.

"Hunter ate a human?" He'd turned back so Jamie saw the shock, and then denial, before Ghost spoke.

"No, or probably not, but even if he did, Hunter would not be able to utilise the DNA to change shape. We were nearer and could see better. He is using a portable version of what hides the pod and ship." Ghost gestured towards her pod. "The field can be used to show a different image, shape, to the real one, but with a portable power pack the result is only precise from one direction."

That was a relief—Jamie had started to wonder if every race except humans could do the shape-changing. "He looked sort of fuzzy and flickered at the edges, but I thought it was the flashing lights. That dog changed shape, so how common is it? How many aliens are wandering around Earth in human shape?"

Ghost shook her head. "Earth is not on the contact list, so there shouldn't be any other aliens here. The shape-copying ability is very rare. The dog is related to us, and we only know of one other race that can shapeshift. It might be extinct." All the joking was gone—for once Ghost looked and sounded dead serious. "Normally we would have eaten a sample from the dead Hellbats to help us perfect this shape, but we realised that was inappropriate with you there."

~~

She stopped, possibly because of the horrified look on Jamie's face, but then she continued. "Your implanted sample would have died in time, leaving no trace we had visited. Just now, when we kissed, I realised that your Slashtail signature is too strong. You must have absorbed a little Slashtail, something that isn't possible with the usual method."

The cautious tone, and look, must be a response to whatever showed on Jamie's face—mostly confusion if it reflected his thoughts. "You have only absorbed a little, but that means that you are nearer to shape-changing than any other known race. Even so it is only a tiny amount, not enough to develop the ability. That would take an injection to deliberately force the change, which you might not survive."

A quick smile momentarily banished the serious look. "Though many years of kissing, or possibly those other habits, might be enough? We will never know as we will be gone long before you have collected enough kisses, unless you would like to travel the stars with us, see our homeworld?"

Jamie had absolutely no intention of discussing kissing or other habits—that had been a big mistake. "Space travel? I'll have to think about that." Sometime when he'd gotten over the shock of finding out Ghost ate things to copy them. Jamie skipped past his momentary curiosity about copying a lettuce or tree. "I thought I saw something flying, just before you came back."

Ghost didn't seem worried now—maybe because Jamie hadn't freaked at the explanation. "Since you have now seen us change form radically, you deserve the truth. We became a flock of small fliers from another world, very useful if we have to evade close surveillance or travel difficult terrain. Rarely used because that one is not a true copy, and we temporarily lose our comms. We can only maintain it for about two of your hours, as anything not needed for flying and navigating is replaced by our brain, to retain memory and intelligence. Then we must keep close together, in a tight flock, so the parts of our consciousness remain connected enough to think rationally."

She hesitated, then answered Jamie's next question before he asked. "We do not keep the blueprint, the information, for many creatures, just a few to deal with emergencies. A swimmer, the night hunter, that sort of thing, all of them larger than the flock." Ghost's smile came back. "If you ever collected enough kisses, those blueprints would come with the ability."

Neither kissing nor his shape would be the problem if Jamie decided to leave earth. "I'm good with this shape, thanks, but I've realised I should work out more if I'm going to be around you for long." Which might not happen if he fixed her pod, but Jamie really was considering the offer. He'd already realised he couldn't go back to his old life. "Is there any exercise equipment in the pod?"

"Only on Starlight Ghost, though you could use this workshop to make up some weights?" Ghost turned away with a shrug. "If there is time. We must leave before workers arrive."

~~

Jamie realised that Ghost wouldn't realise that the day of the week made a difference. "On Saturday? Maybe not. Wait to see if anyone turns up. After all, after Hunter's exhibition, an invisible something zooming out of a workshop might not even make the news. Either way, we should take the opportunity to sleep. I'm shattered so if nobody turns up, don't wake me."

He smiled because the next bit was true, but wouldn't make sense to Ghost. "We're going to have to change our plans, but with a bit of luck, my brain will work on it while I'm asleep. I might wake up with a solution, a way to get around all the problems without leaving Hunter any clues."

"You will work while you sleep?" Her little smile meant Ghost was sure that wasn't possible.

He tried to explain, at least partly to give her something to think about instead of tonight's disaster. "Not quite, but if the problem is fresh when I sleep, if I've worked out what I've got and what it needs to do, my head sometimes sort of rearranges it all. Then I wake up with a way to get there, but it doesn't always work." Jamie laughed, because that wasn't really helpful.

Ghost didn't think so either. "We will sleep on that so our human brain can make it into sense. Will you be buying the computer components tomorrow?"

"No." Jamie didn't need sleep to realise one thing—moving from here too soon would be a bad idea. "Hunter can't find us, so we should take advantage of this workshop as long as possible, two days with a bit of luck. There will be stocks of piping for repairing equipment, and there might be more. There could be cable and pipe for the actual building stored on-site."

As he followed Ghost up the ramp, it took a moment for Jamie to realise she was already singing a version of her night-time happy song. Ghost wasn't going to miss out on her pelt-stroking.

Though before they went to the night-nest, Jamie checked the news. The local disturbance hadn't hit the news desk yet, so the main interest was on Oklahoma, and another appearance of the Salome Malone clone. There were a lot of pictures, at least twenty selfies, and phone videos of Salome laughing and talking with fans.

Jamie had to comment. "I thought you were just going to let a few recognise you."

Ghost looked over his shoulder. "We realised that if they weren't sure, it might not make the news. When we saw a young man staring, wondering, we took off the hat and shades and confessed he'd caught me. He has three selfies, and a lipstick kiss on his cheek."

When he jerked around to look at her lips, Ghost laughed. "No, it wasn't lipstick, but he won't be getting it analysed so it won't matter. If it had been lipstick, it wouldn't have lasted long enough for all the kisses." Pointing at the screen, Ghost gestured. "Keep going, and you'll see some of the women wanted lipstick as well. Is that one of those habits you warned me about?"

"It is, so you'd better be careful who you kiss." Jamie had done as he was told and there was a threesome with Ghost/Salome in the middle. Both the women had lipstick kisses on their cheek. "And how many." A short video clip showed the front of the parking lot, then the next was a slow sweep of a crowd, all waving and shouting. "You did say they'd followed you back."

"We didn't even need the pheromones. Some of them asked about the copy." Ghost sniggered and walked away and back, swinging her hips. "We pretended to be insulted, and asked if they thought this was real or not. They were all convinced."

Jamie started laughing, and pointed. "Either Salome or her agent have realised nobody can tell the difference. She's claiming it was a surprise appearance to help advertise her new movie, and there will be more. Now there's even more publicity, because the cops said it was the copy."

"If I'm going to be making more appearances, I should sleep. Though after all the excitement, I hope someone will stroke my pelt so I can relax?" She strutted off towards the night-nest with a very exaggerated Malone walk. Watching the news had accomplished one thing—it had banished Ghost's worries.

~~

When Jamie woke up, Ghost was in the cleanser. He'd barely thrown back the sheet when she came out, starkers, with her clothes in her hand. "Since you are used to this now, I will put on coverings out here, then you won't have to wait."

As Jamie closed the door behind him, he had to smile. Ghost had a little smile when she said that, so it was another of her jokes. It would back-fire because he'd spoken the truth, she didn't have the same impact. She was still attractive, but he really could more or less ignore it. Unless she kissed him, that still caught him out, but so would a kiss from any attractive woman.

She had left when he came out, and when he went for breakfast, Ghost was dressed. He'd bought cereal and milk, and when he filled a bowl, she dumped her pod gloop. After trying some of his, she filled a bowl as well and joined him. While they ate, she confirmed that no workmen had arrived, so the pod was still in the workshop.

After breakfast Jamie inspected the damage again, and although he hadn't had a eureka moment, he found himself looking at the problem in a different way. At least part of the reason was because the pod computer had been busy. Several new readings had appeared, and a few error readings had disappeared. The system must have installed backups, or extrapolated from salvaged code on the damaged chips.

There were still too many errors, and messages reporting lack of space—Jamie had totally misjudged the gap between pod computing systems and Earth's. Unless he cleaned out a warehouse, he'd never have enough storage and processors. Even if he did, the processors might not be fast enough to run the software, and that was if he figured out what software would work. The best bet was to revert to his first idea—on/off switches.

That meant isolating the thruster controls, and installing an entirely new version. He'd have to literally replace it all, run a bundle of new wiring from the control room to the physical pipes and valve controls. There would be a bundle of cables along the floor from Ghost's seat to the engines, then they'd split up in all directions. It would be slow and clunky compared to the originals, but it would definitely activate and shut off the propulsion and steering.

Bottom line, if it didn't work, Ghost would just have to do a Malone on a top computer programmer, give him a dose of those pheromones. Hopefully enough of his brain cells would survive to fix her ship. Jamie was confident any problems would be programming, not mechanical, because the remains of the original mechanics and piping were still there.

There'd be no fine control; in fact, Jamie wasn't sure there'd be much control at all—direction relied on balancing the output of steering jets. He was absolutely certain the amount of thrust wouldn't match the instruments and controls, but Ghost had asked for basic. He'd warned her it might be scary, and this would qualify.

As long as Ghost practiced first, very carefully, and only wanted to go straight up, it should do the job. Once again, she reassured him straight would do—as long as the pod got far enough from Earth to activate the Stellar Jump. Jamie had worried about fuel, but Ghost showed him the dials. The pod was automatically scavenging fuel from the atmosphere. Earth's air was richer than some other places, so the tanks were already almost full.

~~

Real food relaxed both of them and Ghost followed him back to his work, asking about the repairs so far. "Why did you climb into the main thruster outlets? They were new, and are very tough so the linings should still be intact." Ghost seemed genuinely puzzled, and Jamie realised he still hadn't asked what had hit her.

"I wasn't sure what might have been affected. How did you get damaged? Did something hit you?" Jamie remembered his first impression. "Either something blew up and overloaded the wiring, or damage to the wiring and processors caused a pressure build-up and it blew. I can see from the ruptures the damage came from inside."

The sigh suggested it wasn't a happy memory. "The second, but the damage was inflicted from outside. Our ship has a larger version of what we suggested using on the nearest cameras, as does the Starborn Circus. It hit the pod as we escaped, but at the edge of its range or all the systems would have burned out immediately. The damage must have affected the navigation, or caused a fluctuation in the Stellar Jump, or we would have gone home instead of arriving here."

Ghost patted the nearest wall. "Luckily escape pod systems are simple, and tough. The damage didn't destroy us completely, or leave us stranded in interstellar space, but we knew the systems had been affected. We didn't go into deep-sleep in case it malfunctioned."

From her face, Ghost was remembering something incredibly sad, and Jamie instinctively opened his arms. She moved closer, and as he hugged her, she laid her head on his shoulder. "As the journey carried on past when we should have arrived home, we had no idea where we would arrive, or when. Our instruments gave us no hint, and as a two-hundred-day journey became four, we wondered if we would travel forever, until the last of our clan starved."

She sounded close to tears, and now Ghost put her arms around him. He'd no idea how space travel worked, but Jamie had to ask. "Couldn't you cut the engines or something, and maybe change course?"

Her arms tightened, and Ghost sighed. "There is no way to affect a Stellar Jump once it is initiated. If we had forced a shutdown, that may have destroyed the pod, or we could have ended up between stars, light-years from any planet. We managed some repairs to other systems but even so, by the time we came out of the Between, near Earth, the propulsion was still barely functional. We knew nothing about your world, so we celebrated when our instruments confirmed we could breathe the air."

She glanced up-ship again, towards the front, as she had the last time she mentioned jumps. "As it isn't an original part of the pod, the Stellar Jump has no backup power and takes time to recharge. We skipped towards the inhabited planet, hoping to hide among the orbiting facilities, but it was millions of kilometres away."

Jamie thought he remembered the skip jump being short-range, and Ghost confirmed it. "Using the skip facility to move the whole pod should only be used to refine an approach for docking or orbit, but the thrusters weren't working properly. We saved them for landing, and skipped repeatedly without waiting for it to recover. That is not recommended, but we were desperate. We had to reach orbit before more systems failed, or we would be stranded out in space."

Caught up in the story, Jamie hadn't realised he was stroking her pelt. He stopped, and eased off on the hug, not sure what it meant to Slashtails, and Ghost looked up. There was no hint of teasing or joking in her wan smile. "Please don't stop. This form finds this comforting." She hugged him. "Unless it is inappropriate?"

He couldn't help it, Jamie laughed. "Not really, humans find it comforting as well. I know you like the pelt-stroking."

Rather than make a comment, Ghost snuggled back in, which was an indication of how upset she was. "Our celebrations didn't last long. The damage must have allowed Hunter or the Starborn Circus to plot our course and follow. Hunter arrived in our ship, but we had moved out of range of the disruption beam so he launched a missile."

Her voice sounded strained, so that hadn't been a happy moment. "He only launched one, which should have been enough, but this pod carried two counter-missiles. We kept skipping, waiting until his missile was close before stopping it, but it cost us both our missiles. By that time, we thought we were safe, too near the planet for him to risk another, so it was a shock when he launched again. We dropped into the atmosphere to evade, but a near miss overloaded the damaged systems."

~~

Ghost stopped, but she was holding on tight and either

sobbed or shuddered. When she looked up, her face looked frightened—so Jamie hugged her again and stroked her pelt.

He was sure a missile exploding among the satellites would be noticed, which reminded him of his last visit to Shania. "Damian was talking about some problem with satellites. Some of them stopped working, which messed up communications, delayed some business deal. No mention of spaceships, but I guess the military would keep mystery explosions a secret."

The pause seemed to have given Ghost a chance to recover—she sounded more like her usual self. "There wasn't an explosion. The missile was meant to disrupt our electronics, leave us dead in space without propulsion or even life support. Then Hunter would have pulled the pod inside his ship, where we couldn't escape." The little chuckle was unexpected. "The effect really did look like balls of lightning, electrical discharges around any satellites that were affected."

Her voice sobered as she continued. "Your satellites triggered it early. There weren't many close enough to be caught, but then the effect used them to spread, jumping from one to the next. The nearest will be dead, but some systems might survive further away. The effect weakened as it spread, which is why we survived. The main thrusters failed completely, but we used the steering to kick the pod out of orbit, then turn so they could slow our re-entry."

The glance up had a hint of humour, black humour from her next words. "Our trajectory probably looked a lot like a fall, then something exploded and we really did fall the rest of the way. The levitation facility softened the impact, but pods only have a small unit so it had no effect until it was close to the ground, which is why we left a crater." Ghost reached out with one hand to pat the nearest wall. "Luckily, life pod hulls are very strong, built to handle impacts with wreckage or small asteroids."

Jamie already knew about the crater, and that the hull was more than very strong. "From the sound of it you were very lucky. The TV would go crazy if they knew about spaceships near Earth, firing death rays and missiles and crashing."

He realised he'd started stroking her pelt again, too easy with Ghost snuggled up like this. "I'd better get your pod fixed before someone finds you."

Ghost laughed and stepped back, then patted his chest. "Instead of pelt-stroking. With the hug, I suppose it was also human greeting-to-kin, which might be why this form enjoys it." She spun on a heel and headed for the control room, and Jamie watched her for a few moments. When he turned away towards the engines, he was even more determined to make it work—somehow.

~~

Before he could fit new electronics, Jamie had to work out how to make the individual thrusters open and shut, and rotate. His equipment couldn't read the alien operating systems—he couldn't even recognise individual programmes or files on his updated cracking kit. That meant he couldn't copy, edit, or in any other way adapt the pod's programmes, or even split the thruster controls from the rest.

Ghost found him poking at the equipment with a probe, running current into different places to see the reaction. Her voice pulled him out of his mental rabbit hole, or maze, which is what it would look like. "We will try to leave Albuquerque tomorrow, but first I will scan very aggressively for drones. That will alert Hunter and possibly your own military, but if I destroy any drones I find, we can disappear again. We must find another source for piping, but will you be able to purchase the equipment elsewhere?"

It took a moment for Jamie to realise she was talking to him, then make sense of what she said. "I can't buy elsewhere, or not yet, so I'll still have to contact some locals." He gestured towards his diagram. “At the moment I’m still not sure what I’ll need.”

~~

Jamie realised he didn’t know when Ghost meant to move. “If we stay here over the weekend, I can use the tools in here to modify the scaffold poles outside the door for the piping. As long as I can work out what signal to send and when, and scrounge up enough smaller stuff for the fine control, we could be ready for a test in four or five days.”

“Really?” Ghost’s voice was right in his ear and Jamie jumped. “We will work on the decoy to take Hunter’s ship out of the way.” She kissed his ear and danced away, singing happily, and Jamie dragged his mind back to the problem, again.

Jamie had the pipe side worked out, as long as Ghost could manage without the steering thrusters actually moving. In theory it should work as long as she could vary the thrust through each one. That still left a lot of welding, bending, and cutting, and then probably alterations when reality didn’t match the tentative diagram on his laptop. Getting thicker pipe into some places wouldn’t be easy.

As he took more piping from some hydraulic equipment and the stockroom, and commandeered some equipment, Jamie began feeling guilty. With luck Ghost would come back to repay the firm, unless she had something in the pod that was worth a lot on a primitive planet?

A few data storage modules, RAM chips, and processors from the ship’s controls would do it—they had to be years ahead of the current stuff. With that in mind, Jamie considered leaving a few, if he could work out which ones weren’t needed. He thought he could probably trade a few of them for all the stuff he needed to replace the ruined components, but then remembered the bit about advanced tech on primitive planets.

Actually thinking about replacing Slashtail tech with Earth

stuff gave Jamie the final piece of the puzzle. If he was fitting new pipework, why use the old control equipment? Fitting all new valves also simplified his diagram, as he didn't have to get to some of those fiddly places. With Earth equipment, Earth electronics and computing would do the job. Even so, the computing side would be expensive, and not the sort of thing he'd find in a corner hardware store.

Splitting bills and keeping the smaller ones meant he had over nine hundred dollars now, so he could buy the small stuff. Going back to the same few places for nine hundred dollars' worth of the expensive parts, then the next day for the same stuff, could be a problem. Even if the staff weren't curious, sooner or later the identical numbers on the notes would be spotted. Jamie knew the answer, had known from when he left his car in Santa Rosa, but he kept hoping there would be another way.

~~

Ghost must have seen his hesitation when he went to the gloop dispenser. "We feel the same about pod food, but we would like something fresh, not the frozen packets. We will hunt." The sound of a closing door stopped any attempt at questioning.

Jamie was feeding lengths of hydraulic pipe into scaffold poles when a fluttering caught his attention. Something like a cross between a rainbow-coloured bird of paradise and a large eagle flared its wings and dropped a small deer, then landed on a fork truck. Catching that was a neat trick in the middle of Albuquerque.

A rising series of musical notes were answered from up above, and Jamie looked up to see another bird come through the skylight. It had to close its wings to get through the gap, but then snapped them open to glide around the building before landing. This one carried two ducks, and the other five had a pheasant, two geese, a goat, and another pair of ducks.

"Ghost?"

All seven answered with a low musical warble, enough like Ghost's for identification. With that they all turned and flew inside the pod, but Jamie held back—Ghost didn't like witnesses when she changed. He looked down at the bleeding corpses, and didn't fancy them raw, so it was a good job there were more frozen meals. In Ghost's case this lot would mean she could turn into a deer or goat herd, or a flock using the birds. Some inane part of his mind wondered if Ghost had split personalities, or did one control them all?

Before his mind went any further down any alien rabbit-holes, Ghost came out of the pod in the bikini top and shorts, brandishing two large, wicked-looking knives. "Better than pod gloop or frozen meals. Catch." Jamie let the knife bounce on the floor, rather than lose a couple of fingers catching it. "Are you plucking or skinning?"

"I'll try plucking, because skinning isn't going to happen. Do you have a barbecue in there?" He tried, but Jamie couldn't remember any sort of cooker. "Or an oven? I'll settle for microwaved, because I know we've got one of those. Or I'll thaw one of those meals?"

"We'll cut the raw meat thin so your teeth can manage. Or mince it with a hammer?" Ghost burst out laughing, pointing at his face. "Don't worry, there is a full autochef in the kitchen on the lower deck. It needs food that is skinned and drawn or washed and peeled, but the hopper for the gloop provider isn't as fussy."

Which explained some of the tastes, and two decks explained where all the other bedrooms were. Two seconds thought and the passage and control room were above the airlock, and the cargo hold now he'd seen it. Even so Jamie didn't usually deal with food until it was already bacon or burger, so he went for humour. "No bolts or screws, so dismantling this stuff is outside my skillset."

"In that case I'll deal with it while you keep bolting and things like that." To his huge relief Ghost started picking up a selection of bodies, then paused. "Here, a souvenir if you don't come with me." Jamie took the feather, which started crimson and worked through a deep orangey-yellow to an electric-blue tip. "You can wear it in a hat, but nobody will believe it's real."

"If you leave enough mauve hairs I can braid them, then hang it from my rear-view mirror. You don't think Hunter might have noticed those birds?" He hadn't thought of it until she'd given him the feather, but the birds were too big to belong around here, and the colours would have caught everyone's attention.

"Colour is easy. Outside they were mottled browns on top and grey-blue underneath, but we thought you would like to see the real plumage." Ghost hung the deer around her neck, tucked the goat under one arm, picked up the collection of birds by the legs in two bundles, and started for the pod. Once again Jamie promised himself he'd start exercising. "Dinner in thirty minutes, roast with some of the vegetables we bought. I'll freeze the rest down."

Which meant the pod also had a freezer. Looking at the sixty-foot length, twenty feet high and wide, Jamie realised there must be a lot of it he hadn't seen. Even if the back third was all engines and fuel, he'd only seen five rooms, none of them very big, so there could be a lot more. From the size, ten or eleven rooms, less the Stellar Jump and the levitation and skip drive, but still probably more living space than his home.

Jamie knew the screens in the control room weren't windows, but had assumed the pilot sat at the front. Now he thought about the distance from the hold, and the control room wasn't anywhere near the nose. Later, maybe—Jamie got back to sliding piping into scaffold poles.

~~

Roast venison and duck, with carrots, peas, and a baked

potato, completely stuffed Jamie and tasted a lot better than frozen meals. Once he could move again, he set into the heavy metal work, and by midnight he'd collected the rest of what he needed. After the first attempt, Jamie knew that fixing the sets of pipes together like tubular Russian dolls, one inside another, wasn't going to be a quick job.

Once the multiple pipes were assembled, he tried to fit ninety and forty-five-degree joints rather than actually bend them. Sharp bends were nearly impossible without kinking the inside pipes, so he tried to manage with gentle curves. So far, he was torn over filling the gaps with foam.

He wasn't sure how the exhaust gasses would react with it, but he wanted to stop the outer set heating up too much before the inner ones actually leaked. Looking at the size of the original piping, Jamie figured he'd need at least one of the nearest bedrooms to accommodate the convoluted mass of new metalwork.

That would leave bolting everything else back in place, connecting the new, extended wiring, and matching it to the controls to give Ghost some graduated thrust. Most of that just needed time and sweat, but he still needed the expensive stuff. As he came closer to crunch time, there was still only one viable option, and he couldn't put it off forever.

His hesitation was because it meant burning bridges back to his old life—maybe all of them. Jamie definitely wouldn't be going home afterwards. He would also have to be very careful —the cops at least must be watching his workshop by now.

If nobody worked Saturday, it was a safe bet they wouldn't be here tomorrow, so Jamie would use all this equipment to get the bulk of the bending and welding completed. Fitting could be carried out in the middle of nowhere, hovering over the sea if necessary. Before that, he would use Monday to get the rest of the parts, and say goodbye to his home, forever. Maybe not to Earth, in which case maybe he could open a workshop fixing jet-skis in the Maldives.

No workers turned up on Sunday, except the same security van that drove around the perimeter and left. Ghost was very upbeat about the idea of getting all the brute work done, and helped out where she could. Her strength came in handy, holding lengths of scaffold combined pipes in place, or turning them to make the welding easier and much neater.

When bending ruined some of Jamie's work, she also helped him pull more of the workshop's equipment apart for joints, and raid the stores. That gave Jamie an opening to ask about compensation. She promised to find some way to repay the owners, though it wouldn't be advanced tech.

No DNA-stealing kisses, but Ghost definitely teased now and then, and coming out of the cleanser naked was here to stay. Twice Jamie got a quick hug and kiss to say thank you for the pelt stroking, but on the cheek, and she broke away straight afterwards. He began to believe this was Ghost's real personality regardless of form—it would have taken too much effort to maintain a fallacy without any slip-ups. At least Jamie hoped so, and that she meant it when she told him he was welcome to visit her home, and see Ghost Claw at play.

What Jamie didn't realise was the probable reaction of the galaxy's other sentients. If they found out a native of Earth had joined Ghost Claw voluntarily, they would probably quarantine the whole solar system—forever.

HEAVY METAL MAYHEM

Dawn wasn't Jamie's favourite time, especially on a damp, overcast Monday, but it was text time again. The first thing he noticed when he put the phones together was that there were a lot of missed calls. Shania wanted to talk rather than texting, which was a really bad idea. One of them would say the wrong thing, and the FBI would be knocking on Damian's door. There was also a very innocent text on Papa's phone, a hint and also a diversion for any stranger reading them.

"Hi Jamie, hope you caught your flight. I expected to hear from you by now, but you must be too busy sunbathing." Shania was trying to give him an alibi, a holiday, and it might be a hint the Maldives option was still open. He daren't answer it because the phone was in the wrong country. Jamie shut it down, quickly.

The phone he'd used to send the last text had one reply. *"Frankie says the bedroom, and the spare, are aired out and ready. Your friend looks like the bikini type, so she's put out the sun beds. Be careful, there are all sorts of odd characters sneaking about these days. See you soon, both of you."*

Shania had been checking her clothes. The sun bed, and two rooms, might be another Maldives hint, but he didn't know how to tell Shania it was a good idea. If Damian had actually bought it, and some guy called Jamie was staying there, it would be a good diversion. Jamie wondered if the odd character part meant the FBI or cops had been knocking on her door.

The other phone was the one with all the missed calls, and five texts. They all more or less asked the same thing, without being specific. Were he and his friend all right, had they been anywhere near the weird alien story on the internet, and would he ring so they could talk? Jamie decided not to answer that phone, as it might have been picked up by the FBI.

Instead, he answered the text about sunbeds. *"Sorry, been very busy. Did you see the story on the internet, about Albuquerque? Pleased we are a long way away from all that. Sunbeds sound wonderful. We will really need them after this, somewhere we can relax without crowds, or any of those characters we mentioned. That place we were talking about sounds ideal, unless someone is already sunning themselves there. Hoping we can still call to see you, or maybe we can meet somewhere. Don't worry, we are having a really exciting time."*

~~

A half-hour later, Jamie was looking down on his workshop, and it didn't look any prettier than the view from street level. A thirty-foot-by-seventy timber box, most of it ten feet high, with a two-foot step in the roof above the back eighteen feet, the live-in part. It was all timber, sleepers ten inches wide by six deep, except for one small barred window at the back, a side door, and the front doors.

He'd never seen it like this, and despite the lounger and the inflatable paddling pool on the roof, it looked more like a bunker than a home. There had once been a lot of homemade toys and diversions, things like swings and slides, all made by Papa. With a mesh fence around the edge, they were meant to keep him and Shania safe and occupied while Papa worked—especially during the school holidays.

They'd wrecked some of it, and removed the fence and most of the rest when they were older. The roof became somewhere safe to relax, do homework in good weather, or get away from each other. If they were both on the roof, Jamie and Shania argued about who got the chair, which usually meant Jamie was stuck with sitting on a towel. The pool had been useful for keeping feet cool, or splashing a sleeping Shania if Jamie was willing to suffer the inevitable payback.

Ghost broke into Jamie's trip down memory lane. "Your home is well constructed, difficult to scan for heat, but seems to be empty. There are three pairs of humans watching, but none are using any equipment that will detect us. We may have to move if there is rain, as the disguise is much harder to maintain with water moving erratically over the hull. Hunter will not see us, but anyone close will notice irregularities."

She was watching a bank of instruments, confident that Hunter's ship would be too high to detect the pod among all the metal and emissions in Albuquerque. "The equipment the watchers are using will not penetrate the walls, unless you are loud or turn on heating or electrical equipment."

Jamie thought, and there was a simple solution. "Once I'm in, you can fly off and come back when it's all ready to lift, tonight if necessary. I won't make the second and third calls until you are back, in case someone gets nosy."

Ghost gave a quick smile. "If we leave, we will try to stay as close as possible. We would not like to lose our pelt stroker now, and Ghost Claw try to look after kin. How will you get inside without the watchers seeing you?"

As long as the pod was invisible, that was child's play, literally. "Just behind the lounger, the square bit sticking up and the four steps leading down to nothing are another entrance. Once I'm stood on the bottom step, the square bit is high enough for a door, and inside it are more stairs. Those lead down to the kitchen, where we ate, but they're hidden behind what looks like a cupboard door."

Jamie had to smile at the next part. "There's an electronic pad on both doors. As we got older, Papa fought a losing battle to stop us cracking the code. He was worried about us falling off the roof."

"Is it coded now?" One of the screens zoomed in on the steps.

"Will you know if it has been cracked?"

Jamie held up his car keys. "It's deadlocked as well, then the lock on the door at the bottom needs a code in case a burglar gets through the top one. That might be the real reason Papa installed the locks. I'll know if the lock has been broken and nobody will guess the code—it's Shania's name." He smiled wider, because...

"Shania, six letters, that doesn't seem secure." Ghost caught his smile. "You never told me your second name, or third?"

"No need, Shania isn't her real name. The code is Frankie Madonna and the date she switched to Shania. The name on her birth certificate was Francesca Madonna, and a few people might remember it. They won't know I called her Frankie in private, to wind her up. I daren't use it in public—Shania has a really vicious side if she's truly upset."

Jamie let the laugh come. "Shania came from a website of names, something that wouldn't have any connection with her origins. Papa didn't think much for Shania's real name either, so he didn't mind the change." He stood up and headed for the door. "I'll let the cable down so I can slide straight into the stairwell."

"Take your pistol and wrench, since you will not use a knife." Ghost sounded serious. "Hunter might have left something inside."

A corpse, maybe, but Jamie humoured Ghost. Anyone who managed to get through the first alarms without setting them off wouldn't hack the second one. It wasn't that hard to get through—the code was dead easy, literally, as Jamie had added an extra. If the intruder didn't know about the simple on-off switch, just touching the second keypad would connect them to the main electrical panel. The first crispy would-be burglar stopped any more attempts, and Jamie felt sure it would be just as dangerous for one of those robots.

He took a good look before dropping down, then inspected

the door before tapping in the code and using his key. No corpse or even a smell of burning, but Jamie checked the other two doors once he was inside the workshop—they had a similar backup. Ghost, and that otterish and the alien pistol, had him on edge, but the back door was still barred. When he checked in the cupboard, the beam across the garage hadn't been broken.

Jamie stuck his head out of the door upstairs and waved, long enough for Ghost to see him and flash a light, then began to strip his home of anything that might be useful. A long look at the parts salvaged from his racer, and Jamie realised that somewhere in the last couple of days he'd decided he wasn't just leaving his life behind.

The Maldives would be boring after this, so if Ghost was serious about taking him to see her planet, he was leaving Earth. The idea he'd had on Saturday settled in, and simplified his finances. He could sell the parts for his next racer as well as the workshop and tools.

The heap of salvaged parts would be useless in a society with spaceships, but were valuable to the right people. One man in particular would pay top price for some items, and some of the stuff from Shania's old bedroom, or exchange them for part of what Jamie wanted. The workshop reminded him he didn't have to take anything upstairs.

A big section of the roof hinged upwards, Papa's way of making room if he had to lift a small truck on the big vehicle lift. Jamie had to hammer the bolts, and lifting one side wrecked the waterproofing, but then the cable and box had plenty of room. Working quickly, Jamie went back to the bedroom and packed the rest of his clothes, and then the contents of the freezer and his fridge.

With a smile, Jamie left the broken dishwasher, the pots in the sink, his furniture and all his dishes apart from a Little Pest mug from Shania. Ghost used bowls for drinking, and had wider flat-bottomed ones with a smaller lip for solid food. She winched everything up and out of sight while Jamie collected any tools and spares that might be useful in the pod.

It was a wrench, but Jamie abandoned the rest. The contents of his old bedroom were all repair projects, so he left them as well. The spares in Shania's old room were all useable, but very little went up to the pod. A selection went into a mesh skip with the spares from his racer, valuable kit that wasn't strictly legal as the protection had been cracked. The rest would be primitive junk out in space, but might help him get a better price for the workshop.

Ghost was confident the pod was low enough to stop anyone at ground level seeing the cable, but warned Jamie not to get near the edge of the roof. Even so, there was already a light drizzle, so he moved as fast as possible to get finished before it rained—or cleared up enough to tempt someone up onto a roof. The gear from the workshop took longer than his personal stuff, and neither took long, a sad reflection on his life.

Once he'd sent up the skip the last time, Jamie disconnected the lethal part of the security. Now he could sell the place, and if someone torched it, anyone trying to save the contents wouldn't be in danger. If Ghost was only joking or leading him on, he'd just have to live in the Maldives, but it would be a bit tame now. Though if he couldn't get the pod into orbit, Ghost would be there as well, and Jamie thought he could live with that.

That brought Jamie up short. Ghost had only been in his life for less than a fortnight, but he was already used to her being there. He'd even decided he didn't mind following her to the stars. Bad idea, he didn't even know what she looked like, but now that didn't worry him. He thought more about that, and it wasn't because he liked Ghost, or that she'd accepted him into her clan, or not completely.

Jamie didn't think that how she treated him was an act, but bottom line, it didn't matter. Even if Ghost dumped him at the first stop, he couldn't turn down a chance to see spaceships, aliens, new worlds, and all that advanced tech. He smiled at what Shania would say—refusing to move to the Maldives to running off to the stars was a hell of switch.

Though he couldn't reach the stars yet, and getting there meant taking another chance.

~~

The next part would be risky, but would cut down the time spent shopping. Jamie thumbed the little button pinned to his shirt—a comm Ghost had given him so she'd know when he needed the winch. *"I'm going to make those three calls, Ghost. One will, I hope, buy the workshop, and lend me a car without asking too many questions. That way I can buy better electronics from the second, closer to what I need rather than working around it with a ton of cheaper parts. The third one will deliver some advanced stuff, stolen because even if I found a supplier, I can't afford to buy it over the counter. We'll have to be careful because he isn't the most reliable type."* Solly was an arse Jamie wouldn't get within a mile of most days, but could get pretty much anything.

The fence was a regular at the street racing, selling spares and kit and buying crashed vehicles—or stealing them if the driver went to hospital. Solly would steal pretty much anything, and sell his granny to three different people then let them argue over who got which organs. He was also the only person who would buy the spares in the mesh skip, the cream of Jamie's stock, because none of them were legal.

They were specialised parts from his and several other wrecked racers, taken as part-payment for other work. Jamie had fixed them and tidied up the software, then kept them until the right buyer came along. Right now, Solly was the right buyer, because he would buy it all They'd fetch up to five times the price he'd pay if they were sold as legitimate, so the fence would want them safely packed away before any trouble started.

Jamie used his trolley jack to move the heavy-duty mesh basket to the front door, where Solly could see it but couldn't run off with it—it was too heavy. Busy with that, and thinking about dealing with Solly, he was startled by Ghost's voice. *"You are selling your burrow, your home?"* She must be startled—Ghost didn't make many mistakes over translations like that, not lately.

He realised he hadn't actually explained fully, but she'd been unloading the box and realised. *"It will save us days hopping about buying bits."* Jamie didn't ask about coming with her. He'd rather do that face to face, when he asked what Ghost really looked like. *"We will have to buy everything else and load up before Solly arrives, and hook the winch onto a big basket ready to go. If necessary, we'll let him see the pod, or the airlock at least, rather than take too long. Solly will be swapping for a heap of valuable spares, so he won't shop us until he's got them, but then he might try to repossess his stuff as well."*

Jamie jumped as Ghost's arms came around him. She must be confident the pod was invisible because she'd come down to help. "Does that mean you want a long-term job repairing our ship?" She pulled him around but kept her arms around his waist. "Will you stroke our pelt, please? It is feeling neglected."

Jamie obliged, but now they were face to face, and there was the beginning of a curve at the end of her pelt. Was she deliberately growing it? Ghost snuggled in again as she had last time, and that diverted him from her pelt. "Mmm, even if we don't need a mechanic very often, maybe we can hire you as a permanent pelt stroker." She kissed him on the nose. "Maybe an occasional DNA supplier?" With a big grin she spun away before he could answer.

~~

By now Jamie was sure the watchers knew someone was in here, but were waiting for more information. They couldn't even be sure how many people there were because the walls were ten inches of solid timber. Jamie could never decide if Papa really had bought cheap second-hand sleepers, or just stolen them, but he must have had help. They hadn't come from the railway sidings a mile away, because the railway didn't use oak.

Jamie only knew they were oak because a neighbour knew a guy who wanted some, and he wanted Jamie to sell fifty and give him a finder's fee. The big steel beams supporting the roof might have come from the sidings. They looked a lot like railway lines, with RSJs on end to support the middle. Jamie was thinking about the sleepers because now he was selling up, he'd looked up prices, and now he was bloody sure Menhir would buy the place.

Stripped of everything he personally needed, his own home looked strange as Jamie sat on the settee, waiting for the first two contacts to be up and about. He mulled over what Ghost said, and hoped she meant the part about him being the repairman on her ship. He could learn more—aliens had to have instruction books or videos. The pelt-stroking made him smile. If he was her repairman, he'd end up doing that anyway, but maybe not in the night-nest once she re-joined her people.

The DNA part worried him, but not as much as it should. Jamie was almost sure that the parts about purple hair and shape-shifting were a tease, that Ghost just wanted enough to make her switch easy. If she kept asking, there were two big questions Jamie wanted answering. Was the Ghost that teased and laughed an act, or her real personality in a human body? If it was the latter, he'd probably keep giving her DNA in her human form, and like her as an alien unless she was truly gross.

Even if it was all an act, and the sight or smell of her real form turned his stomach, giving DNA might not be optional.

He could only resist up to a point. If Ghost's human body stripped off, slid into his bed, and gave him a blast of that perfume, his alien cherry would be jelly even if he threw up afterwards. If she wasn't repulsive as an alien, the human version might not even need the human pheromones.

He was just wondering why Ghost still used "we" when the others were frozen or computerised, when Jamie realised it was nine. He shelved that debate and used a new phone, one he'd bought in Oklahoma, to call the first number, Menhir. Lottie would buy or sell any amount of legitimate new or second-hand kit for cash, no strings, but she wouldn't deliver.

He wouldn't even ask. Nobody delivered anything valuable to the Pits, not without an armed bodyguard, and that went double for women. That was why he needed transport as well as cash, which meant giving Menhir a good enough deal to leave him feeling generous.

He was still worried about a raid, but the weather had brightened so the pod wouldn't have to move. Bottom line, Ghost promised she could immobilise the cars, and knock out any humans without killing them.

~~

Getting Menhir to come and discuss buying the workshop was easy, but getting a sensible price was a lot harder than expected. Some of that might be because Jamie warned him the cops would ask questions, even though the sale was legal. Menhir was wary, because Jamie wanted him to tell the police he didn't meet Jamie, just a guy who claimed to be a cousin. The last problem was convincing him to loan the Jeep Cherokee, not a pickup. Jamie was worried about Hunter when he collected from Lottie.

If it came down to a chase, his purchases could be damaged if they were in the open, or might bounce out of the back. The Cherokee wasn't a street racer, but it had a manual shift and plenty of power, and could handle going off-road if necessary.

Jamie insisted that loaning it was part of the deal, because he knew the price was a steal. Menhir was a businessman, not a crook, but his first offer for the workshop and equipment came close to attempted robbery.

It was a good price considering the state of the place, but Jamie now knew the walls and roof were worth several times more than all the rest. When Jamie first told him it was a job lot, Menhir had asked if that included the sleepers, the only thing he'd been specific about. That meant that despite the disparaging remarks, he knew what they were worth. The comments about firewood and scrap metal were true, but that would probably be left behind.

For the fourth time, Menhir asked about rot under the paint. "No chance, Menhir. Papa was always careful to repair the paint, and the overhang keeps most of the rain off. Even if a few aren't perfect, there are seven hundred and sixty."

Menhir tapped the wall, which had no effect on ten inches of oak. "Are you sure? Some are cut in half, so less than that."

By now Jamie was just impatient enough to bite back, gently. "Me and Shania counted them one summer, so I'm sure. I looked up the price of second-hand oak sleepers this morning and was surprised, but I'm in a hurry. Otherwise, I'd have sold them in lots."

Instead of arguing, Menhir laughed. "Taking them apart might not be as easy as you think. They are all drilled, with steel bars covered in plastic going down through the holes to tie them together. Sometimes I wonder if your Papa knew what was coming, or was just a very careful man." This time he thumped the wall, hard. "I never saw them, but someone said the men who delivered acted like soldiers, old soldiers."

"Papa never said." Though Jamie wasn't really surprised. The tin box in the safe with the rifle held five medals, though Papa had never mentioned them. The tin was in the pod now, destined for Shania if possible. "He once said the sleepers were bankrupt stock."

Menhir chuckled and turned to inspect the garage floor, thirty feet by fifty with two pits running most of the length. "Maybe the diggers were as well. There were a lot of stories about machines digging trenches all over the Pits, and then it was all levelled out. The diggers didn't have any company markings, and they disappeared without trace. I've asked what it was all for, and some mentioned drainage or power cables but I never got a straight answer."

Any other time Jamie would have been interested, but right now he was on the clock. "No idea. Right now I've got to decide if I should take your price, or just sell the equipment and find buyers for the walls. I'd rather sell now, but unless I can borrow wheels and finish my business, I'm going to be stuck here anyway."

"Is that why you want cash?" Menhir waved a hand. "Never mind why, but that's what makes me wary. If I pay in cash, then the cops or another buyer turns up and stops me loading up, I'm stuck. The price has to be low enough to take a chance."

"It's me, Jamie, not bloody Solly. When have I ever cheated *anyone*?" He'd been his usual self, trying not to offend, but now Jamie firmed up. "Don't take me for an idiot, Menhir. Even if some are cut in half, the going price for used oak sleepers is forty dollars each, thirty thousand for it all. I'd get nearly twenty-three grand if I sold them as damaged, which they aren't, or not enough to matter. A reclamation firm will buy them for that, and the hundred three-foot lengths over the Pits, but then you'll lose out on some very cheap equipment. Once the walls are down it will be gone overnight, and neither of us will ever see it again."

Jamie pointed to the big lift. "Six-point-five-ton four-post vehicle lift, six grand new and you know it works. The spares in Shania's old room are worth a grand, minimum, because I've overhauled them all. Then there's trolley jacks, the pillar drill, and all the other tools. Give me a decent price for the rest and forget the sleepers, and I'll offer them to a reclamation firm for twenty thousand. I bet they'll pay cash, probably within the hour."

Maybe he believed Jamie, or he already had an agreed sale for the sleepers, but either way Menhir went up to twenty-five grand—and agreed to loan the Cherokee. He took one last walk all around the workshop and Jamie's rooms, and confirmed everything was in with the price. Nearly everything—it didn't include one skip of parts.

The racer spares were obvious, but Jamie refused to deal—Menhir was honest so he wouldn't pay the same as Solly. From the way he inspected the workshop, Menhir would strip out everything else, including the wiring and plumbing, which would be easy once the walls were down. Once he'd agreed to the price, Menhir wanted to gossip, especially about the Hellbat bodies.

Jamie admitted he'd ran when he saw them, but denied actually killing any of them. He confessed he was scared of someone blaming him, either a gang or the police, and was leaving town. He had an alibi, as long as nobody saw him before he left. Once he understood the reason, Menhir seemed happier about the cousin part.

Leaving town cut out any talk about Menhir's family. Menhir, and most of his family, kept trying to hook his only single daughter up with various young men, including Jamie, but neither was keen. Eventually Menhir's eldest son arrived with three men, all carrying shotguns, to deliver the cash and persuade Menhir to leave. Jamie wrote down the code for the doors, gave him the spare keys, and promised to phone when he was done with the Cherokee.

He confirmed he'd be here until mid-morning tomorrow, but Menhir could start dismantling everything straight afterwards. From a couple of comments about light-fingered locals, Jamie was sure there'd be a work crew and a couple of trucks waiting for him to leave. That might help, as Solly wouldn't want too many witnesses if he tried to cheat.

~~

Ghost had told Jamie the sleepers would stop anyone hearing what was said inside, and then while they were gossiping, Menhir had mentioned sleepers being used to build shooting ranges. That meant he'd already got a sale but Jamie didn't care—though he was really happy with the idea his walls were bulletproof.

The cops had to be tapping the phone lines, hoping for leads, but they wouldn't know about this phone. Jamie was just hoping the watchers were patient. Ghost had been listening to comms, and the cops were waiting until they were sure they'd got the whole gang, including both women. Alternatively, they had cars and a chopper waiting to tail him.

The third pair of watchers only communicated occasionally, using code so they could be from the FBI or someone like Solly. By the time Menhir left, a van full of police had arrived, a snatch squad, but they were hanging back still. Jamie didn't need much of a delay—neither of these calls would take long. In an emergency, the cable hanging down in the workshop would whisk him away in seconds.

The call to Lottie worked out better than expected, mainly due to Jamie having a lot more cash than expected. There was stuff she didn't have, but she did some checking while Jamie waited. She could get the rest very quickly if the price was right, and Jamie was willing to pay the extra. He arranged to pick it all up later, and confirmed he'd bring cash.

The first part of the call to Solly took no time at all, and Jamie could have written the script in advance. Solly wanted the salvage from Jamie's car—he'd tried to get it straight after the crash. As expected, he would also take the other spares and could get what Jamie wanted, and Jamie didn't care how much profit the arse made as long as he got the parts. The difficulty was making sure Jamie was paid, and wasn't ripped off or robbed afterwards. The waiting coppers might catch Solly, but that wouldn't help Jamie.

"No offence, Solly, but I'll want to look through everything before I part with my gear. You know as well as I do that packaging doesn't mean much." Since Solly would repackage some of what he bought and sell it as new, he couldn't argue with that. "My stuff stays locked in my garage until I've run a test kit over everything I'm buying, and put it on a pallet."

"As long as you don't try to run off with anything until I've checked the spares. We could carry out both checks at the same time?" From his voice, Solly didn't expect that to fly.

"I check first, then we leave my purchases outside, and you come in the back door with me to check your payment. I can't run off with a pallet, can I? Once I open the main garage door you load up, and I move my stuff inside." Jamie would make a frantic dive for the pallet and ride it out of there. That would trigger the cops, and they should keep Solly busy. "Don't come early. You remember the last asshole who tried to come in without knocking?"

"Yeah, super-crispy. That's illegal you know. What happened to those Hellbats?" That was out of the blue, and much too casual.

Jamie was torn. Did he say the killer was still here, and hope it would keep Solly honest, or would that just mean he brought more men and possibly guns? "No idea, I was out of town. That's why I wasn't there to answer the cops, and why they stuck me on the TV. All sorted now, but I'm a bit nervous because whoever did it is out there somewhere."

After a couple more attempts to get Jamie to admit he knew more, Solly dropped it and agreed on the delivery and collection. When he rang off, Jamie still wasn't sure if the arse thought Jamie knew the killer, was the killer, or was innocent.

Probably not the last one—Solly never assumed anyone was innocent.

The call made him nervous, so Jamie attached the heavy basket and winched it up into the pod. Solly was the type to try and arrive early, through the back door, with help. He was already wondering if he should change the meeting with Solly to somewhere else, but if not, Ghost could drop the basket again. When Ghost winched him up, and reported that the watchers hadn't noticed him leaving, Jamie heaved a sigh of relief.

As they flew away, Jamie occupied himself by phoning Menhir, to say he'd moved out early. He was tempted to ask Ghost to aim a screen backwards, but then he might change his mind. In retrospect, that might have been a good idea.

~~

Since they were in the neighbourhood, sort of, Jamie asked for a favour. Within minutes he had a bird's eye view of Damian and Shania's mansion. The gaggle of skinny women were near the pool, but this time Shania was hosting a barbeque. No chops and steaks, the man and woman in spotless white were setting out bite-sized morsels on sticks, with a lot of fruit, salad, and booze.

Ignoring the view for now, Jamie used the pad and pencil from his toolbox to write a note. Shania might consider the oil stains proof it wasn't a hoax.

"Hi Shania, it's your favourite charity project. Just heard your brother Jamie moved to that place in the Maldives last week. Someone said he sold his garage; he should have stuck a sign on the door. Probably a good idea because he'd only just gone on holiday when someone stole his car, so they would have stripped the place by the time he came back. Good job he left his Papa's medals with me. I've passed them on because I've finally met someone I'd follow anywhere. She's still in some trouble, but it should all work out. Hope I can pop in to see you some day. Love, always."

Jamie daren't mention aliens and all the rest in a note, in case the FBI raided Damian. He looked at the viewscreen, and Jamie really was tempted. If he dropped the message tied to the tin, the splash would drench several of the skinny trophy wives and girlfriends. It might also wipe out his message, so he settled on dropping it onto the grass near the path back to the house. As he looked in his toolbox for tape, a faint, familiar scent swept around him.

"Give the letter to me and I'll make sure she sees it." Ghost seemed torn, as if she wanted to tell him something, but then she took the folded note and tin and went through into the airlock. Jamie watched the screen, but there were just the dozen women and a few birds flying about, and then Ghost came back.

She flicked a couple of switches and zoomed a screen in on Shania's lounger, and there was his note and the tin. Jamie watched his sister come back to her seat, double-take, pick up the folded paper with her name on it and look around. She picked up the tin, called out to her friends, and headed for the house.

Jamie turned to Ghost, but she was busy putting the screen back into standby mode, so she didn't want to talk about it. Jamie let it be—though he was fairly sure who that flock of birds had been. He remembered they weren't a proper change and wondered if she was embarrassed.

The main thing was that Shania knew he'd sold up and wasn't coming back, so he wouldn't wreck any alibi she set up. Damian wouldn't want Shania connected to the killings, so without DNA or fingerprints, expensive lawyers and wads of cash would make sure Jamie wasn't blamed. There were both in his car, but he'd covered that part.

Jamie was certain there'd be someone with his name living in a small private villa in the Maldives within days, possibly hours. There'd be people to swear he'd moved in last week, and an army of lawyers would trample anyone trying to get details or an interview. Now Jamie could concentrate on getting Ghost off-planet.

~~

It was early afternoon when Ghost and Jamie left the pod hovering at the back of an empty warehouse. The final delay was for Ghost to run off three copies of the payment from Menhir, though Jamie kept the originals separate to make sure Lottie got them. At least that solved any problems with getting additional spares if he needed them, and buying new clothes for both of them.

There wouldn't be any human clothing out there, so Jamie took Ghost shopping to stock up, everything from a thick jacket to underwear. Ghost decided she should buy more clothes for her Earth body, but then wouldn't say what. Her voice and expression meant there was some sort of joke or tease involved, but Jamie had no idea what she'd find funny.

A cab dropped them around the corner from Menhir's Cherokee with time to spare. Ghost was worried about not having much ammo, and Jamie had a pocket full of cash, so they did some more shopping.

It made a dent in one wad of counterfeits, but now they had enough ammunition for a real firefight, except for the magnum and full jacketed for the rifle. Solly was bringing both, but the ammo might be blanks if he was contemplating a double-cross. Ghost compensated by purchasing solid loads for the shotgun—the guy selling them reckoned they'd stop an elephant and might break an engine.

That bit of information persuaded Jamie to buy another shotgun, or steal it since he used counterfeit cash. He was keeping track, but still couldn't work out how to pay everyone back. Maybe there was an interstellar Fed-Ex?

He was still early, so Jamie called into a couple of big stores and bought a lot of standard spares, the ancillary stuff. Hard drives, chips, CPUs, motherboards, connectors, wiring, more fuses, he wanted spares for anything he thought might blow if he installed it wrong the first time. He twitched several times when police walked or drove past, but the Cherokee was anonymous.

It wasn't just possible recognition that worried him. There was a big canvas bag full of weapons and reloads in the front footwell, with extra pistols and ammo in the glove box.

~~

By the time he drove up to Lottie's, Jamie was on edge, expecting Hunter to pop up any moment. When she looked out of the smaller door and beckoned, the two obvious heavies opening the big warehouse doors didn't help his nerves. He drove in and opened the door, but didn't get out. "What's with the bodyguard, Lottie? I thought you couldn't afford them, and that's why you don't deliver?"

"Slow down Jamie. You never seen them because you don't usually need enough gear to drive inside." The tall, painfully thin middle-aged woman glanced over at the two men, who were closing the door again. "Those boys are always here, heavy labour for the bigger stuff a frail creature like me can't manage. They double up keeping an eye on my customers, but usually low-profile if it's someone like you. If they came with me to someplace like the Pits, everyone would know that they weren't here, and the place would be stripped bare."

The easy smile looked the same as usual, and when Jamie glanced at Ghost, she looking relaxed. Lottie's eyes followed Jamie's glance and she smirked. "So, have you finally found a girl, or got your own bodyguard?"

That was worth a smile—Lottie had no idea how good a bodyguard Ghost was. "Sort of. The job is for her, and I need an extra pair of eyes." Jamie was still watching the two heavies.

"Relax, will you? They're out here because you're buying a lot of valuable gear." Lottie looked pointedly at the stack of boxes on the counter. "I've had to source some elsewhere and pay for immediate delivery, so the ungodly might be curious. This is better gear than your usual purchases, and a lot of it, so there's always a chance you might not want to pay once it's loaded. You aren't known for having a lot of readies." She hooked a thumb over her shoulder. "Those boys give me peace of mind."

"Here's some peace of mind, but it stays with Ghost until I've loaded up, yeah?" Jamie took the wads of cash from inside his jacket, riffed the edges to prove the colours stayed the same through the stacks, and passed them to Ghost.

"This will keep it safe until you want it, Jamie." Ghost put the cash inside her barely-fastened shirt, but at least she had a bra on now. Jamie had suggested underwear several times, but even though she'd finally bought some, the one on show meant Ghost still didn't understand the under part. She took out a pistol, and leaned forward to pull the stock and action of a shotgun out of the bag on the floor.

With Jamie's door wide open, Lottie saw both weapons. "From the name, Ghost, and the weaponry, I'm guessing she's a bodyguard." The tall half-Mexican nodded approvingly. "You always were the trusting sort, too trusting. Come on then. Sooner you check, sooner I'm paid."

As Jamie got out, Lottie pointed at the counter. "I'll want to run the bills through there, or a random selection. I'd do it anyway for that amount, but I'm being even more careful right now. There are some damn good counterfeits out there, near enough identical is what I hear."

"These are real, or I'll be calling on Menhir. He's buying the heavy equipment from my place at a very good price, so I doubt he'll cheat." Jamie realised he'd said too much when Lottie glanced suddenly back at the Jeep. "Yes, I'm doing this last job, a big one, then moving out. Got a good offer." He smiled, because it was true. "Repairman on a ship."

"I was wondering if that amount of storage was to build someone a standalone Wikipedia, though I suppose you could be putting it on a ship. From the way you fix most things, and some of this gear, better try and remember ships are only supposed to float on water. With petabyte processors, you could probably turn it into a spaceship." When Jamie glanced at her, the big grin meant Lottie was joking.

Jamie managed to laugh. "The first spaceships didn't need anything like that, and if that's what I was doing, I'd want a lot more money. Modern ships are a bit like cars; they use computers for everything."

"Spaceships as well, modern astronauts are more like tourists. Some of them *are* tourists." Lottie gave Jamie a list, then began passing boxes and ticking them off her own copy. "Even if it doesn't get to space, the way you adapt stuff, it might forget and start flying." She stopped dead, then cursed under her breath. "Does Solly know you're leaving? He was asking questions about why you'd need some very expensive kit, so if a birdie told him I've been buying a few of these items?"

Jamie wanted to curse as well. "He's trading with me. I'm swapping everything I salvaged off my racer when I wrote it off, and some other kit from racers. The software is all cracked so it will fit on anything, but Solly gave me a good deal because he'll sell it as genuine. You're strictly legal, so you'd give me peanuts even if you bought." Jamie thought hard about what was said. "I never said I'm leaving. I never told you until just now."

"I just told him I knew you were working on something bigger than usual, but I hadn't heard you were going." Lottie glanced back at her guards, and kept her voice down. "Is this something to do with Hellbats? I've just realised that if Ghost is the real thing, well, they wouldn't reckon a woman." A big smile lit up her face. "I bet the first three dropped while they were still eyeing up her ass."

Jamie was nervous again, but couldn't help smiling at the big grin on Lottie's face. The Hellbats always tried to beat her down on prices, pressure her, or shoplift while they were buying. "I can't say, but please don't repeat that guess to anyone. I'll be gone in a few hours, but I need those hours."

Refusing to sell to them could have resulted in a fire-bombing, so like a lot of other retailers, Lottie watched their hands and kept an iron bar handy. He'd always liked her, so Jamie gave her a parting gift: peace of mind. "But when you're done here tonight, relax and raise a toast to Hellbats, in memory. The rest of them caught up with Ghost, so they're extinct."

Lottie laughed, walked around the other side of the counter, and reached underneath. She slid a disc box across the worn wood and winked. "Latest crack for Porsche spares, a thank you."

"Ta." Jamie didn't know if it would be any good in a spaceship, but refusing would have been odd and he really did appreciate the thought. "Well, that list and this one agree with the heap in the car, so I'd better pay." He raised his voice. "Ghost, the cash please."

She slid across to the driver's seat and leant out of the window, then pulled out the cash. Jamie heard Lottie snigger when Ghost pulled her shirt further open and checked inside. "Nothing else in here, Jamie." He caught the humour in her voice and eyes as she slid back and sat down. Jamie turned around to find Lottie trying hard to keep her face straight.

"Oh yeah, probably four or five down before they stopped perving. Nothing else in here?" She gave up and laughed, but that didn't stop her taking the cash and putting in into a note counter, then extracting several for testing. "If she isn't your girl, Jamie, you really should consider the idea. All clear here, so good luck." Lottie stuck out a hand. "You watch your mirrors until you're a long away from here, and never come back."

"Not unless I need specialist kit from someone I can trust. I'll try to send a postcard." Jamie climbed into the Cherokee, and since there was room in the warehouse, turned around. Lottie waited until he was lined up with the door, then looked through the peephole before telling the two men to open up. "Keep your eyes open, Ghost. Lottie is nervous."

~~

He pulled out and headed down the street, and everything looked fine until Jamie reached the T-junction. A quick look showed cars blocking the road each way, and a glance in the rear-view revealed a big SUV coming up the road behind. As it came past Lottie's warehouse a fork truck shot out, the forks going underneath the big car before the steel uprights hit the side panels and pushed.

The SUV tried to keep going, but the forks were lifting and the wheels lost traction, and then it was airborne. A hand came out of the car window, pointing a pistol, but Lottie's heavies stepped into view, both aiming shotguns. The gunman in the car thought better of it, even when the fork truck dropped the vehicle onto a four-foot brick wall and it rolled onto its side. A hand waved from the fork truck cab.

Jamie had waited to be sure the SUV was out of it, but he'd been looking at both road blocks. "Be ready for a big bump, Ghost, and maybe someone shooting from your side." He turned right, accelerated towards the cars across the road, and at the last moment swung off the road. A smaller or lower car wouldn't have made it, but electronics didn't weigh much so the Cherokee was riding high.

The front bounced up and over the high kerb, but the back of a pick-up still half-blocked the sidewalk. The wheel bucked in Jamie's hands as he put one front wheel through the low wall and hedge, and the Cherokee faltered. He dropped it down a gear and rammed the pedal down, and it scrabbled forward, crushing the bushes. A crash and roar of engine noise meant that either the low wall or the trampled greenery had torn off the exhaust—not a problem as long as the tyres didn't lose traction.

The other problem, someone shooting at them, wasn't as bad as expected. Ghost hadn't waited to see what anyone else was going to do—she'd started shooting before Jamie hit the kerb. By the time he was past the blockage and trying to pull back onto the road, she'd tossed one pistol into the footwell and was well into the magazine in the second. Jamie couldn't get the angle to force his front wheel back over or through the wall, but there was a gap coming up.

The brick pillar disintegrated, and as the Cherokee bulldozed the broken gate aside, Jamie swerved back onto the tarmac. He glanced over as the heavier beat of a shotgun replaced the pistol. Ghost had both elbows outside the window, clamping herself to the door to keep the gun rock steady as she emptied it back down the road.

The barrel angled further around, almost backwards as Jamie straightened up and floored it, taking a quick look in his mirrors. There were five people lying in the road, two of them still moving, but none were shooting. He almost said something, but Jamie hadn't told her not to shoot, just warned her someone else might. He'd forgotten Ghost believed in being proactive, and meeting violence with at least equal violence.

Though as yet he didn't know that the current level of violence barely registered on the Ghost Claw scale.

~~

When he worked out where he was heading, Jamie muttered curses under his breath. He'd have to take a detour, a fairly big one, because without an exhaust he'd be picked up going through town. He'd have to keep the speed down even along a quieter route, so he didn't attract too much attention. A traffic stop and a fine weren't the end of the world, but the stink of gunfire would lead to a search, then Ghost would get proactive.

"Lottie has a big trophy." Ghost was feeding shells into the shotgun, while two empty clips on the floor meant the pistols were ready to rock again. It hadn't taken her long to adapt to primitive Earth weapons. "Will they follow?"

Jamie thought quickly, and there'd been no chase car so the survivors would take too long to get going. "I doubt it. That was set up quickly, a last-minute smash and grab. I reckon someone heard that Lottie bought in expensive kit, immediate delivery, and waited to see who turned up." Jamie might have wondered if Lottie sold him out, but the stranded SUV was convincing. "Driving with no exhaust is illegal, so we'll have to take a long detour and hope to avoid the cops. They'll investigate the shooting, and the noise means we'll be noticed, then the cops will check surveillance cameras."

With a grin he turned onto the forecourt outside a workshop with a huge tyre logo on the front. "Or maybe not. I forgot we've still got Menhir's payment, or a version of it. Hide the weapons, then this place will fix us up while we wait."

~~

The wait was longer than expected—dusk was starting to creep into the corners and alleys when Jamie paid up and drove away. The delay was because the tyre workshop sent out for a fender and fixed that as well as the exhaust, but Jamie preferred sitting in a garage to worrying about police or an ambush. When he got out, he'd seen three bullet holes in the back of the Cherokee, and he didn't want a repeat.

He parked out of the way of any other customers, and the staff hadn't minded him waiting. They'd been entranced, at least partly because Ghost really wanted to know about the reason for different tyres and exhausts, and why some tyres had worn in different places. The other reason was that she was climbing the stacks and bending to inspect treads. No scent this time, so nobody was blatantly looking down her shirt or taking close-ups of her ass, but those shorts should be classified as a weapon.

The crew seemed to think she was famous—maybe it was the mauve hair—so they all wanted a selfie when they'd done. Jamie took an extra picture, using one of their phones, so they had a group shot in front of a tyre rack.

He'd been worrying about the drive home, and all the cameras he'd been on, but the pictures suggested a way to throw some doubt on any identification. It relied on Ghost, and Jamie wasn't sure how Ghost would feel about it. Around the corner from the workshop, he pulled up to the kerb. "Um, would you mind doing something for me, if you can?" A glance showed Ghost looking inquisitive. "Er, well, can you look like me, enough to fool a camera as we drive past? Then there'll be some doubt if it was ever me, or just several disguised men."

"It will take a little while?" The tone was teasing, and when he looked, so was Ghost's look. "It would be easier if we had DNA to copy that hadn't been absorbed, as it will still have your exact pattern? You will be parked for the change, so you won't have to drive at the same time."

Driving a little further, Jamie parked in the shadow of a taller building, so the inside of the Cherokee would be darker. He'd kissed her when Ghost took DNA, a reaction, but never done so deliberately. Now he wished he could pretend he wasn't looking forward to it—the kissing-DNA part anyway.

Ghost wasn't pretending at all—she was enjoying teasing him. "Should we emit pheromones to help you concentrate? Maybe remove coverings? Are you sure this won't lead to those other things? You never explained, so should we be worried?" The laugh at his shaking head meant she'd been expecting it. "You must kiss us as well, properly, or it will look strange if someone comes past." She must have noticed his reluctance.

He'd been trying to persuade himself to ignore the mouth hoovering, but her joking about it made kissing much more appealing. Even if he tried to hold back, that might upset Ghost, and she was doing him a big favour. Jamie ended up laughing at himself because if any other woman looking like her asked for a kiss, he'd be happy to oblige.

He put his arms around Ghost and kissed her, thoroughly and with absolutely zero regrets. At least they were dressed and on a public road, and he remembered the alien part so he wasn't tempted to go further.

"That was much better, lots of DNA." Ghost's smirk was much too appealing, especially after the kiss. It disappeared as she looked down for a moment. "Now we must concentrate. You might not like us after this, as we will look very strange for a while."

He'd wanted to know what she looked like, but if Ghost didn't like the idea, it might be a bad idea. Then Jamie realised that Ghost's reluctance was because she never shapeshifted where he could see, but there was an easy fix. "You could get in the back? I won't look, I promise." Now he didn't want to look, and still wasn't sure he wanted to see Ghost as a man—let alone his twin.

The next few minutes seemed like hours. Jamie could hear scrabbling, and Ghost's scent was stronger for a while, then a stranger's hand was on the back of the passenger seat. A quick glance showed that although it was larger, a man's hand, it wasn't identical to Jamie's. The hairy legs below the shorts might look like his as Jamie had never memorised his legs, while the exposed chest had a similarly sparse amount of hair.

Ghost's face and hair didn't look quite right, but when Jamie looked in the mirror it was closer than he thought, just not identical. Jamie/Ghost might not be as broad across the shoulders, and was a little shorter, but they could definitely be taken for brothers, possibly twins at first glance. The resemblance was obvious enough for Damian's lawyers to use, because regardless of any photos, Jamie didn't have a brother.

"We approximated the body, so that we looked like a different male disguised as you." The mouth was Jamie's, but the voice and faint scent were still Ghost's—which was confusing. "A perfect match would take longer and is not necessary." She/he glanced down, and she/he'd taken off the shirt and bra. "We noticed that naked male chests are acceptable, very strange."

Jamie tore his eyes away from his/her face and cleared his throat. "That's perfect, thank you. Now let's hope we are on some cameras. I might jump a few lights to make sure." He concentrated on the road, and driving, and set off. After a couple of turns the temptation to keep looking died back, and Jamie relaxed. There wouldn't be an attack here, not with stores, crowded pavements, and traffic. He didn't even mind queues at traffic lights—after all, he wanted witnesses when he jumped them.

Ghost was people and store-watching, with occasional questions, while Jamie was already thinking about tomorrow morning, and Solly. He kept an eye on his mirrors of course, so he couldn't help noticing the monster truck. With the giant tyres it took up two lanes, and the high suspension meant it wasn't inconspicuous. Jamie had never seen one in town before, and hadn't realised they were allowed to mix with ordinary traffic.

At the next two junctions, Jamie wasn't near enough to the lights to jump the red and get his picture taken. When he stopped at a crossroads, the truck had moved up and was only a few cars back, then something beeped and Ghost grabbed her pistol. "Hunter is here. The detector has noted advanced technology in the vicinity, and it can only be him." A slow scan through the windows revealed nothing, then Ghost put her head out of the passenger window and looked back. "Behind us. Drive!"

Jamie hit the accelerator, pushing the two cars ahead but turning the wheel so they were shunted aside, and hurtled across the crossroads against the lights. Ghost was already shooting, but he didn't have time to check his mirrors. He clipped the back of a van, then something hit his back wing, but he straightened up. The Cherokee left glass from front and rear lights, and strips of rubber on the tarmac, but Jamie made it across.

He glanced in his mirror, and even if the police now had a picture of him and his twin, they wouldn't care. They'd be concentrating on Hunter's vehicle, because it was following. The cross-traffic had either braked or swerved to avoid Jamie, which had blocked the road, but the big tyres were clambering over vehicles.

Jamie did a double-take, because the vehicle wasn't climbing —it was somehow crushing a wide track through the vehicles like a road roller. Ghost's voice grabbed his attention. "Swerve!" Jamie did so with a convulsive jerk, and saw something shoot past the Cherokee. It splattered on the road like a bucket of tar, just ahead, and the passenger-side wheels passed through the edge. It felt like the brakes went on for a moment, but only at one side.

He swerved back onto his side of the road, just in time to avoid a head-on, wondering how the hell that truck would fit down a single lane. It might just run over the oncoming traffic, unless it met a truck or bus. Another look in the mirror showed that it was half on the sidewalk. It mowed down a succession of lampposts, then instead of the wheels passing each side of a cyclist, he was picked up and thrown.

A shimmer went across the empty space under the truck, turning a metallic silver for a moment before Jamie could see right underneath it again. "Ghost, there's something underneath the truck."

The sound of a shotgun answered him, then a low growl. "It is an armoured ground car, disguised as a big Earth vehicle. The solid shotgun will not penetrate armour. Try to find a narrow road."

A glance back showed that the ground car, whatever that was, had started gaining now it wasn't smashing road users aside. He'd lived here all his life, but the town centre wasn't Jamie's usual stomping ground so he didn't know his way around, and there wasn't time to check a map. He wrenched the wheel over and the tyres squealed, but kept enough contact as the Cherokee fish-tailed down the next side street.

Jamie turned right at the T-junction, almost too late. The green beam that went past behind him hit the back of a parked car and a house front, so Hunter had given up on secrecy. This road was long, straight, and there weren't any side roads. Quick, desperate glances showed that some garages were set back, so the driveways went back past the house. "This might get rough, Ghost. Hang on."

Before he could find the right spot, the monster truck swung around the corner to follow him. Jamie saw the silvery stuff appear between the big wheels, so he swung the wheel across, paused until he daren't wait any longer, and swung back. The driver coming the other way slammed on his brakes and looked horrified, but Jamie was clear, and then a much bigger blob of black tar buried the front of the oncoming car.

The skid stopped dead, as if it had hit a wall. Jamie swerved again so he was behind it, then saw an opportunity and turned up a driveway. The driveway extended past the back of the house, and just before he reached the garage, Jamie swung the wheel—Menhir wasn't going to be happy about the state of his car. The hood buckled but stayed down, while the wooden fence splintered, then a dog ran for its life as the vehicle charged across the backyard and trampled a flower bed.

Trash cans went flying before Jamie smashed through another fence, and across the next garden. More boards, three wire fences, and a hedge later he swerved back down a driveway, and stopped.

"Listen for that truck. If it comes up behind the houses, I'm going back along the road." Jamie listened, mostly to his pounding pulse as it tried to settle. He lowered his voice, sure he'd still hear that monster truck widening the track through the gardens. "What was that stuff?"

"The black will pin you in place, then set. The green will destroy solid material and leave living creatures unconscious, helpless. Hunter must be alone in there, as he is only firing straight ahead. If he had a gunner to aim, we would not have been able to dodge. Try to keep him turning, so he can't stop steering long enough to activate the weapons."

She might be a ferocious fighter, but for the first time Ghost's male-human expression looked frightened. "If we are trapped, or the car is hit, you escape while we face him and try to lead him away. Go home and wait."

Jamie didn't like that idea, not with the watchers and Solly visiting, but right now he didn't have time to argue. "Hold tight, here we go." The racket behind meant that Hunter was coming through the gardens. He'd see where Jamie came down this drive, but that huge thing would never fit between the houses. Accelerating smoothly out onto the road, Jamie headed back towards the stopped car.

The driver was stood in the road, looking at the black stuff all over the front of his car, but ran for cover when he saw Jamie coming. Jamie almost lifted a hand to hide his face when he saw a woman in her front garden with a phone raised, taking pictures—then remembered he wanted publicity. She wasn't the only one, so he made sure they all got a good shot.

He stared at a house with a missing front, the rooms on view, then remembered the green beam. Most of the car had disappeared, leaving the chassis and engine and parts of the front third of the bodywork. Jamie checked the rear-view mirror—and nearly ran off the road. A shower of brickwork shot out across the road, followed by the front of the monster truck. No pretence now—it was definitely alien, and military.

The disguise had failed, and the gleaming silvery machine with three big tracks, one around the centre, explained the squashed cars. The bits poking out of the angled plates between the tracks looked too much like weapons, presumably the tar and green beam, but were pointing the wrong way. The turret on the top, off-set to avoid the tracks, was already on target. Jamie swung back down the way he'd come, back into town.

A crackling noise was followed by bright light, a lightning bolt across the rear-view mirror that left an after-image on Jamie's retinas. The house on the corner exploded in flame. "What was that!"

"That is a larger version of what we considered using to stop the camera, but this one really is like a bolt of lightning. Using it on Earth is illegal, but so are the other weapons and revealing the ground car. Hunter will kill us if we cannot be captured, to avoid prosecution." Ghost was twisted in her seat, looking back, and she looked shocked.

"Why kill us? He'll never cover up the evidence, not with all the cameras." Though right now that wasn't the most urgent problem. "What will stop that thing? It went through a house!"

"Only one end wall of a single-storey brick building. It might not break through in the middle, or if you can find a stronger structure." Ghost was looking through the bag, and now she pulled out Lucie's magnum. "If he follows on foot, we may get a clear shot. We believe this or the rifle will penetrate his personal protection."

"Something more solid?" She had to mean concrete, an old industrial building rather than one of the lightweight modern units, but Jamie couldn't think of a narrow gap between two. Inspiration struck. "I'm going to drive around some back streets. There's a shorter route but there will be traffic, and that bastard will flatten anything in the way, leave a trail of bodies."

This time Jamie slowed, making sure the Hunter saw him turn. Thirty yards down the street he slowed a little more, trying to judge the ground car's progress.

He nearly misjudged, because the turret was already facing this way, but the Cherokee was out of the line of fire when the lightning struck. This time the beam only clipped the corner of a house, but flames shot out of the nearest windows. "You never did say how he thinks he'll hide the evidence. Even if we disappear, he's killing dozens at least." Jamie was beginning to wonder if it was a man-in-black beam or a nuclear bomb solution.

"Killing indigenes isn't a crime, as you aren't a recognised race." Ghost leaned out of the passenger window, the magnum in both hands, then sat back down. "Tell me if we are turning and we will try to hit the driver's cameras. This might damage them, or at least make him wary."

"Murder isn't a crime?" Jamie didn't risk being shot this time —there was only one turning they could have taken to get out of sight. He cut the next corner by driving across the lot behind the house, but abandoned any thought of repeating it. The ground car did the same but tore a corner off the house.

"No, the crime is technical pollution, and if we die or are captured, nobody will ever know." Ghost didn't sound happy, but Jamie was horrified. "It could be hundreds of years before Earth is visited officially, inspectors to decide if humans are fit to join the civilised worlds. In the interim, any rogue traders or tourists that visit will keep quiet, or they might be prosecuted for being here."

~~

Instead of thinking too much about alien laws, Jamie concentrated on his driving, but was careful to take roads with room for the ground car. He daren't turn down an alley. The buildings were bigger here, but Hunter had already used the green beam to cut a corner. The front third of a house had crumbled, which might be enough to bring down something bigger. Jamie didn't want to be responsible for collapsing a tower block full of flats or office workers.

That was still a possibility, as the ground car tore the corner off another building, cutting across to keep up speed. The alien machine took the next three corners properly, and Jamie realised Hunter wasn't confident he could smash through the bigger buildings. He didn't use the beam either, so maybe he wouldn't survive if the building collapsed. By now Jamie was wondering why he hadn't seen flashing red and blue lights.

A bright beam pinned the Cherokee, a helicopter, but Jamie couldn't slow so he hoped the pilot realised he wasn't the problem. Spike strips would reduce him to a crawl, but wouldn't slow Hunter up at all. He didn't think there'd be anyone already laying strips or raising barriers on the road ahead—he was taking turns almost at random so they'd never plot a route.

The light swept away towards Hunter, then lighting flashed from around the last bend. Jamie took a turn just so he could look back, and risked taking his eyes off the road. The helicopter was easy to see—the spotlight beam was sweeping across the night sky as it spun away trailing smoke. From the brief look, it wasn't falling, so it must be under some sort of control. Jamie couldn't watch long enough to find out if it crashed.

Though what he saw made one decision for him. "I'll have to cut this short. I've no idea how many people he's killing in those buildings, and now he's started on the police." Jamie caught sight of flashing lights ahead, and took the next left. He didn't want to lead this maniac to a roadblock, or even a cop car. It crossed Jamie's mind that if he took too long there'd be National Guard choppers and tanks, but he had a nasty feeling that even modern armour wasn't designed for that lightning bolt, or the green beam.

When Jamie crossed a main road he saw very little traffic, and wished he had a scanner so he could hear what the squad cars were saying. They had to be diverting traffic, but he didn't know what routes would be clear. By the time he remembered Ghost's comms, it didn't matter. "Here we go. If this fails, I'll drive around a corner and slow for you to jump, then I'll lead him to the river. I'll turn a corner so he doesn't realise the water is there, and with luck, Hunter will be going too fast and drown."

Ghost dived over the seat into the back. "You will leave first, then we will drive into the river as we can change form to swim clear very quickly. When we leave the water, it is dark enough for us to evade detection if we become the night hunter. Can we save your purchases first? Drop them off?" A glance showed that she was pulling boxes together, trying to bundle them.

"We'll try, but first we're going caving. I want to see him smash his way out of this." This time Jamie slowed, crawling down the ramp so Hunter would definitely see him. The lightning bolt cracked the concrete wall at the opposite side of the entrance, but only a few pieces came loose. "Seems like concrete will slow him up."

Ghost's voice was muffled, then clearer. "That depends on which weapon he uses. The green ray, you would probably call it a molecular disruptor, will crumble rock. It loosens molecular bonds in solids—the more solid the object, the better it works." She looked shocked when she climbed back into the front and saw where they were. "We are trapped!"

"Not quite, and we can dodge the green beam. You said he can't aim it sideways so he has to get the front pointing towards us. Now buckle up, because this could get rough." Jamie drove down the centre of the cavern, through the gap in the next wall. As the ground car charged down the ramp, the top clipped the height bar. The turret jutted up another two feet so it tore through the beams above, and the ceiling collapsed—sealing the entrance.

Jamie had been hopeful, but neither stopped the damn thing and the turret survived. He swerved sideways, out of sight, and stopped part-way across the next section of the underground garage. The last view showed the turret wasn't quite hitting the roof, but only because it was retracting.

Quick glances in the mirrors showed that Jamie had guessed right—Hunter wasn't going to try smashing down a concrete wall, and the ground car wouldn't go through the gap. He saw a green glow instead of the familiar flash, then green cracks showed in the concrete wall dividing the bays. Once the wall began to crumble, Jamie accelerated, swerving back into the centre.

The beam wouldn't have reached him anyway, though it had enough strength left to reduce the first two parked cars to skeletons. So far so good, as Hunter had swerved across to trample the collapsing wall. The turret had fully retracted, so it wasn't tough enough to break through the concrete beams holding up the roof. Jamie had half-hoped breaking them would bring the lot down on top of the vehicle.

When the armour smashed through the disintegrating concrete, Jamie was just driving through the next opening. He was taking it steady, so he could make the bend without making it obvious he wasn't going any further. Even so, Jamie still had enough speed to bounce the Cherokee when he hit the ramp. The engine roared in the confined space, but as he drove back up to street level, Jamie could still hear the metallic carnage behind. The ground car was bulldozing its way through the parked vehicles at full speed.

Jamie began to smile. "If he uses the green beam, how good are his brakes when he sees what's behind the concrete?"

Ghost's head whipped around to look back, then she turned to Jamie with her own smile starting. "He thinks it's a wall, the same as the last one." A green glow seeped through the part of the wall above the lower end of the ramp, but the Cherokee was already clear. "Even if he realises, he has to stop about one hundred of your tons, on metal tracks, on concrete..."

Ghost stopped speaking as the whole Cherokee bounced upwards, concrete shot across the ramp behind them, and dust flew out of every seam and crack of the walls and ceiling. Jamie slowed for the exit, then turned left and drove sedately away. "A hundred tons versus however many thousands of tons of earth, rock, and foundations are holding the ramp and building up. Even if the ground car will still drive, Hunter has just demolished the only other ramp out of there. The cops will be too busy cutting him out to bother us."

Jamie had a twinge of conscience as he saw the glass and light rubble covering the road behind—the impact hadn't done the hotel much good. He wondered if the protesters would finally get their way and get the "concrete monstrosity" demolished. He'd chosen that basement garage because he figured the building was solid enough to survive.

He drove steadily away, hoping the cops were too busy to worry about his missing headlamp. Just in case, he pulled off the road as soon as he saw flashing lights, with the front as close as possible to a parked car. There were a few tense moments as three cop cars and then an ambulance came past, but none of them even slowed up.

Jamie was surprised, and relieved, as the Cherokee's grille and hood, and the new fender, had been used as a ram. After waiting a little longer, he set off nice and steady, but once he was clear of the area, he turned into a multi-storey parking lot. As he parked up in a shadowy corner, Jamie finally relaxed—they'd made it.

Though he immediately realised they hadn't—there was still the meeting with Solly.

DOUBLE-DOUBLE CROSS

Within two minutes, another realisation hit Jamie. "How much advanced tech will the police find in that thing?" At least he was leaving the planet. A few advanced processors might not be too bad, but an army with that green ray, or the lightning, would create havoc. Worse, as soon as another nation found out about it, they'd try to steal it, or attack before it was used on them.

Ghost was relaxing as well, and she didn't seem worried. "None. That may have damaged the ground car and even injured Hunter, but the driver's pod is close to indestructible without advanced weaponry. It will survive simple crushing, but the rest of the ground car is immobilised at least." She/he sniggered and turned to face Jamie. "Even if Hunter gets out, we have escaped. He will have to stay long enough to destroy all traces of advanced tech, even the metal in the armour."

"If nobody will visit Earth, why does it matter if he leaves some bits of metal?" Though Jamie was remembering her melting the bits of robot when they'd picked up the pod.

From her voice, Ghost was confident. "Stories of green beams destroying buildings, or a large, alien machine, are just rumours. Proof will have to be something more convincing than pictures that might be special effects. Though if any actual tech survives, even a section of advanced armour plate, the first official visit to Earth will have solid proof of pollution. They will scour every record and rumour, and will never give up looking."

Ghost's laughter was probably at least partly relief. "Not because of the pollution. That is only a fine, and isn't worth chasing if enough time has passed. What will annoy them is that the idiot blatantly broke their laws, literally drove a ground car through them in full view of indigenes. If he doesn't make sure he wipes out any physical evidence, the inner worlds will make an example of him."

"Inner worlds?" Jamie was looking in the direction of the hotel, relieved there was no gunfire. Ordinary cops would have no chance against that green beam pistol.

Her voice caught Jamie's attention, and when he looked, Ghost's lip was curled in disgust. He wondered if his sneer really looked like that. "They are the oldest worlds, the first ones civilised and very proud of it. Much too high and mighty to do their own dirty work, but they will pay for top-class investigators and mercenaries if their precious pride is dented. The next ring are very advanced, but have only been civilised for three or four millennia."

She/he glanced at Jamie and something, maybe his expression at the sight of his own sneer, prompted her to explain. "They aren't really rings, though level twos tend to be near a level one and are partly surrounded by level threes. The levels aren't clear, one shades into the other, especially when it comes to the outer ring. Those are level five or six, depending on who counts."

Her hand patted Jamie's leg. Another glance showed that she had recovered her humour and was smirking. "You will have a better idea if you visit my home. We are technically a level four, but still have some outer ring rough edges. Beyond the outer ring are the probation planets, worlds that are trying to gain official recognition, and outside them are worlds like your Earth."

She'd definitely diverted Jamie from worrying about Hunter, the police, or even Solly. "It must take hundreds of years to travel all the way to the inner worlds." He'd have liked to see all that, but Jamie knew he'd never live long enough.

“That depends as they are scattered, not in a neat group. The nearest is within a hundred lights. If you didn’t stop at all the worlds in between, you might visit half of the oldest civilisations in a human lifetime.” A glance showed that Ghost still had a little smile. “More if you lived as long as a Slashtail, or perhaps all of them if you became true Ghost Claw.”

It occurred to Jamie that he might have found a really good reason for swapping DNA. “How long is a Slashtail lifetime?”

Ghost held her hand out, palm down, then rocked it. “Variable, as natural lifespans are not totally applicable. The reason worlds strive for recognition, and then to advance, is that level four qualifies the inhabitants for regeneration treatments, technically eternal life. On our world, there is a quota. Every thirty-seven of our years, one in every two-hundred of our population must give up their lives or permanently leave the planet. That allows the creation of new Slashtails without overpopulating the planet.”

Her hand patted his leg again, and Jamie could hear a deep sorrow behind her light tone. “Ghost Claw have no rules, so we live as long as we wish. Be warned though, no rules means that many Ghost Claw die much too soon.”

“I’m sure I would need a lot of DNA for that, and you already said that might not be wise.” Jamie pushed on before she told him any details, like scales or ten legs and poison fangs. “Killing your population to keep the numbers down seems drastic, or is that a rule for all members?”

That brought a sigh. “No, the rule is that any member planets using regeneration must avoid over-population. A maximum population is agreed, but the method is left to the locals. There are many variations, though suspended animation is not counted, as they are still alive and using resources. Wealth often helps, while random poison, or competitions so the strongest survive, are popular. Sometimes a member of a family must die to allow one of them to give birth."

Jamie would have bet on wealth helping, but one part of that sounded really nasty. "Random poisoning? Does that include young people, kids?"

The nod was accompanied by a sneer, so Ghost didn't like the idea. "Yes, in some cases. One world consists of cities all holding approximately the same population, and periodically gasses one of them, chosen by lottery. An occasional world decides against a cull, they ban procreation. Those worlds usually stagnate eventually—no new blood. Or worlds overpopulate when the population procreate without permission. Their societies collapse and are culled by starvation or war, but before their ecosystem is irreparably damaged, mercenaries from the class one worlds rebalance the population."

"So it isn't eternal life at all." Jamie tried to work out what Earth would do, and was sure billionaires and politicians would find a way to live forever. He wondered if Damian and Shania would qualify, or their descendants.

Ghost shook her head. "Leaving your native world forever reduces the population, and the one who leaves has no need to die. No need for a cull if enough of the population choose permanent exile, but there are never enough volunteers."

"Why not?" Jamie was sure there'd be thousands of people on earth who would be happy to tour the universe and never come back.

"They aren't accepted anywhere else." Ghost gestured towards herself. "Ghost Claw aren't accepted at home, but our whole clan are wanderers so we don't care. It is a lonely choice for others. None of the other worlds grant citizenship to other races, or allow long-term residents—that would raise the population and prevent a birth. Changing worlds after twenty or thirty years and starting a new business, time after time after time, is possible but far from easy. Living on primitive worlds would work, but you'd have to hide your regeneration, and even visiting them is illegal."

He would have liked to spend the rest of the night talking about alien worlds and Ghost's life, but Jamie had an urgent problem first. "I'd love to hear about some of the places you've been, but first we'd better work out where to meet Solly. After the number of people who will have taken our picture, I'm guessing there will be a lot more police outside my garage. They'll pounce as soon as I appear. There will be an all-points alert for Menhir's Cherokee, and it's got my fingerprints all over it. If the police get them, even Damian's lawyers can't keep insisting I'm in the Maldives."

"Will Solly still swap?" Ghost was worried again—without those spares they'd be back to shopping and stealing, and maybe alerting Hunter.

He hadn't expected to laugh, but Jamie did. "Solly is greedy. He'll do the trade but now he'll definitely try to cheat, and then sell us to the highest bidder. We'll have to work out someplace with a back door and two escape tunnels." He suddenly remembered the pod's talents. "Or an invisible elevator. That won't solve the problem of my fingerprints in here, too many to clean them all off. I'll have to burn it, but I haven't any real cash to pay Menhir. If he's too upset he might tell the police he met me, not a cousin."

~~

A combination of Google and Jamie's memory decided on a location, then Ghost collected the pod, and followed Jamie and the battered Cherokee out of town. He parked where he'd be able to spot an ambush and probably any watchers, then Ghost flew them back towards his garage. Jamie had totally misjudged the number of police.

Menhir hadn't wasted any time. There were a score of people working under floodlights, dismantling the place and loading trucks. Two trucks with cranes were lifting sleepers from the walls onto flatbeds, and now Jamie could see the row of steel bars sticking up. All the secret watchers had gone, but the police van had stayed, keeping an eye on the crowd of locals. Menhir's extended family, with baseball bats and shotguns, were making sure the neighbours stuck to just watching.

Ghost flew out of town, slowly to make sure Hunter didn't spot them, and parked to eat and refine their plan. By the time they'd eaten, watched the news on the TV, and plotted, it was early morning and Jamie was shattered—but relieved.

Jamie's name wasn't mentioned, even though his face was the one the police wanted to talk to. He was wanted in connection with the deaths of thirty-nine civilians and seven police officers, injuries of nearly a hundred more, and a trail of destruction right through Albuquerque.

The police sketch of a suspect was followed by several blurry pictures of a Jamie-like man driving, and then a few clearer pictures where he had a nearly identical passenger. There were two blurry versions of a female Ghost on the news, both with light brown skin and hair, and more blurred pictures of Jamie, Jamie-Ghost, and Ghost on the web.

Ghost admitted she'd been using a localised, low-level distortion since they'd collected the pod, and her pelt had some camouflage abilities. It diffused radar signals, its heat signature was always the same as the background, and it bent light so that digitisation would always result in a muddy brown. She'd turned the blurring off to let the police get the Malone pictures, and after copying Jamie. The human brain compensated to give a clear view, though it might need a blink or squint, but the slight visual vibration had more effect on recordings.

The TV issued a warning the terrorists may be a gang of men who all looked similar, or a family as the only clear pictures showed possible twins—Ghost's disguise had worked. There were at least two women wearing different wigs, neither of whom seemed to be related. The police still didn't give out Jamie's name, which had to be down to Damian, but now Jamie worried about the cost of the lawyers. Damian might decide to economise, though he didn't seem the type to send an assassin.

Despite the body count and charges, the nameless picture wasn't the main story. Most of the news concentrated on the ground car, allegedly driven by other members of the gang, or a rival gang, with several attempts to guess a motive or target. Various commentators included or discounted the monster truck, while the ground car was allegedly a stolen secret weapon. There was plenty of footage of the chase, with both vehicles and burning cars and buildings, but no close-ups of the ground car.

Some pictures were almost pure white, followed by the aftermath, but the lightning beam had been too bright for pictures. The green beam was tied to the previous disturbance, with sketches of glowing green spiderwebs and pictures of fallen masonry, but once again no actual pictures of the beam.

Ghost explained that one—the ground car's version of her distortion would have caused temporary malfunctions in electronics without advanced protection. She hadn't realised that included any nearby phone cameras, but that had to be why there were no close-ups. The car stuck in black stuff had disappeared, leaving a big pothole, which sparked plenty of internet conspiracy theories.

Absolutely nobody could agree on what had happened at the hotel, which had to be down to the authorities. It would be weeks, maybe months, before anyone actually got to see the crushed vehicles under there. With one corner slowly sinking into the Earth, even a concrete monstrosity hadn't been strong enough to survive intact. At least Jamie got an explanation of why the hotel were blaming a subterranean collapse for the subsidence.

According to Ghost, Hunter's ground car must have been

stuck in the garage, so he'd overloaded the green beam generator. The beam wouldn't have penetrated the armour from outside, but from inside the feedback would have eaten the whole vehicle. A globe of rock and concrete about thirty feet across would have been reduced to dust.

Hunter would have made sure there wasn't any physical evidence. He would have waited, using his personal shield to hide, then destroyed the actual weapon and anything it missed with the hand weapon. The same weapon would let him tunnel out.

Ghost had changed back to her mauve-haired female version before retrieving her pod, and now she stretched and yawned. Arching her back she glanced down at her chest, and then at Jamie, and smirked. "You seem to find this covering more interesting than the first, or a hairy chest." Jamie didn't answer —she'd put on the bra, just the bra, instead of the bikini top. She licked her lips. "Mmm, time for your version of greeting-to-kin. Lucky really, as we are in just the right mood to have our pelt stroked."

When she looked towards Jamie, Ghost had a downright wicked smile. He shook his head, as convincingly as he could. "But without DNA, because you already have a lot to absorb." Her smile never faltered, so Jamie just hoped she didn't use pheromones.

From her singing, Ghost really did enjoy having her pelt stroked, and for a long time. No pheromones but she was teasing again—by the time he'd finished, Jamie was absolutely certain her pelt was longer. The cover was pulled down below her waist so he could stroke it all, which showed the beginning of an intriguing curve. At least she stayed face down, and pulled up the covering afterwards.

~~

Ghost roused Jamie not long enough after dawn, as soon as the sky was bright enough to force Hunter up high. Jamie texted Shania before they moved, because she'd be worried. He only put together the one phone, and the only text told him Damian hadn't wasted any time setting up the Maldives alibi.

"Two surprises, but I didn't like the second one. Too late for the place we discussed, there's a guy moved in there who wanted some privacy. Hope you don't treat whatever you've borrowed the same as your car. Let Frankie know when you want to meet. We are both very keen to meet your new friend."

Jamie wasn't sure he'd get to meet her, unless Ghost landed on the lawn for a quick meet and greet. The guy who wanted privacy would be called Jamie, so he had to make sure he didn't leave a drop of blood or a single fingerprint. The second surprise had to be the TV news, so Jamie stuck with reassurance. *"Hi, everything fine here. We're staying well clear of all the stuff on the TV, and will be keeping our heads down. If I were you, I'd have a family day at home. No telling where that armoured thing might turn up."*

It wouldn't turn up, but Solly might kick off a gun battle. Then Hunter's drones would spot it, and from his reaction last night, he might settle for blasting the pod into scrap. He could probably do that from up high, and since he didn't seem to mind collateral, wouldn't need a precise fix.

Jamie tried to work on the repair, but he couldn't concentrate properly, so he gave up and phoned Solly with the third burn phone. From his lack of reaction, Solly had expected a new location, and agreed to drive west along I-40 at eleven a.m. Ghost headed that way so they'd be in position early, but suggested a diversion.

"After you explained aces and wild cards, we investigated card games." There was a gotcha coming, it was in her expression. "We tried playing some and you are right, it would be very easy to lose the pod, or even Starlight Ghost, but that led to discovering digital currency. When we investigated ways to acquire some, for the repayments you requested, we discovered mining for bitcoins."

With a flourish, Ghost produced what Jamie recognised as four of his plug-in data sticks. "The technology in this pod is not really advanced, but is far beyond Earth normal." Jamie nodded—he'd already found that out the hard way. "We set several components on mining coins, once we found the process, and left them to it. There is a digital wallet on each of these, with bitcoins that add up to just over one million dollars. Would you like to burn the Cherokee, or shall I?"

Jamie looked at the amounts written on each stick, and smiled. He held one up. "Let's make a delivery first. I'd love to burn the Cherokee, but not until Solly gets the full benefit. It will keep him from getting too confident."

Fifteen minutes later Jamie dropped a parcel, literally, then texted Menhir on the third burn phone. *"Parcel on the doorstep."*

He watched from above as someone took the almost-empty cardboard box inside. The note told Menhir to report the Jeep Cherokee stolen sometime yesterday, and the password for the data stick. The bitcoins were compensation for the vehicle, as it would be burned out when the police found it. Since the repayment was more than the cost of a new Jeep Cherokee, and bitcoins were anonymous, Jamie was fairly sure Menhir wouldn't upset. He might claim the insurance as well, but Jamie didn't care.

A slow flight across the river and out of town, and Jamie lowered two mesh skips. The one containing the spares he was trading was big and heavy, so Solly couldn't run off with it. Jamie disembarked and arranged the cable to the second, lighter one with a lid, and spread out a groundsheet. After that, all he could do was sit and worry, and he had a lot of worries. The big one was that Ghost insisted this was the last time they could be caught.

Once he had these spares, the pod could fly off and submerge. They could surface hours later, someplace remote where they could hide ashore, or just hover in the middle of an ocean. Ghost was confident that she could avoid Hunter once they weren't shopping or moving about.

~~

At least part of the worrying was because when Ghost scanned the immediate area, to find Solly's spy, there were two watchers. Neither of them was looking the right way, or using advanced surveillance gear, but someone had managed to follow or find the Cherokee. Ghost had scanned all the packaging from Lottie so there wasn't a tracer, but Solly might have had someone watching Lottie's place.

Solly was suspicious enough to have Menhir watched after he'd visited Jamie, so maybe the Jeep had been followed from his home. Maybe they'd just put trackers on all Menhir's vehicles, or someone had spotted it after he'd escaped the Hunter. Considering the state of the bodywork, that wouldn't have been difficult. Jamie gave up trying to guess, it was too late to matter, but it still nagged at him. A message from Ghost cleared Jamie's mind—Solly had arrived.

Jamie didn't send precise directions, but Solly pulled up near Enchanted Trails RV Park, and the abandoned Cherokee. There was open ground in every direction so Jamie knew there were no police, and Solly hadn't brought a small army. He called, wishing he'd bought another burn phone. This one might be compromised by now. *"Change of plan, mystery dealer man. Head for the airport, five miles north. I spotted your friends."*

Solly got the message about avoiding names, or he usually avoided them anyway. *"Okay, fair enough, mystery seller, but I'm bringing one with me. From the stories I heard about what happened outside your supplier's place, you've hired muscle."* Ghost had connected the pod's optics to a small, alien pad in Jamie's hand, so he saw Solly turn his pickup around, and a man run from one of the RVs.

When Solly was halfway along the wide-open road, over a

mile from the nearest buildings or cover, Jamie called again to give him the actual meeting place. *"Tell your friend to ditch the long gun."* When Solly started to argue, Jamie had his bit of fun. *"Look back at the Cherokee."* He pressed the button, and as promised, whatever Ghost had done turned the vehicle into a small, intense fireball. *"The gun won't help."*

Once the weapon was thrown out of the pickup's window, Jamie gave him the rest. *"Take the left turn, and park outside the main entrance."* That was the SW Aeronautics Mathematics and Science Academy, a flat-topped building a mile short of the airport, totally isolated, and deserted during the holidays.

~~

The dealer would be annoyed anyway, but now he started to show it. *"I hope this is it, or the meet is off. You'd better be dealing straight, or even a fireball and your muscle won't be enough to get you out alive."*

"This is it. I'm just a bit nervous after the gang war, the ambush, and the trouble in town last night." Jamie crouched in the bushes beside the building, next to an empty mesh basket. A wire cable led away across the ground until, just past the corner, it went up to the roof. Ghost and the pod were up there, hoping nobody looked too closely and caught a distortion.

The fence had been doing his homework. *"I know someone who lost several men near your supplier's, and he reckons you've got hired help, but he said your car was barely fit to drive. I recognise the one that just burned, and it looked as if it had been used for a ram-raid but it hadn't been shot up. The damage was more like the one on TV, playing tag with coppers and a tank."* He sounded intrigued, but then Solly laughed. *"That tank was supposed to be under the hotel, but a birdy tells me the scans can't find it. It got away, somehow."*

He paused, then sounded more thoughtful. *"If it was after you, any solid information is worth cash. If you know where it went, I know people who would pay a lot of money for the information, and a lot more for the hardware. Hard cash will come in useful if you're skipping town."*

"Who says I'm skipping?" Jamie had asked Menhir to keep quiet, but maybe he'd let it slip, or maybe Solly had checked this morning.

Laughter answered. *"A work crew turned up with a crane and put most of your place onto trucks. The cops were really excited, but then they left, and when someone asked, you'd sold the lot."* Solly laughed again. *"From what I was told this morning, there isn't enough left for a decent bonfire."*

"There is someone on top of one of the airport buildings, with binoculars." Ghost had a perfect view, and better optics. *"He does not have a weapon. A vehicle is blocking the road from the airport, and another is parked two miles the other way."*

Jamie turned off the phone, and spoke into the badge. *"Let me know if any vehicles head this way, from any direction."*

~~

When Solly pulled in and climbed out of his truck, Jamie called out from the bushes. "Everything is in the wire basket in front of the main doors. There are bricks in the bottom so you can't run off with it, and if you try, you get a smaller version of the Cherokee. Your man stays in the truck, my muscle stays out of sight. You bring one item to the bushes and put it on the groundsheet, then you pick up one bundle. I check the goods while you check the payment, then we both load up. We repeat it seven times, until it's all swapped. If anyone comes past your vehicles, from any direction, boom and I'm gone."

There was no laughter this time—Solly had dropped the act and was stone cold serious. "Damn Jamie, you finally wised up. Turns out you're more like your papa than anyone thought. From what I was told, and this setup, you found a professional, but the reports can't decide if it was a man or a woman. One very reliable source reckoned it was your brother, but I've known your family for years. Who is it?"

"Goes by the name of Ghost; nobody you will know." For a moment Jamie nearly laughed, but bit it back. "She's not from around here."

"With a name like that I'm guessing retired spec-ops. I bet the Hellbats didn't know what hit them. She? I'll let them know, if there's a survivor, just to piss them off." Solly must have been listening to the bug in one ear, because he nodded, straightened, and his voice was suddenly more business-like. "One seventh at a time, right?" He dropped the back of the pickup and pulled out a box.

"One-seventh. Head this way, but bear a little to the right. It'll be obvious." Jamie watched the man in the cab, because Solly wouldn't try anything without backup.

Solly saw the groundsheet, then spotted Jamie and the wire cage. He grinned and nodded. "Guess you won't be running off with that either."

Jamie smiled back. Even if he'd had his car it wouldn't fit, though he might have crammed it in the Cherokee. "The Double Eagle II Airport is just up the road, so I might fly off with it. I'll be in clear view all the way there, with plenty of witnesses if trouble starts, so I guess your men will let me past."

"At least I'll get to see your new friend. Leave a number, I can always use someone discreet." When Jamie didn't answer, Solly shrugged and went to look at his payment.

~~

Solly didn't seem to be in any hurry, but Jamie wanted to get this over with as fast as possible. The tests showed that the payment was all genuine, and included the two loaded magazines for the magnum and a box of jacketed rifle ammo, but Jamie didn't relax. He didn't trust Solly to play it straight.

Ghost reported more vehicles arriving, a pickup truck and two quad bikes. They stopped a mile to the west, on a parallel dirt road, which confirmed Jamie's fears—Solly was closing the back door. There were plenty of buildings to the east, towards the river and Albuquerque, but even a dirt bike would have trouble crossing the three miles of broken ground to get there.

When he put down the last part of the payment, Solly paused. “Where the hell did you get hold of genuine Formula E kit, off the books? I thought you'd got a rip-off version, but it isn't, so it should only work on the original vehicle. It reads like a clean factory setup, but with the codes entered so it can be fitted to anything. Now I've got another offer, I can find a job for a man like you.”

“Sorry, I've got a better offer.” Even if he hadn't, Solly would steal the cracking kit once he realised that was doing all the work. Papa had cracked the Formula E kit—Jamie wouldn't have known where to start. He was barely a mediocre hacker without the kit, and useless at modifying anything but simple software. At least the question explained why Solly was taking so long—he'd been double-checking the software.

Ghost sent a message, so Jamie warned Solly. “A word of warning. Flying those expensive-looking drones near an airport can be dangerous, they might crash.”

“Not if you pay enough, and those are military.” Solly stopped and frowned, worried now. “Ghost. She's cracked the damn things.” It wasn't a question so Jamie didn't answer. She hadn't even tried—Ghost was poised to gift each one a personal lightning strike if the warning didn't work. The drones wouldn't stop the pod, but Ghost wanted Solly off-balance, trying to guess what other backup Jamie had. “Okay, I'll pull them back. You really should have accepted my offer, Jamie.” With that Solly headed for the last of his goodies.

~~

Jamie skimped the check on the last box, but still nearly took too long. Ghost had already reported the drones pulling back, but now the alien pad gave a shrill beep. Jamie didn't look—he slammed the lid on the skip shut and started running.

He heard a car door slam, then his earpiece told him the problem. *"Solly is getting back into his truck and the guard is running towards the bushes. There are two men coming out from under the tarpaulin in the back, they must have used thermal shielding. Five vehicles and two bikes heading this way from every direction but east. The small plane that is taking off might be coincidence."* Ghost obviously didn't think so.

"Hold fire." Jamie didn't want a bloodbath, even if Solly deserved it. He'd reached the wire running up the side of the building, and grabbed it with both gloved hands. *"Pull me up, please."* By "please" he was running up the wall. Behind him the cage slid across the ground, then followed him upwards. The pod moved out from the roof so he lost contact with the wall, but Jamie kept going up until the airlock appeared around him.

The cable paused, Jamie grabbed the ladder, and then the cage finished its journey much faster than it started. If any of Solly's men saw it, they'd be reporting that it disappeared into a hole in mid-air. Jamie scampered up the ladder and out into the corridor, to find Ghost grinning from the doorway.

He glanced down to where the door had shut, and scowled. "I expected him to try something, but that was a bit much. It's a pity the bomb wasn't real. At least it would have given the asshole a shock."

Ghost held something up. "Ghost Claw don't know how to make fake bombs, or small ones, so he parked a bit too close." She turned back towards her seat. "Come on, we added a three-second countdown, a loud one. You can watch them run and dive for cover, then try to put out a burning pickup and his expensive purchases."

~~

Jamie closed the hatch and started after her, then the pod lurched and threw him into the wall. "What was that?"

Through the door he saw Ghost clamber into her seat, then the view on the screen spun and dipped. She shouted one word.

"Hunter!"

As Jamie staggered into the control room, the pod dived, almost standing on its nose, before spinning and heading towards Albuquerque. Until then he hadn't realised it had its own gravity, though the mismatch between what his eyes and feet thought made him feel dizzy and sick. As Jamie dropped into his seat, bands extruded to pin his chest and thighs in place, just in time as another shock tried to toss him at the ceiling. The internal gravity had limits.

Ghost was also pinned in her seat, but her hands were busy flipping switches and sliding controls. The panels in front of her flashed different coloured lights, a lot of them yellow, while a robotic voice kept shouting something. Alarms howled until they suddenly shut off, then as the cameras panned, Jamie saw a pillar of smoke rising beside a building. Ghost had triggered her surprise.

The big screen suddenly zoomed across the buildings ahead, and a tall, gleaming shape shimmered into view. "Found him." Light flashed halfway up, then the screen whited out and the pod lurched sideways again. Alarms wailed, and Jamie could smell something burning.

This time the alarms kept going, but the volume reduced as the pod steadied again, and dived for the ground. The globe shimmered into view again, but when the weapon flashed, the pod was already sliding up and sideways and it missed. "We used the decoy that we made to help us get away, but we only made one."

As Ghost's hands danced across the controls, Jamie saw a flash on a smaller screen. A lightning strike tore a big crater next to the road behind them, and Solly's men scattered away from a pickup as smoke billowed from the hood. Ghost was still talking. "That won't work again now he knows we can still manoeuvre, and we are too slow to get out of range before he hits us again."

Jamie felt helpless—he *was* helpless even though there were some controls in front of him. "I'm going to crash." Ghost's human laugh mixed with an odd chittering. "Only half-crash, but it will look real because it almost is. We hope there is enough water in the river or it might be too real." The river expanded to fill a screen, the pod shuddered and tried to stop, and Jamie was really grateful for the seat belts, again. Most of the screens showed swirling brown but several had blacked out.

"Yes! Now you know why Ghost Claw turn off failsafes so we can hit things." Ghost was still slapping switches and pressing buttons, but it wasn't quite as frantic. "We are too low for him to hit us, and Hunter dare not take off in daylight."

"Why not? Half of Albuquerque must have seen the big dome thing. Is that your ship, Starlight Ghost?" Jamie had accepted the ship was big, but that thing had towered over the nearby buildings—it had to be twice as tall as the high-rise towers and much wider.

"Our instruments picked up enough discrepancies to extrapolate the position, and the energy surge when he fired weapons was obvious. The ship will still be invisible, but the diffraction of light will be noticeable to anyone in the vicinity. The emissions from the weapon, and the damage, will have set off alarms in any nearby military base, and witnesses will be trying to report lightning bolts from nowhere. If he uses enough power to lift in a hurry, rather than sneak away, your military will get a fix."

Ghost sounded distracted, still hitting switches. "Our hull is breached, but the flooded compartments are sealed off. Look up Jamie, and tell us how to get close to him without being seen. Quickly, before he sends a drone and finds out we aren't a wreck."

~~

Jamie looked up to see a street map with a big yellow cross, and a smaller one in the river. The smaller one was moving slowly downstream. He leant forward, looking at the control panel and wondering how to tell her where to go, but Ghost was ahead of him. "Just put your finger on the screen, Jamie, and draw the route."

A closer look at the screen explained how Hunter had landed without smashing anything. He'd set down just south of the Wisebuys baseball stadium and Dreamstyle Arena, just across the road from the University Stadium. The rough ground was sometimes used by off-roaders, as there were no buildings or trees. At least the university was shut down for the holidays, and he didn't think there was a game at the baseball stadium.

There'd still be some staff, but the bastard wouldn't be slaughtering hundreds of students or spectators. Running his eyes back and forth, Jamie tried to compare the height of that dome with the taller buildings near the river, and some of them might do the job.

Even so, Jamie hesitated. If Hunter spotted the pod coming up over the bank, then even if Ghost tucked away behind a building, he'd just level it. He'd do that anyway, as soon as Ghost opened fire. Jamie just couldn't do it, put a building with an unknown number of people inside on the firing line. "There's nothing big enough, but you can come up under a bridge, then you can nip out and take a shot. The steel in the bridge might soak up a shot or two."

"This pod has no weapons that can damage Starlight Ghost. Even if we rammed her, we would not breach the armour, but if we can reach the airlock we can open it. Then we will take our ship back or Ghost Claw will die as they should, fighting." Her voice was sombre, with no hint of humour, and when Jamie looked across, her face was set. "This is not your fight, Jamie, so we will set you down first."

~~

He almost agreed, but then Jamie realised—if he let her go

and she died, he'd never get to the stars. He'd live out his life here on Earth, in the Maldives, knowing what was out there, but he'd never be able to tell anyone. If he did, he'd be black-bagged, squeezed dry, and never see daylight again.

Jamie didn't think Ghost was suicidal, so she thought she could win, and if she did it on her own, he would lose—she wouldn't take someone who ran away from a fight. From what she'd said, Ghost Claw were always in trouble, so he'd better start getting used to the idea.

He hesitated for a moment longer, and sniffed, but Ghost hadn't used pheromones so this was free choice. Jamie rethought, but despite the dying thing, Ghost must think she had a decent chance. "Don't be silly. If you get the ship back and it's damaged, where are you going to find another starship mechanic?"

Ghost turned towards him with a blinding smile, and for a moment Jamie thought he saw some relief. "Where is the bridge?"

Jamie reached out, and tried really hard to stop his finger trembling as he drew in the course. The route was easy enough, just stay in the water under one bridge, then levitate under the next one. "There is an island with trees under the bridge. Can the pod still levitate?"

Ghost checked her instrument panel before nodding. "Yes, and the water has dealt with the smoke and cooled the hull. We scanned the bridge we just passed, and there is enough metal to interfere with Hunter's search, unless he takes off to get a better angle or sends a drone. Our deception system is damaged, so we will hope nobody notices a small spaceship stuck to the bottom of the road."

More of the chitter/laugh surprised Jamie. "If we fail, and Hunter leaves without finding the pod, we will be avenged. There will be enough evidence to set real hunters on his trail, eventually, especially with the memory modules we have been dropping."

Within minutes, dirty water was pouring off the screens as the pod shot upwards, then it was among treetops. One screen turned almost black while others showed ironwork or greenery, and one showed tree trunks disappearing downwards. "We have moved all remaining shielding to the bottom half, and with the shadows it might be enough. Nobody will take pictures of anything. Hunter is emitting interference and blocking police communications, but your military will be heading this way."

~~

Jamie didn't care about pictures—he was more worried about how to get out of the pod. "Can we get onto the bridge from here? I thought we could take the bike, blend in with the traffic until we get close."

"There are individual levitation packs, but we will leave the bike here. Starlight Ghost has the images from the news and will be watching for matches." Ghost glanced over and looked worried again. "There used to be protective clothing and weaponry in this pod, but they were removed after we made our mistake, before we escaped. We cannot offer anything to help you against Hunter's weapons, but can provide a radio and translator?"

"Okay." Jamie suddenly realised it might be an internal one, but before he could ask, the lights went out.

He woke up with Ghost cuddling him. That was enough to distract him, so he didn't notice the sore spots on his neck and shoulder straight away. "We are sorry, but there was no time to explain. It will feel strange until the module adapts to your personal DNA, but then you won't feel it." Her hand stroked the back of his neck. "There is a bump just here. Press to turn on the radio, again to turn it off." Her hand moved behind his left ear. "This turns the translator on and off."

Jamie put his hand to the back of his neck and found a small bump, then another one behind his ear. A press on each and when Ghost spoke, he could hear an echo. "There is a small incision at the top of your back, which is sealed. The radio is protected from Hunter's interference unless we move too far apart. It is set to the same frequency we are using, but once it has integrated you will learn to change that. The levitation unit includes a shield to stop anyone seeing you flying, but we will turn them off. Hunter would detect the emissions once we weren't masked by the bridge, which is why your transmitter is turned down, and will only reach about forty feet. Do you feel well enough to continue?"

He would be feeling fine—if Jamie could forget the murderous alien and life-or-death battle. He wasn't keen on a living alien radio in his head, but understood why, and anyway Jamie was more worried about Hunter. He remembered what Ghost said before offering the radio. "You can't help? Does that mean we haven't anything that will get through Hunter's protection?" Jamie stood up, and Ghost helped him as he staggered for a moment, then found his balance.

The short laugh was a relief. "Not quite. He will believe he is safe, even if we get inside the ship, as advanced worlds do not use weapons like yours. His personal shield will be set to deflect beam weapons like the green web and lightning, not physical assault. We believe the shock from the rifle and magnum bullets, and probably the shotgun, will strain a personal emitter. Enough hits will either drain the power pack or blow it."

Ghost's lips were peeled back in a snarl that should have had more teeth. She pressed several buttons on the pod controls, nodded, and stood up. "With you providing a diversion, and both the rifle and magnum, we can overload his shield or get to the airlock. Once inside there are weapons that will definitely break his shield, and then Ghost Claw will not need weapons."

"I can't use the magnum, and Solly only provided twenty jacketed rounds for the rifle." Jamie confessed his main worry.

"I don't know if I can stick a knife in anyone, or shoot in cold blood if Hunter's shield is down." He was talking to Ghost's back as she headed along the corridor past her nest-room.

~~

This room had lockers—they were too near the Earth version to be anything else. Ghost put her hand on one, there was a click, and she opened the door to retrieve two small packs with half a dozen straps. "Use whichever straps you need so it doesn't come off. Take the controller off the side before you fasten it on."

The controller had to be what looked like a small, slim cell phone, with odd letters on the buttons and a strap to go around his wrist. "Do I need straps between my legs?" Jamie didn't fancy that without padding, but didn't want to fall out while the pack flew away.

"No, the unit will include you in the field." Ghost fastened hers around her waist with straps over her shoulders. No buckles, the straps attached to any other strap wherever they touched. "This is so you don't drop it."

Reality poured an iceberg's worth of ice water over Jamie, as he realised what Ghost expected him to do. He had to create a disturbance that fooled an alien with advanced weaponry, using a primitive rifle and a wrench. His mind stuck on one thing—disturbance. "Hang on, I need some of the stuff from my car if you want a real diversion." It didn't take long, since what he wanted had red warning stickers all over them. Jamie came back with one of the rucksacks bought for shopping. "Will the harness work if I carry this?"

She looked curious, but Ghost didn't ask. "Easily, but hang it around your neck, then you can hold a weapon as well as the control. We'll just set the unit to negate your weight, then you only need to move the slider up and down a little. Not too far or you may reach orbit."

There was enough tease in that for Jamie to hope she was

joking. Just in case, he was going to be very careful, and the cord that Ghost fastened to his belt hopefully dealt with steering. Ghost passed him the rifle and two pistols, put the shotgun, ammo, and the wrench into the pack, then opened the hatch to the airlock. She dropped through, but when Jamie tried to put a foot on the ladder, he floated. He heard a chuckle as Ghost pulled the tether and he followed her down.

No stopping—the door opened and they dropped through into open air. Jamie realised what negating weight meant when Ghost stopped pulling. He floated, but not for long. Ghost towed him clear of the bridge, then up and over the railing.

~~

Cars screeched to a halt and a woman screamed, while a dozen people scattered as a man and woman floated down onto the sidewalk. Maybe it was all the weaponry rather than the floating, but either way Ghost used the space to run to a stopped car. She opened the door, pulled the driver out, and slid across his seat to the passenger side.

"Push the control down to use your feet, and hurry." Jamie didn't have any option about hurrying—he was still tied to her. He was careful with the slider, but his feet hit the ground with a thump and he staggered. Diving into the passenger seat, he slammed the door as he took off with a squeal of rubber. Ghost put a hand on his arm. "Slow down and join the other traffic. Drive normally. The ship computer will alert Hunter to any disruption in traffic patterns, especially if it is approaching."

She held up a pad with an overhead view of the university, without any alien ship. "This map shows earth walls here, along the other side." Her finger drew a line on the far side of the big open space. "Park there, and use them as cover when you open fire."

"What will you be doing?" Ghost had the magnum, the long-barrelled pistol, at least four ordinary pistols, and a lot of knives, but the Hunter had that ray gun.

"Surrendering." Startled, Jamie glanced across, and Ghost's lips were peeled back from her teeth in a snarl. "Just until we are near enough. Then your rifle and this magnum will get us through his personal shield, or past him and into the ship. He can't stay in an armoured vehicle if he wants to fit control collars."

Jamie had been worrying about shooting someone in cold blood, but now he remembered the ground car crushing vehicles and blowing up houses. He reminded himself that no matter what Hunter looked like, he was an alien, so not a person, but that didn't work too well. After all, Ghost was an alien, and very much a person.

He'd been driving more or less on auto as he thought, following the traffic, but had a sudden urge to turn off. The road was clearing fast as the vehicles ahead did just that, disappeared down side roads, then Ghost must have noticed. "Follow the traffic, but turn towards some sort of cover so we can sneak up."

~~

Jamie figured that if he wanted to be on the other side of Starlight Ghost, he may as well detour right around it. That way he could sneak up from the other side. Even so, as he drove past a couple of streets, he had to fight an urge to turn away. Something dropped past his eyes and the feeling disappeared. He jerked his eyes over to find Ghost smiling.

She tapped his chest, and Jamie felt something hard. "Sorry, but that was quicker than explaining. The necklace is neutralising the aversion emissions. Hunter has tuned them to deflect indigenes, so that only Ghost Claw can approach." Ghost turned her head towards the ship, her face hardening. "If he is using aversion, he may not bother to monitor indigenes. Make your first shot count."

Jamie remembered the warning about the ship watching

traffic. With the aversion thing clearing the streets, he was able to drive on sidewalks and the wrong side of the road, so he used buildings to mask his approach. "That's as near as I can get. If I accelerate around this corner and down the road, then across the dual highway and into that opening, we'll be where you wanted. It won't take long but we'll be out in the open, so Hunter will have a clear shot." He was sure that anything that damaged the pod, with a hull that could make a crater when it landed but still fly away, would turn the car into a brief firework.

Ghost's voice sounded strained, so maybe she wasn't as certain as her words suggested. "He wants us alive, so he will hold fire. Park so that when we get out, you can crawl out the same door, hidden by that earth wall. Then find a good place to shoot from. Stroke our pelt for luck?" There might have been some tease in that, but she looked hopeful and a little fragile, so Jamie reached out.

"I need all the practice I can get for when I join the crew." Now he was certain she'd been playing games with the length, because her pelt ended around waist-level, clear of her shorts. "Better?"

"Once more, and we should wish you luck as well." This smile was stronger, then as Jamie stroked her pelt again, she connected for a full DNA-stealing kiss. Jamie didn't fight it—he needed all the luck and encouragement he could get. Ghost pulled back, sighed, and then her face set. "Drive." Jamie hit the accelerator.

MEET THE RELATIVES

All the way down the short stretch of road in full view of the ship, then across both highways and into the parking area, Jamie was expecting flame and death—but nothing happened. He ducked down as he pulled up close to the earth bank, and when Ghost got out, he scrambled after her. Dragging his rucksack, he crawled along behind the bank, well clear of Ghost, then eased up to peer between the grass and weeds on the top.

This close, Jamie could see the distortion as the ship tried to divert light, and almost succeeded. He looked up and there simply wasn't anywhere to hide from that thing. From halfway up, a camera would be looking down behind his cover.

The ship's disguise reminded him of something else—unless Hunter turned his gadget off, the alien would be invisible. Even as Jamie wondered how Ghost expected to get into an invisible ship, he heard her, and not just her shouting. He immediately wished he had a volume control for the comms in his head.

"Ghost Claw Clan of the Purple Hills Slashtails challenges the thief in our ship. Come out and fight, coward." When he glanced that way, Jamie saw that she'd taken off the harness, shorts, and top, though she'd kept the belt and boots holding her weapons.

Jamie wondered why she'd done something that stupid. Not the naked thing, that meant sod all to an alien, but the guy in a spaceship wasn't going to come out where she could get to him. When a square hole appeared about thirty feet up, and a fuzzy figure floated out and down, he reassessed.

The fuzzy moved quickly, heading straight towards Ghost,

then stopped and jerked back as the first bullet hit. She ran forward, firing the magnum, and the fuzzy shape flashed as each bullet hit and went back a little. When it flashed brighter and disappeared, it revealed a big metal four-legged shape, a giant K-9.

Maybe not, Jamie conceded, when it reared up onto two legs. It was over nine feet high and maybe five feet wide, a giant robot, but definitely not the tin man from *The Wizard of Oz*. This one tended more towards a Rambo version of C-3PO—or a small Optimus Prime as it had been sprayed all the colours of the rainbow.

It was definitely tough, as the last three magnum rounds knocked it back a couple of steps but bounced. Ghost stopped dead, but before she could move, the robot had caught her arm with a wire lasso. Jamie took careful aim at the robot's head, worried a ricochet might hit her.

~~

"Stupid animals. Did you really think I would risk myself brawling?" Another two aliens were floating down from the opening, one of them holding the other, the purple otterish, by its neck. The bigger one was surrounded by a faint shimmer, but wasn't concealed. Jamie's first impression was of a huge tulip bulb with a harness like his, a smaller bulb upside down on top, and four stubby legs. Where the bulbs met was a frill of half a dozen ribbons, frayed on the ends, though Jamie quickly realised the fraying was small tentacles or fingers. Three 'hands' held the otterish's lead, a pistol of some sort, and a small device with flashing lights.

With a scream of rage, Ghost's human form peeled apart into seven sections, hideously grotesque but already morphing as they shed the lasso, belt, and boots. By the time they landed, long, pale mauve hair was sprouting, and then each one uncurled to reveal furry versions of the purple otterish. They all stood up on their long back legs, and reached for weapons.

The new voice spoke again. "Tenndix, catch Ghost Claw alive, all of them."

The comms in Jamie's head jerked him back to reality. *"Jamie, shoot the Hunter!"* Despite her appearance, Ghost was still in there someplace, and, as the seven creatures grabbed knives or pistols with their front paws, Jamie realised they weren't any sort of otter or meerkat. He also realised that when Ghost kept saying "we," she meant it, but he'd think about that later.

Jamie swung his rifle towards the tulip-bulb type and pulled the trigger, retargeting at the last minute to hit its legs. It wouldn't have mattered, as the shimmer flashed and momentarily became a semi-transparent egg shape protecting the alien. The alien raised its pistol so Jamie dropped and rolled aside. The earth bank glowed green, but only slumped a little so the weapon had limits.

Popping up, Jamie fired at the Hunter again, not too worried where he hit as the glow protected it. Another of the ribbons grabbed a different pistol, so he did the drop and roll again. This time his cover steamed and then cracks appeared, while the weeds burst into flames. Jamie was beginning to see why Ghost told him to use the earth bank as cover.

~~

When he came up again, Jamie hesitated for a moment as a shriek split the air. The dark purple otterish on the lead was thrashing about, presumably in agony. "Surrender, Ghost Claw, or I will kill your male." Any reservations disappeared and Jamie aimed for the little tulip bulb at the top. He assumed it was the head as it had a band around it with flashing lights, and was in the right place, though it crossed his mind he could be wrong.

The glow flashed again, and this time a few sparks flew off it. *"Shoot it again, Jamie, break it."* He glanced towards Ghost and her clan, and the robot had lassoed three of them, and grabbed another as it tried to get past and attack the Hunter. When Jamie looked back at the Hunter, it pointed the flashing box at the bald otterish, which screamed and thrashed about again.

Jamie fired three times before the alien holstered both pistols, and pulled a longer weapon off its back. There were definite sparks, but then Jamie had to duck away as the longer weapon came up. The new weapon didn't seem to have any effect on the earth or weeds, but Jamie felt as if the inside of his skin itched, all of it. It only lasted for a moment, but he didn't want a full dose of that!

The rifle was empty, so Jamie had a few moments to think as he reloaded. He released the magazine and opened a box, and swore. The box said jacketed, but Solly had given him soft lead, presumably so Jamie couldn't shoot holes in the vehicles when he was double-crossed.

Too late now, though now Jamie hoped the shite had been too near the fire bomb. He rammed in five rounds and put the magazine back, then came up and started shooting as fast as he could. There were flashes, but only a few sparks and the alien ignored him, torturing the bald otterish again.

Before he ducked to reload, Jamie glanced towards Ghost Claw Clan. Five of them were lassoed now, around the neck, though two still had knives and were trying to cut themselves free. The others were beating on the lasso or the robot with their big fluffy tails, and clawing at whatever they could reach, but didn't seem to be having any effect.

One of the free ones reloaded the magnum and started shooting at the robot, while the other used one of the other pistols to target Hunter. Only the first shot had any effect. The otterish with the magnum switched to Hunter, but the bullets had no more effect than Jamie's soft-nosed rifle ammo. Solly had switched the magnum ammo in the magazines, all except the first round, the one that Jamie could see.

~~

Jamie dropped and thumbed in fresh rounds, wondering what the hell to do now. The magnum stopped, but he waited for the Slashtail to put in the last magazine. When the first shot rang out, he came up, hoping to combine their fire on one target and overwhelm it. Too late, the robot was brushing aside the bullets and closing fast, another two lassoes snaking out. Jamie fired three times, but the tin man ignored the bullets as a lasso caught a leg, and the robot reeled its last target in.

The robot transferred the lasso to the hand already holding six, then as the last captive came near enough, snatched the gun and tossed it away. The big metal figure made a perfect target as it put a lasso around the Slashtail's neck, and released the leg, but Jamie daren't shoot. He wasn't good enough to be sure he wouldn't hit an ally, either a miss or a ricochet.

Jamie fired the last two at Hunter, who also ignored him, then dropped out of sight. He was wondering if there was anything he could do to help Ghost, then as he reached for more rifle rounds, Jamie remembered why Ghost had bought solid shotgun ammo. It was supposed to be able to bust a car engine block.

Tossing the useless rifle aside, Jamie jacked the shotgun to get rid of the buckshot and fed in five solid rounds. As he did, he could hear the Hunter telling Ghost Claw Clan to surrender and accept control collars, and Ghost refusing. Each time she did, the bald otterish screamed—that decided the target.

The shotgun wouldn't be as accurate as the rifle, but the bottom tulip shape was a big target and only about fifty yards away. The flash, sparks, and alarmed yell after the first shot were gratifying. Jamie started shooting as fast as possible, relieved that he'd taken the Hunter's attention off torture. That might not be good for Jamie's health as both his translator and comms repeated the next instruction. *"Tenndix, secure Ghost Claw and kill the savage."*

~~

A quick glance through a patch of the remaining weeds showed the robot disconnecting the bright yellow arm, the one with all the lassos attached. The hand on the end grabbed hold of the metal railing blocking a gap in the earth bank, and held on despite Ghost Claw's struggling.

Ghost's voice broke into the screaming and yelling. *"Jamie, turn off the radio, or the Mekk-Hive will use it to locate you."*

As Jamie ducked again, he reached for the bump on the back of his neck, then rolled frantically away. Flame spilled over the bank and down his side, much too close—the robot had a flamethrower. He crammed in more rounds, then popped up and fired, shocked to find the robot much closer. The clang of the shot hitting, and the way it went back half a step, were encouraging, but by the third shot it was raising its arm again.

The volume immediately dropped as only the translator passed on Hunter's next words. "What is the problem? It is only a savage."

The robot's 'voice' was unmistakable, literally robotic even through a translator. "My sensors cannot penetrate the earth well enough for accuracy." They were too close for Jamie's comfort, though while they were shouting, the lack of a radio didn't matter.

"You can see smoke from the weapon and locate its noise. Use explosives and then you only need to get close." Bald otterish screamed again, and Hunter switched back to threatening Ghost Claw. "If you do not surrender soon, your male will die, and then Ghost Claw will be finished. Without your clan my employers can gather as many Slashtails as they wish."

"We are our people's knife, but do not think they will be helpless without us." Though Jamie thought he detected some desperation in Ghost's voice. He would have been more interested in what they both meant if he wasn't busy trying not to get killed. Though if the robot was using smoke and noise to locate him, Jamie had just the thing—road flares.

He'd thrown them into the rucksack when Ghost said she'd need a diversion, then forgotten them once the shooting started. The bigger ones were used for crashes during road-racing, and between the ones from his car and his wrecked racer, and spares, he had fourteen. There was even a gun and a few distress flares for starting races, or stopping them if there was a big pile-up.

~~

Jamie put his hand in his pack and felt around for a road flare and the flare gun. He pulled the tab and threw the road flare along the ground, then aimed the gun as low as possible and pulled the trigger. The flare skipped along the ground until the parachute kicked in. The road flare had started smoking by then, so Jamie popped up, and when he saw the robot turn away, emptied the shotgun at Hunter.

He missed at least once, but the sparks and the glow were impressive, then Jamie had to roll away before the robot got him. The earth glowed and as the assault continued, the bank melted and half-slumped as lava flowed down the sides. While it did, he reloaded and listened to Hunter berate the robot and threaten Ghost Claw. Otterish screamed as the next flares went off, and when he popped up behind a low bush Jamie saw why.

Hunter was using a gun on the otterish, presumably low-power as it wasn't fatal, but it was obviously very painful. The robot was melting the bank near the road flare so Jamie emptied the shotgun at Hunter, and this time the shield popped. There was no time to celebrate or take advantage—the robot had given up on hand weapons. As it turned, the light blue right arm shortened and thickened, and the palm it aimed at Jamie had a big hole.

Jamie rolled towards the flare, hoping to fool the robot, but he hadn't got far when earth flew everywhere. Something punched right through the earth bank, leaving a trail of smoke right across the road before blowing a hole in a building. The metallic voice blared out. "Using these weapons will attract investigators."

Jamie didn't think Hunter cared, and the alien confirmed it. "There will be no evidence of who we are. Why didn't that blow it up?" At least the alien sounded harassed, and the otterish's screams had changed. They were less like pain and more like Ghost's rage. Jamie had finished pushing rounds into his shotgun, so he fired a flare past the gap, then another. He came up slowly, sliding the barrel through a clump of grass and weeds, cautious. The robot was moving away at an angle now, the other side of the gap as it turned towards the smoke from the pair of flares.

He had all the time in the world to shoot, but Jamie couldn't. The purple otterish had leapt on Hunter, even though the growls were mixed with screams of pain as lights flashed on that box. Two pistols were on the ground and it was fighting for another, the pair of them twisting and turning so Jamie might hit the wrong one. That left one target.

The shotgun rounds had knocked the robot back, but the detached hand was around a metal tube. It couldn't move so it would take the full force, like hitting metal that was on an anvil. Jamie ignored everything else, including the chance he might hit Ghost, as he aimed and fired—and missed. He didn't even check on the robot, though the sound of an explosion was reassuring—Jamie moved the barrel down just a little and fired again. Hit! The hand let go and the arm fell to the ground.

~~

He aimed again, wanting to break it, but Ghost's voice rang out. "Look out Jamie, the Mekk-Hive is coming!"

Jamie dropped and rolled frantically, further than he wanted to as the explosion was near enough to give him a boost, but he held onto the shotgun. He lost the pack, but an open box of ammo landed nearby, spilling rounds. Buckshot, but

Jamie didn't have any options. He threw the road flare in his hand towards the site of the explosion, then heard Hunter. "Tenndix, help me."

Hunter's call, and the rising chorus of growls and snarls, nearly killed Jamie as he popped up to see what was happening. Ghost Claw were free, and the first three were swarming Hunter, wielding knives and thrashing it with their tails. The tails tore lines into Hunter's skin or bark, which spouted dark brown liquid—Slashtails! Tenndix was looking right at Jamie, with that cannon or rocket launcher aimed right at him, but when Hunter called, it turned away.

Jamie fired at the robot anyway—if it reached the fight Ghost Claw would lose. Most of the buckshot probably missed, but when a few from the second shell hit it, the robot stopped dead. Jamie fired again but it didn't move, so he looked towards Hunter. He was just in time to see it levitate up towards the opening, knocking two Slashtails free.

The Hunter's belt, weapons, and that flashing box were scattered around on the ground, so it was running away. Some of the Slashtails were hugging bald otterish, but others picked up guns. The weapons didn't fire, but the Slashtails did something and when they tried again, Hunter screamed in pain. Only for a moment—it was near enough to lunge into the airlock and the opening began to close.

~~

Two groups of three Slashtails rose into the air to follow, leaving one laid on the ground, so Jamie ran forward. He might not be much good in the fight, but he had a levitation unit. He could give it to the bald otterish, since it could obviously fight but the others had taken the harnesses. As he ran, Jamie watched that opening. Once it closed, Hunter could take off, so if he saw a hint of a glow or smoke, Jamie was running for the earth bank. Then he'd have to hope the rockets didn't fry him.

The door closed before the Slashtails reached it, but they

clustered to one side, and after a few moments it began to open again. Those with weapons began shooting through the gap, bullets and ray guns, and the translator meant Jamie understood Hunter's yell. "No! How?" The next yell was pain, from further into the ship as Slashtails scrambled through the gap, shooting as they went.

Ghost's voice rose above the rest. "Spread out, find control panels. It doesn't matter what, doors or hull armament, get into the software and seize control of as much as you can. Drive Hunter into a corner and pin it so we can finish it." The last Slashtail went in through the almost-open door and their voices faded, interspersed by the clang of metal, shots, and yells.

Jamie had finally reached bald otterish. It had a lot of cuts and burns, enough to put a human in intensive care, but was on its hind legs, shouting at the ship. The translator struggled, but the gist was that it wanted to disembowel Hunter, slowly, and feed him his own entrails.

~~

The furry mauve shape laid nearby wasn't moving, so Jamie called to the bald purple creature. "Er, hello? I'm Jamie."

The otterish turned, and sniffed. "Ghost Claw know our kin, Jamie. Our thanks." The voice had hints of Ghost, but definitely wasn't. "My name is Rend."

"Hi, er, Rend." Jamie gestured to his harness. "I'm not much of a fighter, so do you want this or are you out of the fight?"

"Never." Rend's answer was nearly impossible to understand through the growl and the bared, sharp teeth. All the Slashtails had heads that looked too large for their bodies, to Jamie's eyes, and the short, wide muzzle looked as if it had a hell of a bite. "If I hold, you lift us both. Gratitude." With that Jamie was up-close and personal with a bald purple alien, with what he could now see were hands, and a long-toed foot, firmly gripping his harness. Rend's tail was stuck straight out, clear of Jamie, to his great relief—as he came past the robot, he'd seen all the scratches and gouges in its paintwork.

"Right. It'll be slow because I've never done this before." He'd hardly spoken when Rend's other foot reached for the control, and they both shot upwards. Ghost Claw had ambidextrous hand-feet.

As they landed in the entrance, Rend's hand unclipped the harness and dropped it out of the ship. "Hunter will not escape. Clan feud, to the death." With that the bald Slashtail staggered to the other two belts and tossed them out. It reached out to pull a knife from Jamie's belt. "You have a weapon to hurt Hunter. I will find more."

Before Jamie could answer, Rend turned and limped/tottered towards a screen and controls beside the door. Jamie looked down at his shotgun and shrugged—it only had two shots left. He cheered up as he remembered the pistols, and cautiously looked through an open door in the back wall. The corridor was empty, so he ran to the end and peered around the corner, both ways.

~~

As he made his way deeper into the ship, Starlight Ghost was like Jamie expected, but also totally different. Spaceships were always depicted with metal corridors, either all welds, rust, and rivets, or smooth, neatly painted ones with pastel colours and soft lights. These corridors had started out the blatantly metal type, with door frames and equipment bolted or welded on, but had been painted so there wasn't any rust or dust.

He thought the base coat had been cream, but now hatches, bolt heads, or sometimes whole walls were painted bright colours. The continuous lines of colour probably helped Slashtails to navigate, but the rest had to be decoration. There was no theme, and sometimes the colours clashed, but what really threw Jamie was the graffiti.

The translator tried to tell him what the wording meant, but he didn't always need it. The graffiti was art of varying quality, from cartoons to lifelike depictions of Slashtails, all fighting or hunting with alien weapons or sharp steel. One was a huge creature peeling apart into Slashtails, at least thirty of them even though half of it was still splitting, and another had a horde of mauve Slashtails swarming over a wall, waving alien guns. There was also a bewildering variety of scenery behind the figures, presumably different planets.

Jamie thought the mishmash might be because this was a lower deck, so it didn't matter. He found a box with the door open, and a row of buttons—it couldn't be anything but an elevator so Jamie poked the top button. The doors slammed shut and it rocketed upwards, which was when he remembered Ghost's opinion of rules and safety measures. He swayed and grabbed the wall as it stopped, and the doors slammed open.

Hunter was there! It was running towards him along a corridor painted with underwater scenery, faster than those stumpy feet should allow, and had definitely been in a fight. Half its harness had been torn away, so it couldn't fly away, and Jamie thought there were less ribbon-arms. There were definitely more cuts, burns, and holes in its skin.

Hunter stopped dead. "The savage?" A ribbon curled, bringing around a pistol that had been aiming back along the passage, but Jamie hadn't hesitated.

~~

He nearly lost the shotgun as he didn't raise or brace it against the recoil, but that meant the buckshot hit before the alien weapon was lined up. At short range, aiming wasn't a problem, and nine holes appeared in the bottom tulip bulb. Hunter made a low grunting noise and spun halfway around, which gave Jamie time to raise the gun and aim at the top bulb. The flash was disappointing—Hunter's head had its own shield, though Jamie got second prize.

Some of the shot hit the ribbons, and the weapon fell to the deck. A ribbon elongated to retrieve the gun, so Jamie snatched out his pistol and opened fire. He'd never be sure if he hit the limb, but the target was in front of Hunter so every shot hit its body. The alien was tough, because it didn't go down, though after the seventh it ran off, staggering and bouncing off the walls.

Jamie kept shooting so Hunter kept running, around the corner and out of sight even when the pistol ran out of bullets. Jamie was relieved. He wasn't a knife or wrestling type—especially with something a head taller and twice as wide.

Another elevator flew open and a Slashtail leapt out. "Jamie!" That was Ghost's voice. "I heard you shooting. Did you get it?"

"Yes, but I ran out of bullets. It ran off down there and turned left." He didn't get a chance to say more.

"Turn on your comms." Ghost pounced on the dropped alien weapon, and plugged in a wire from a belt around her waist. It beeped, and she smeared a cut onto a panel at the side, then grabbed Jamie's hand. Before he could object, she nipped his finger, smeared the panel, and then put his finger to her cut. "Now it will work for you. Don't keep the trigger down too long or you will damage the walls."

She tapped her cut with a long, clawed finger. "I will smear this on a main panel when I find one, so the ship knows you. My blood on your finger should activate most weapons you find." The chittering after that had more than a hint of manic adrenaline junky. "You should stroke my pelt, fair return for the DNA?"

Despite her appearance, the combination of scent and her pelt ran over any reservations and Jamie stroked her. "My thanks. I will fix these elevators so Hunter cannot go higher, and if he tries, he will end up on the airlock level." Ghost plugged her belt into each elevator in turn, then raced off down the passage, drawing a short, fat pistol. "Come on!"

Jamie didn't even try to keep up. A quick experiment showed that his new pistol 'fired' jagged lightning bolts, leaving scorch marks on the paintwork, which was reassuring. He held his second human pistol in his left hand and headed towards the sound of shouting and screaming, checking each corner in case Hunter was coming back this way.

~~

Jamie could never really piece together the fight—it was hide-and-seek with weapons over dozens of floors and what seemed like miles of corridors. At least he knew he wasn't going in circles, because all the walls had different scenes on them, some with living creatures and others showing planets from space. He could hear the Slashtails reporting as they took over more and more of the ship, and soon realised the master plan. They had closed down the internal defences so the ship wouldn't shoot anyone, and then concentrated on doors.

The references were meaningless, so Jamie had no idea which doors were locked, but when he found the first one he couldn't open, he realised it didn't matter. He was being herded the same way as Hunter, so he'd find the fight sooner or later. Remembering what Ghost was doing to the elevators, he used one. Just as she said, it didn't matter what button he pressed—when the door opened, he'd found the fight.

Not directly, luckily, but the sheer volume of shouting and shooting from one direction was a big signpost. He checked each corner, but when he reached the entrance airlock, Jamie wasn't in any danger. Hunter was too busy trying to hide or shoot the Slashtails, who were all more accurate than Jamie.

He got one more good look at a decidedly battered-looking pair of tulip-bulbs, but the sheer volume of fire meant he'd never know if he hit it with either weapon. Hunter's last weapon fell, and moments later it was buried in shrieking, snarling, biting, clawing purple fur. When the furry tide drew back, they left an inert lump leaking light brown liquid from most of its surface. Some of the wounds reminded Jamie of the road ambush, and wondering about chainsaws, but now he knew what caused them.

There was brownish liquid on most of the tails, but he still couldn't see how they inflicted damage—he sure as hell wasn't stroking one to find out. As the Slashtails formed a tight group, they began to sing, and he realised that Rend, the bald one, wasn't moving. They all cuddled and stroked it, then one detached and came towards Jamie. It looked like all the rest, but the voice meant it was Ghost.

"We did not realise how badly Rend had been hurt by Hunter, or we would not have allowed him to fight. Though he was Ghost Claw, so perhaps we couldn't have stopped him anyway." She sighed, a very human-like sound, and Jamie realised that unlike human translation devices, this one retained her individual human voice.

"Can't you, you know?" Jamie brought his hands together. "Join, or blend, or is it too late?"

"Too late for an intensive care pod, and we cannot meld as Rend is what you would call our male." She sounded defeated, and maybe it was the voice, the scent, or just sympathy but Jamie reacted without thinking—he hugged her. Ghost's head only came part-way up his chest so he knelt, and stroked her head and down her back, then froze. He'd just realised the 'hands' on his back had long claws, the mouth breathing onto his ear had sharp teeth, and he might have just done something really offensive.

~~

The gentle hug in return was a relief, as was the half-chitter-laugh, half-sob. "Thank you, Jamie. We might kidnap you before we leave, as a pelt-stroker." Her voice sounded uncertain. "Would you greet the rest of your kin, stroke their pelts?"

"No problem. After all, I guess I already did that, sorta." That would take some getting used to, but now wasn't the time. Maybe it was some sort of mental communication, because even though Ghost didn't call them, the other five Ghost Claw gathered around. As they did, Jamie realised where his wriggly furry dreams came from—Ghost must have split in the night.

Ghost's voice murmured in his ear. "Not all our pelt, this form has a Slashtail." He'd remembered, sort-of, but had become used to stroking her pelt to the end so it was a timely reminder. Ghost Claw were helping—all the tails were straight out away from Jamie. He tried to share the stroking, but then realised the wriggling was partly so they rotated to get a share, and to rub against each other.

With them all together like this he could see that some were slimmer, or had thinner faces or were taller. Ghost was definitely the biggest, both height and weight even if she would be very slim without the fur, maybe more ferretish. As they hugged him and each other they murmured their names, and he began to fit them to features. Ghost was actually Nightclaw, while Quicktail was the smallest and Shortfang had one shorter tooth.

~~

An alarm, and a speaker relaying a demand that the aliens surrender and give up their robot, broke up the hug-fest. Ghost, because Jamie couldn't get his head around Nightclaw just yet, sent four Slashtails to finish taking control of Starlight Ghost. She went to answer the demand, and to collect Tenndix. Even if he'd recovered, the robot couldn't resist the ship's weapons or grav-lifter.

Jamie was left to keep Quicktail company as she stood vigil over Rend's body, as that needed two Ghost Claw clan members. Despite a blistered stripe across her chest and a sling on her arm, she was armed to the teeth, presumably in case Hunter miraculously recovered. While they waited, the shortest Slashtail explained that Cutvoice's body would be brought up as well, to join Rend. Ghost Claw dead were always escorted by two of their kin, and they were the least able of the survivors.

Although Ghost had said he was part of the clan, Jamie had thought it was at least partly a tease. Now he found that Quicktail treated him as if he had fur and a tail, as Ghost Claw, though as she pointed out, his education and claws needed work. She seemed to think he was coming with them, as a pelt stroker at least, and that had a hint of Ghost's teasing. When she turned towards the airlock door, he understood the least able comment. Quicktail had a savage wound on her leg, a partly-cauterised gouge, and a long, sheathed weapon strapped to it as a splint.

When the airlock door opened, Jamie got a shock. There were three gunships in sight, hovering near enough for him to see they were carrying missiles. Moments later an invisible elevator brought Cutvoice, the dead Slashtail from the fight below, and deposited her in the entrance. By the time he'd carried her to join Rend, the invisible elevator had deposited the levitation harnesses and various weaponry that had been left down there.

That included Jamie's pack, rifle, and the scattered ammo, so he reloaded the shotgun and pistol. They might not stop the robot when it arrived, but the shotgun would knock it back until Quicktail got the right weapon lined up. Jamie's comms told him not to worry; the internal weaponry was back under control. *"Keep clear if the Mekk-Hive moves or you might be injured."*

A clicking noise was a long-barrelled weapon up on the roof lining up, then a panel whirred up and a squat weapon slid out. Jamie stopped worrying about the robot, or not a robot, according to the message. "Quicktail, what's a Mekk-Hive?"

The Slashtail inspected Tenndix, then pointed a pistol with

coils around the barrel at the yellow arm laid on its own. “If that moves, electrocute it with Hunter’s gun. Mekk-Hives are a collection of independent entities who have transferred most of their life support into tech. They combine for mutual advantage and defence, but can change shape and operate on their own.”

Jamie put his shotgun down and pulled out the alien weapon. “So that arm can do what, crawl off on its own?”

The chitter was definitely humour. “It can change shape, dramatically, and then will have wheels, tracks or anti-grav, and at least one weapon. From the colours this is a ten-fold hive, it has ten members, and the Slashtail translation of its name means ten-ten. The entities rely on computers for memory and most decisions, but the speck of bio means they are people, not machines.”

~~

The discussion was interrupted by a much larger Slashtail, with Ghost’s voice. She paused when she saw Jamie’s face and shook her head. “No, we have not combined. I have taken on mass to deal with the human authorities, as experience suggests primitive societies do not take small entities seriously. They have agreed to a one-hour delay. I must go and add more weight while the others secure our prisoner.”

The four Slashtails who followed her carried manacles, chains, a mesh helmet, and a long mesh coat. As Ghost disappeared back into the ship, the manacles fastened the Mekk-Hive’s detached yellow arm to the light blue one, at the wrist, and the dark green ankle to the scarlet right ankle. The mesh helmet was dropped over the bright pink head and tightened at the neck, then thin chains tightened it across the white optics and speaker grille.

Thicker chains tightened the mesh coat against the light acid-green upper-left chest, the reddish-brown upper-right chest, the black midriff, and the orange hips. As the Slashtails drew back, Jamie had to ask. "Can't it, they, change shape and wriggle out?"

"They could." Quicktail's humour meant that wasn't likely, then she gestured to the big squat weapon. "The Tickler, the atomic exciter, is a cousin to the green ray, and affects any type of matter. It really does tickle at first, then it vibrates any bio into sludge. If the Tickler is turned up far enough, and keeps going long enough, it can reduce anything to a puddle of exotic alloys and chemicals."

A scrape of metal and then a loud click attracted Jamie's attention, and Quicktail explained. "Once everything is attached, and activated, the current freezes all the external plates in position."

The other four were pulling a floating machine of some sort, attached to the wall by a thick cable, and they set it down next to the Mekk-Hive. A variety of thicknesses of wires were clipped to the restraints until they were all attached, then one turned to Jamie. "Our new kin should throw the switch."

Another broke in. "Why? We did more damage to it." This one sounded grumpy, annoyed.

Quicktail cut in. "Shortfang is right, Sourspit. Jamie should have the honour. He broke Hunter's shield, then freed us, and offered himself as a target to keep the Mekk-Hive distracted."

Rather than argue, the grumpy one, Sourspit, produced a short bow that Jamie recognised. It was the same as Ghost's when she agreed Pills could live. "That is just. The honour is yours, Jamie. You should have a proper name."

The Slashtail still sounded grumpy, but wasn't arguing, so maybe it was just the way she talked. Jamie returned the bow. "Thank you. What do I do?"

Five long clawed fingers pointed, and five voices chorused. "Press the big red button!" From the chittering that was a Slashtail joke, and considering the usual results of pressing big red buttons in movies, Jamie could relate. He pressed it, stepping back smartly as sparks flew, and a ripple of lights ran across the front. The Mekk and restraints glowed, just faintly, so he assumed it was working.

~~

The other Slashtails left Jamie and Quicktail to their vigil, scattering back into the ship. They were joking about giving Jamie a proper name, with Peltstroker the favourite before they went too far to hear. He was sure those weren't their real names, just the translator's approximation, though Shortfang's must relate to her tooth.

Thinking about the names made it obvious there weren't many to operate a ship this size, though Tenndix and Hunter must have done so. "How big a crew does Starlight Ghost need?"

"Four can move Starlight Ghost from place to place, but fighting the ship needs a minimum of a hundred. Ghost Claw Clan was fifteen hundred strong, as we needed many fighters, and operators for our landers, flyers, and other mobile weaponry." The Slashtail's voice was thick with grief, and she paused for a few moments. "Many died when we were betrayed and captured, using gas so those who survived awoke wearing control collars."

The paw up to her neck was probably involuntary. "For a short time, we obeyed without fighting, but only until we were ready. Ghost Claw are nobody's slaves! But we were unarmed, and many were killed before they could close with the enemy. More died to make way for our escape, while others fell to delay the pursuit, and even more as we fled. Too many, but if we had reached home, we would have bred back eventually. Now our male is dead."

He didn't want to ask, but Jamie had to. "Are there no other Slashtail males on your world?"

As the silence stretched out, he began to think he wasn't getting an answer, but Quicktail must have been thinking.

"You are clan, so you should know. There are very few Slashtail males, as the longevity treatment killed most. Not immediately, that was not apparent until many years later, too late to save them."

This pause lasted long enough for Jamie to consider telling her to drop it, but then Quicktail continued. "Ghost Claw Clan is different, so no male will join us voluntarily, even if their clan would allow it. Each clan holds their males close, safe from any cull, as the other effect of the treatment is that no males have been produced since."

~~

Jamie couldn't answer at first—the sheer scale of the tragedy struck him dumb. He thought of almost every human male dying, and Earth's countries would do the same, jealously guard any they had. There'd probably been clan wars. "I'm sorry for asking, and for Ghost Claw, and all Slashtails."

"You are clan. You must know." Quicktail took a deep breath, and changed the subject. "We remember very little from the meld, as Nightclaw is dominant. As we split, we are gifted impressions of what happened, as if it had been a dream. Some things make a stronger impression. Pelt stroking is better when we are me instead of us, and even Sourspit might laugh if she rides a motorbike."

She was trying hard so Jamie went with it, trying to add some humour. "Can all Ghost Claw do that, the melding thing? Apart from me. I can't even manage a little patch of purple pelt."

The chittering laugh was a welcome response. "That will take a long time, or we could inject you. Then it would be over in tens of days, but you would be ill and might die. The kissing method is slower but safer, though melding could take hundreds of your years. We can all meld, but must have a dominant to lead, to take control of the shape and thinking."

The Slashtail concentrated, and the back of one hand lost

the fur and changed colour, slowly until it looked more like human skin. "Each one can change to any creature if we have the information, the biological pattern, and there is a freezer full of preserved samples for if we need a particular form. We can take on bulk if necessary, by eating a large amount of meat. If it has a similar makeup to whatever we want to be, that helps. Any indigenous creature on a planet is usually near enough to help with copying any other. Your cows are close enough to human for Nightclaw to use for adding bulk, now she has your pattern."

That rang a big alarm bell for Ratter. "Is that what Ghost, er, Nightclaw, is doing now, trying to pass as human?"

"Yes. Primitives usually prefer dealing with someone familiar."

"Not on Earth." Jamie realised he still didn't know how to transmit. "Can you warn her, please? No problem with being larger, but we need to talk before she chooses a shape." By the time Ghost arrived, now the mauve-haired human version, Quicktail had taught Jamie to transmit, but everyone would hear. Changing the channel, or even the volume, would take practice, and there wasn't time.

Because Ghost's plan might not kill him, but Jamie might be the only human left.

GOODBYE EARTHLINGS

The big smile from Ghost was familiar, and welcome. "All the humans we saw seemed to like this form, so why can't I use it to talk to the general or the president?" Her shorts and bikini top had been rescued with everything else, which made the number of cuts, burns, and bruises obvious.

Jamie though he'd need a stretcher and a lot of painkillers, but although she moved carefully, Ghost didn't seem to be in pain. She was well enough to tease. "Perhaps with less clothes, but I thought that was inappropriate?" At least that settled one thing, the copy's personality had always been Ghost, or Nightclaw, and not a mix.

Instead of reacting to the teasing, Jamie thought about how to explain. "If you appear like that, the general and the five hundred hidden experts watching the exchange will think you are human. No matter what you say, they'll assume you are from a rival nation. Everyone will be trying to work out which one rather than actually listening to what you say."

He didn't pay much attention to global politics, but Jamie knew there'd been several moments when mankind almost wiped themselves out. The latest had been before Jamie was born, near Russia in a country called Ukraine, and there were still people who remembered it. "Once they think they've narrowed it down, worked out which country sent you, they'll demand you surrender. If you stop their attack, they'll threaten your home country, or so they'll believe. That country will go on alert and threaten to retaliate, then the reason will leak and other governments will go on alert. Eventually, someone will launch the first missile, and start a nuclear war."

"But nuclear weapons won't damage Starlight Ghost. Why would you destroy your own planet?" Ghost looked at Quicktail, obviously baffled, but the Slashtail didn't have an answer.

Jamie tried again. "If this ship was built on Earth, a nuke would work. They'll use one if you don't surrender and nothing else works, but hopefully not until you are a lot higher. I don't think they'll sacrifice Albuquerque. I hope not." Jamie stopped dead, and reassessed. "The USA and allies won't, but others might." Which would kill Shania, he realised, and wondered if he could warn her in time, or get her aboard.

Though Ghost still hadn't gotten the message. "That might destroy satellites, but apart from an uptick in radiation levels, won't hurt anything else."

There wasn't time to get Shania clear of a nuke, so Jamie concentrated on persuading Ghost she shouldn't annoy the US Army. "It will hurt humans. There aren't many nations with nukes but some have hundreds, and they're all poised, ready to retaliate if one of the others attacks. They know it'll knock mankind back to the Stone Age, but if someone lets one off, the rest might not wait to see why."

He shrugged as he remembered something his brother-in-law once said about nukes. "According to nearly everyone we're wrecking the planet anyway, but I'd rather not speed things up."

Jamie stopped as a light bulb went off in his brain. If Ghost would agree, he might do some good, give humanity a reason to try a bit harder. "I know you can copy a person you see on a movie. How about nearly copying a human's version of an alien?"

"We have twenty of your minutes. Do these human aliens wear clothes as well?" The smile knew they would.

~~

Twenty minutes later, Jamie, Quicktail, and the bodies were

to one side of a carefully staged set, where they wouldn't be seen by either the cameras or through the open door. With luck he wouldn't be needed, but just in case, he had three screens. One showed what Ghost could see through the door, one was the picture coming in, and the third showed what she transmitted.

Ghost wore a pale lemon night-nest cover, a sheet that covered everything but her eyes, and shaded those. She must have contacted Sourspit, as the airlock door opened. The screen that was receiving messages had a logo on it, the USA seal, and for the last five minutes, Starlight Ghost had transmitted a similar design. The Slashtail version used the colourful winged alien Jamie had seen, and the wording around the edge read United Civilised Entities in one of the common galactic languages. The English translation was across the bottom of the screen.

Now the screen showed a cloaked Ghost, with a chained Tenndix behind and to the left, and Hunter's body behind and to the right. Beyond them was the open airlock, with four gunships in the distance. The other screen switched to a man in uniform, sat at a desk with a little Stars and Stripes on one corner. He covered his mouth for a moment, and shortly afterwards one gunship rose up, and then moved back into place. Jamie understood his doubts—from the gunships, it would look as if a door had opened in mid-air.

Jamie whispered to Quicktail, who transmitted to Ghost's internal com, in Slashtail in case the humans had managed to hack it. "Good. Now he's sure it's live and thinks you are vulnerable." Not according to the Slashtails, even though there'd be a LOT of missiles locked onto the opening. "Start."

"Greetings, Earthling. We apologise for the transgressions of the criminal who invaded your world. He is dead, and his war machine is being taken to a specialised facility for decommissioning."

The glances to the side had to be the general looking for the reaction of his experts. He was good—there'd been no hint of surprise. His eyes centred on the screen, and Ghost. "We demand the, the war machine, and the body so we can ascertain if it really is an alien. Your ship killed several people with a lightning ray, then injured more when it blew up a building. We expect you to turn over whoever was responsible for trial."

Jamie didn't speak—the rehearsed replies covered that, more or less, and Ghost was definitely smart enough to improvise a little. "If you tried to dismantle the war machine, a considerable area of your world would become uninhabitable. We apologise for the deaths, injuries, and destruction inflicted by this spaceship, the criminal's human Hellbat mercenaries, and the assault vehicle.

She gestured towards Hunter's body. "One of our citizens was captured when that criminal stole the ship, but escaped when it reached your planet, so the criminal tried to kill them. The ship has now been recovered by a special operations team of races suited to Earth's gravity and atmosphere, and the citizen has been rescued. Our operatives were careful not to harm any humans, though some groundworks nearby were damaged."

The general was speaking as soon as Ghost finished, so he'd been ready for a refusal. "Show your face. Witnesses saw two humans hijack a car, and now it's parked next to your ship. The alien excuse isn't going to work, so who sent you?"

Jamie had hoped the two hadn't been connected, but there was a plan. "Show them the fakes."

~~

Ghost ignored the general's last question, concentrating on the identification. "Our operatives were disguised as humans, their appearance based on pictures found on your news services. Our laws forbid showing our true selves or advanced technology on primitive planets, as it can cause alarm."

The shrug was exaggerated enough to be clear under the loose covering. "Now I have a problem. We are meant to individually adjust the memories of witnesses, but your media means billions have seen too much. Adjusting those numbers would require a task force, at a significant cost, so standard operating procedure in such cases is a mass mindwipe. The same applies to electronic records. The costs of removing specific evidence would be prohibitive, so we would blank it all."

The shrouded figure began pacing, three paces one way then six the other, then six back again. "Written or printed media is immaterial, as Earthlings would forget how to read, and the more susceptible would forget language, and perhaps how to walk." Ghost paused, but not long enough for a reply, and then sighed. "Even if your race recovers, you would take centuries to reach this level again. That does not seem fair, as this situation was not caused by an Earthling, but the rules are clear. I have no option, unless—"

Stopping suddenly, Ghost turned to face the camera and leant forward, her eyes narrowed. "I would be taking a risk, personally, but Earthlings are so close to true civilisation that I am willing to take a chance. Even so I must insist on two things. The first is that the whole incident must be dismissed as a hoax. Then, if you can assure me the pictures will be destroyed immediately afterwards, I can prove that your witnesses did not see humans."

"I agree." That came without the general checking anything, and Jamie wanted to shout liar.

"One moment please." Behind Ghost, rough copies of Jamie and Ghost, a little larger than life-size and dressed as they had been for the attack, walked into view. They turned their backs. "I am sure the cameras on your primitive flying machines can see these are not humans." The two figures fuzzed for a moment, then sharpened again, and now they had weapons belts, some armour, and backpacks.

When the two figures turned back, one was a wrinkly, red-skinned eight-foot bipedal with a large fanged mouth and four compound eyes, two on the sides of its head so it could see backwards. The other had a slit sprouting two large fangs in a smooth head with large white eyes, perched on a short, smooth tube covered in short, light blue fur. Five short, barbed tentacles sprouted from each 'shoulder,' while ten longer tentacles at the bottom held it off the ground, though two were holding big brutal blades. The rest of their weapons, apart from blades, were nothing like human, and included Jamie's pistol with all the coils.

Shortfang and Oneless had created the human versions, using the backpack shields that Hunter and Tenndix used to pass as policemen. They'd also stuffed themselves with meat, then visited the hold for suitable 'combat alien' patterns for when the disguise was turned off. Ghost gestured. "As I explained, combat specialists."

This time the general couldn't hide a flinch, maybe at the thought of his soldiers meeting either creature. He quickly recovered. "And yourself?"

~~

As Ghost began speaking, Jamie crossed his fingers. "Please do not jump to conclusions. From images in your media, some visitors in the past may have been careless with memory adjustment." Ghost, or Jamie, was hoping at least one watcher was a Trekkie, and then that the experts jumped to the right conclusions—a visitor had been spotted at some time.

She removed her covering to reveal a figure that would be familiar to a *Star Trek* fan. Ghost had copied a picture of T'Pol, the female Vulcan, then altered her but kept the face and figure very close to the original. She wore a quickly-created loose top and trousers in a silky yellow, and the clothing wasn't the only difference. This version's eyes had horizontal slit pupils, as close inspection of the film would show, while her hair was a short purple Mohican, an adapted pelt.

When Ghost turned, she had a long braid, but the sides of her head, and her pointed ears, were clearly visible. The last touch was her skin—it was light green, which hadn't been obvious with her hood shadowing the small strip showing around her eyes. Jamie had giggled when he suggested it, pointing out that little green men was a common term for aliens. She turned back and smiled, showing a neat set of pale pink pointed teeth, a stark contrast to her dark green lips. "Are you satisfied?"

The general was definitely thrown, but he had his own script. "That proves nothing. It could be faked."

Ghost frowned, just enough to show she was getting impatient, or annoyed. "Ask your flying machines to fire their weapons at me. Their missiles as well. Please move all humans clear as our shields will not protect them."

She smiled again, but this time with more teeth and it wasn't friendly. "Or we could cause enough damage to force them to land, or vaporise one? Please understand we are being polite. Your weapons cannot harm us and we can leave whenever we wish, but I felt sorry for you. I have no wish to reduce your race to ignorant savages. I would rather explain your race's options, encourage you to advance and prosper."

The general wasn't conceding she could leave, or damage his gunships, but he had to ask. "What options?" Jamie and Ghost both thought that he'd be expecting threats.

~~

Instead, he would get Jamie's parting gift to his planet. "Please give me your word this information will never become public knowledge, as it may cause alarm."

"This discussion will remain a national secret." Jamie was sure the general and his handlers meant that. He was also stone certain the entire discussion, including the movie, would be sold to several countries and media outlets, and probably be dumped anonymously on the internet.

Ghost paused, then sighed and her shoulders slumped just a little. Jamie hoped the watchers concluded she was reluctant, perhaps worried that she could get into trouble. "Despite your advances, your world is still considered primitive, but all civilised races pass through a similar phase. Normally they are left alone until they learn better, or destroy themselves, but I believe we owe you something for the damage and loss of life. Earth is capable of reaching the minimum requirements within decades, if humans were to concentrate on doing so, and then you will be invited to join the civilised worlds."

From the way the general's eyes were moving, there were at least six screens or people feeding him information or prompts. Even so, there could only be one answer. "What minimum requirements?"

On their screens the alien figure straightened a little, which should be read as recovering her confidence. "The cessation of wars, one planetary government, and due care for the planetary environment and its flora and fauna. Nuclear weapons and biological warfare must be abolished before you can even be considered."

Ghost made a casual throwaway gesture. "There will be benefits of course, such as advanced tech, better medicines, and longevity… perhaps immortality for some. Trade and tourism, so there will be weaponry to defend the planet, more powerful than yours but with little or no side effects. The types are strictly controlled, and preclude any that damage the ecosystem."

With a short bow, Ghost finished. "I have already said too much, but I have lived seventeen hundred of your years, and seen too many races fail and fall into barbarism or extinction. Please ensure any record is destroyed. Do not try to prevent our leaving, as your citizens may be harmed by mistake." She raised a hand which only had two thick fingers and a thumb, so it looked like the Vulcan gesture on *Star Trek*. "Live long and prosper."

The camera cut out, the airlock door began to close, and sure enough the gunships opened fire and launched everything. Jamie couldn't look as he'd have been seen, and anyway he wasn't putting his favourite head in the target zone. He watched on his screen, and in fact his head would have been safe.

~~

Lightning reached out to barely caress the missiles, and some exploded. The rockets propelling the rest cut out and they headed earthwards, as did two of the gunships. At least Ghost had listened to Jamie as they didn't explode or drop like stones. Missiles from the other launchers and aircraft surrounding the ship met the same fate.

The cannon shells, and probably bullets from however many troops had sneaked up, created pretty sparkles when they hit Starlight Ghost's shields. None of it had any effect inside the ship, except for a firework display across the airlock entrance before it closed.

Jamie had worried about blast if the spaceship took off, but there wasn't any. None of the troops were in any danger of being incinerated when the still-invisible spaceship left the ground, and Jamie would have been safe behind the earth bank. As Fliptrip slowly engaged the controls, massive generators fed enough electricity to power a city into exotic machinery.

Without any visible sign of the immense forces in play, Starlight Ghost neutralised the effect of local gravity, then repulsion pushed the ship away from the planet. The only outward sign of the effort required to levitate hundreds of thousands of tons was a hollow. A combination of the ship's weight, and then the repulsion field, had compressed the earth into something very close to stone.

The attackers couldn't see the starship, just ripples and distortions in the air, and smoke being deflected. The shield, however, was stopping or annihilating the huge amount of metal being thrown at it, which created a rough outline. A giant, bottom-heavy, egg-shaped firework over fifteen hundred feet tall, and over eight hundred feet across at the widest point, rose into the sky above Albuquerque.

The ship drifted southeast as it rose, towards the international airport, because Jamie cared more about the poor schmucks down below than their government did. It wasn't entirely selfless—he wanted all the falling crap a long way away from the Pits. He had a nasty feeling the military wouldn't care what fell there, and anyway, the newer-build houses could take the punishment better.

He thought the assault would ease off as Starlight Ghost passed over the airport buildings, but it intensified, which can't have done the planes much good. The spaceship moved out across the runways, and the assault intensified. More warplanes and gunships arrived, adding their autocannon, gatlings, and missiles, while something ground-based volleyed missiles from the airfield.

For a moment the attackers must have thought they'd overwhelmed the defences, as two missiles managed to 'evade' the defensive weapons. As they struck the shield, it faltered, or so it seemed, and the spaceship was in plain view. Only the disguise wavered, so nothing hit the ship, because the glimpse was deliberate.

Jamie wanted to make certain nobody thought this was a hoax, that another nation was responsible, but Ghost didn't want Starlight Ghost identified by interstellar investigators. Since then, Tripflip had been working hard on reprogramming the masking, mostly to divert the investigators elsewhere.

As Ghost had once explained, the pod could either hide, or pretend to be something else about the same size and shape. Starlight Ghost could take that to a whole new level, though an emitted field made sure only the long-range military cameras got a clear picture.

All the eyes looking at the disturbance had a brief, flickering view of a truncated, five-sided pyramid nearly fifteen hundred feet tall, two hundred and fifty feet along each side at the top, widening to four hundred and fifty feet along the bottom. The whole exterior was grey metal studded with angular turrets, hatches, and dishes, unlike the real hull's smooth black curves.

The spaceship was taller than any building in the USA, or the longest super-tanker stood on end, and much longer and wider than the largest aircraft carrier ever built. To Jamie, each face had a similar style to the Empire's warships in *Star Wars*, but it actually resembled genuine warships from several civilised worlds. The whole thing was too big for anyone on Earth to have built and launched secretly, and was pristine, undamaged despite the onslaught.

Once the spaceship was high enough that it wouldn't harm the people below, the repulsion eased off and the main drives took up the strain. Still moving slowly, and trying to avoid satellites, Starlight Ghost passed through Low Earth Orbit, then accelerated. The onslaught had almost stopped as the ship moved higher, with one last volley of what might have been ICBMs as it cleared the satellites.

Rather than blow them up, Oneless carefully targeted them with micro-missiles. The guided bullets matched courses, and each one contained the same technology as Ghost's little grey drones. With all the electronics shut off, including guidance, the missiles would just keep going, then when the fuel ran out, the micro-missiles would detach and self-destruct. It wasn't the easiest way to deal with them, but Jamie didn't want radioactive material or a nuclear bomb falling on Earth.

FAREWELL FRANKIE

The following morning, after the scramble to use the cleanser, Ghost's first words meant that none of them were leaving yet. "I will take the larger shuttle to collect the pod and any other evidence, or destroy it completely."

Jamie didn't think it would be that easy. "Won't the Army have found it? They've already talked to people who saw us fly up from under the bridge. It will be on the way to a secret underground government base, guarded by tanks and planes." He remembered his thoughts about how long a tank would last against Hunter's beams, and this would be a massacre.

The sad smile still had traces of Ghost's grieving-for-kin. "It isn't there. Once we were on the bridge, and you were driving away, I used my remote controls to submerge it again. When we gained control of Starlight Ghost, I transferred my link. That allows more precise remote control of the pod, and it has been moved downstream. It was a controlled drift using the current, so there were no disturbances, then it came out into woodland. A drone is watching."

She hooked a furry purple arm in Jamie's. "I'm not hungry after putting on all this bulk, but everyone else should eat. We will make sure Starlight Ghost is secure, then once you have recovered enough, I will teach you to fly something better than an escape pod."

Jamie wasn't the only one who needed recovery time. Ghost and the other Slashtails were limping and aching, a lot worse than Jamie. Jamie's were mostly bruises and sprains, as he hadn't been in the actual fighting. All the Slashtails had been bleeding, and last night, Jamie had been sure some of the burns and slashes would have put him in a hospital.

Now the worst wounds seemed much better, but the Slashtails all seemed to have collected more cuts and burns, and bruises from the way they moved. Since she'd been so helpful after the fight, Jamie asked Quicktail, and she showed him her leg. The savage wound was now a scabbed slash that didn't need a splint. "Last night, while you slept, we melded." He understood what that was, the six-into-one, but it didn't explain the healing.

Quicktail chitter-laughed, probably at Jamie's baffled look. "The individual injuries can't survive the blending. The amount of trauma does, but we heal quickly, quicker like that. A few hours later we split, but unless we have all been very badly injured, rebuilding our individual bodies will not reinstate broken bones or internal injuries, or any crippling or life-threatening injuries. It is a survival instinct, but there is a price. We all retain a share of the trauma, but as less dangerous injuries, sprains, bruises, and burns."

Since Jamie had seen Ghost turn into seven purple ferrets, that made sense in a weird alien way. The Slashtails all looked battered, worse than yesterday, but they were all mobile enough to clean up the debris from the fight. For Fliptrip and Shortfang that meant making sure all the Starborn Circus's and Hunter's code was eradicated. As he winced and limped, Jamie knew his problem wasn't melding, or cuts and bruises—he just wasn't fit enough for fighting aliens. Sourspit showed him a room with exercise equipment and weights to suit all shapes and sizes—a big hint.

Just as Ghost promised, mealtimes were much better on Starlight Ghost. The starship already carried provisions, and Hunter had collected more, from Earth. Unlike the pod, the ingredients were kept separately, without dirt and excess foliage or bugs, so they all retained their taste. The Slashtails liked a diet heavy on meat, some of it raw, but Jamie was shown the kitchen and a selection of joints and vegetables.

The bank of gleaming ovens, microwaves, and hotplates was alien but recognisable, though Jamie needed a crash course in reading Slashtail. The translator was literal, and if it didn't get the exact shade of meaning, medium rare might mean charred or semi-raw food. He found a hotplate and threw some slices of beef on it, then tested until it was cooked.

Sometime after lunch, Ghost asked Jamie if he was fit enough to come and collect the pod. Since the best he could do was clean debris that was too big for the cleaner bots to pick up, he was ready for a change. When he saw the shuttle, Jamie wasn't as keen.

"You expect to fly that along the river and through Albuquerque, in broad daylight?" The escape pod had been much bigger than expected, but this was a whole new scale. He should have known, he realised, because the pod was meant to go inside.

Ghost patted the gleaming black metal. "We will adjust our speed to reach Earth orbit at nightfall in Albuquerque. The camouflage system isn't as efficient as the ship or pod, but between that and darkness, we should remain unseen." She gestured to a turret with a short fat barrel, then an open hatch that revealed lines of missile heads. "If we are unlucky or careless, we will evade, or destroy a persistent attacker. The pod cannot make orbit by itself so we need this, the largest shuttle."

A door hissed open, leading to a small room—an airlock with Slashtail-sized spacesuits. "We will need new suits, both of us, as I will retain this bulk. Since we are few in number, Ghost Claw Clan cannot combine to increase size, and some may think we are vulnerable."

~~

Ghost took human form before setting off, but wore the loose 'Vulcan' clothing and there was no teasing. Once the shuttle left Starlight Ghost, Jamie was immediately given a basic lesson on steering and accelerating—just in case. That was followed by basic skipping—very basic as it was just the maximum distance, straight ahead. A hundred thousand kilometres a time soon ate up most of the three hundred and eighty thousand kilometres to Earth, but then a yellow light warned them about Earth's gravity.

Ghost used a reduced skip to reach the gravity limit, then the shuttle went on automatic for most of the remaining thirty thousand kilometres. Jamie's next lessons concentrated on the shields, masking, and different weapons systems. Some seemed complicated to Jamie, but Ghost assured him he was only learning the basics.

Learning to operate even a shuttle took time, first for the theory and virtual reality flights, then a lot of practice in space. Ghost might have meant to be reassuring when she pointed out that if he was doing the fighting, they were already in real trouble. Jamie had to agree with what might have been a joke —that his best bet would be to fire everything at full power towards anyone in range.

They both slept on the way, but in their seats in case the autopilot woke them. Ghost reclaimed control to refine the course, before giving Jamie more lessons on operating the shuttle. Those weren't too stressful as there wasn't any traffic out here. He handed control back to Ghost for re-entry, but watching her would be a good lesson. With the USA and probably most of Earth's militaries on alert, Ghost had to avoid leaving the usual streak of fire across the sky.

For normal re-entry, the turrets and hatches were all closed down, and pulled in flush with the hull so they didn't burn off. This time the turrets could have been deployed, but the atmospheric disruption might disturb clouds or leave a vapour trail. As she made contact, Ghost had to match the speed and direction of the first wisps of atmosphere. When the shuttle came lower, she continually changed course and speed to copy the way the planet affected the air.

Jamie sat at the co-pilot controls, fascinated as he read the translated screens and dials and tried to follow what she did. The descent was slow and sometimes erratic, to match local conditions, and was only possible with the use of the repulsion, what Jamie thought of as anti-gravity, as well as manoeuvring thrusters. When the flight levelled out there was starlit water underneath, and Jamie had no idea where he was. A map appeared on a screen, and they were crossing the Pacific Coast just north of California.

As the shuttle came closer, the lights of Albuquerque seemed normal, though Jamie had only seen this view on the TV. Not quite this view—a patch of brighter light was Starlight Ghost's landing area, surrounded by floodlights. The little lights in the air explained the other screen, the one tracking dots with distances and speeds. There were helicopters over the scene of the fight, and the faster, higher ones must be jets.

With the floodlights as a marker, Jamie spotted the bridge, with floodlights shining up from the river as well as downward. The lights of the Double Eagle II Airport were distinctive, well clear of the city lights, as were three nearby patches of very bright lights.

One was where he'd made the exchange with Solly, and one the pickup Hunter nearly hit, but the third was a mystery. Jamie used his new training to zoom in, and there was a team investigating a tangle of blackened metal. They'd connected Menhir's Jeep Cherokee with the rest, but he was sure there'd be no fingerprints or even a stray hair.

The shuttle's optics, and the floodlights around the damage, showed a large burned patch next to the charred front of the SW Aeronautics Mathematics and Science Academy building. The blackened remains of Solly's pickup truck were well inside the half-circle where all the greenery had been burned. Ghost's bomb had made sure Solly's purchases would burn, too fast for any rescue. From what the internet said about crime scenes, the cover over the cab meant there was a body.

He wasn't usually the murderous type, but Jamie was hopeful—the last Ghost saw, Solly was getting into the cab. His theory was reinforced by the third set of lights, set up around a crater and an uncovered pickup with a burned-out engine and melted front tyres.

~~

Ghost pulled back and dropped lower, skirting all signs of activity until she could descend into the river valley. There was one other job before retrieving the pod—she wanted the info-packets she'd dropped on the way to assault Starlight Ghost. They'd been meant to make sure Hunter was caught by interstellar inspectors, but now they'd cause trouble for Ghost Claw.

The big shuttle hovered over the water upriver of Albuquerque, safely hidden while Jamie practiced his new piloting skills. He wasn't aboard his new craft—the hold was big enough to hold a fairly plump goose and there was no room for a pilot—but he was responsible for flying it. The drone drifted downstream until it reached the spot the first info-package had been dropped, then hovered and began to search.

There was a distinctive return when he found the alien artifact—deliberate so once aliens were official visitors, one of them would notice it. The next part wasn't as easy. While maintaining position as the current pulled at the target, he had to lock the tractor beam onto the cigarette-packet-sized box, then lift it out of the water and into the hold.

Not really the ubiquitous tractor beam of so many sci-fi stories, but Jamie had read too many of those books. The Slashtails called it a variable repulsor, and they actually knew how it worked. It didn't even act like a beam, and according to Ghost it was a version of what let the pod float around. The result was that the target was lifted, so Jamie's head insisted on thinking of it as a tractor beam. Luckily, that didn't affect how it worked.

Four times Jamie extended the repulsor/tractor beam sensors down into the water, locking onto each small target. He had to be careful, as when the repulsor field activated around the package, the river tried to drag it downstream. It also pulled up a little of the water around it as it came out, so he couldn't spend too long lining it up on the hold.

The drone was just above the water, and it was dark, but Jamie still sweated over each one. Afterwards he realised that if anyone had noticed the splashing from his mistakes, they probably wouldn't have been alarmed. Even if they'd seen a ball of water floating upwards, then disappearing, a spectator would have probably dismissed it as shadows, a trick of the light. At the time he worried over each one, while Ghost spent the whole time relaxing with her feet up on the instrument panel, watching screens.

~~

Eventually Jamie had all four, and the drone was back in the shuttle's hold. The pod was south of Albuquerque, but Ghost couldn't follow the river—the intense activity around the bridge straddled the Rio Grande. Despite the disguise, Ghost didn't want to risk going upwards, as the air over the city was full of military aircraft. Flying low and very slowly, she looped right around the city, well away from any buildings, and came back to the river downstream.

This time there wasn't any need to search. A signal alerted the drone watching the pod and the surroundings, and it guided Ghost in. Jamie flinched when she knocked down two trees to land in front of the battered craft—Ghost must have been fed up with slow and careful.

She opened the rear doors, remote-controlled the pod and drone inside, and was flying away across the countryside within minutes. Jamie tried to look, but if anyone had reported the racket the military hadn't responded yet.

Once it was out in the countryside again, well away from

the city or river, the shuttle slowed and hovered. "One last look at Earth, Jamie. One last chance to stay?" Ghost pointed back towards the hold and pod. "Your trophy is there, your motorbike?"

~~

He wasn't tempted, but Jamie paused, taking a last look at familiar trees and grass. "No thanks, though I would have liked to talk to Shania. I can text her, or even call her, but it isn't the same. I'd also hoped to introduce you." He tried to remember what he'd said to Ghost about his texts, and couldn't remember if he'd mentioned his sister knowing Ghost was an alien. Jamie thought his sister would be utterly blown away by either the human or Slashtail version, but there might be a rule against it.

The long silence wasn't promising, but it ended with a sharp nod. "Since nobody has noticed us, you can visit, to prove you are alive and tell her where you are going." When Jamie looked at her, Ghost was dead serious. "I should say no, as she might notify the authorities, but you are clan so that would not be just."

There was another silence, but this time Ghost was looking at a map. "This shuttle cannot land in the garden where I arrived. The camouflage isn't as good as the pod or Starlight Ghost, so a neighbour might see us coming in. I can use the river again, and then land in the fields next to Rio Grande Nature Centre? You can walk from there, or use your trophy."

Jamie had to laugh at that—a Hellbat bike was the absolute opposite of stealthy—but then he nodded.

~~

Both of them were silent during the trip, Jamie because he was trying to work out what to say to Shania. Once she'd checked there were no late-night wanderers, and the shuttle settled in the fields, Ghost sighed. She glanced at Jamie, then inspected the instruments, looking embarrassed for some reason. "I will wait here, unless you call to say you are staying.

I would ask for pelt-stroking, in case you don't come back, and perhaps a little DNA, but that would not be fair."

Right now, Jamie was past all the double-talk—he admitted the truth. "I don't think I'll be staying, but either way I'd like a kiss before I go in there. Not for DNA or luck, just a kiss, though I'm pretty sure you'll get your pelt stroked." He smiled as he remembered some of his worries, and some of Ghost's threats. "Without removing coverings or emitting pheromones, or it might be a very long kiss."

Ghost didn't answer—she was already moving across and onto his knee, and her arms wrapped around his head. By the time Jamie surfaced her pelt had been thoroughly stroked, right down to that tempting curve, and he'd seriously considered removing coverings from both of them. He was actually surprised to see it was still dark outside—the kiss felt like it had lasted several hours.

He didn't know what to say, and Ghost apparently had the same problem, at least until he'd followed her to the door. "Stamp on the ground as you walk away, leave footprints so you can get near enough to see the shuttle. If you get lost, I will guide you in." She tapped the back of her head. "Remember, you have my number if necessary."

Jamie nodded and headed across the fields, and then along the deserted streets, hoping Shania was at home. The garage opener was still in the pod, among the parts he'd stripped from his car, so he used the number pad on the front gate. As expected, his code was for the house door so it didn't work, but a man in uniform came out of a brick building.

"Please tell Shania there is a visitor for Frankie." The guard didn't seem impressed. "Please. I swear she will know exactly who you mean, and won't want me saying any more."

The guy still didn't answer, just talked to his sleeve, and one of the cameras moved a little to centre on Jamie. The guard finally nodded, and put a hand on his pistol. "One moment, sir, while we open the gate. One of our men will escort you."

Jamie had to walk through a metal detector, which beeped, but it must have been able to see he had no weapons. He was shown into the back of what looked like an adapted golf buggy, with a screen so he couldn't snatch the driver's pistol. The winding driveway and underlit greenery was no doubt meant to be impressive, but Jamie was busy going through his story and hoping Shania would accept it.

~~

He couldn't ignore the front of the huge house, something he'd never seen. The main worry was the empty steps leading to the big double doors when the buggy pulled up. Not for long—one of the doors opened and Shania ran down the steps. "It *is* you!" She turned to the guard and smiled. "Thanks Saul. Please make sure the surveillance tape is blank, and there's no record of Jamie. He's supposed to be somewhere else, sunning himself."

The guard smiled and nodded. "No problem, ma'am." He saluted and turned away. "What visitor, why am I here?" Shania was laughing as the buggy set off, but then she hugged Jamie before stepping back to inspect him. "I'd ask what the other guy looked like, but you look as if you lost." Before he could answer she tugged him sideways, along the front of the house. "Come on, we'll walk around to the back and you can explain—without inquisitive staff."

She turned towards the door and waved to Damian, and he waved back, then raised a hand to Jamie before going indoors. Once they were on their own, she looked up at him, and then burst into tears! For some reason she was smiling as well, and then she hugged him, hard. "All this time, twenty-four years. I'd almost given up hope, but then when Papa died, you looked after Mama's grave. Is that why you wouldn't move?"

Jamie stared down at her in total shock. "Mama's grave? She died? When?" He knew Mama left when they moved to the garage, but... He suddenly realised what Shania meant, because there was only one place he'd looked after. "The flowers and grass? Mama is buried there?"

"Oh shit, I'm sorry. Papa wouldn't let me tell you, but he promised to explain when I left home." She patted an ornate stone bench. "Sit down, Jamie." Once they were sat, Shania took both his hands. "What do you remember about moving to the garage?"

He usually steered clear of those memories, but now Jamie tried. "There were flames, and shouting, lots of noise. Then it was dark and safe, for a long time. You were there, and a lot of people, but Mama wasn't. Papa was, or sometimes he wasn't but I knew he'd come back. Then the others went away and we moved into the garage, but couldn't go out because it was dangerous. That was it, from then on it all sort of blended into growing up in the garage with you and Papa. What happened? I always thought Mama left."

Shani scrubbed at her eyes, then grabbed his hands again. Her voice was very quiet and gentle, and cautious. "She did, in a way, Jamie. Papa said we weren't to talk about it, but we both thought you knew. We realised you didn't recognise the house, not after it burned down, but Papa thought that might be a good thing. It might have been a bomb or a tank, or a freedom fighter with explosives who got hit, but Papa couldn't get Mama out."

She sighed, then pushed on, and now the tears had started again. "You were only three, so I guess you didn't realise the place across the street was Papa's garage. Once all the fighting was over, he heaped up what was left of the house and burned it. Then he covered what was left with earth, planted bushes and flowers, and grassed the rest. Some of the neighbours brought ashes, people they lost, and put them on the heap, and they helped him. That's why it was kept so nice, no trash or beer cans. I put Papa's ashes on there, when you said you didn't want to go to the memorial garden."

~~

Jamie tried to take it all in, but it was too much, and then one thing caught his attention. "The garage was across the street? That was the dark place?"

"Yeah." The shrug was barely noticeable. "Papa put us in the pit, and then put the boards over the top and filled a big skip with scrap to stop anyone finding us. It was on that big lift, and was raised to let people in and out. Did Papa ever show you the pipes?"

The look on Jamie's face must have answered. "He promised, but I guess he never worked up to it. Some of the grating at the bottom of the pit, the part under the lift, can be removed. There are big concrete pipes down there, with heaters, bed frames, and air blowers. There weren't many kids living nearby, but we all stayed in there for days. The mothers and old folk lived in the garage, and jumped in the other pits if there was trouble. They left the covers on except for a small gap by the steps. Papa said the place was like a bunker, and he was right, not a single bullet came inside. He used to go out with that rifle, and come back with food."

She sighed, a big shuddering release of tension, and hugged him tight. "It changed you, more than it did me. Maybe because I was older, and came out now and then to collect hot food or take out the trash. Afterwards, Papa stopped joking, he just worked and looked after us, and you were really quiet. You'd follow us about, mostly Papa, but you never laughed or played. Even when you got older you didn't play with the other kids."

"I liked the garage, and helping Papa." Jamie had already realised that when Ghost took him camping. "We used to play on the roof?"

"Most of the time you played by yourself, but now and then you'd say or do something and I'd know my little brother was still in there, hiding. I loved that stupid Frankie name. It was so normal, the sort of thing a little brother should do. I used to pretend I hated it, because it made you laugh." She had a half-smile, but then Shania looked guilty. "I told Papa you needed to talk, maybe see a doctor, but he said you'd sort it out eventually."

~~

The short laugh was mixed with tears, and Shania fumbled for tissues. Jamie had some, and she used them as well before she was ready to speak. "You did, but it took an alien invasion. You wouldn't sell up, and stayed shut up in that bloody place for days on end, and I just didn't know what to do. Then there were bodies all over, and you'd run off leaving one little note that said bugger all. Now you've turned down the Maldives to run off with some woman."

The smile faltered, and her hands squeezed. "Are you sure? You don't have to; Damian will still find you somewhere. I'd like to spend some time with my brother, the new one, or the old one that just came back."

That hit Jamie as hard as anything. He'd thought Shania wanted sod all to do with him, but now he knew she just wanted to get him away from the garage, and the memories. He thought about staying, but then he shook his head. "It's the chance of a lifetime, Shania. I can go to the stars, and see all those wonders and aliens, but if I don't go now the chance is gone."

Jamie stopped, but too late, he'd told her. Before he could try to recover, Shania's eyes opened wide. "Go to the stars? What sort of alien do you mean? Are any of those women going, the ones you've been dragging around the countryside? I though you meant someone from abroad, and that was a hell of a disguise. Did she look like Salome Malone when you went camping?" All the sympathy and tears were done, his big sister wanted some answers—now!

She grabbed his wrist, inspecting the friendship bracelets. "Ha, the Salome in Oklahoma had some of these. That was her again, wasn't it, but you only said one, so is she the brown-haired woman as well? Are either of them the alien? And how the hell did you get that note delivered, it nearly gave me a bloody heart attack. So did the medals, I'd never seen them." Shania stopped for a moment to inspect his cuts and bruises. "How did you get in that state? Was it anything to do with all the bodies near your garage, and why you sold it?"

Before Jamie could answer she'd carried on. "The TV has been ranting on about aliens and spaceships, and think you are an alien, or a gangster, or a mass murderer. Who was the double? Is that why you look like this, you were too near all those explosions yesterday? All that business about keeping off the streets, did you know that bloody great whatever was coming?"

~~

At first Jamie fended off some questions, just explaining disguises without mentioning shapeshifting. He also tried to skirt around technology, but half of Albuquerque had seen Starlight Ghost, and the pictures of the ground car had been on TV. Shania knew him too well—she knew he was hiding something and kept digging. "Hold on Shania, just give me a moment to think, right?"

"To think of more bullshit?" The hands on the hips and narrowed eyes made Jamie smile—he knew that look from back when they were barely teenagers. He put a finger to his lips, and then tried to work out what to do.

~~

In the end he could only think of one thing—he put a hand to the back of his head and pushed. Ghost must have been waiting. *"I understand, Jamie. Good luck. I will drop the remaining bitcoins on the lawn."*

"No!" Shania looked startled but Jamie waved a hand, "Not you." He should have been able to do this silently, but hadn't got there yet so he ploughed on. *"I want to show Shania. I want*

her to meet you, so she can see why I'm off to the stars." Now Shania's eyes went to Jamie's hand, on the back of his neck, and she looked around—then up.

"Just Shania, and only in the shuttle, but she can't tell anyone." He could hear the humour in Ghost's voice as she continued. *"Will she want her clothes back, or would that be inappropriate?"*

"Give me a minute." Jamie grinned at Shania. "Yes, I've got a radio in my head, yes, I was in the middle of all those explosions, and my new alien friend is in a spaceship, parked in the fields next to the Rio Grande Nature Centre. If I take you to meet her it has to be a secret forever. Ah, she's wearing your clothes, because she didn't have any when we met."

As he spoke, Jamie could see Shania winding up to blow. She thought he was teasing, but the last bit caught her out. She giggled and looked past him, in the general direction of the fields. "I sometimes wondered what it would take for a girl to get you thinking of her instead of engines and oil, but never thought of *that*!"

Her face straightened, and a finger jabbed Jamie in the chest. "You swear it's true? It had better be, because I'm not keeping it a secret from Damian. Go on, ask your head for permission." The grin came back. "No need to ask who's in charge."

~~

Damian agreed, eventually, but he definitely thought Jamie was pulling some sort of stunt. He'd heard more than what was common public knowledge, because he pointed out anything that size would be spotted by the armed forces if it landed in the fields. When Jamie insisted this was a shuttle, a smaller version, he agreed, but only because Shania threatened to go on her own. Even so, Damian insisted on travelling to the edge of the fields in a big off-roader, with an armed chauffeur.

The chauffeur waited in the car, with a two-way radio in case Damian needed him, then Ghost's voice in his head guided Jamie into the darkness. Damian and Shania both paused, squinting as they spotted a darker something against the lights of the city, but Jamie urged them forward. When a dimly-lit doorway appeared in mid-air, in the middle of the hazy black shape, Jamie heard two gasps.

At the last moment he wondered if Ghost would meet them as a Slashtail, but she was human, and had removed the loose clothes to show Shania's shorts and bikini top. When Jamie glanced back, that was probably the right thing to do—both Damian and Shania looked surprised but not frightened. From the twitch of her lip, he knew when Shania recognised her clothes.

Ghost bowed, her short formal version. "Welcome, Jamie's kin. Please come inside. Opening the door affects the disguise, so a military aircraft might notice an anomaly."

With a quick glance upwards, Jamie's human relatives hurried through the door, then waited as Ghost closed it and opened the inner door. Jamie thought he should explain. "Airlock." From the startled looks, maybe he should have kept quiet. "It's all right, the air is the same inside." He assumed so, but he'd never asked. Jamie took a firm hold of his nerves.

Once in the control room, Damian and Shania were looking everywhere, but as Jamie followed, Ghost held out her hand to them. Jamie hadn't even realised she knew how to shake hands. "I understand this is a traditional human greeting."

She beckoned to Jamie and when he joined her, his comms activated. *"Stroke my pelt, greeting-to-kin."* The kiss wasn't as intense as the good luck one, and the pelt-stroking stopped short of the curve. Ghost turned to two amused humans. "My clan has adopted Jamie, and that is our greeting-to-kin. He has agreed to join us as an engineer, as ours died recently."

~~

That broke the ice, and then Ghost was the perfect host —she even offered hot or cold drinks. She never mentioned girlfriend, or her relationship to Jamie, but held his hand, occasionally hugged, and kissed him several times. By the time she'd done, Shania had a version of what had happened that didn't sound too bad. It covered all the parts on the news, and enough extras to cover what might leak from the government, but avoided shapeshifting—and gave the impression Jamie and Ghost were an item.

Damian definitely knew more than he should, so either money, social status, or the right contacts had already loosened lips. Vaporising the ground car matched the facts he'd heard, even though nobody knew how it had disappeared. Damian didn't think anyone would believe him even if he told them. He asked why Ghost hadn't spoken to the military instead of the Vulcan, then nodded when Jamie explained.

Damian agreed with the logic, and swore to never mention seeing her—he didn't fancy the idea of living with an annoyed Shania. He added that a nuclear war might not be quite as bad, but he'd rather avoid one. Damian's sense of humour had apparently recovered from the shock.

Jamie already knew that Damian loved his sister, or he'd never have married her despite her origins. Shania had always been fiercely protective, making sure nobody got any hint that might embarrass Damian, so it had taken longer to realise she didn't do it just to protect her new life. Even so, they'd always been more formal when he was there.

Perhaps it was because there were no servants to see them, or maybe it was the shock, the circumstances, but they held hands and had their arms around each other most of the time. It was so natural that Jamie was sure that's how they usually acted when nobody else could see them. More surprising was that Damian discussed it all with Shania, and listened to her answers. She always gave the impression he was in charge, and she was just the decorative wife.

Damian had known all about Jamie's escapade, as he'd brought armed guards and accompanied Shania when she picked up the note. Shania reckoned it was like an invasion, four cars full of men holding machine guns or shotguns. It was Damian who suggested a burn phone, and the innocuous, innocent message on Papa's, but the other messages were Shania's.

Once they'd discussed Jamie going to space, Damian offered cash, or something else so Jamie could pay his way. He pointed out he'd get it back when he sold the Maldives villa, but laughed when Jamie apologised. Shania confessed they'd both enjoyed the subterfuge and excitement, a break from their usual life, but she could have done without the worrying part.

The money suggestion reminded Jamie of one thing he'd never sorted out. "If you like sneaky spy stuff, you could do me a favour, pay off some debts?" When Damian nodded, he'd obviously got the wrong idea. "No, I don't want you to use your money. There's the best part of a million bucks in bitcoins on these three drives, and I've got a list of people I cheated." Now Shania was scowling, so Jamie hurried on. "Sort of. I paid them with copies of my cash, absolutely identical but the serial numbers are the same."

"Do they know?" When Jamie shook his head, Damian looked really puzzled. "You expect me to tell them they were robbed, then give them the cash?"

Jamie realised that sounded a bit stupid since he'd got away with it. "No, sorry, I just thought you could arrange for the right amount of real money to reach them, hopefully without a hint of why. Then my conscience won't nag." He pointed to one address. "I did rob this place. I took two big boxes of pipe fittings to fix a sort-of spaceship."

Damian seemed to find that funny. "Spaceships need a lot of them, do they?" He took the drives, and glanced at Shania. "We'll work out something, a bundle of notes under the door if necessary. After all the practice, a bit more undercover work will be easy. I'll lurk with a balaclava and a jetpack, while Secret

Agent Frankie climbs a drainpipe to stuff the money through a window."

Shania mock-scowled at Jamie. "That's your fault. It's a good job you're leaving, or Secret Agent Frankie might be looking for payback."

A relieved Jamie handed over the list of people he'd cheated or stolen from, but then Ghost had a request. "If you pay for the damage when we broke into the pipe store, would they give you the evidence? The ropes and clamps are alien technology, even if it isn't obvious, and we could get into a lot of trouble if other aliens ever find out."

Between them, Jamie and Ghost explained the technological pollution laws, and that they were serious. Even so, getting evidence from the police wouldn't be easy. Shania came up with a way, once she'd looked down Jamie's list. "This doesn't come to anything like a million. What do you want us to do with the rest, Jamie?"

"It will be no good to me where I'm going. Stick a proper memorial up for Mama and Papa, and all the rest? Buy a new bikini, or car?" Damian and Shania had plenty of money, so he really had no idea.

Shania smiled and nodded. "I wanted to put something on the grave, but Papa wouldn't let me. He made me promise I wouldn't use a rich man's money to pretty up what the rich man's army did." Both of them looked uncomfortable with that, but she pushed on. "I'll talk to a couple of people with relatives to remember. I'll explain the cash comes from you, that it's for a memorial and to keep it tidy."

Glancing at Damian, she gave Jamie a little half-smile. "I can put the rest in trust? Maybe to help the kids in the Pits or something? They won't take charity from the likes of Damian or me, in case it's got strings, but they'll probably accept something like that if it comes from you."

Jamie liked that idea. After all, even if he hadn't really

socialised, he'd eaten a lot of homecooked food that he'd never paid for. "Done, but that doesn't get the tech back."

"That depends on Damian." Shania held up one of the drives. "I'm betting that he knows whoever owns the place, or one of his friends does. If he lets them know a friend of a friend's son was involved, very embarrassing, he could pay for any damage and stolen goods. Then if he offers an upgrade for their security, and suggests the owner could ask the cops to drop the investigation? Then rope and clamps wouldn't be evidence, so if the owner said they were his? I'm not sure how to get him to hand them over, but they'd be out of the police station."

"That part is easy." Damian's mock-scowl wasn't fooling anyone. "The idiot son stole them from a friend of his father's, and giving them back would soothe some ruffled feathers. The first part, however, is going to mean calling in some favours, or owing one or two."

Shania hugged him, then came across to put her hands over Jamie's ears. "I'll make it up to you. I've got all this money, so instead of a bikini, I could buy something you'd like better, just to say sorry?" Her face didn't look even slightly guilty, and Damian just smiled and shook his head.

Though he hadn't dropped the subject. "How alien is the rope and these clamps? Do I have to melt them down, or just throw them in a lake?"

Three pairs of eyes turned to Ghost, but she didn't answer immediately. Then instead of answering Damian, she turned to Jamie. "Do you trust this man, Jamie? Will he keep his word?"

He would have liked to say yes, but Jamie didn't really know the guy. "I trust Shania, and Shania trusts him, I reckon." Shania nodded, still looking curious. "Why?"

Ghost left, and came back with a clamp, and a coil of rope. "As you can see, they are not obviously alien." She looped the rope, activated the clamp, and handed it to Tania. "The clamps won't work unless they are recharged. If you destroy the power source, thoroughly, then added an Earth battery, I believe the rest could be mistaken for a natural human development."

Tania had tugged at the rope, then passed it to her husband. As he tugged it, Ghost turned to Damian and bowed. "If this technology would be useful, maybe profitable, I will show you how it works, fair return for your efforts to hide our mistake. Once you have built a human version, I would like you to melt the original down so there is no evidence."

Damian tugged again, and looked at the buttons and light. "If we can make one that isn't too bulky, it should sell. I'm sure a lot of people will stick with using knots, but there will be a few who have to clamp two ropes together quickly, and with one hand." He nodded, turning the clamp over. "Thank you. I would have done it anyway, for Shania's brother, but this might help with the favours. I can offer someone a share in a new business."

Ghost explained how the clamp worked, and how to release it, then suggested analysing the rope. The materials might be available, and the treatment might be feasible, in which case it was very strong. Once he could duplicate them, or if he couldn't, Damian agreed to put the ropes in a furnace.

Shania drifted across to Jamie and nudged him. "I was hoping for something to remind me I've got a brother out there somewhere, but a clamp and a list of your crimes?" The smile meant she was joking, which was a relief. "Though I suppose if you gave me a present it would be stolen. After all, you gave Ghost stolen clothes."

Ghost overheard, and missed the meaning of the smile. "If you wish, I will give them back. After I find more, or I will be inappropriate."

Shania burst out laughing, pointing at the shorts. "Not really, I doubt they'll ever fit me again. Keep them, please, a souvenir of Earth since I won't be at the, er, whatever."

The look at Jamie was a question—would there be an alien wedding?

Although she didn't realise, Ghost let Jamie off the hook. "Wait one moment, please." She came back with a handful of shimmering material. "This is a skinsuit, and will remind you where Jamie went. It is advanced technology, powered by your body movement, body heat, and any light source. Don't worry about it looking too small, it will stretch and then adjust to fit whoever wears it. It is designed to maintain a comfortable internal temperature, regardless of external conditions."

Jamie was about to ask why Ghost was handing out banned technology, but she turned to him. "The media coverage will mean that sooner or later, news of the Vulcan visit will spread. It will be at least a hundred years before any officials check on Earth, and then they will find records. Movie of the Vulcan includes mention of a fugitive and pictures of Hunter's body, which will explain traces of banned tech."

She shrugged and held up the suit. "Most spaceships carry these suits, so even if this one is found, it can't be traced to Starlight Ghost. I doubt anyone on Earth will notice it is alien, unless Shania is trapped and uses it to save her life." That was true. The thin, glittery material looking like foil, not some advanced alien material.

Turning back to Shania, Ghost pointed. "The colours can be changed, here, so it can also be used as camouflage or to be easily found in an emergency. It will extrude a hood, gloves, and boots if required, and keep you alive in a fire, underwater, or in a vacuum for a little under two of your hours. This is where you set the internal temperature."

Damian broke in to cast his vote. "If that happens, I will swear I bought it from someone who met the alien." He put an arm around Shania. "After that description, I might insist she wears it every time she goes out."

~~

Once Shania had used her phone to take a picture of what looked like a label inside the suit, and had a lesson in how to use it to set the temperature and colour, Ghost had a warning. "Don't ever let anyone know where it really came from, or Jamie will be in a lot of trouble. There are severe penalties for leaving advanced tech on primitive planets."

"I'll put it in my will; I'll be cremated wearing it." Shania held the glittery material against her and posed for Damian. "High-tech thermals will be handy when I'm old and doddery. I think Ghost lost out in the exchange."

"Just don't leave it in a changing room somewhere." Damian sounded dead serious, and Shania looked guilty, but then he smiled and gestured towards Jamie. "Jamie has just been explaining how even an escape pod has better electronics than Earth, so your thermals would bring the Feds."

"These electronics are not much better than yours." Ghost held out two small boxes. When Damian opened them, Jamie recognised the scorched contents, three in each. He looked at Ghost, puzzled, so she explained. "Damian should have a leaving present as well, and the clamp is a payment."

She turned to Damian. "There is a practical reason. These will help you reach the right people and encourage Earth to advance, which is important to Jamie. Swear that someone found them near the hotel after the alien machine was destroyed, and sold them to you."

Damian took them, puzzled, so Jamie enlightened him. "The processors are at least one generation ahead of whatever is currently being developed, the ones that haven't been declared yet. The construction might be totally different, or just boost modern knowledge, and someone might have to develop new tools. The smaller ones are RAM chips that hold the equivalent of a petabyte hard drive. You'll need a specialist firm to work out how to duplicate them, then you'll have a supercomputer in your phone. Please don't say where you really got them."

"I swear it." Damian held up his prizes. "I'll get a few people I trust involved in this; people who worry about the world their children will live in. These will get us into the discussion about how the USA reacts to the alien visit, and will prove that they really were aliens."

He reached out to shake Ghost's hand. "Thank you, for these, and for the attempt to mend our world." Ghost claimed it was Jamie's idea, but Jamie made them all laugh when he said it was Shania's fault really, for nagging him to recycle properly and stop using gas just racing about.

Ghost finally explained she had to get moving, to be clear of Albuquerque before the military noticed an anomaly, as this shuttle wasn't as tough as the ship.

Both Damian and Shania were smiling in a bemused sort of way as they left, reluctantly as they both still had a million questions. Instead of going back to the car, they stood on the field with their arms around each other, squinting at the dark shape as it drifted away from them. They were both still waving long after they must have lost sight of the shuttle, but turned back to the car just before Ghost dropped into the Rio Grande valley.

~~

Jamie turned from the screen, and just had to ask. "You kept telling me you had to avoid technical pollution, and keep aliens a secret. You even melted little bits of metal, so why did you change your mind? The clamp part made sense, but the rest didn't."

Although she was smiling, Ghost looked a little apprehensive, and possibly guilty. "Once we met, I thought your sister would keep one secret, the clothing, and it seemed fair that her mate also had a gift. Even if they tell everyone, this way you said goodbye properly, and left them something, a souvenir."

The smile had just a hint of mischief. "It might not have

been wise, but Ghost Claw have never been cautious. The hugging was because I thought your kin would accept it better if you left because you'd found a mate." Jamie hadn't asked about the kissing and hugging, though he'd wondered. Now he knew it was just to fool Shania.

Ghost had hesitated, and now she blurted out the rest in a rush. "And this body enjoys the kissing without it being just for DNA. The kiss for DNA to copy you, and the one before you left, when you relaxed, were much nicer than the others, and I wanted to try it again. I did not take DNA?" A flash of wicked humour came and went. "Not much, but it seems to be a natural result."

After asking for a kiss, Jamie couldn't really object, and he'd enjoyed it as well—too much for his peace of mind. He thought Ghost was right about the rest. Shania wouldn't want to cause possible trouble for her brother, or Damian, and he didn't think Damian would do or say anything to harm Shania. His sister would definitely be much happier thinking of him somewhere among the stars with human-Ghost. She'd imagine some sort of alien house, garden, and kids instead of worrying about monsters.

Damian had seemed really interested in the criteria for being considered civilised. He wasn't a politician, but had some local influence, and knew others who might like the idea. There were already leaks, and now the new tech meant Damian could get involved without mentioning Jamie's visit. If something slipped, it would be ignored among all the garbled information that would hit the internet.

He realised Ghost was still waiting for some reaction to her 'confession.' "Okay." That wasn't enough really, so Jamie confessed as well. "You are right about Shania, and Damian, and this human body enjoyed the kissing. I'm sure you know that I always have." Before Ghost could start teasing, Jamie switched to the view ahead. "Are we going back to Starlight Ghost now, or do you want to pick up half a dozen motorbikes first?"

That was the right thing to say—Ghost smiled and glanced down at her chest. "By removing coverings and asking? Maybe we will call back when we have finished our feud, if we survive? It is forbidden of course, but if you are Ghost Claw, that is a good reason to come." She pointed at Jamie's controls. "In which case you need to practice flying a shuttle. You can take us to orbit, very gently, and I'll shoot down anyone who spots your mistakes."

Jamie wasn't totally sure that was a joke. When they'd been discussing talking to the general, some Slashtails had suggested shooting down half a dozen aircraft if he started making demands. As a result, Jamie's flying was probably too cautious, and took much longer than necessary, but that meant he made orbit undetected.

After that, the flight back to the moon was easy—the seats reconfigured and they slept while the autopilot took them to the skip limit. Not that Jamie was allowed to sleep for the whole trip. There were a lot of other systems and equipment to learn about, which helped to take his mind off leaving home.

Though when he reached Starlight Ghost, Jamie found out he might not be leaving after all.

~~

While Ghost and Jamie had been away, the others had finished cleaning up and making sure they were in full control of Starlight Ghost. They had also been talking. Jamie had barely gotten out of the shuttle when the other Slashtails took Ghost off for a discussion.

When they came back, there was one anomaly Jamie had to ask about. "It makes no difference to me, but why are you all different sizes? You were all the same at first." Ghost had reverted to fur, which meant she was taller than Jamie. Shortfang and Oneless, called that because she only had five digits on one hand, were still the same size as the combat aliens they'd copied. Sourspit was about halfway between that and what Jamie thought was normal Slashtail. Tripflip was smaller but definitely bigger than Quicktail, who didn't seem to have altered.

The Slashtails exchanged looks, and if they'd been human, Jamie would have thought the body language suggested embarrassment. "Forget it. It doesn't matter, as long as you don't get too big and crush me in the night-nest, or suffocate me."

"Perhaps we just wanted more pelt for you to stroke?" Quicktail looked at Nightclaw, but she had her eyes on the instruments, deliberately maybe. "Ghost Claw have a natural advantage over other Slashtails, so we are feared on our homeworld. Your translator would call it Earth or Dirt. About half the worlds inhabited by sentients are called more or less the same thing, while worlds with avian or aquatic dominant species tend to refer to the atmosphere or oceans."

"Which is avoiding the real issue." Ghost interrupted, gesturing to include the others. "Most Slashtails live peaceful lives, though it was not always so. Our people fought for survival, and then each other, and our main weapon was our Slashtail." She pointed at Quicktail, who stuck her tail out and the bushy fur flattened.

Jamie flinched as he saw why Ghost warned him not to stroke one. The tail was studded with dark purple triangular blades, like cartoon spikes on a club over two feet long. With a little wiggle, Quicktail whipped her tail through a complicated series of curls and strikes that might explain her name. She ended up with her tail out straight again, all the blades bared. She relaxed and the fur fluffed up to hide any sign.

Jamie was speechless, but Quicktail was obviously waiting for his reaction so he tried. "Wow doesn't really cover it. It's definitely a step up from a knife up the sleeve."

Turning back to face him properly, Quicktail flicked her tail back behind her, and Ghost carried on explaining. "But when a naturally belligerent race have a Slashtail, creating a civilised, peaceful society is difficult. A moment's annoyance can lead to serious injury, and as they can't be withdrawn like our claws, accidents can happen. Our pelts usually keep the damage down to scratches, unless it is deliberate, and there is more tolerance within a clan. As population densities grew, and we became more civilised, that changed. Eventually our violent natures, and tails, became the only thing stopping us from true civilisation, acceptance by other races, and immortality."

She tapped the nearby seat, a dished circle of scratched leather. "This is much tougher than Earth leather, and armour plating every cable in an advanced society would be costly."

~~

Jamie had noticed armoured cables, and when he looked around, any wires he could see were protected. There weren't many, which made sense—the Slashtails presumably kept them to a minimum or built them in. Though since the Slashtails had built a starship… "I guess you found a solution."

"We did." Despite her furry appearance, Ghost produced a very human-like sigh. "The blades are softer while they are growing, and covered by a thick layer of skin that blunts their edges. When we attain full size, at about fourteen years old, the blood supply to the covering begins closing off. The soft tissue dies, and the blades are exposed. There is a four-year period where what you would call teenagers have to wear a sleeve over their tails, but once the process is completed the blades are removed. It is painless, and doesn't even bleed."

Her shortened chitter had no humour. "Unfortunately, that caused another problem. It was found that removing the spikes alters our body chemistry, making us much less belligerent. Slashtails can still defend themselves, using a wide variety of very dangerous weapons, but have no inclination to do so unless it is life or death. Even if Slashtails are forced to fight, most tend to try to wound, or surrender. That is ideal for living in a peaceful society, but not if our citizens or world are attacked." There was a brief silence, then just as Jamie was about to ask, Ghost answered his question.

Her tail flicked out sideways and the blades showed, briefly. "So one clan, a poor one whose ancestral lands are mostly bare rock, and have little prey, agreed to be our planet's warriors. As you can guess from our name, Ghost Claw already survived by raiding, so we used those skills to become the defenders of our race. Since that means keeping our Slashtails, and violent natures, we are also outcasts, unable to live in normal society."

Her lips drew back, showing her fangs, and there was a growl in the next part. "Now one of the clans, or perhaps all of them, has decided they can manage without us." Other growls answered, and a quick glance showed that all the Slashtails had their fangs and claws showing, and some were displaying the blades in their tails.

Despite her having an alien body, Jamie could see Ghost forcing herself to relax, suppress her anger. "Someone gave or sold our male to Hunter. Rend was safe on our world, protected by adolescents from all the clans as part of the agreement. We defended the other clans; they kept our male safe. You asked why we are putting on bulk." A paw gestured to take in the rest. "We are going to find out why we were betrayed, and deal with the culprit."

~~

That seemed to be the explanation, and Jamie didn't want to push for more but he was still baffled. Nightclaw, Ghost, must have realised. She came across and faced Jamie, reaching to take his human hands gently in her six-digit Slashtail hands. "Adding bulk before battle is shameful, an unfair advantage as other Slashtails cannot do the same. Our honour is essential. It ensures we are protectors, not predators, but this time we have little choice. If we fight with weapons, six against a whole clan, we will die very quickly. If we declare clan feud, then weapons will not be allowed. Even so, some other clans have hundreds of thousands of members."

"Thousands? How can you win against thousands?"

"We can't." Nightclaw squeezed his hands, gently. "Regardless of what happens, Ghost Claw is finished. When Rend died, so did our clan as we cannot breed." Her voice strengthened, with a savage edge to the deep sorrow. "But we are Ghost Claw, so we will not die quietly. No clan has more than six males. If we tear our way through their fighters and kill their males, our enemies will die with us. Despite their extended lives, accidents will whittle them down, until eventually their clan will follow Ghost Claw into oblivion."

He couldn't help it, Jamie stepped forward and hugged her. She hugged back and he stroked her pelt, safely above her tail. If he closed his eyes the voice in his ear could have been human-Ghost, but then he realised what she was saying.

"While we were on Earth, the others discussed you. It is right that you should have a choice. If we die, the life-pattern we exchanged will be the only trace of Ghost Claw left in the universe. You will also be the only human who is not confined to Earth, so you should have one last chance to stay here." She hugged, then moved back. "Or you can come with us, and if Ghost Claw die, you can be the final bitter drop of our vengeance."

Six furry faces wanted an answer, but Jamie didn't really understand the question. He'd had second and third thoughts, then decided to leave, and now he had to decide again? "I already knew I'd be the only human out there, and that Ghost Claw would eventually die out. Why will it be quicker, and how can I be your vengeance?" He smiled and held up his hands. "No claws, ghost or any other sort."

Ghost, or Nightclaw, held up one hand with the six claws extended. "You will not need claws. When we challenge whoever is responsible, if they accept, killing us will cost them many of their clan. They may accept the losses because when we are gone, they should inherit our lands and possessions, including Starlight Ghost. They will be disappointed." She pointed at Jamie. "You will inherit it all."

He could see exactly what would happen next. "Then they challenge me, or just wait for me to die."

The chittering meant Jamie was wrong, or they all found the idea of him dying very funny. "You are human, so they cannot challenge, but our swapping means that you have enough Slashtail to be related, and inherit. As an adopted Ghost Claw, you are entitled to the longevity treatment, but there is no cull on Earth, so you can live as long as you wish. They will die before you do, as their turn will eventually come around."

Nightclaw took two long steps back, and gave a short, formal bow. "If Ghost Claw Clan die, will you be our vengeance, Jamie?"

It should have taken a lot of thought, but only two things mattered. Ghost Claw might not die, in which case Jamie really would like to join them in whatever came next. But if some asshole killed them all, especially Ghost, then Jamie wanted to hurt them as much as possible. "I will."

Behind her, Jamie saw the rest of the clan were on their hind legs, facing him and looking somehow more formal than their usual posture. "Then with your help, we will be true to our nature even when we are gone." All six held up their hands, digits hooked but the claws retracted.

At some unseen signal they spun on one foot with their blades exposed, six chainsaws slashing across and then back out of sight. The Slashtails stamped to stop the spin and crouched, and now a single digit had a claw extended, and slashed across the other way. "Ghost Claw!" The translator didn't attempt to translate the short, sharp shriek that followed, but it didn't need words to be a threat.

Ghost, or Nightclaw at the moment, stood up straight again, her voice crisp and official. "Fliptrip, fire the main drives and break orbit. Once we have enough clearance, activate the Standard Jump and take us above the elliptic, and far enough from the star to activate the Stellar Jump. Ghost Claw are going home."

~~

As the others sat back down, Jamie still stood, frozen in shock. "But." An alien finger covered Jamie's mouth.

"No. It is decided. Your clan leader has spoken." Ghost's voice softened. "You can hire a crew and roam the galaxy for a thousand years, see all those wonders, or set up a spaceship repair shop. If you get lonely, sneak back to Earth and find a girl, one who likes her pelt stroked." She chittered quietly. "You can call in to see your kin, and tell them about your adventures."

Jamie kept quiet, though he answered in his mind. But it won't be the same without you. Jamie didn't want to be all alone in the universe even if he had a spaceship, or all alone on Earth, and even if he found a girl, he didn't want to lose his friend. He rethought that and it was true. In or out of her pelt, he liked Ghost, more than any other man or woman he'd met.

Not love, even though he liked kissing her when she was human. If she never put on her human shape again, he'd still like her, and he'd still want to stay. He liked Nightclaw's personality, her sense of humour, her scent, and stroking her pelt, but now that stupid honour was going to kill the only real friend he'd ever had.

No, whoever handed Rend over had killed Ghost, and her clan, so if Jamie did inherit the ship, he'd make sure they paid. Jamie daren't say anything, but he didn't subscribe to the Slashtail honour code, and she'd just told him what to do. If he used whatever else he inherited to hire a crew, it shouldn't be too hard to find however many enemy males had survived.

After that he might get away or he might not, but the bastards who started all this would be doomed.

Though that would be a last resort, because Jamie thought he might find another way. Despite saying they were rebels, Ghost Claw Clan weren't totally off the reservation, but Jamie was. If they'd been willing to break every rule, the first hint that any Ghost Claw survived would have been assassins in the night or a nuclear bomb. The defences around the males would be established with Slashtail rules in mind, so they wouldn't stop Jamie.

The same applied to the clan surviving. If exchanging biological code would eventually give Jamie shapeshifting, then converting a Slashtail should be easier. There must be a Slashtail rule or reason why not, but he wasn't going to ask, or not directly. Stealing a male and forcing a conversion would be a no-no, and Ghost wouldn't accept it, but if some asshole had sold one male, maybe Jamie could do a deal for another. A warship would help with negotiating. Questions about his own conversion might give Jamie enough information, and then he could spring it on them.

~~

Jamie shelved his plotting, because the rest were preparing for the journey home. Before any Stellar Jump, all the external doors had to be checked physically, and the turret seals after they were retracted. There weren't a huge number of doors, and checking the turrets only meant someone running a sensor around the access hatch, but it took time for seven of them to cover them all.

Finally, cameras inspected each section of hull to make sure nothing jutted out, then they were retracted. Sourspit complained they were taking too long, though Jamie was realising that was just how she was. She knew that seven weren't really enough for a ship this size.

The crew had moved Tenndix and his chains into a cell, still connected to the power supply to immobilise the Mekks. Ghost Claw took imprisonment seriously—there were half a dozen big weapons poised to annihilate anything that escaped. The cell block was encased in a warship-strength shield, then a second layer of armour, as full power might damage the cells and walls. Hunter's body had gone into storage, in case Ghost Claw ever needed the pattern.

When the crew gathered in the main control room, the number of empty seats and unmanned banks of instruments and controls emphasised Ghost Claw's losses. The survivors were quiet now, no joking at all as they rechecked instruments. Everyone was worried they might have missed a bit of the code the Starborn Circus used to take control.

As everyone took a seat, Nightclaw pointed to a bank of dials. Jamie was to sit and watch them, to make sure none of them went too far from the optimum. There were markings to show when it was dangerous, but he was to report long before then. Jamie was sure automatic reactions would be better, but now he found that the programming wouldn't react until the readings hit the green.

If there'd been a full crew, someone would be sat at the controls and react immediately. Now Jamie was an early warning, to give one of the others time to switch seats and access the right controls before it was urgent. Hunter would have managed by having Tenndix split up to cover ten stations, which might be why it chose to bring a Mekk-Hive. Then Nightclaw mentioned a couple of possible scenarios if Jamie missed a warning, including his atoms in a long smear orbiting the sun—after that he was happy to watch dials for hours.

Or not, as the Standard Jump only lasted a few minutes. Even so, it had moved Starlight Ghost from the elliptic, where all the planets orbited, to a point nearly two billion miles 'above' the sun. With no objects near enough to interfere, the crew began checking all over again, ready to activate the Stellar

Jump.

The amount of checking was because the crew still worried about a few stray scraps of Hunter's or the Starborn Circus's code. Even so, it only took an hour, then Fliptrip announced that Starlight Ghost had activated the Stellar Jump, and slipped out of normal space into the Between. When all the Slashtails but Fliptrip stood up and left their posts, Jamie was confused. "What about watching for problems?"

Nightclaw turned and came back to him. "Unless the drive malfunctions, we are safe until we arrive home. We will take turns to keep watch, but any problems usually involve it not activating properly."

Since he'd read some sci-fi, Jamie was still worried. "What about pirates, or hitting stray rocks?"

That was worth a chittering Slashtail laugh. "Nobody really knows where we are until we arrive. *We* don't know, but there has never been a collision, and the instruments can't even find a star out there. A field can be set up around a specific area, usually a solar system, to pull any ship out of the Between in a particular place. Our solar system pulls them out next to a heavily armed orbital. Most class four worlds do the same, to ensure any visitors coming out of the Between are peaceful. The chances of setting up an intercept for a specific ship in open space are small enough to be considered zero."

"So how long will the trip take?" Skipping had been nearly instantaneous, and the Standard Jump had only lasted minutes and moved them halfway across the solar system. Jamie had expected the Stellar Jump to be the same.

"On board, just over half an Earth year, but on your world several years will have passed, and a different amount of time on our own homeworld. Time is slippery in the Between." From the chitter, Jamie's expression amused Nightclaw. "We will arrive at a location approximately eighty light-years from Earth, but some scientists claim we don't actually move; our position and our destination become the same place. There are nearly as many theories about the Between as there are scientists, but only a few are still trying to investigate it. The Stellar Jump and the Between were discovered at least five millennia ago, so those who knew are dust. Most of us believe that as long we can put in a destination, activate it, and arrive at the right place, why mess with it?"

"So what do we do for six months?" Jamie remembered one thing he'd once promised himself. "I suppose I can start with exercise, to try and build up my strength. I'm guessing there are instruction manuals and spare parts, so I could try to fix the pod, properly this time?"

"Some space travellers sleep." Ghost gestured downwards. "There are slowtime capsules that reduce your natural bodily functions so you age very slowly, useful for those who are not immortal, or who get bored easily. Starlight Ghost has a few for visitors, but Ghost Claw never use them. We will be busy checking Starlight Ghost again, slowly and thoroughly this time, so you could help with that. That would teach you more about how our ship works."

She turned towards the door, and if she'd been in human form, a wicked smile would have accompanied her last words. "Then there are six pelts that need stroking."

~~~~~

Meet Ghost, Jamie, and the Slashtails again in *Fur and Fury*, the conclusion of Starborn Circus
~~~~~

STARBORN CIRCUS – ENTITIES AND MISCELLANY

Damian: Old money, inherited a business empire, Shania's husband

Fiend: Leader, Hellbat biker gang, drug dealers, extortionists, and street racers

Ghost Claw Clan of the Purple Hills Slashtails: Slashtails with mauve pelts. Can combine, meld, to become a larger creature. Ghost Claw clan members in the meld translate as Nightclaw, Quicktail, Shortfang, Sourspit, Tripflip, Oneless, Cutvoice

Ghost Hill: Mystery woman – dark-skinned look-alike of Salome Malone, sex goddess

Hunter: Alien hunting a fugitive who landed on Earth

Jamie – James Ricardo Salas: Twenty-six, broke, mechanic with rundown workshop, hopeful street racer

Lottie: Electrical vehicle spares and computerised equipment supplier

Lucie aka **Lucifer:** Second in command, Hellbat motorbike gang, and street racer

Menhir: Second-hand engineering equipment and vehicle dealer and parts supplier

Nightclaw: Ghost Claw Clan leader – her personality dominates her meld

Rend: Male Slashtail, purple and bald except for tail

Shania: Jamie's twenty-nine-year-old sister, Damian's wife. Dedicated exercise, diction lessons, deportment classes, makeup practice, semi-starvation, and hair bleach fulfilled her ambition, marrying into money

Slashtails: Alien race, furred, big-headed, long-legged, slim, ferretish, about thirteen kilos, with very bushy tail. Able to stand or run on two or four legs, with dexterous clawed fingers on front paws/hands, long enough to use human weapons, and gripping toes.

Solly: Automotive parts dealer, fence, and thief. Will buy or sell almost anything, or steal it.

Starlight Ghost: Heavily armed interstellar starship, a bottom-heavy egg-shape approx. 1500 ft from the domed top to the bottom, with the widest point almost 800 ft in diameter, close to the upper practical limit for planetary landings

Tenndix: Ten-fold Mekk-Hive, a qualified interstellar pilot, currently in bipedal robot configuration. Each section is a mech with a speck of bio-sentience to qualify as alive, not machinery. Scarlet left leg, dark green right. Yellow left arm, light blue right. Bright pink head with white eyes, antennae, and speaker grille. Body: orange loins, light green upper left, reddish-brown upper right, black midriff

Between: A mysterious place, perhaps another dimension, where the laws of space and time are flexible. Spaceships in the Between can travel long distances, apparently faster than light, though the time elapsed on the ship and at both the start and destination may differ by years

Immortality: Longevity treatments theoretically allow immortality, but qualifying planets must prevent overpopulation. The methods vary, but effectively, only entities not registered as inhabitants of any world can live forever (barring accidental death).

To maintain a stable population while allowing the creation of new children, an equivalent number of adults must die. The race may choose their own method, from lotteries to banning procreation. Over-breeding, exceeding the agreed limit, will be corrected by a cull, organised by the class one planets.

IF YOU LIKED THIS BOOK, CHECK OUT THE REST OF VANCE HUXLEY'S BOOKS!

Science Fiction

The Shattered Stars: Breach of Contract

The Shattered Stars: Riding the Spear

Up, Up and Away

Dystopian

Fall of the Cities: Planting the Orchard

Fall of the Cities: Putting Down Roots

Fall of the Cities: Branching Out

Fall of the Cities: A Mercedes for Soldier Boy

Fall of the Cities: Last Man Standing

Fall of the Cities: Uprooting the Orchard

Fall of the Cities: Country Living and Dying

Fall of the Cities: Legends Never Die

Fantasy

Ferryl Shayde

Ferryl Shayde 2 A Student Body

Ferryl Shayde 3 A Very Different Game

Ferryl Shayde 4 Storm and Steel

Ferryl Shayde 5 The Talisman

Ferryl Shayde 6 Animal Magic

Ferryl Shayde 7 Witch Snitch

Ferryl Shayde 8 Adepts, Apprentices and Ascention

The Forest and the Farm

Path of Mist series:

Cloud Runner

Path Finder

Children's

Harriet the Hornet

VANCE HUXLEY

Vance Huxley lives out in the countryside in Lincolnshire, England. He has spent a busy life working in many different fields – including the building and rail industries, as a workshop manager, trouble-shooter for an engineering firm, accountancy, cafe proprietor, and graphic artist. He also spent time in other jobs, and is proud of never being dismissed, and only once made redundant.

Eventually he found his Noeline, but unfortunately she died much too young. To help with the aftermath, Vance tried writing though without any real structure. As an editor and beta readers explained the difference between words and books, he tried again.

Now he tries to type as often as possible in spite of the assistance of his cats, since his legs no longer work well enough to allow anything more strenuous. An avid reader of sci-fi, fantasy and adventure novels, his writing tends towards those genres.

AND NOW THE STORY COMES TO A CLOSE.

But you can find out what happens next – for free! Simply visit:

www.EntradaBooks.com

And sign up to receive books, updates and news and we'll send you a book of your choice for free!

Onward and upward, and tally-ho.

-Vance and the (allegedly) neglected divas (catimals)

Printed in Great Britain
by Amazon